Alexander Douglas Thomson

Euripides and the Attic Orators

A comparison

Alexander Douglas Thomson

Euripides and the Attic Orators
A comparison

ISBN/EAN: 9783337428754

Printed in Europe, USA, Canada, Australia, Japan

Cover: Foto ©Andreas Hilbeck / pixelio.de

More available books at **www.hansebooks.com**

EURIPIDES

AND

THE ATTIC ORATORS

A COMPARISON

BY

A DOUGLAS THOMSON, M.A., D.Litt.

LECTURER IN GREEK IN THE UNIVERSITY OF EDINBURGH

London

MACMILLAN AND CO., Limited

NEW YORK: THE MACMILLAN COMPANY

1898

PREFACE

In writing these pages I have consulted a large number of works bearing more or less closely on the subject under treatment; and of particular cases of indebtedness to these I have endeavoured to make full acknowledgement in the notes. The books which I have found most helpful are the following:—

Berlage, *De Euripide Philosopho.*
Blass, *Die Attische Beredsamkeit von Gorgias bis zu Lysias.*
Butcher, *Demosthenes* (in Macmillan's Classical Writers Series).
   Some Aspects of the Greek Genius (1st ed.).
Coulanges, *La Cité Antique.*
Jebb, *Attic Orators.*
Mahaffy, *Euripides* (in Macmillan's Classical Writers Series).
Paley, *Euripides* (in Bibliotheca Classica).
Wilamowitz-Moellendorff, *Euripides, Herakles.*

I must make special mention of Berlage's *De Euripide Philosopho*, the work which I have found most useful for my present purpose, and to which I can scarcely overrate my obligation. I have followed Berlage's method and arrangement almost throughout, extending to the Orators what he had done for Euripides only. But even in the case of Euripides I have written chiefly from manuscript notes; and any errors that may occur in the matter of references are my own.

Professor Decharme's *Euripide et l'Esprit de son Théâtre*—a book at once brilliant and judicious—I had not read till the present work was completed, but I have been able to add numerous references to it in the foot-notes.

If this study of Euripides and the Attic Orators has, in the matter of comparison, proved less fruitful than I had anticipated, and if the conclusions are frequently of a negative rather than a positive character, it has had, I hope, at least one result which makes it not altogether useless. It has been the occasion of doing for the Orators what had already been done for Euripides—of grouping together and so converting into a whole which is more εὐσύνοπτον their thoughts on those problems of life which must always be of interest to thinking men.

The work was originally presented to the Senatus of the University of Edinburgh as a thesis for the degree of Doctor of Letters, and owed its inception to a suggestion of Professor Butcher, to whom I would here record my gratitude for much kindly interest shown during its progress. The fact that it was written as an academic dissertation may perhaps be regarded as a sufficient reason for quoting the Greek texts rather than translations.

I have used the Oxford text of Euripides, with Nauck's *Tragicorum Graecorum Fragmenta* (2nd ed.) for the Fragments, and the Teubner texts for the Orators.

EDINBURGH,
October, 1898.

CONTENTS

EURIPIDES AND THE ATTIC ORATORS

CHAPTER I

INTRODUCTION

§ 1. AFTER Marathon, Salamis and Plataea had secured
Greek freedom against Persian encroachment, there came
a period of repose. Already there had been indications of
a wider intellectual life. The exclusive sway of Poetry was
beginning to break down. A feeling was arising that thought
might be beautifully expressed in prose as well as in verse,
and thus there was being removed one of the greatest
hindrances to clear, untrammelled reflection. Practical life
began to occupy more and more the minds of thinking men:
mythology was no longer the sole object of literary study.
From the Persian Wars and their consequences this new
intellectual tendency received the stimulus it needed to rouse
it to life and vigour. Not only have we their direct result in
the history of Herodotus, and in much of the Aeschylean
drama, but they gave the first great impulse to that period
of enterprise, alike in practical and in speculative life, which
reached its culmination under Pericles.

A century and more before the Persian Wars, the Greeks,
dissatisfied with the mere personification of natural agencies
which constituted their theology, and true to their natural
bent for inquiry, had begun to ask what those natural
agencies really were. Originally there had been no dividing
line between philosophy and theology, but now that dividing
line began to be traced. The earliest philosophers were
physicists, who devoted themselves to the study of nature

B

as a whole, under the belief that the study would lead them to the discovery of truth. The most important name for us is Anaxagoras (470 B. C.), who exercised a strong influence on Euripides [1]. He was the first to recognise νοῦς as the ordering principle of the universe, and in this way made a tremendous step in advance of his predecessors.

Between the physicists and Socrates came the Sophists, who represent the birth and growth of Scepticism. This scepticism was a natural and necessary step in the progress of thought. When so many and so widely different schools sprang up, each claiming to give the true interpretation of the universe, and yet giving out doctrines so contradictory; when these doctrines had become more or less popularly known, and had been the cause of endless debate and discussion, it was an inevitable result that scepticism should spread. And this spirit was fostered also by the social and political conditions of the time; for over the whole of Greece, as we have seen, and above all in Athens, there took place in the fifth century B. C. a great and rapid development in all departments of life. The victory over Persia, combined with the steady growth of democracy, had given a stimulus and promoted an activity which was quite unprecedented. The power of speaking was becoming more important, and was the chief weapon in the hands of ambitious citizens; and men were eager to acquire powers of argument and debate, and to learn the opinions of the greatest thinkers of the day. The sophists came forward to satisfy these wants, and in so doing they incidentally rendered a great service to Greek prose. The most important of them was Protagoras [2], whose treatise on Truth began with the words, 'Man is the measure of all things,'—meaning that there is no such thing as objective truth, that truth is not absolute but relative, and similarly that, in matters of conduct, right and wrong depend on opinion.

---

[1] It can hardly be said, however, that Euripides was a *disciple* of Anaxagoras.

[2] For the relations existing between Euripides and Protagoras see Decharme, *Euripide et l'Esprit de son Théâtre*, pp. 48–49 ; and for Euripides and the sophists generally see the whole section (pp. 47-58).

Socrates (469-399 B. C.) shared in that part of the general scepticism which believed it impossible to arrive at certain knowledge with regard to nature and physical science ; but, unlike the sophists, he did maintain the certainty of moral distinctions, and instituted a new method to discover error and establish truth. And this method he applied, not to physical questions, but to questions of conduct. Socrates was the first ethical philosopher.

Between the physicists and Socrates, as has been already observed, philosophy was cultivated exclusively by the sophists. By them the study of philosophy had been combined with that of rhetoric. Socrates effected a separation of the two. Between the sophist—as the word was subsequently understood—and the rhetorician it is impossible to draw a sharp line of distinction. The same man is at one time termed a rhetorician, at another a sophist[1].

No more congenial soil for the cultivation of sophistry and rhetoric could have been found than Athens. If we consider the small size of the state and the extremely democratic nature of its institutions, especially after the changes effected by Pericles, it will at once appear that it was an absolute necessity for a public man to possess some skill as an orator[2]. It was the citizens themselves who transacted all public business whether judicial or political : they administered as well as made the laws. As in time of war the Athenian could not delegate his duty to a mercenary, so in time of peace he must be cognisant of his country's laws and interests in order to be able to follow the discussions on the Pnyx, to act as πρόεδρος, πρύτανις, or ἄρχων,—in short, to discharge all public

[1] No doubt the name σοφιστής suggests the East and the practical culture of Ionia, while ῥήτωρ suggests the West and the Sicilian rhetoric. See Jebb, *Attic Orators*, I. Introd. cxii-cxxiv ; and cf. Blass, *Attische Beredsamkeit*, p. 15 :— 'Sophistik und Rhetorik sind durchaus nicht identisch, aber doch mehr dem Namen als der Sache nach getrennt.' 'In both instances the aim was ability in practical life, and the difference between the two was rather of theoretical than of practical importance' (Holm, ii. p. 425). Cf. Plato, *Gorgias*, 464 C.

[2] This movement really had its beginnings in the Solonian constitution, and received a still stronger impulse from the reforms of Clisthenes. The career opened to eloquence was widened after the Persian Wars.

offices to which appointment was made by lot. By the
constitution of Solon it had been made imperative for every
citizen to hold a political opinion, and in case of civil discord
to take one side or the other. The severance between the
individual and the state came later, when Athens had fallen
on evil days. Under such conditions political success was
hardly to be attained without eloquence; and thus the art
of the orator, which flourishes best under a free government, — and a free government implies always a certain
amount of turbulence and strife—was brought to perfection
at Athens.

Yet it was clearly impossible that any and every citizen
should become an accomplished speaker. In many cases that
would be prevented both by poverty and by lack of ability.
Public instruction at Athens did not go so far as has sometimes
been supposed: the higher education was left to private
initiative. Only those who could afford it attended the lectures
of grammarians, of rhetors and sophists. It is true that some
Athenians, such as Cleon and other demagogues, became
famous as speakers without such education, but, especially after
the Peloponnesian War, it was the exception. The growing
power of rhetoric and sophistry, which at least helped a man
towards ready and persuasive speech on any topic under
discussion, put a wide difference between those who were and
those who were not versed in these studies. The ordinary
citizen, when brought face to face in the Assembly or the
law-courts with a trained speaker, found himself at a great
disadvantage.

The Athenians were always inordinately fond of litigation:
Aristophanes is continually making fun of τὸ φιλόδικον at
Athens. And the number of civil and judicial suits was
enormously increased by the Peloponnesian War, more especially by the confiscations of the Thirty. When the democracy was restored, many wrongs as to property and
other things had to be set right. But the Athenian citizen
could not, as we do, retain counsel to plead his cause before
the judges. Such a course was against all law and tradition.
He must be able himself to discharge this as well as all other

civic duties. And so he devised the expedient of employing
a trained speaker to compose a speech for him, and this
speech he committed to memory and delivered himself. It
was this custom that established the profession of the λoγo-
γράφος. Most of the orators—even those who, like Demosthenes,
devoted most of their attention and energy to deliberative
oratory and questions of public policy—occasionally acted as
λογογράφοι: Isaeus never acted in any other capacity.

The internal condition of Athens during this period was
thus extremely favourable to the development of forensic
oratory. Her external relations in the age of Demosthenes
were no less favourable to the development of deliberative
oratory. Gradually, by force of circumstances, the number of
speakers in the Assembly had grown smaller and smaller,
until none ventured to mount the βῆμα except professional
ῥήτορες like Aeschines and Demosthenes: the rest, like many
of our Members of Parliament, contented themselves with
recording a party vote. After Philip embarked on his course
of encroachment, these speakers found ample stimulus and
occasion. Political passions were at a white heat, and the
fervour of the passion is transfused into the spoken word.
It is just to this time, when Athenian degradation and de-
moralisation were progressing with fatal steadiness, that we
owe the masterpieces of Athenian oratory [1].

It must not be supposed, however, that the New Culture
succeeded in establishing itself at Athens without opposition [2].
It was too much at enmity with the popular religion for that.
Religion was one of the bases on which the Greek state

---

[1] Cf. Tacitus, *Dialog. de Orator.* c. xxxvii (Church and Brodribb's translation) :—'We are speaking of an art which arose more easily in stirring and
unquiet times. Who knows not that it is better and more profitable to
enjoy peace than to be harassed by war? Yet war produces more good
soldiers than peace. Eloquence is on the same footing. The oftener she has
stood, so to say, in the battlefield, the more wounds she has inflicted and
received, the mightier her antagonist, the sharper the conflicts she has freely
chosen, the higher and more splendid has been her rise, and ennobled by
these contests she lives in the praises of mankind.' Cf. also *ibid.* c. xl.

[2] See Holm, ii. pp. 281-2. For an exceedingly able discussion on the
New Culture—and especially on Euripides' relation to it—see *ibid.* c. xxvi,
pp. 423-465.

rested [1] ; and anything which tended to subvert the national
religion could not but be viewed askance by many of the
citizens. So long as science was pursued in such a way that
it did not clash with religion, so long it was not actively
resisted ; but, as soon as it appeared to contradict religion,
it met with strenuous opposition. So far Athens was em-
phatically intolerant. Anaxagoras,—though he was the friend
of Pericles—Protagoras and others suffered exile ; Socrates was
condemned to death. Men of the old school—the Μαραθωνομάχαι,
the ideal citizens according to the conservative Aristophanes
—were strongly adverse to all those new ideas, which seemed
likely to subvert the morality and religion which had become
established and traditional ; and hence they regarded with
disfavour the instruction of the sophist and rhetorician, even
while they realised that such instruction was a necessary
instrument to influence and power.

On two of the great triad of tragedians the New Culture
exercised but little influence. True, neither Aeschylus nor
Sophocles is free from sophistry or regardless of rhetoric [2].
No true Athenian could be, for sophistry is characteristic of the
Athenian mind generally. But in Aeschylus and Sophocles
these things are not continually obtruded as they are in
Euripides [3]. It was after the Persian Wars that the study of

---

[1] Coulanges goes further (*La Cité Antique*, pp. 375-380 : Livre iv. c. ix.—
Nouveau principe de gouvernement ; l'intérêt public et le suffrage) :—' La religion
avait été pendant de longs siècles l'unique principe de gouvernement.' See
the whole chapter, and cf. *ibid.* p. 415 :—' L'État était étroitement lié à la
religion ; il venait d'elle et se confondait avec elle, &c.'

[2] One need only instance the trial-scene in the *Eumenides* of Aeschylus,
especially the speech of Athena (681-710) with its formal ending, εἴρηται
λόγος : Sophocles, *Oed. Col.* 939-1013 ; *Antig.* 639-725 ; *Ajax*, 1047 ff., 1226-1315 ;
Electra, 516-609. For the progress of Rhetoric as seen in Tragedy, and
especially in Euripides, see Blass, pp. 41-42 :—' Die Tragödie also wenigstens
theilweise mit dem Strome schwamm.' Cf. also Campbell, *Greek Tragedy*,
pp. 127-8. 'Tragedy,' he says, 'reflects an instructive light upon the
growth of rhetoric and of rhetorical casuistry in Athens.' Comedy struggled
against the stream. See Jebb, *Attic Orators*, Introd. cxxxi :—' While Comedy
set itself against that culture, Tragedy had been more compliant.'

[3] See Blass, pp. 41-42. Euripides, however, is a philosopher as well as
as a sophist. Cf. Wilamowitz-M., *Herakles*, Einleitung, p. 30 :—' und φιλόσοφος
im echten sinne ist er auch, obwol er auch σοφιστής ist, im echten, wie im
üblen sinne.'

sophistic and rhetoric came into vogue. In 480 B.C.—the date of Salamis and of the birth of Euripides—Aeschylus was forty-five years old, Sophocles fifteen. Hence, other considerations apart, they were not exposed to the new influence in the same way as Euripides was; for Euripides may be said to have been born with the New Culture[1]. The influence which it exercised on him was enhanced by his natural bent: he was a student, not a statesman; a man of thought, not a man of action. He was profoundly affected by Anaxagoras, and helped to popularise his theories. In fact his dramas, with all their inconsistencies and changing opinions, reflect faithfully the general course of thought which had its beginning in the time in which he lived—the modern spirit, the growing doubt and scepticism in matters of religion and philosophy, the advance of the democratic movement with its accompanying freedom of speech, the solvent condition of ideas on society, the rationalistic tendency of thought, the desire to probe the secrets of the universe and solve the insoluble.

In the inner Greek life of the fourth century B.C. we can perceive the growth of those tendencies which had their beginning in the time of Euripides. Religion in its outward aspect—the celebration of festivals &c.—was as punctiliously observed as ever. But, though there was a reaction to outward orthodoxy[2], it was now little more than a matter of external observance. Religion, attacked before by the philosophers, now practically ceased to exist as a motive—as a

[1] Euripides is much further removed from Sophocles than the mere difference in age might lead us to expect, for Sophocles was never affected as Euripides was by the New Culture. Cf. Wilamowitz-M., *Herakles*, Einleitung, p. 4:—'In solcher zeit geht das leben rasch und machen ein par jahre einen gewaltigen unterschied.' Cf. also Abbott, *Pericles*, &c. pp. 318-319; and Westcott, *Religious Thought in the West*, p. 97:—'Though he was only a generation younger than Aeschylus, his works, when compared with those of his predecessor, represent the results of a revolution both in art and in thought.'

[2] See Mahaffy, *Euripides*, p. 12. Even in the Periclean age the many clung to ancient beliefs. Cf. Coulanges, *La Cité Antique*, p. 12:—'Mais la foule qui, même à Athènes, restait attachée aux vieilles croyances, &c.' But the orthodoxy was perhaps one rather of religious *observances* than of *beliefs*. For the pietism of the Athenians and their scrupulous discharge of religious observances, see Coulanges, *ibid*, p. 261.

living power in Greek life[1]. The moral fibre of the Greeks
had also become weakened, and morality had gone from bad
to worse. Public morality openly countenanced what private
morality condemned. The moral degeneration was as strongly
marked as the political degeneration. As Euripides reflects
the life of his time, so do the Orators of theirs. There is in
Isocrates and Demosthenes no theme of more frequent recurrence than the degeneracy of the Athens of their day as
contrasted with the Athens of bygone times.

§ 2. In view of these facts, it will not surprise us if we
find that both in form and in matter, in style and in thought,
Euripides has much in common with the Orators,—far more
than either Aeschylus or Sophocles has. In the present discussion I have restricted myself to a comparison of the
thought alone. But it would not be difficult, I think, to show
that Euripides is even more rhetorical than the Orators[2].
We constantly meet with rhetorical phrases and turns, and
he abounds in regular trial-scenes and debates. In fact, every
kind of oratory is to be met in his plays—dicanic, symbo-
leutic, epideictic. He is brought near the Orators also by
the large number of technical rhetorical terms which he
employs, and his use of every-day language, proverbs, and
colloquialisms; and he follows the rules of rhetoric even more
closely than they do in the disposition of his ῥήσεις[3].

Mr. Earle[4], speaking of the essentially oratorical nature of
the actor's part, of the fact that the history of the Attic drama
—which was thoroughly democratic in character—coincides

---

[1] It had become largely 'un culte d'habitude'—'vaines cérémonies'
(Coulanges, *La Cité Antique*, p. 417).

[2] Cf. Wilamowitz-Moellendorf, *Herakles*, Einleitung, p. 27:—'Wol aber hat
er die kunst des ἀντιλέγειν so sehr ausgebildet wie nicht einmal ein rhetor,
und seine ganze technik ist davon durchdrungen.'

[3] Cf. Quintilian, x. 1, 67-68:—'Illud quidem nemo non fateatur necesse
est, iis qui se ad agendum comparant, utiliorem longe fore Euripiden.
Namque is et sermone magis accedit oratorio generi, et sententiis densus et
in iis quae a sapientibus tradita sunt paene ipsis par, et dicendo et respon-
dendo cuilibet eorum, qui fuerunt in foro diserti, comparandus; in adfectibus
vero cum omnibus mirus, tum in iis qui in miseratione constant, facile prae-
cipuus.' See also Pflugk and Klotz's edition of the *Helena*, Prooemium, p. 14;
and Jerram's edition of the same play, Introd. p. xiii.

[4] In his edition of the *Alcestis*, Introd. xxxii–xxxiv.

with the history of the great Attic democracy, and of the manner in which that drama reflects all the strongest influences of the time—the Persian invasion, the growth and spread of the Athenian empire, the consequent widening of geographical knowledge among the Greeks, &c.—remarks:—'So then, if not in its origin, yet in its supreme development, the actor's part goes hand in hand with the growth and development of Attic oratory under the Clisthenian democracy. Thus we may say that the stage represents Athenian oratory,—nay, even that the Aeschylean stage would be but the βῆμα of the orators in holiday guise at the festival of Dionysus.' If this is true of the Aeschylean stage, still truer is it of the stage of Euripides [1].

One other point is here worthy of notice. Euripides was ahead of his time. He was one of the foremost standard-bearers of the New Culture. He was a philosopher as well as a poet, and, like many of the philosophers, had become discontented both with the popular religion and with the narrow view of public life fostered by the city-state. With regard to both his attitude tends frequently to become one of despair. He longs for a wider outlook, and now and again has dim visions of cosmopolitanism. That is one thing among many which makes him less distinctively Greek than Sophocles, and brings him nearer not only to the life of the century immediately following his own, but also to the life of our own day. Besides, he brought tragedy down to the level of every-day life, and painted men 'as they are.' To quote Berlage (p. 33):—'Nam, ut teste Cicerone Socrates philosophiam, sic Euripides tragoediam de coelo revocavit et in hominum animis collocavit.' The consideration of all these facts is enough, I think, to justify the attempt to institute a comparison between Euripides and the Attic Orators [2].

---

[1] On the close connexion in form generally between poetry and oratory cf. Cicero, *De Oratore*, i. 16:—'Est enim finitimus oratori poeta, numeris adstrictior paullo, verborum autem licentia liberior, multis vero ornandi generibus socius ac paene par: in hoc quidem certe prope idem, nullis ut terminis circumscribat aut definiat ius suum, quo minus ei liceat eadem illa facultate et copia vagari qua velit.'

[2] In the fourth century B.C. 'many of the playwrights were either professed

On the other side there are considerations which might lead us to modify our expectations as to the fruitfulness of such a comparison. Apart from the fact that the nature of the poet's work and the Orators' is, in part at least, determined by the literary form in which that work is cast, there is the further important consideration that the lives they led were diametrically opposed. Euripides was a student, a theorist, courting the quiet of retirement and privacy: the Orators were politicians, men of action, occupied in the storm and stress of public life, and that too at a time when public life was peculiarly full of difficulty. Hence it is that the poet, dealing with imaginary cases, is full of moralising and generalisation: the orator, dealing with a special case, has no time to moralise, but tends always to particularisation and directness. In proportion as he possesses directness and force—for the two are closely allied—the orator is a great orator; he is weak in proportion as he lacks them. Demosthenes is an illustration of the former case, Isocrates of the latter[1].

The position of Isocrates relatively to Euripides calls for special notice. He is not, in the strictest sense, an orator at all. Rather he might be designated a philosophical and political essayist. But as a philosopher he lacks the keenness which characterises Euripides, and as a politician he is a mere dreamer of dreams. Yet, from the nature of the case—for he too was a student who lived a life of retirement and took no active part in public life—we shall find that on many subjects he offers far more material for comparison with Euripides

orators or statesmen.' See Symonds, *Greek Poets* (Second Series), p. 324. Cf. also *ibid.* pp. 327-8 :—' The intrusion of professional orators into the sphere of the theatre might have been expected in an age when public speaking was cultivated like a fine art, and when opportunities for the display of verbal cleverness were eagerly sought. We are not, therefore, surprised to find Apharcus and Theodectes, distinguished rhetoricians of the school of Isocrates, among the tragedians. Of Theodectes a sufficient number of fragments survive to establish the general character of his style ; but it is enough in this place to notice the fusion of forensic eloquence with dramatic poetry, against which Aristophanes had inveighed, and which was now complete.'

[1] 'Suavitatem Isocrates, ... vim Demosthenes habuit' (Cicero, *De Oratore*, iii. 7).

than do the other orators. This is perhaps another proof that the ideas which Euripides and men like him had striven to disseminate in the latter half of the fifth century had reached a wider audience in the fourth, and gained more general acceptance.

As we might expect, the subjects where there is least material for the present comparison are those of philosophy and religion; those where there is most, public life and politics, ethics, private life, and life in its general aspects. Of politics and public life Euripides has a good deal to say—much more than might at first sight seem probable—and this constitutes in many ways the most fruitful section of the comparison.

In pursuing the following investigation I have, with a view to greater clearness, adhered to a definite arrangement; and the various subjects are treated in the following order:—

(1) Philosophy, including physical, geometrical, astronomical, and geographical questions.

(2) Religion.

(3) Death.

(4) Life in its general aspects.

(5) Ethics.

(6) Public life.

(7) Politics.

(8) Private life.

I would add one caveat. Let it here be said, once for all, that, in dealing with any subject whatever, we must beware of attributing to Euripides himself all the opinions he puts into the mouths of his characters. It is always a difficult matter to discover a dramatist's own views from his plays. The dramatic proprieties must be observed. Yet in certain cases, when an opinion is expressed again and again, or when we feel that it is expressed with a certain fervour, we may with more or less certainty put down that opinion as held by the writer. Further, in the case of the Greek drama, the Chorus may very often be regarded as employed to give utterance to the poet's own ideas. And, lastly, there are those soliloquies, of such frequent recurrence in Euripides, which do not contribute to the progress of the play's action, and in which the immediate subject of the play is lost in wider reflections and generalisations. It is, however, more with the thought itself that we are here concerned than with the question whether it is or is not the writer's own opinion; and so I have very seldom attempted to express any judgment on a point where certainty is generally impossible of attainment.

CHAPTER II

PHYSICAL THEORIES—GEOMETRY—ASTRONOMY— GEOGRAPHY

It is clear from many passages in Euripides that, though
he is 'nullius addictus iurare in verba magistri[1],' and is
always the poet as well as the philosopher, he had devoted
a good deal of attention to the theories of the Ionic physicists
and especially to those of Anaxagoras[2]. From the nature
of the case, such studies are almost never alluded to in the

[1] Cf. Wilamowitz-M., *Herakles*, Einleitung, p. 26:—'Als philosoph ist
Euripides keineswegs ein anhänger des Anaxagoras, sondern gibt mit der-
selben zustimmung auch widersprechende lehren anderer wieder.' The
influence of Anaxagoras on Euripides is, as it seems to me, somewhat
underrated both by Berlage (*De Euripide Philosopho*, Pars II), by Wilamowitz-
Moellendorff *loc. cit.*, and by Decharme, *Euripide*, &c., pp. 36–42. M. Decharme's
conclusion is couched in more moderate language than might be expected
from the arguments which precede it :—'Si donc Euripide n'a pas adopté
la doctrine entière d'Anaxagore, s'il s'en est quelquefois séparé ouvertement,
on n'en doit pas moins reconnaître qu'il s'est inspiré de lui et de son esprit.
Cette influence générale exercée sur le poète par le philosophe peut expliquer
l'assertion trop absolue des critiques grecs qu'Euripide est de l'école d'Anaxagore.'

[2] It seems very probable that Euripides had Anaxagoras in his mind when
he wrote ll. 903–911 of the *Alcestis*, and also when he wrote these lines
(*Frag. 910*) :—

ὄλβιος ὅστις τῆς ἱστορίας
ἔσχε μάθησιν
μήτε πολιτῶν ἐπὶ πημοσύνην
μήτ' εἰς ἀδίκους πράξεις ὁρμῶν,
ἀλλ' ἀθανάτου καθορῶν φύσεως
κόσμον ἀγήρων, πῇ τε συνέστη
καὶ ὅπῃ καὶ ὅπως.
τοῖς δὲ τοιούτοις οὐδέποτ' αἰσχρῶν
ἔργων μελέδημα προσίζει.

Orators. Isocrates indeed—who was an essayist rather than an orator—is the only one who mentions them.

In *Frag.* 913—which can hardly express the opinion held by one who studied astronomy with Anaxagoras—Euripides says :—

> τίς τάδε λεύσσων θεὸν οὐχὶ νοεῖ,
> μετεωρολόγων δ' ἑκὰς ἔρριψεν
> σκολιὰς ἀπάτας ; ὧν ἀτηρὰ
> γλῶσσ' εἰκοβολεῖ περὶ τῶν ἀφανῶν
> οὐδὲν γνώμης μετέχουσα [1].

Isocrates says that most men have considered the study of astronomy, geometry, and eristic as mere prating and small talk (*Antid.* § 262):—

> οἱ μὲν γὰρ πλεῖστοι τῶν ἀνθρώπων ὑπειλήφασιν ἀδολεσχίαν καὶ μικρολογίαν εἶναι τὰ τοιαῦτα τῶν μαθημάτων.

In his own opinion such studies are beneficial as a mental training (see the whole passage, *Antid.* §§ 261–265). Elsewhere (*Panath.* §§ 26–28) he says that they are beneficial to the young, but not suitable for older men [2].

In the way of actual theory we may quote from Euripides the following lines (*Alc.* 243–244):—

> ἅλιε καὶ φάος ἁμέρας,
> οὐράνιαί τε δῖναι νεφέλας δρομαίου ...

This theory of *rotation* we find again in *Orestes*, 982–984 (where we have Anaxagoras' theory of the sun):—

> μόλοιμι τὰν οὐρανοῦ
> μέσον χθονός τε τεταμέναν
> αἰωρήμασι πέτραν
> ἀλύσεσι χρυσέαισι φερομέναν
> δίναισιν βῶλον ἐξ Ὀλύμπου ... [3]

[1] See Decharme, *Euripide*, &c., p. 34 :—' Si l'on prenait ce texte à la lettre, quelle condamnation d'Anaxagore et d'Euripide lui-même!'

[2] Cf. Demosthenes (?) *Erot.* § 44 :—τῆς γὰρ γεωμετρίας καὶ τῆς ἄλλης τῆς τοιαύτης παιδείας ἀπείρως μὲν ἔχειν αἰσχρόν, ἄκρον δ' ἀγωνιστὴν γενέσθαι ταπεινότερον τῆς σῆς ἀξίας. For a full discussion of the ' philosophy ' of Isocrates, see Thompson's edition of Plato's *Phaedrus*, Appendix ii ; Schandau, *De Isocratis doctrina rhetorica et ethica* ; Jebb, *Attic Orators*, II. c. xiii.

[3] See Paley's note *ad loc.* ; Adam, in his edition of Plato's *Apology*, Appendix i. (M. Decharme, *Euripide*, &c., pp. 36–37, explains the πέτρα as

and in *Frag.* 593 :—

> σὲ τὸν αὐτοφυᾶ τὸν ἐν αἰθερίῳ
> ῥύμβῳ πάντων φύσιν ἐμπλέξανθ᾽,
> ὃν πέρι μὲν φῶς, πέρι δ᾽ ὀρφναία
> νὺξ αἰολόχρως, ἄκριτός τ᾽ ἄστρων
> ὄχλος ἐνδελεχῶς ἀμφιχορεύει.

We may add here that Diog. Laert. in his Life of Anaxagoras (ii. 10) has these words :—ὅθεν καὶ Εὐριπίδην μαθητὴν ὄντα χρυσέαν βῶλον εἰπεῖν τὸν ἥλιον ἐν Φαέθοντι—with which compare the lines just quoted from the *Orestes.*

The earth and the encircling aether are the origin of all things, and nothing perishes :—

> Αἰθέρα καὶ Γαῖαν πάντων γενέτειραν ἀείδω (*Frag.* 1023).
> κοὐκ ἐμὸς ὁ μῦθος, ἀλλ᾽ ἐμῆς μητρὸς πάρα,
> ὡς οὐρανός τε γαῖά τ᾽ ἦν μορφὴ μία·
> ἐπεὶ δ᾽ ἐχωρίσθησαν ἀλλήλων δίχα,
> τίκτουσι πάντα κἀνέδωκαν εἰς φάος
> δένδρη, πετεινά, θῆρας οὕς θ᾽ ἅλμη τρέφει
> γένος τε θνητῶν (*Frag.* 484) [1].

---

the rock suspended over the head of Tantalus, and the δίναισι as the whirling winds.) Cf. also *Her. Fur.* 650–654 (with Paley's note).

[1] See Paley's note on *Helena,* 34 ; and cf. Berlage, p. 43 :—'Anaxagoras praeceptor Euripidis principium finxit infinitam multitudinem particularum tenuissimarum inter se cohaerentium, quae vocantur ὁμοιομέρειαι. Ejus libri περὶ φύσεως initium servavit Simplicius ad Aristot. Physica (pg. 33 b) "ὁμοῦ χρήματα πάντα ἦν, ἄπειρα καὶ πλῆθος καὶ σμικρότητα ... Πάντα γὰρ ἀήρ τε καὶ αἰθὴρ κατεῖχεν, ἀμφότερα ἄπειρα ἰόντα. Ταῦτα γὰρ μέγιστα ἔνεστιν ἐν τοῖς σύμπασι καὶ πλήθει καὶ μεγέθει." καὶ μετ᾽ ὀλίγον· "καὶ γὰρ ὁ ἀὴρ καὶ ὁ αἰθὴρ ἀποκρίνεται ἀπὸ τοῦ πολλοῦ τοῦ περιέχοντος καὶ τόγε περιέχον ἄπειρόν ἐστι τὸ πλῆθος. Postea autem, ut exponitur apud Simpl. (in Aristot. Phys. pg. 33 a) ὁ νοῦς πάντα διεκόσμησε Schaub. fr. 8), contorta scilicet celeri motu (pg. 67 a, Schaub. fr. 18). Quo facto (pg. 38 b, Schaub. fr. 19) τὸ μὲν πυκνὸν καὶ διερὸν καὶ ψυχρὸν καὶ ζοφερὸν ἐνθάδε συνεχώρησεν, ἔνθα νῦν ἡ γῆ. Τὸ δὲ ἀραιὸν καὶ τὸ θερμὸν καὶ τὸ ξηρὸν ἐξεχώρησεν εἰς τὸ πρόσω τοῦ αἰθέρος."

Wilamowitz-Moellendorff maintains that physical questions have no interest whatever for Euripides *Herakles,* Einleitung, p. 33 :—'Aber auch mit Perikles und Anaxagoras ein physisches problem erörternd ist er nicht zu denken : alle die physikalischen einzelfragen interessiren ihn nicht im mindesten, selbst die μετέωρα nicht, wenn er auch einmal die sonne eine χρυσία βῶλος nach Anaxagoras nennt (Phaeth. 777, Or. 983). Und wenn er im Phaethon einen lieblichen sternmythos dramatisirt, so vermenschlicht er ihn ganz.'

Γαῖα μεγίστη καὶ Διὸς Αἰθήρ,
ὁ μὲν ἀνθρώπων καὶ θεῶν γενέτωρ,
ἡ δ' ὑγροβόλους σταγόνας νοτίας
παραδεξαμένη τίκτει θνητούς,
τίκτει βοτάνην, φῦλά τε θηρῶν·
ὅθεν οὐκ ἀδίκως
μήτηρ πάντων νενόμισται.
χωρεῖ δ' ὀπίσω
τὰ μὲν ἐκ γαίας φύντ' εἰς γαῖαν,
τὰ δ' ἀπ' αἰθερίου βλαστόντα γονῆς
εἰς οὐράνιον πάλιν ἦλθε πόλον·
θνήσκει δ' οὐδὲν τῶν γιγνομένων,
διακρινόμενον δ' ἄλλο πρὸς ἄλλου
μορφὴν ἑτέραν ἀπέδειξεν (*Frag.* 839)[1].

There is nothing like this to be found in the Orators; but we may here quote from Hyperides a passage in which he speaks of the sun as determining the seasons and fructifying all things (*Epitaph.* ii–iii):—

ὥσπερ γὰρ ὁ ἥλιος πᾶσαν τὴν οἰκουμένην ἐπέρχεται,—τὰς μὲν ὥρας διακρίνων εἰς τὸ πρέπον καὶ καλῶς πάντα καθιστάς, τοῖς δὲ σώφροσι καὶ ἐπιεικέσι τῶν ἀνθρώπων ἐπιμελούμενος καὶ γενέσεως τῆς τροφῆς καὶ καρπῶν καὶ τῶν ἄλλων ἁπάντων τῶν εἰς τὸν βίον χρησίμων[2].

Euripides in several passages mentions the Pleiades, three times with the adjective ἑπτάπορος:—ἑπτάποροι Πλειάδες αἰθέριαι (*Rhes.* 528: cf. *Iph. Aul.* 7; *Or.* 1005).

In one of the passages (*Iph. Aul.* 7) he also mentions Σείριος by name[3].

In *Frag.* 594 we have the ἄρκτοι and the ᾿Ατλάντειος πόλος:—

. . . δίδυμοί τ' ἄρκτοι
ταῖς ὠκυπλάνοις πτερύγων ῥιπαῖς
τὸν ᾿Ατλάντειον τηροῦσι πόλον[4].

Nowhere in the Orators is any mention made of the stars.

---

[1] See also *Hipp.* 601; *Troad.* 884.
[2] Cf. Antiphon (the sophist, not the orator), *Frag.* 103 a, 104, 105 (ed. Blass).
[3] See Paley's note *ad loc.*
[4] On Euripides' fondness for astronomy see Paley's notes on *Ion*, 1146–1158; *Rhes.* 529; *Alc.* 962; and Earle's note on *Alc.* 962.

In connexion with the Greek notion of the world and Greek ideas of geography[1] we may quote the following passages :—

ὅσοι τε πόντου τερμόνων τ' Ἀτλαντικῶν
ναίουσιν εἴσω φῶς ὁρῶντες ἡλίου (*Hipp.* 3–4)[2].
Δαναὸς ὁ πεντήκοντα θυγατέρων πατὴρ
Νείλου λιπὼν κάλλιστον ἐκ γαίας ὕδωρ,
ὃς ἐκ μελαμβρότοιο πληροῦται ῥοὰς
Αἰθιοπίδος γῆς, ἡνίκ' ἂν τακῇ χιὼν[3]
τέθριππ' ἄγοντος ἡλίου κατ' αἰθέρα,
ἐλθὼν ἐς Ἄργος ᾤκισ' Ἰνάχου πόλιν·
Πελασγιώτας δ' ὠνομασμένους τὸ πρὶν
Δαναοὺς καλεῖσθαι νόμον ἔθηκ' ἀν' Ἑλλάδα (*Frag.* 228).

and Demosthenes, *Epist.* iv. 7 :—

καὶ ἑῶ Καππαδόκας καὶ Σύρους καὶ τοὺς τὴν Ἰνδικὴν χώραν
κατοικοῦντας ἀνθρώπους ἐπ' ἔσχατα γῆς.

[1] Euripides is not much interested in foreign peoples or questions of geography. Cf. Wilamowitz-M., *Herakles*, Einleitung, p. 31 :—'Fremder völker sitten, fremder länder wunder kennen zu lernen ist er nicht beflissen ; mit geographischen namen zu prunken verschmäht er.'

[2] See Paley's note *ad loc.* For Oceanus as environing the earth see *Orestes*, 1376–1379 (with Paley's note).

[3] This theory of the Nile seems to have been commonly held. Cf. Eur. *Hel.* 1–3 ; Aesch. *Suppl.* 559 (where Egypt is called λειμὼν χιονόβοσκος) and *Frag.* 300 (Nauck) ; Herod. ii. 19 ff.

CHAPTER III

RELIGION—MYSTERIES—BLOODGUILTINESS

§ 1. LIKE every religion which has its origin in the personification of natural forces, the religion of the Greeks was poly-
theistic. These natural powers, against which men seemed so
weak and helpless, would originally be regarded with fear:
the feeling of reverence would come later, when their movements were thought to be due, not to blind force, but to an
immanent mind and will. The recognised presence of this
mind and will would lead men more and more to attribute
to them all human emotions and qualities, and even a human
appearance and form. The inventiveness of the Greek mind
would do the rest. Hence, even in the earliest Greek literature which we possess, we have an elaborate, anthropomorphic
mythology [1].

It was only in power, however, not in virtue that these
gods were superior to men. Human justice and temperance
exceeded the divine. Greek morality was a much purer
thing than Greek religion, and acted as its corrector [2].

In Homer the depravity of the gods and their mutual
quarrels are set forth without hesitation or disguise. Even
Zeus may be successfully opposed by the inferior gods.
'L'essence de la société divine est l'anarchie.' And so men
believed that over this turbulent democracy there was a
higher divinity to which even the Olympic gods must render
obedience. To this they gave the name of μοῖρα.

[1] For some general characteristics of the Greek religion see Holm, i.
pp. 132-133; Coulanges, *La Cité Antique*, pp. 136-142. Coulanges contrasts
the worship of ancestors with the worship of the gods of physical nature.
[2] Cf. Lloyd, *Age of Pericles*, ii. pp. 196-198.

If we compare the gods of the *Odyssey* with those of the *Iliad*, we find that already a purer conception of their nature exists. Their immorality is much less frequently obtruded: they are far more often spoken of as aiding the good and taking vengeance on the evil. From the time of Homer Zeus is consistently regarded as the avenger of perjury, the protector of the suppliant and the guest.

In Hesiod the gods are universally considered as the destroyers of the wicked, the protectors of the good. A host of watchers reveal to Zeus all that passes on the earth.

This advance is continued in the lyric poets. Higher opinions of the gods began to prevail as men made progress in civilisation and humanity. It was at this time that the phrases ὁ θεός and τὸ θεῖον began to be used. Zeus is now commonly regarded as the *censor morum* who punishes all evil-doing. The popular opinion of this time is perhaps best expressed by Pindar[1], who also declares that gods and men have the same origin, and that the thing wherein they chiefly differ is strength, men being weak and fragile, the gods strong and immortal. As to the divine power all the lyric poets are agreed: Zeus is coming more and more to be identified with μοῖρα.

In Pindar especially a new and important feature may be noticed,—*the suppression of myths which had for their subject immorality on the part of the gods.* To disparage the gods is depraved wisdom[2]: 'de dis nil nisi bonum' is his motto[3].

In Herodotus the thought ever present is the weakness of man and the folly of trying to rise above it. If one does make the attempt, he is speedily humbled. The god is a jealous god, and suffers none but himself to be proud[4]. Happiness and prosperity are of themselves a sufficient cause to bring a man low; and the iniquities of the fathers are visited upon the children unto the third and fourth generation. This notion, like that of the divine jealousy, was clearly a popular one. The views of Herodotus are more crude than those of the lyric poets.

---

[1] *Nem.* vi. 1-9.
[2] *Ol.* ix. 40-41.
[3] *Ol.* i. 35, 52.
[4] *Herod.* vii. 10.

Aeschylus, of a philosophic bent, endowed with a bold and comprehensive mental grasp, and eager to know the causes of things, could hardly be content merely to shut his eyes to difficulties in the popular conception of the divine nature, and adopt Pindar's policy of suppression. In the few dramas which have come down to us, and which contain numerous conflicting ideas, he frequently mentions the unconquerable necessity of fate. But the Aeschylean Necessity is not capricious: it always works for righteousness. To its laws all are subject—not men only, but also the gods. Transgression of these laws brings sure punishment (δράσαντι παθεῖν). The Aeschylean conception is higher than that of Herodotus. Mere prosperity is not enough to bring down the jealous wrath of heaven: men are not hateful to the gods, if only they are just and moderate. Even in the case of the Hereditary Curse it is not guilt that is inherited, but only a tendency to guilt. There must be an initial, voluntary act on the part of the man himself. 'The soul is its own fate.' But Aeschylus does not always represent the gods as guiltless. In the *Prometheus* Zeus is a cruel tyrant: in the *Eumenides* (640 ff.) the Erinyes reproach him with throwing Kronos into chains. Aeschylus, though he so often assigns to the gods the care of justice, cannot quite break away from the tormenting tradition which assigns to them so many transgressions [1].

In Sophocles the influence of fate is not present as it is in Aeschylus, nor is it separated from the divine supremacy. He is less speculative than Aeschylus, and his moral grasp is not so comprehensive. But none ever showed a greater hatred of arrogance or more earnestly inculcated moderation. There is no maxim truer to the Greek character than μηδὲν ἄγαν, and nowhere is this seen more clearly than in Sophocles. In him men recognise the justice of the gods, and very rarely presume to accuse them of wrong. Like Pindar, Sophocles was of opinion that stories which had for their subject immorality on the part of the gods should be passed over in silence. With him the gods are holy and just, and observe

[1] Cf. *Frag.* 156, 350 (Nauck) in Plato, *Rep.* ii. 380 A, 383 B.

the evil and the good. The 'unwritten laws[1]' are closely connected with the divine supremacy[2].

So far the poets. But philosophers also had given attention to these questions, and waged war with the popular beliefs[3]. Xenophanes was the first to assume the aggressive. He maintained that God was one and unchangeable and in no way resembled men; and he attacks Homer and Hesiod for attributing to the gods conduct which would be disgraceful even in human beings. Heraclitus substituted for the popular and traditional notion that of universal law. This law is his Zeus. The ground of revolt both in Xenophanes and in Heraclitus is a moral one.

Later philosophers made no direct attack on religion, but the doctrines to which reason and natural science led them were directly opposed to it. With Democritus Nature was τὸ θεῖον, with Anaxagoras νοῦς.

The position of the sophists was a purely negative one. They could not believe in the popular traditions, but for these traditions they offered no substitute[4].

In Aristophanes, the burlesque critic who so unsparingly lashed Euripides as a quibbling atheist, we find many things which at first sight look much more impious than anything Euripides ever wrote. But these things are said merely in jest, and not with a view to disturb religious conviction. The impieties of Aristophanes are only apparent[5].

---

[1] *Oed. Rex*, 865 ; *Ajax*, 1343 ; *Antig.* 454.

[2] See Butcher, *Some Aspects of the Greek Genius* (1891), pp. 83-129 ; Campbell, *Greek Tragedy*, pp. 103-118.

[3] For the manner in which religion regards poetry as contrasted with that in which it regards science see Holm, ii. p. 165. See also Coulanges, *La Cité Antique*, pp. 415-424 (Livre V, c. i, *Nouvelles croyances: la philosophie change les règles de la politique*).

[4] Cf. Protagoras *apud* Diog. Laert. ix. 51 :—περὶ μὲν θεῶν οὐκ ἔχω εἰδέναι Berlage cj. εἰπεῖν) οὔθ' ὡς εἰσὶν οὔθ' ὡς οὐκ εἰσίν. πολλὰ γὰρ τὰ κωλύοντα εἰδέναι, ἥ τε ἀδηλότης καὶ βραχὺς ὢν ὁ βίος τοῦ ἀνθρώπου. And see Coulanges, *La Cité Antique*, p. 419 :—'On les (sc. les sophistes) accusa de n'avoir ni religion, ni morale, ni patriotisme. La vérité est que sur toutes ces choses ils n'avaient pas une doctrine bien arrêtée, et qu'ils croyaient avoir assez fait quand ils avaient combattu des préjugés.'

[5] See Perrot, *L'Éloquence politique et judiciaire à Athènes*, pp. 162-164 ; Verrall, *Euripides the Rationalist*, pp. 82-84.

Thucydides makes hardly any mention of the gods of mythology. He is concerned with human affairs, and seeks to explain things by natural causes. He lays little stress on oracles [1], and treats with a slight touch of sarcasm the superstition of Nicias [2].

Socrates and Plato are both said to have been pious worshippers of the gods, and that though they by no means thought with the people on the subject of religion. Apparently they were either of opinion that the popular religion was better suited than philosophy to the ordinary citizen, or they considered that it would be dangerous to overthrow what was one of the bases of the political constitution. Yet both certainly believed that the gods did nothing but what was right, and 'needed nothing.' Socrates (*Phaedrus*, 229 E) considers allegorical interpretations of the myths as proofs ἀγροίκου σοφίας: he is convinced of the obscurity of divine things, and would let well alone [3].

Both poets and philosophers, therefore, had sought to purify the popular mythology. But they had employed different methods. The poets retained what seemed good, destroying only what was positively immoral: the philosophers declared the myths to be wholly untrue, and swept them utterly away. The two movements were united in Euripides, who was at once philosopher and poet. But Euripides shows considerable weakness on this side of his work as well as on the artistic. In both he held a *media via* between the old and the new [4]. He could not break

---

[1] Cf. ii. 21. 3 :—χρησμολόγοι τε ᾖδον χρησμοὺς παντοίους, ὡς ἀκροᾶσθαι ἕκαστος ὥρμητο. In this respect Thucydides resembles Euripides.

[2] vii. 50. 4 :—ἦν γάρ τι καὶ ἄγαν θεασμῷ τε καὶ τῷ τοιούτῳ προσκείμενος.

[3] In the *Euthyphro* Socrates declares that τὸ ὅσιον cannot be learned from the gods : the gods themselves are not agreed as to its nature. For a full discussion of the whole subject see Grote, c. lxvii ; Coulanges, *La Cité Antique*, pp. 418 ff. ; Decharme, *Euripide, &c.*, pp. 59–64.

[4] This inconsistency shows itself also in dealing with political, social, and ethical questions. It was hardly to be avoided by one who lived in a time of free-thought and inquiry, and who was himself deeply imbued with the sceptical spirit. See Jerram's *Alcestis*, Introd. pp. xxi, xxii. For an interesting essay on Euripides' religious views see Westcott, *Religious Thought in the West*, pp. 96–141 ('Euripides as a religious Teacher'). But Westcott does not make

away from the tradition which compelled a tragedian to
choose his subject from mythology, and yet that mythology
he entirely undermines and destroys when he says, 'If the
gods do anything base, they are not gods[1].' But to this
position Euripides did not at once attain.

Berlage is, I think, right in distinguishing three main
stages in the attitude of Euripides towards the popular
religion. In the first stage he accepts the popular religion:
in the second he becomes sceptical, rationalistic, vituperative:
in the third, while not indeed returning to his first position,
he refrains from active hostility, deeming it only useless
labour. The dramas falling under the first division—to
mention only complete plays—are the *Alcestis* (438 B.C.) and
the *Medea* (431); under the second division, *Hippolytus* (428),
*Hecuba (423), *Andromache (430–420), *Hercules Furens*
(424–416), *Supplices (420), *Ion (420–418), *Troades* (415),
Helena and *Electra (412) **Iphigenia Taurica* (411), *Orestes*
(408); under the last division, *Bacchae* and *Iphigenia Auli-
densis* (406), *Phoenissae* (405)[2].

In the *Alcestis* and the *Medea* Euripides hardly deviates
from the orthodox path of the traditional religion. The
sovereign power of Necessity is a theme of frequent recurrence. We need only refer to the famous ode in the *Alcestis*
(962–990). 'I have found nought mightier than Necessity,'
the poet says:—

$$\kappa\rho\epsilon\hat{\imath}\sigma\sigma\sigma\nu \ o\dot{\upsilon}\delta\dot{\epsilon}\nu \ \dot{a}\nu\dot{a}\gamma\kappa\alpha\varsigma$$
$$\eta\hat{\upsilon}\rho\sigma\nu.$$

Necessity is the only deity who has no altar to which we
may approach, and who will accept no sacrifice:—

$$\mu\acute{o}\nu\alpha\varsigma \ \delta' \ o\mathring{\upsilon}\tau' \ \dot{\epsilon}\pi\grave{\iota} \ \beta\omega\mu\sigma\grave{\upsilon}\varsigma$$
$$\dot{\epsilon}\lambda\theta\epsilon\hat{\iota}\nu \ o\mathring{\upsilon}\tau\epsilon \ \beta\rho\acute{\epsilon}\tau\alpha\varsigma \ \theta\epsilon\hat{a}\varsigma$$
$$\mathring{\epsilon}\sigma\tau\iota\nu, \ o\mathring{\upsilon} \ \sigma\phi\alpha\gamma\acute{\iota}\omega\nu \ \kappa\lambda\acute{\upsilon}\epsilon\iota.$$

sufficient allowance for conflicting opinions, or for any change or development
in Euripides' thought.

[1] *Frag.* 292. l. 7:—εἰ θεοί τι δρῶσιν αἰσχρόν, οὐκ εἰσὶν θεοί.

[2] The dates of those marked with an asterisk are uncertain.

Without Necessity even Zeus cannot accomplish what he
wills:—

> καὶ γὰρ Ζεὺς ὅ τι νεύσῃ,
> σὺν σοὶ τοῦτο τελευτᾷ.

In several fragments belonging to this period Necessity is
coupled with the gods:—

> . . . . σκαιόν τι δὴ τὸ χρῆμα γίγνεσθαι φιλεῖ,
> θεῶν ἀνάγκας ὅστις ἰᾶσθαι θέλει (*Frag.* 339).
> σὺ δ' εἶκ' ἀνάγκῃ καὶ θεοῖσι μὴ μάχου (*Frag.* 716).

Apollo rescues Admetus from the death to which he had
been doomed, but it is only by tricking the Fates (Μοίρας
δολώσας. *Alc.* 12 : cf. *ibid.* 33) that he succeeds.

The popular notion of the φθόνος of the gods we find in
Alc. 1135. Heracles prays that it may not fall upon Admetus
in his hour of happiness:—

> ἔχεις (sc. τὴν γυναῖκα)· φθόνος δὲ μὴ γένοιτό τις θεῶν[1].

The gods are spoken of with reverence: their power and
justice are extolled: they are the avengers of wrong-
doing:—

> θεῶν γὰρ δύναμις μεγίστα (*Alc.* 219).
> λίσσου δὲ τοὺς κρατοῦντας οἰκτεῖραι θεούς (*ibid.* 251).
> Ζεύς σοι τάδε συνδικήσει (*Med.* 157)[2].
> οὐκ ἔστι τὰ θεῶν ἄδικ', ἐν ἀνθρώποισι δὲ
> κακοῖς νοσοῦντα σύγχυσιν πολλὴν ἔχει (*Frag.* 606).
> φεῦ, μήποτ' εἴην ἄλλο πλὴν θεοῖς φίλος,
> ὡς πᾶν τελοῦσι κἂν βραδύνωσιν χρόνῳ (*Frag.* 800).

It is true that in later plays also the power and justice
of the gods is frequently extolled: what is chiefly to be
noticed is that in neither the *Alcestis* nor the *Medea*—though
both these plays furnished occasion enough—are the gods
made the objects of impious invective.

Even at this time, however, we see indications of the poet's
later scepticism (*Med.* 409-413)[3]:—

---

[1] See Jerram's note *ad loc.*; and cf. *Orestes*, 974.
[2] Cf. *Med.* 492-495.
[3] Mr. Jerram thinks that even in the *Alcestis* the poet 'is at war with
his materials,' though the play 'exhibits no overt signs of rebellion against

ἄνω ποταμῶν ἱερῶν χωροῦσι παγαί,
καὶ δίκα καὶ πάντα πάλιν στρέφεται.
ἀνδράσι μὲν δόλιαι βουλαί, θεῶν δ'
οὐκέτι πίστις ἄραρε.

Divination is uncertain: the gods are unknowable (*Frag.* 795):—

τί δῆτα θάκοις μαντικοῖς ἐνήμενοι
σαφῶς διόμνυσθ' εἰδέναι τὰ δαιμόνων;
οὐ τῶνδε χειρώνακτες ἄνθρωποι λόγων·
ὅστις γὰρ αὐχεῖ θεῶν ἐπίστασθαι πέρι,
οὐδέν τι μᾶλλον οἶδεν ἢ πείθειν λέγων.

There is an interval of three years between the *Medea* and the *Hippolytus*. In these three years (431-428) great changes had taken place at Athens. Pericles had died; the city had been wasted by the plague; the seeds of moral disorder had been sown, and were already beginning to bear bitter fruit; religion and morality had been shaken to their foundations. The difference between the Athens of 431 and the Athens of 428 is no greater than that between the Euripides of the *Medea* and the Euripides of the *Hippolytus*.

In the dramas of the second period Necessity is not emphasised by Euripides as it is in those of the first. It is indeed often mentioned, but in a vague way: ἀνάγκη, χρεών, μοῖρα, τύχη are more or les interchangeable terms. In *Iph. Taur.* (1486) Necessity is said to rule both gods and men:—

ΑΘ. αἰνῶ· τὸ γὰρ χρῆν σοῦ τε καὶ θεῶν κρατεῖ [1].

orthodox beliefs,' and that what he says in effect to his audience is—'These be the gods ye worship!' (See his *Alcestis*, Introd. xxii xxiii.) Still more emphatic is Dr. Verrall in his *Euripides the Rationalist*. The *Alcestis*, he says, belongs to 'a type of dramatic work whose meaning lies entirely in *innuendo*' (p. 77). 'The creed of Euripides was that of nascent philosophy, science, and rationalism' (p. 79). I cannot help thinking that Dr. Verrall has read into Euripides a good deal more than Euripides himself—not to speak of his audience—would have imagined to be there. Despite the keenness and brilliancy of the work, it is not, to me, convincing. His premises, I think, do not apply to the *Alcestis*; and even in the case of the *Ion*—where they do apply, at least in part—the conclusions seem overdrawn.

[1] But the date of *Iph. Taur.* is uncertain. The play perhaps ought to be classed with those of the third period.

Necessity is hard and invincible (*Hel.* 514; *Hec.* 1295; *Or.* 488): it is unavoidable (*Heracl.* 614; *Hipp.* 1255; *Ion,* 1388): it brings many things to pass (*Heracl.* 898). Fate and Zeus are almost identified (*Andr.* 1268: cf. *Electra,* 1248): the Fates sit nearest the throne of Zeus (*Frag.* 620): Fate and Zeus are superior to Hera and Iris (*Her. Fur.* 827): Castor and Pollux are inferior to Fate and the gods (*Hel.* 1660; *El.* 1298 ff.): the labours of Heracles are imposed either by Hera or Necessity (*Her. Fur.* 20): to the gods are due the vicissitudes of fortune (*Heracl.* 608).

A study of these passages will make it clear that Euripides uses the various terms—as they were no doubt used in the language of common life—to denote vaguely that something which men find it impossible to escape. Of infinitely greater importance is his attitude towards the gods themselves. We shall first look at some passages where the gods are blamed, then at some passages where they are praised, and finally try to explain the discrepancy.

Hippolytus, in the play of the same name, is represented as one who has sought to exceed the bounds of human nature. He slights Aphrodite—with consequences. Yet it is with Hippolytus and Phaedra that our sympathies lie, not with the avenging goddess. Phaedra is merely the instrument of vengeance, and is morally innocent. Artemis, who appears in order to disclose the truth of the matter, speaks in no mild terms of her sister Aphrodite, on whom she lays the whole blame :—

τῆς γὰρ ἐχθίστης θεῶν
ἡμῖν ὅσαισι παρθένειος ἡδονὴ
δηχθεῖσα κέντροις παιδὸς ἠράσθη σέθεν (1301–1303).
ἀνθρώποισι δὲ
θεῶν διδόντων εἰκὸς ἐξαμαρτάνειν (1433–1434).

But she will yet be on even terms with her (1420–1422):—

ἐγὼ γὰρ αὐτῆς ἄλλον ἐξ ἐμῆς χερὸς
ὃς ἂν μάλιστα φίλτατος κυρῇ βροτῶν
τόξοις ἀφύκτοις τοῖσδε τιμωρήσομαι.

Hippolytus is conscious of the injustice of his fate (1060–1061):—

ὦ θεοί, τί δῆτα τοὐμὸν οὐ λύω στόμα,
ὅστις γ' ὑφ' ὑμῶν, οὓς σέβω, διόλλυμαι[1];

No wonder if the Chorus feel that the ways of the gods are perplexing, and exclaim (1102–1110):—

ἦ μέγα μοι τὰ θεῶν μελεδήμαθ', ὅταν φρένας ἔλθῃ,
λύπας παραιρεῖ· ξύνεσιν δέ τιν' ἐλπίδι κεύθων
λείπομαι ἔν τε τύχαις θνατῶν καὶ ἐν ἔργμασι λεύσσων·
ἄλλα γὰρ ἄλλοθεν ἀμείβεται,
μετὰ δ' ἵσταται ἀνδράσιν αἰὼν
πολυπλάγητος ἀεί[2].

We can imagine that another writer might have treated the subject in such a way that the death of Hippolytus would have been felt to be a fitting vengeance for his contempt of the goddess of love, and no indignation against Aphrodite would have been aroused. But, when we read the play of Euripides, all our sympathies are with the human personages. The wrangling of the two goddesses[3], the spite of Artemis, the cruelty of Aphrodite—are all painted in the most glaring colours. The only effect which the play could have on the spectators must have been to make them indignant at such gods, and to awaken in their minds serious questionings of the truth of the traditional religion. 'Ab uno disce omnes.' In the dramas of this period Euripides never misses an opportunity of hurling at the gods his strongest indignation and fiercest invective.

---

[1] Cf. 1363–1369:—

Ζεῦ Ζεῦ, τάδ' ὁρᾷς;
ὅδ' ὁ σεμνὸς ἐγὼ καὶ θεοσέπτωρ,
ὅδ' ὁ σωφροσύνῃ πάντας ὑπερσχὼν
προὔπτον ἐς Ἅιδαν στείχω κατὰ γᾶς,
ὀλέσας βίοτον·
μόχθους δ' ἄλλως τῆς εὐσεβίας
εἰς ἀνθρώπους ἐπόνησα.

[2] The meaning of this difficult passage I take to be as follows:—'The thought of the gods' care for men, when it comes to me, doth greatly relieve my pain: but, when I would hopefully cherish (a belief in) a Providence, I am at a loss when I compare men's fortunes with their deeds: for all things change in divers ways, and the life of man shifts and wanders evermore.'

[3] Cf. Cypris and Hera in the *Helena* (see Jerram's edition, Introd. xiii).

In no play are the sceptical doubts of Euripides more plainly shown than in the *Hercules Furens*. Amphitryon questions the justice of Zeus (211–212):—

> ὃ χρῆν σ' ὑφ' ἡμῶν τῶν ἀμεινόνων παθεῖν,
> εἰ Ζεὺς δικαίας εἶχεν εἰς ἡμᾶς φρένας:

and exclaims loudly and passionately against his immorality (339–347):—

> ὦ Ζεῦ, μάτην ἄρ' ὁμόγαμόν σ' ἐκτησάμην,
> μάτην δὲ παιδῶν γονέ' ἐμῶν ἐκλῄζομεν.
> σὺ δ' ἦσθ' ἄρ' ἥσσων ἢ 'δόκεις εἶναι φίλος.
> ἀρετῇ σε νικῶ θνητὸς ὢν θεὸν μέγαν.
> παῖδας γὰρ οὐ προὔδωκα τοὺς Ἡρακλέους.
> σὺ δ' ἐς μὲν εὐνὰς κρύφιος ἠπίστω μολεῖν,
> τἀλλότρια λέκτρα δόντος οὐδενὸς λαβών,
> σώζειν δὲ τοὺς σοὺς οὐκ ἐπίστασαι φίλους.
> ἀμαθής τις εἶ θεός, ἢ δίκαιος οὐκ ἔφυς.

'The god is stubborn,' but Heracles will meet obstinacy with obstinacy (1243):—

> αὔθαδες ὁ θεός· πρὸς δὲ τοὺς θεοὺς ἐγώ.

Hera is unjust and slays the innocent. Who would pray to such a goddess (1307–1310)?—

> τοιαύτῃ θεῷ
> τίς ἂν προσεύχοιθ'; ἢ γυναικὸς οὕνεκα
> λέκτρων φθονοῦσα Ζηνί, τοὺς εὐεργέτας
> Ἑλλάδος ἀπώλεσ' οὐδὲν ὄντας αἰτίους.

Theseus, seeking to pacify Heracles, says it is not seemly that a mortal should bear so ill misfortunes from which even the gods are not exempt. It is better to follow the gods' example, and do evil contentedly (1316–1319)!—

> οὐ λέκτρα τ' ἀλλήλοισιν, ὧν οὐδεὶς νόμος,
> συνῆψαν; οὐ δεσμοῖσι διὰ τυραννίδας
> πατέρας ἐκηλίδωσαν; ἀλλ' οἰκοῦσ' ὅμως
> Ὄλυμπον ἠνέσχοντό θ' ἡμαρτηκότες.

The effect of such words on the minds of the spectators must have been even greater than that produced by the

Hippolytus. There the invective was limited: here it is extended to all.

Heracles will give credence to no such poets' tales. The god, if he be in truth a god, can stand in need of nothing (1341-1346):—

> ἐγὼ δὲ τοὺς θεοὺς οὔτε λέκτρ' ἃ μὴ θέμις
> στέργειν νομίζω, δεσμά τ' ἐξάπτειν χεροῖν
> οὔτ' ἠξίωσα πώποτ' οὔτε πείσομαι,
> οὐδ' ἄλλον ἄλλου δεσπότην πεφυκέναι.
> δεῖται γὰρ ὁ θεός, εἴπερ ἔστ' ὄντως θεός,
> οὐδενός· ἀοιδῶν οἵδε δύστηνοι λόγοι[1].

These words, though they imply a denial of the very basis of the play, show that Euripides had now reached a conception of the gods far purer than the traditional one. So also Iphigenia will not believe the story of the 'cena Tantalea' (for which she finds a rationalistic explanation): none of the gods is evil (*Iph. Taur.* 386-391):—

> ἐγὼ μὲν οὖν
> τὰ Ταντάλου θεοῖσιν ἑστιάματα
> ἄπιστα κρίνω, παιδὸς ἡσθῆναι βορᾷ,
> τοὺς δ' ἐνθάδ', αὐτοὺς ὄντας ἀνθρωποκτόνους,
> ἐς τὸν θεὸν τὸ φαῦλον ἀναφέρειν δοκῶ·
> οὐδένα γὰρ οἶμαι δαιμόνων εἶναι κακόν[2].

I will only add here some similar passages from other plays belonging to this period. No tragedy furnishes so copious a supply as does the *Ion*.

The gods are audacious and unjust (252-254):—

> ὦ τολμήματα
> θεῶν. τί δῆτα; ποῖ δίκην ἀνοίσομεν,
> εἰ τῶν κρατούντων ἀδικίαις ὀλούμεθα[3];

---

[1] Cf. *Frag.* 210.

[2] Cf. *Frag.* 292 :—

> εἰ θεοί τι δρῶσιν αἰσχρόν, οὐκ εἰσὶν θεοί.

In the same tragedy, however, the existence of the gods is plainly denied (*Frag.* 286):—

> φησίν τις εἶναι δῆτ' ἐν οὐρανῷ θεούς;
> οὐκ εἰσίν, οὐκ εἴσ', εἴ τις ἀνθρώπων θέλει
> μὴ τῷ παλαιῷ μωρὸς ὢν χρῆσθαι λόγῳ.

[3] Cf. *ibid.* 877.

Apollo's injustice is frequently mentioned (e. g. 384–385):—

ὦ Φοῖβε, κἀκεῖ κἀνθάδ' οὐ δίκαιος εἶ
ἐς τὴν ἀποῦσαν, ἧς πάρεισιν οἱ λόγοι[1].

Shame prevents him from appearing in person (1557–1558):--

ὃς ἐς μὲν ὄψιν σφῶν μολεῖν οὐκ ἠξίου,
μὴ τῶν πάροιθε μέμψις ἐς μέσον μόλῃ.

He is a base paramour (912):—

κακὸς εὐνάτωρ[2].

He has power: he should have virtue also (439–440):—

μὴ σύ γ'· ἀλλ' ἐπεὶ κρατεῖς
ἀρετὰς δίωκε.

The gods break their own laws, yet they punish sinners (440–443):—

καὶ γὰρ ὅστις ἂν βροτῶν
κακὸς πεφύκῃ, ζημιοῦσιν οἱ θεοί.
πῶς οὖν δίκαιον τοὺς νόμους ὑμᾶς βροτοῖς
γράψαντας αὐτοὺς ἀνομίαν ὀφλισκάνειν ;

Is it just to speak of men as evil, when the gods do wrong (446–451)?—

σὺ καὶ Ποσειδῶν Ζεύς θ' ὃς οὐρανοῦ κρατεῖ,
ναοὺς τίνοντες ἀδικίας κενώσετε.
τὰς ἡδονὰς γὰρ τῆς προμηθίας πάρος
σπεύδοντες ἀδικεῖτ'· οὐκέτ' ἀνθρώπους κακοὺς
λέγειν δίκαιον, εἰ τὰ τῶν θεῶν κακὰ
μιμούμεθ', ἀλλὰ τοὺς διδάσκοντας τάδε.

True, Apollo is justified (1595), and Creusa is reconciled to him (1609 ff.). But the justification is only partial: the writer's purpose has been fulfilled.

Apollo is no better than a κακὸς ἄνθρωπος (Andr. 1161–1165): he is σκαιός (El. 972), and unjust (Or. 28, 162, 285): he lends no aid to one who has obeyed his behests (Iph. Taur. 711). The gods deceive (Hel. 704, 708): they are false as dreams (Iph. Taur. 570).

---

[1] Cf. Frag. 355, 426, 438, 912, 919, 952.
[2] Cf. ibid. 894.

But in these plays the gods are not always blamed; and I will now instance some passages where they are the objects of praise.

The gods justly destroy evil-doers (*Suppl.* 504-505):—

ἢ νυν φρονεῖν ἄμεινον ἐξαύχει Διός,
ἢ θεοὺς δικαίως τοὺς κακοὺς ἀπολλύναι.

They are beneficent, and to them is due the growth of civilisation and all the benefits it brings (*Suppl.* 201 ff.). A man should not charge the gods with folly in order to screen himself (*Tro.* 981-982). The gods hate violence (*Hel.* 903), and their word is true (*ibid.* 1150): they pity the woes of mortals (*El.* 1327): they observe the evil and the good (*Her. Fur.* 772 ff.): they aid the just only, not the unjust (*El.* 1349), and give justice the victory over injustice (*Ion,* 1117-1118). Zeus, though late, has regard to the suffering (*Heracl.* 869). The power of the gods is frequently mentioned. It is impious folly to say that they have no power (*Her. Fur.* 757-759). If a man has the gods on his side, he needs nought else (*Suppl.* 594-597). Hence frequent injunctions to honour and worship the gods (*Suppl.* 301-302; *Hipp.* 88, 107; *Heracl.* 902-903; *Ion,* 1619-1620; *El.* 890-891; *Iph. Taur.* 1475-1476).

Now how is this apparent discrepancy to be explained? In large measure, no doubt, by the dramatic proprieties. But there are other considerations also. Of these the most important is that, just as on the more formal side of his art Euripides was unable to free himself from the bonds of tradition and strike out a line wholly new, so also, even after he had come to the conclusion that the deity must be perfectly holy, and hence could no longer be a pious worshipper of the gods of mythology, he was still unable to find any satisfactory and permanent standpoint. He was destructive rather than constructive, negative rather than positive. He was not completely master of the material with which he worked: it was very often master of him. So it was that his position frequently resembles that taken up by the poets who preceded him: when the gods show

themselves just and 'needing nothing,' he is ready to accord
them reverence; when the myths represent them as cruel
and immoral, he maintains that such gods are no gods, and
assails them with indignant invective. Hence his uncertainty
and vacillation. In his mind feeling and tradition were
at war with reason; he could not follow his rationalistic
method to its legitimate conclusion [1].

In connexion with the above-quoted passages in which
the gods are blamed, it may be noticed that evil-doers turn
this conception of the gods to their own account, and blame
the gods to screen themselves. In *Hipp.* (433–481) the nurse
advises Phaedra not to resist Aphrodite, but to give the
rein to her passion. Even Zeus is not able to resist; and
it is pure ὕβρις to desire to be superior to the gods [2]. In
Heracl. (990) Eurystheus throws the blame of his cruelty
on Hera. Orestes (*Or.* 285–287) says that Loxias incited
him to the impious deed [3].

Similarly suffering and misfortune come from the gods
(*Tro.* 691):—

νικᾷ γὰρ οὐκ θεῶν με δύστηνος κλύδων [4].

There was an absence of dualism in the Greek religion.
They had no devil, and, in order to rid themselves of the
blame of their wrong-doing, they were forced to lay it upon
the gods.

We are now in a position to investigate more fully
Euripides' conception of the nature of the gods. We have
already seen that, after he had reached the conclusion,
δεῖται γὰρ ὁ θεός, εἴπερ ἔστ' ὄντως θεός, οὐδενός (*Her. Fur.*
1345–1346), he could no longer accept the myths of the
popular religion. His studies in physics must have helped

---

[1] Wilamowitz-M., *Herakles,* Einleitung, pp. 29-30, says :—'Seine eigene
ansicht von den ἀρχαί, ein dualismus von geist gott aether und stoff körper
erde, ist *ein compromiss* zwischen der philosophie des ostens und der theologie
der heimat und des westens.'

[2] Cf. *Her. Fur.* 1320-1321 ; *Tro.* 948 950.

[3] Cf. *ibid.* 28-30 (with Paley's note..

[4] Cf. *Hipp.* 867, 1347 ; *Hec.* 202, 721 ; *Her. Fur.* 1189 ; *Tro.* 770, 1201.

to confirm his disbelief[1]. But he was not able at once to
form any definite opinion as to what their true nature was.
Often his words are of the vaguest: sometimes he doubts
whether they exist at all.

The ways of the god are inscrutable (*Hel.* 711-712):—

> ὁ θεὸς ὡς ἔφυ τι ποικίλον
> καὶ δυστέκμαρτον[2].

In *Frag.* 480 we have these words;—

> Ζεύς, ὅστις ὁ Ζεύς, οὐ γὰρ οἶδα πλὴν λόγῳ.

So again (*Her. Fur.* 1263):—

> Ζεύς, ὅστις ὁ Ζεύς.

And cf. *Or.* 418:—

> δουλεύομεν θεοῖς, ὅ τι ποτ' εἰσὶν οἱ θεοί.

His sceptical doubts thus frequently intrude themselves.
Yet rationalism is folly and lawlessness (*Iph. Taur.* 275 ff.):—

> ἄλλος δέ τις μάταιος, ἀνομίᾳ θρασύς,
> ἐγέλασεν εὐχαῖς, κ.τ.λ.[3]

Zeus is sometimes identified with Aether (*Frag.* 941):—

> ὁρᾷς τὸν ὑψοῦ τόνδ' ἄπειρον αἰθέρα
> καὶ γῆν πέριξ ἔχονθ' ὑγραῖς ἐν ἀγκάλαις;
> τοῦτον νόμιζε Ζῆνα, τόνδ' ἡγοῦ θεόν[4].

Cf. *Troad.* 884-888, where we have, perhaps, the doctrine
of Anaxagoras[5]:—

> ὦ γῆς ὄχημα κἀπὶ γῆς ἔχων ἕδραν,
> ὅστις ποτ' εἶ σύ, δυστόπαστος εἰδέναι,

---

[1] So Helen doubts the story that she was born from an egg (*Hel.* 21).
Cf. *Tro.* 971 ff.; *El.* 737-738 ; *Frag.* 506.

[2] Cf. *Frag.* 793 :— ὅστις γὰρ αὐχεῖ θεῶν ἐπίστασθαι πέρι,
  οὐδέν τι μᾶλλον οἶδεν ἢ πείθειν λέγων.

[3] Dr. Verrall, however (*Euripides the Rationalist*, p. 174), regards the incident
as 'a little triumph for "the insolent fellow, disorderly and rash".' Perhaps
it is so meant : I am not sure that it is.

[4] Cf. *Frag.* 839 :—Γαῖα μεγίστη καὶ Διὸς Αἰθήρ, κ.τ.λ.; and see Decharme,
Euripide, &c., p. 84 :—'L'éther et Zeus ne font qu'un.... Euripide dépouille
donc Jupiter de sa personnalité divine pour ne voir en lui qu'un nom de
l'éther, et pour le transformer en un élément essentiel de la nature.'

[5] See Paley's note *ad loc.*

D

Ζεύς, εἴτ' ἀνάγκη φύσεος εἴτε νοῦς βροτῶν,
προσευξάμην σε· πάντα γὰρ δι' ἀψόφου
βαίνων κελεύθου κατὰ δίκην τὰ θνήτ' ἄγεις[1].

The "κατὰ δίκην" in this passage is worthy of notice.

Alcmena does not think that Zeus has been just towards her (*Heracl.* 717-719):—

IO.   καὶ Ζηνὶ τῶν σῶν, οἶδ' ἐγώ, μέλει πόνων.

ΑΛ.   φεῦ·
Ζεὺς ἐξ ἐμοῦ μὲν οὐκ ἀκούσεται κακῶς·
εἰ δ' ἐστὶν ὅσιος αὐτὸς οἶδεν εἰς ἐμέ.

With the "νοῦς βροτῶν" in the passage quoted from the *Troades* we may compare *Frag.* 1018:—

ὁ νοῦς γὰρ ἡμῶν ἐστιν ἐν ἑκάστῳ θεός[2].

Sometimes the poet wonders whether the gods exist at all, or whether chance rules all things (*Hec.* 489-491):—

ἢ δόξαν ἄλλως τήνδε κεκτῆσθαι μάτην
ψευδῆ, δοκοῦντας δαιμόνων εἶναι γένος,
τύχην δὲ πάντα τἀν βροτοῖς ἐπισκοπεῖν[3];

In one or two passages he plainly denies their existence, e.g. *Frag.* 286:—

φησίν τις εἶναι δῆτ' ἐν οὐρανῷ θεούς;
οὐκ εἰσίν, οὐκ εἴσ', κ.τ.λ.

The issues of all things lie with the gods (*Suppl.* 617):—

ἁπάντων τέρμ' ἔχοντες αὐτοί[4].

We meet also with the popular notion of a jealous god (*Or.* 974):—

φθόνος νιν εἷλε θεόθεν.

---

[1] Of this passage M. Decharme says that it is 'prière non de dévot mais de philosophe ... elle était d'un genre nouveau, et Jupiter n'en avait jamais entendu de pareille' (*Euripide, &c.*, pp. 85-86).

[2] Cf. Cicero, *Tusc.* i. 26 :—'Ergo animus, ut ego dico, divinus est, ut Euripides dicere audet, deus.' For the less personal 'temple in the soul,' see *Hel.* 1002-1003 :—

ἔνεστι δ' ἱερὸν τῆς δίκης ἐμοὶ μέγα
ἐν τῇ φύσει.

[3] Cf. *Frag.* 901. In *Iph. Taur.* 1486, τὸ χρῆν rules both gods and men.

[4] Cf. *Or.* 1545.

The gods suffer no man to be proud : they humble the mighty and exalt the weak :—

ἐχθρῶν γὰρ ἀνδρῶν μοῖραν εἰς ἀναστροφὴν
δαίμων δίδωσι, κοὐκ ἐᾷ φρονεῖν μέγα   (Andr. 1007–1008).
            ἀλλὰ τῶν φρονημάτων
ὁ Ζεὺς κολαστὴς τῶν ἄγαν ὑπερφρόνων (Heracl. 387–388)[1].
ὁρῶ τὰ τῶν θεῶν, ὡς τὰ μὲν πυργοῦσ' ἄνω
τὰ μηδὲν ὄντα, τὰ δὲ δοκοῦντ' ἀπώλεσαν (Troad. 608–609).

It is folly to attempt to impose upon the gods (Hipp. 950–951) :—

οὐκ ἂν πιθοίμην τοῖσι σοῖς κόμποις ἐγώ,
θεοῖσι προσθεὶς ἀμαθίαν φρονεῖν κακῶς.

The highest note is struck in the following passages :—

οὐδένα γὰρ οἶμαι δαιμόνων εἶναι κακόν (Iph. Taur. 391).
ἐγὼ δὲ τοὺς θεοὺς οὔτε λέκτρ' ἃ μὴ θέμις
στέργειν νομίζω, ...
δεῖται γὰρ ὁ θεός, εἴπερ ἔστ' ὄντως θεός,
οὐδενός· ἀοιδῶν οἵδε δύστηνοι λόγοι (Her. Fur. 1341–1346)[2].
εἰ θεοί τι δρῶσιν αἰσχρόν, οὐκ εἰσὶν θεοί (Frag. 292)[3].

But at this height Euripides never had the courage long to remain. That would have implied a total renunciation of the traditional mythology. The truest index to his normal position is to be found in such a line as this :—

ὡς οὐδὲν ἀνθρώποισι τῶν θείων σαφές (Her. Fur. 62)[4].

The ἀδηλότης of the whole question impresses him as strongly as ever it did Protagoras.

In the plays of the third period (Phoen., Iph. Aul., Bacchae[5],

---

[1] Cf. Heracl. 908 ; Aesch. Persae, 823–824 :—

Ζεύς τοι κολαστὴς τῶν ὑπερκόπων ἄγαν
φρονημάτων ἔπεστιν, εὔθυνος βαρύς.

[2] Cf. Frag. 210.

[3] For Euripides as a defender of the true conception of Deity see Verrall, Euripides the Rationalist, pp. 155 ff.

[4] Cf. Hipp. 1104 ff. ; Tro. 885–886 ; Hel. 711, 1137 (with Paley's note).

[5] Pater calls the Bacchae the 'palinode' of Euripides (Greek Studies, p. 51). Cf. Mahaffy, Euripides, pp. 84–85 ; Paley, Euripides, ii. p. 392. For the view that the Bacchae is not indicative of a real reaction to orthodoxy, see Tyrrell's Bacchae, Introd. xxiii–xxxviii. Bishop Westcott, in a passage which is

and certain fragments) we see a decided change in the
attitude of Euripides towards the popular religion. Not
that he ever renounced altogether his sceptical doubts, or
accepted *in toto* the traditional mythology. That was impossible. But wearied with questionings and heart-searchings
which led to no definite or satisfactory issue, he seems to
have come to the conclusion that his task was a bootless
one and his labour lost, that his philosophic doubt was
barren of benefit either to himself or to others, and that
even an avowedly imperfect religion was perhaps better
than none.

Fate is rarely mentioned in these plays. Unavoidable
calamities are sometimes ascribed to the gods (*Bacch.* 1349:—
τάλα. τάδε Ζεὺς οἶμαι ἐτέλεσεν τατησ· cf. *Phoen.* 379), sometimes to αἰσα (*Phoen.* 1595:—ὢ μοῖ, ἀπ᾽ αὐχὴν ἃς μ᾽ ἔφυσας
ἄθλιον, and must be endured (*ibid.* 1763:—τὰς γὰρ ἐκ θεῶν
ἀνάγκας θνητὸν ὄντα δεῖ φέρειν).

The poet's rationalism[2] asserts itself in *Bacch.* 284-294—
a passage which many consider spurious, and in *Frag.* 210,
the speaker refuses to believe tales of the immorality of
the gods. But such passages are rare.

The power and justice of the gods are often mentioned.
To the gods all things are easy (*Phoen.* 689):—

$$\text{ταῦτα δ᾽ εὐπετῆ θεοῖς.}$$

There is no escape from them (*Phoen.* 872-874):—

$$\text{ἃ συγκαλύψαι ταῦτα Οἰδίπου χρόνῳ}$$
$$\text{χρῄζοντες, ὡς δὴ θεοὺς ὑπεκδραμούμενοι,}$$
$$\text{ἡμάρτον ἀμαθῶς.}$$

---

by no means overawing says:—'Thus the *Bacchae* is no palinode, but
a gathering-up in rich maturity of the poet's earlier thoughts' (*Religious
Thought in the West*, p. 106. M. Decharme however, is quite within the truth
when he says:—'En vérité, il n'est nullement démontré qu'Euripide ait
songé, sur le déclin de sa vie, à faire profession de mysticisme bacchique'
(*Euripide*, &c. p. 90

[2] Cf. *Phoen.* 360; *Iph. Aul.* 443, 1370; *Bacch.* 581; *Frag.* 572.

[3] See Paley's note on *Bacch.* 200 οἶδεν οὐδὲν τοῖς δαίμοσιν: and for
Euripides' rationalistic or symbolic interpretation of myths—a kind of inter-
pretation said to have been employed also by Anaxagoras—see Westcott,
Religious Thought in the West, pp. 106-107.

If a man acts βίᾳ θεῶν, his punishment is sure (*Phoen.* 868 ff.).

When Capaneus utters blasphemy, Zeus smites him with his thunderbolt (*Phoen.* 1172–1182).

The gods are not devoid of understanding (*Iph. Aul.* 394):—

οὐ γὰρ ἀσύνετον τὸ θεῖον.

They see the deeds of mortals (*Bacch.* 391–392):—

πόρσω γὰρ ὅμως
αἰθέρα ναίοντες ὁρῶσιν τὰ βροτῶν οὐρανίδαι.

Divine vengeance is slow, but sure (*Bacch.* 882 ff.).

There are frequent injunctions to belief in the gods[1] and to piety[2], which is better than wisdom[3], and which brings with it a painless life[4].

Impiety is regarded with horror (*Bacch.* 263):—

τῆς δυσσεβείας. ὦ ξέν', οὐκ αἰδεῖ θεούς[5];

It is best to be not over-wise (*Bacch.* 427–431):—

σοφὰν δ' ἀπέχειν πραπίδα φρένα τε
περισσῶν παρὰ φωτῶν.
τὸ πλῆθος ὅ τι τὸ φαυλότερον
ἐνόμισε χρῆταί τε, τόδε τοι λέγοιμ' ἄν.

One should think as befits mortals. Life is short: 'carpe diem' (*Bacch.* 393–395):—

τὸ σοφὸν δ' οὐ σοφία,
τό τε μὴ θνατὰ φρονεῖν.
βραχὺς αἰών· ἐπὶ τούτῳ δέ τις ἂν μεγάλα διώκων
τὰ παρόντ' οὐχὶ φέροι[6].

A man should not know or do κρεῖσσον τῶν νόμων: faith costs little (*Bacch.* 890–896):—

οὐ
γὰρ κρεῖσσόν ποτε τῶν νόμων
γιγνώσκειν χρὴ καὶ μελετᾶν.
κοῦφα γὰρ δαπάνα νομί-
ζειν ἰσχὺν τόδ' ἔχειν,
ὅ τι ποτ' ἄρα τὸ δαιμόνιον,

---

[1] *Bacch.* 1326.   [3] *Bacch.* 199 ff., 325, 635, 795, 1255; *Iph. Aul.* 1396.
[2] *Bacch.* 1005.   [4] *Bacch.* 1002.   [5] Cf. *Bacch.* 476, 490.
[6] See Paley's note *ad loc.*

τό τ᾽ ἐν χρόνῳ μακρῷ
νόμιμον ἀεὶ φύσει τε πεφυκός.

What is specially to be noticed is that, though the calamities of Iphigenia in the *Iph. Aul.*, and of Oedipus, Menoeceus, and the whole Labdacid race in the *Phoen.*, furnished occasion enough, we nowhere find anything resembling the invective which is hurled at the gods in the dramas of the second period. The strongest language the poet employs is found in the following passages:—

> τὸ μὲν σὸν ὦ νεᾶνι γενναίως ἔχει,
> τὸ τῆς τύχης δὲ καὶ τὸ τῆς θεοῦ νοσεῖ
>
> (*Iph. Aul.* 1403–1404).
>
> φόνιος ἐκ θεῶν
> ὃς τάδ᾽ ἦν ὁ πράξας (*Phoen.* 1031–1032).
> τί τλάς; τί τλάς; οὐχ ὁρᾷ Δίκα κακούς,
> οὐδ᾽ ἀμείβεται βροτῶν ἀσυνεσίας (*ibid.* 1726–1727).

There were thus three main periods in the development of Euripides' ideas relatively to religion,—the first period, up to the beginning of the Peloponnesian War, when he acquiesced in the generally accepted beliefs; the second period, beginning with the Peloponnesian War and lasting some twenty years, when he was at open enmity with these beliefs; and, finally, the period of his latest dramas, when, though he never returned to his original position, he came to look on his campaign as labour lost, and desisted from his attempt.

I have gone at some length into an examination of Euripides' religious opinions, partly because of the interest of the question in itself, partly because it is impossible fully to understand his position without a more or less minute study of his plays. But it is more than time to pass on to the Orators, and seek to discover what opinions we can find there. In this field also, as in that of physics, we reap but a scanty harvest. A remark which Schandau makes about Isocrates, to the effect that his opinions about immortality, and about the gods and the manifestation of their will, were the ordinary, current opinions, might be made with equal truth of all the Orators[1]. From the nature of the case, such philosophising and discussion as we find so frequently in Euripides is in them almost entirely absent. One passage in Isocrates, however (*Busiris*, §§ 38–43), recalls such lines in Euripides as *Iph. Taur.* 391, *Her. Fur.* 1341–46, *Frag.* 292[2]. The poets' tales of the gods are, says Isocrates, impious and incredible. The gods can do no evil:—

ἀλλὰ γὰρ οὐδέν σοι τῆς ἀληθείας ἐμέλησεν, ἀλλὰ ταῖς τῶν ποιητῶν βλασφημίαις ἐπηκολούθησας, οἳ δεινότερα μὲν πεποιηκότας καὶ πεπονθότας ἀποφαίνουσι τοὺς ἐκ τῶν ἀθανάτων γεγονότας ἢ τοὺς ἐκ τῶν ἀνθρώπων καὶ ἀνοσιωτάτων, τοιούτους δὲ λόγους περὶ αὐτῶν τῶν θεῶν εἰρήκασιν, οἵους οὐδεὶς ἂν περὶ τῶν ἐχθρῶν εἰπεῖν τολμήσειεν· οὐ γὰρ μόνον κλοπὰς καὶ μοιχείας καὶ παρ' ἀνθρώποις θητείας αὐτοῖς ὠνείδισαν ἀλλὰ καὶ παίδων βρώσεις καὶ πατέρων ἐκτομὰς καὶ μητέρων δεσμοὺς καὶ πολλὰς ἄλλας ἀνομίας κατ' αὐτῶν ἐλογοποίησαν (§ 38) . . . . . . ἐγὼ μὲν οὖν οὐχ ὅπως τοὺς θεούς, ἀλλ' οὐδὲ τοὺς ἐξ ἐκείνων γεγονότας οὐδεμιᾶς ἡγοῦμαι κακίας μετασχεῖν, ἀλλ' αὐτούς τε πάσας ἔχοντας τὰς ἀρετὰς φῦναι καὶ τοῖς ἄλλοις τῶν καλλίστων ἐπιτηδευμάτων ἡγεμόνας καὶ διδασκάλους γεγενῆσθαι (§ 41).

Yet in the *Helena* (§§ 59–60), while illustrating a statement that Zeus and the gods are overcome by beauty, he adduces several of the mythical stories which were not by any means to the credit of the king of gods and men;—ἀλλὰ Ζεὺς ὁ κρατῶν πάντων ἐν μὲν τοῖς ἄλλοις τὴν αὐτοῦ δύναμιν ἐνδείκνυται, πρὸς δὲ τὸ κάλλος ταπεινὸς γιγνόμενος ἀξιοῖ πλησιάζειν. Ἀμφιτρύωνι μὲν γὰρ εἰκασθεὶς ὡς Ἀλκμήνην ἦλθε, κ.τ.λ.

Aeschines declares that wrong-doing has its origin, not with the gods, but with the ἀσέλγεια of men (*Agst. Timarchus*, §§ 190–191):—

μὴ γὰρ οἴεσθε, ὦ Ἀθηναῖοι, τὰς τῶν ἀδικημάτων ἀρχὰς ἀπὸ θεῶν, ἀλλ' οὐχ ὑπ' ἀνθρώπων ἀσελγείας γίγνεσθαι, μηδὲ τοὺς ἠσεβηκότας, καθάπερ ἐν ταῖς τραγῳδίαις, Ποινὰς ἐλαύνειν καὶ κολάζειν δᾳσὶν ἡμμέναις· ἀλλ' αἱ προπετεῖς τοῦ σώματος ἡδοναὶ καὶ τὸ μηδὲν ἱκανὸν ἡγεῖσθαι, ταῦτα πληροῖ τὰ ληστήρια, ταῦτ' εἰς τὸν

---

[1] Towards the end of the fifth century B.C. and in the generation following there was a reaction towards at least outward orthodoxy. See Mahaffy, *Euripides*, p. 12. But see also above, Introd. p. 7.

[2] See above, p. 29.

ἐπακτροκέλητα ἐμβιβάζει, ταῦτά ἐστιν ἑκάστῳ Ποιή, ταῦτα παρα-
κελεύεται σφάττειν τοὺς πολίτας, ὑπηρετεῖν τοῖς τυράννοις, συγ-
καταλύειν τὸν δῆμον.

Demosthenes (?) says that it is against the divine nature to
lie (*Epist.* iv. § 4):—

θεοὺς ... οἷς οὐ θέμις ψεύδεσθαι[1].

In another passage, speaking of the case of Orestes, he says
that the gods would not give an unjust decision (*Agst.
Aristocrates,* § 74):—

οὐ γὰρ ἂν τά γε μὴ δίκαια θεοὺς ψηφίσασθαι.

But apart from these passages we find nothing but the
commonplaces of current beliefs[2]. The gods observe human
actions:—they favour the pious and punish the impious:
vengeance belongs to them, and if it is slow, it is also sure:
they forget not:—

οἶμαι δὲ καὶ θεοῖς τοῖς κάτω μέλειν οἳ ἠδίκηνται (*Antiphon,*
κατηγορία φαρμακείας, § 31).

τούτοις μὲν οὖν ὁ θεὸς ἐπιθείη τὴν δίκην (τετραλογία Γ. β. § 8).

ἐκείνων μὲν οὖν ἕκαστος ἀπώλετο, ὥσπερ εἰκὸς τοὺς τοιούτους
(Lysias, *Frag.* xxxiv. 53, § 3).

παράδειγμα τοῖς ἄλλοις, ἵν᾿ ἴδωσιν ὅτι τοῖς λίαν ὑβριστικῶς πρὸς
τὰ θεῖα διακειμένοις οὐκ εἰς τοὺς παῖδας ἀποτίθενται τὰς τιμωρίας[3],
ἀλλ᾿ αὐτοὺς κακῶς ἀπολλύουσι[4] (*ibid.*).

---

[1] Cf. Plato, *Apol.* 21 B :—οὐ γὰρ δήπου ψεύδεταί γε (sc. ὁ θεός)· οὐ γὰρ θέμις αὐτῷ.

[2] 'All through Greek history scepticism never made way among the
majority even of educated people, but was merely the privilege or pain of
small circles of philosophers and their followers' (Mahaffy, *Social Greece* (1883),
p. 366). 'Take Demosthenes, or the orator Lycurgus, or Hyperides, or even
any obscure contemporaries whose works have been preserved. Do they imply
a public educated by the sophists? Do they preach or suggest sceptical
views? Nothing of the sort. All of them address throughout an
orthodox and even religious public' (*ibid.* pp. 367-368). 'Thus the Demo-
sthenic public was probably more orthodox than the Periclean, certainly not
less so,' &c. (*ibid.* p. 372; cf. also p. 371). But see above, Introd. p. 7.

[3] With this contradiction of the ordinary belief that the sins of the fathers
were visited upon the children contrast Lysias (?), *Agst. Andocides,* § 20 :—
πολλαχόθεν δὲ ἔχω τεκμαιρόμενος εἰκάζειν, ὁρῶν καὶ ἑτέρους ἠσεβηκότας χρόνῳ δεδω-
κότας δίκην, καὶ τοὺς ἐξ ἐκείνων διὰ τὰ τῶν προγόνων ἁμαρτήματα. Cf. Lycurgus,
Agst. Leocrates, § 79.

[4] Cf. Lysias (?), *Agst. Andocides,* §§ 3, 13, 19-21, 33; *Agst. Eratosthenes,* § 96.

χρὴ δὲ καὶ νῦν πλέον ἔχειν ἡγεῖσθαι καὶ πλεονεκτήσειν νομίζειν παρὰ μὲν τῶν θεῶν τοὺς εὐσεβεστάτους καὶ τοὺς περὶ τὴν θεραπείαν τὴν ἐκείνων ἐπιμελεστάτους ὄντας ..... (Isocrates, Antid. § 282).

ἀνὴρ μὲν γὰρ ἀσεβὴς καὶ πονηρὸς τυχὸν ἂν φθάσειε τελευτήσας πρὶν δοῦναι δίκην τῶν ἡμαρτημένων· αἱ δὲ πόλεις διὰ τὴν ἀθανασίαν ὑπομένουσι καὶ τὰς παρὰ τῶν ἀνθρώπων καὶ τὰς παρὰ τῶν θεῶν τιμωρίας (Isocr. De Pace, § 120) [1].

ὃς γὰρ ἂν ὑμᾶς λάθῃ, τοῦτον ἀφίετε τοῖς θεοῖς κολάζειν· ὃν δ' ἂν αὐτοὶ λάβητε, μηκέτ' ἐκείνοις περὶ τούτου προστάττετε (Demosthenes, On the Embassy, § 71) [2].

... ὅθ' οἱ θεοὶ φανεροὺς ὑμῖν ποιήσαντες παρέδοσαν τιμωρήσασθαι (Dinarchus, Agst. Philocles, § 14).

τοὺς μὲν γὰρ ἀνθρώπους πολλοὶ ἤδη ἐξαπατήσαντες καὶ διαλαθόντες οὐ μόνον τῶν παρόντων κινδύνων ἀπελύθησαν, ἀλλὰ καὶ τὸν ἄλλον χρόνον ἀθῷοι τῶν ἀδικημάτων τούτων εἰσί· τοὺς δὲ θεοὺς οὔτ' ἂν ἐπιορκήσας τις λάθοι οὔτ' ἂν ἐκφύγοι τὴν ἀπ' αὐτῶν τιμωρίαν, ἀλλ' εἰ μὴ αὐτός, οἱ παῖδές γε καὶ τὸ γένος ἅπαν τὸ τοῦ ἐπιορκήσαντος μεγάλοις ἀτυχήμασι περιπίπτει (Lycurgus, Agst. Leocrates, § 79) [3].

Both good and bad fortune come from the gods :—

... ἀλλὰ καὶ τῶν θεῶν τοὺς μὲν τῶν ἀγαθῶν αἰτίους ἡμῖν ὄντας Ὀλυμπίους προσαγορευομένους, τοὺς δ' ἐπὶ ταῖς συμφοραῖς καὶ ταῖς τιμωρίαις τεταγμένους δυσχερεστέρας τὰς ἐπωνυμίας ἔχοντας ... (Isocr. Philipp. § 117) [4].

νῦν μέν γ' ἀποτυχεῖν δοκεῖ τῶν πραγμάτων, ὃ πᾶσι κοινόν ἐστιν ἀνθρώποις ὅταν τῷ θεῷ ταῦτα δοκῇ (Demosthenes, Crown, § 200).

It is to the favour of the gods that the safety of the state is due, and piety has its reward :—

εἰ γάρ τις ἐν δημοκρατίᾳ τετιμημένος, ἐν τοιαύτῃ πολιτείᾳ, ἣν οἱ θεοὶ καὶ οἱ νόμοι σώζουσι, τολμᾷ βοηθεῖν τοῖς παράνομα γράφουσι, καταλύει τὴν πολιτείαν, ὑφ' ἧς τετίμηται (Aeschines, Agst. Ctesiphon, § 196) [5].

ἐκ δὲ τοῦ τὰ μὲν Ἑλληνικὰ πιστῶς, τὰ δὲ πρὸς τοὺς θεοὺς εὐσεβῶς,

---

[1] Cf. Isocrates, Ad Demonicum, § 50 ; Archidamus, § 59 ; Adv. Callimachum, § 3.
[2] Cf. ibid. § 239.   [3] Cf. ibid. §§ 91, 94, 148.
[4] Cf. Isocr. Evagoras, § 25.   [5] Cf. ibid. § 130.

τὰ δ᾽ ἐν αὑτοῖς ἴσως διοικεῖν, μεγάλην εἰκότως ἐκτήσαντ᾽ εὐδαιμονίαν
(Demosth. *Olynth.* iii. § 26)[1].

The issues lie with the gods:—

ἐν γὰρ τῷ θεῷ τὸ τούτου τέλος ἦν, οὐκ ἐμοί (Demosth. *Crown*,
§ 193).

We find also the old popular notion that the gods harden
the hearts of the proud, and send upon them blindness and
infatuation:—

. . . ἀναβοήσας τις τῶν Ἀμφισσέων, ἄνθρωπος ἀσελγέστατος καί,
ὡς ἐμοὶ ἐφαίνετο, οὐδεμιᾶς παιδείας μετεσχηκώς, ἴσως δὲ καὶ δαιμονίου
τινὸς ἐξαμαρτάνειν αὐτὸν προαγομένου, κ.τ.λ. (Aeschines, *Agst.
Ctesiphon,* § 117)[2].

δοκεῖ δέ μοι θεῶν τις, ὦ ἄνδρες Ἀθηναῖοι, τοῖς γιγνομένοις ὑπὲρ
τῆς πόλεως αἰσχυνόμενος, τὴν φιλοπραγμοσύνην ταύτην ἐμβαλεῖν
Φιλίππῳ (Demosthenes, *Phil.* i. § 42).

πολλάκις γὰρ ἔμοιγ᾽ ἐπελήλυθε καὶ τοῦτο φοβεῖσθαι, μή τι
δαιμόνιον τὰ πράγματ᾽ ἐλαύνῃ (Demosth. *Phil.* iii. § 54)[3].

οἱ γὰρ θεοὶ οὐδὲν πρότερον ποιοῦσιν ἢ τῶν πονηρῶν ἀνθρώπων τὴν
διάνοιαν παράγουσι· καί μοι δοκοῦσι τῶν ἀρχαίων τινὲς ποιητῶν
ὥσπερ χρησμοὺς γράψαντες τοῖς ἐπιγενομένοις τάδε τὰ ἰαμβεῖα
καταλιπεῖν·

ὅταν γὰρ ὀργὴ δαιμόνων βλάπτῃ τινά,
τοῦτ᾽ αὐτὸ πρῶτον, ἐξαφαιρεῖται φρενῶν
τὸν νοῦν τὸν ἐσθλόν, εἰς δὲ τὴν χείρω τρέπει
γνώμην, ἵν᾽ εἰδῇ μηδὲν ὧν ἁμαρτάνει (Lycurgus, *Agst. Leocrates,*
§ 92).

Fear the gods (Aeschines, *Agst. Timarchus,* § 50):—

τοὺς θεοὺς δεδιὼς κ.τ.λ.

Practise piety and shun impiety (Isocr. *De Pace,* § 135):—

τρίτον ἦν μηδὲν περὶ πλείονος ἡγῆσθε μετά γε τὴν περὶ τοὺς
θεοὺς εὐσέβειαν τοῦ παρὰ τοῖς Ἕλλησιν εὐδοκιμεῖν.

---

[1] Demosthenes makes frequent mention of the favour of the gods to Athens.
Cf. *O'ynth.* ii. §§ 1, 22; *On the Crown,* §§ 153, 195; *On the Embassy,* § 256; *Epist.*
i. § 8.
[2] Cf. (*ibid.* § 133) the use of θεοβλάβεια, a word employed also by Herodotus.
[3] Cf. *On the Symmories,* § 39; *Agst. Timocrates,* § 121.

Submit to what the gods send (Demosth. *On the Crown*, § 97):—

δεῖ δὲ τοὺς ἀγαθοὺς ἄνδρας ἐγχειρεῖν μὲν ἅπασιν ἀεὶ τοῖς καλοῖς, τὴν ἀγαθὴν προβαλλομένους ἐλπίδα, φέρειν δ' ἂν ὁ θεὸς διδῷ γενναίως.

Trust the gods for public and private well-being (Antiphon, περὶ τοῦ Ἡρῴδου φόνου, § 81):—

καὶ γὰρ τὰ τῆς πόλεως κοινὰ τούτοις (sc. τοῖς θεοῖς) μάλιστα πιστεύοντες ἀσφαλῶς διαπράσσεσθε, τοῦτο μὲν τὰ εἰς τοὺς κινδύνους ἥκοντα, τοῦτο δὲ εἰς τὰ ἔξω τῶν κινδύνων.

Men grow better when they approach the gods (Isocr. *Frag.* iii. (α'.) 7):—

οἱ ἄνθρωποι τότε γίγνονται βελτίους, ὅταν θεῷ προσέρχωνται· ὅμοιον δὲ ἔχουσι θεῷ τὸ εὐεργετεῖν καὶ ἀληθεύειν.

It is impious to do, in the name of the gods, what is unjust (Demosth. *Leptines*, § 126):—

εἰ γὰρ ἃ κατὰ μηδέν' ἄλλον ἔχουσι τρόπον δεῖξαι δίκαιον ὑμᾶς ἀφελέσθαι, ταῦτ' ἐπὶ τῷ τῶν θεῶν ὀνόματι ποιεῖν ζητήσουσι, πῶς οὐκ ἀσεβέστατον ἔργον καὶ δεινότατον πράξουσι; χρὴ γάρ, ὡς γοῦν ἐμοὶ δοκεῖ, ὅσα τις πράττει τοὺς θεοὺς ἐπιφημίζων, τοιαῦτα φαίνεσθαι οἷα μηδ' ἂν ἐπ' ἀνθρώπου πραχθέντα πονηρὰ φανείη.

Men should make the gods their leaders (Demosth. *Epist.* I. § 16):—

τὸν Δία τὸν Δωδωναῖον καὶ τοὺς ἄλλους θεοὺς . . . . ἡγεμόνας ποιησάμενοι καὶ παρακαλέσαντες, κ.τ.λ.

The gods should be invoked first (*ibid.* § 1):—

παντὸς ἀρχομένῳ σπουδαίου καὶ λόγου καὶ ἔργου ἀπὸ τῶν θεῶν ὑπολαμβάνω προσήκειν πρῶτον ἄρχεσθαι. εὔχομαι δὴ τοῖς θεοῖς πᾶσι καὶ πάσαις, κ.τ.λ.

Necessity, Fate, Fortune, Chance, are spoken of in the vague manner characteristic of current speech. The words used are ἀνάγκη, χρεία, δαίμων, τύχη: ἡ εἱμαρμένη is found in several of the orators, ἡ πεπρωμένη only in Isocrates, who uses it twice (*Ad Demon.* § 43; *Helena*, § 61).

Deeds done unwittingly are due to τύχη (Antiphon, περὶ τοῦ Ἡρώδου φόνου, § 92):—

τὸ μὲν γὰρ ἀκούσιον ἁμάρτημα ὦ ἄνδρες τῆς τύχης ἐστί, τὸ δὲ ἑκούσιον τῆς γνώμης.

Τύχη is unavoidable and irresistible (Antiphon, περὶ τοῦ χορευτοῦ, § 15):—

οὐ δῆτ' ἔγωγε, πλήν γε τῆς τύχης, ἥπερ οἶμαι καὶ ἄλλοις πολλοῖς ἀνθρώπων αἰτία ἐστιν ἀποθανεῖν· ἣν οὔτ' ἂν ἐγὼ οὔτ' ἄλλος οὐδεὶς οἷός τ' ἂν εἴη ἀποτρέψαι μὴ οὐ γενέσθαι ἥντινα δεῖ ἑκάστῳ [1].

Ἀνάγκη is bitter and hard:—

οὐδὲν γὰρ πικρότερον τῆς ἀνάγκης ἔοικεν εἶναι (Antiphon, τετρ. Α. β. § 4).

σκληρὰ ἀνάγκη (τετρ. Β. β. § 2).

ἡ σκληρότης τοῦ δαίμονος (ibid. γ. § 4).

One should not oppose ὁ δαίμων (Antiphon, τετρ. Β. δ. § 10):—

μήτε . . . ἐναντία τοῦ δαίμονος γνῶτε [2].

Τύχη is common to all (Isocr. Ad Demon. § 29):—

κοινὴ γὰρ ἡ τύχη καὶ τὸ μέλλον ἀόρατον.

It is perplexing (Isocr. Panegyr. § 48):—

. . . ὁρῶσα δὲ περὶ μὲν τὰς ἄλλας πράξεις οὕτω ταραχώδεις οὔσας τὰς τύχας, κ.τ.λ. [3].

It decides and rules all things (Demosth. Crown, § 306):—

τὴν τύχην τὴν οὕτω τὰ πράγματα κρίνασαν [4].

Every man's τύχη is allotted by ὁ δαίμων (Demosth. Crown, § 208):—

τῇ τύχῃ δ', ἣν ὁ δαίμων ἔνειμεν ἑκάστοις, ταύτῃ κέχρηται.

---

[1] Cf. Hyperides, Epitaph. vi. 1:—τῆς δὲ εἱμαρμένης οὐκ ἦν περιγενέσθαι.

[2] Cf. Lysias, Olymp. § 4:—. . . στέργειν ἂν ἦν ἀνάγκη τὴν τύχην.

[3] Cf. Demosth. Prooem. xxxix. § 2:—τὰ μὲν γὰρ τῆς τύχης ὀξείας ἔχει τὰς μεταβολάς.

[4] Cf. Demosth. Olynth. ii. § 22:—μεγάλη γὰρ ῥοπή, μᾶλλον δ' ὅλον ἡ τύχη παρὰ πάντ' ἐστὶ τὰ τῶν ἀνθρώπων πράγματα : Prooem. ii. β. § 3:—πολλῶν γὰρ τὸ τῆς τύχης αὐτόματον κρατεῖ : Prooem. xxv. § 2:—ἐν τῇ τύχῃ τὸ πλεῖστον μέρος γίγνεται : Aeschines, On the Embassy, § 131:—τὴν τύχην, ἣ πάντων ἐστὶ κυρία. See also Demosth. Epist. ii. § 5.

Τύχη and δαίμων (or δαιμόνιοι) are sometimes combined (Lysias, *Agst. Agoratus*, § 63):—

ἡ δὲ τύχη καὶ ὁ δαίμων περιεποίησε [1].

§ 2. If in his philosophical opinions Euripides was greatly influenced by Anaxagoras, no less strong was the influence exercised on his religious and moral views by Orpheus [2], Musaeus [3], and Pythagoras [4]. We are not here specially concerned with the question how far the mysteries go to explain that *theocrasia* which is so noticeable in Euripides; but it may be interesting to quote and compare certain passages in Euripides and the Orators in which special reference is made to the mysteries and to those initiated in them. Most of these passages have reference to purity of life, and to the great care exercised so that the mysteries should be kept secret, and in no way polluted or violated [5].

In the *Rhesus* (943-947) Orpheus is mentioned as the one who introduced these mystic celebrations, and with his name is subjoined that of Musaeus :—

μυστηρίων τε τῶν ἀπορρήτων φανὰς
ἔδειξεν Ὀρφεύς, αὐτανέψιος νεκροῦ

---

[1] Cf. Demosth. *On the Symmories*, § 36 :—ἡ τύχη καὶ τὸ δαιμόνιον : *Crown*, § 303 :—ἢ δαιμονὸς τινος ἢ τύχης ἰσχύι : Lysias (?), *Agst. Andocides*, § 32 :—ὑπὸ δαιμονίου τινὸς ἀγόμενος ἀνάγκης.

[2] It is by no means certain, however, that Euripides was ever strongly attracted by the Orphic sect. See M. Decharme's arguments for and against (*Euripide*, &c., pp. 90-93). A passage in the *Hipp.* (quoted below) describes them as pietistic hypocrites. See also Paley's note *ad loc.*

[3] 'It is now impossible to detach the real Orpheus, the Thracian bard, from the marvellous stories that grew round his name, and from the spurious "Orphic hymns" that were attributed to him in later time, and which were constantly extended and interpolated. Müller thinks that Orpheus is really connected with the cult of the Chthonian Dionysus (Ζαγρεύς) ; and that the foundation of this worship, and the composition of hymns for the initiations connected with it, were the real functions of this poet. Similarly Μουσαῖος was a sort of eponymous representative of the hymns connected with the Eleusinian Mysteries' (Merry, note on Aristoph. *Frogs*, 1032).

[4] See Berlage, pp. 120-121, 162.

[5] See Kennedy, *Demosthenes against Leptines, Midias, &c.*, Appendix vi : Mahaffy, *Social Greece*, pp. 376-378 : Holm, i. pp. 411-412 : Lloyd, *Age of Pericles*, ii. c. xlix.

τοῦδ' ὃν κατακτείνεις σύ· Μουσαῖόν τε σὸν
σεμνὸν πολίτην κἀπὶ πλεῖστον ἄνδρ' ἕνα
ἐλθόντα, Φοῖβος σύγγονοί τ' ἠσκήσαμεν.

The ethical precepts of Pythagoras, like the Orphic rites [1], aimed at preserving the body pure from various things which were believed to pollute it—such as the eating of flesh, bloodshed, &c.—; and a passage of the *Hippolytus* (952–957), where Orpheus is mentioned, contains also perhaps an allusion to Pythagoras [2]:—

ἤδη νυν αὔχει καὶ δι' ἀψύχου βορᾶς
σίτοις καπήλευ', 'Ορφέα τ' ἄνακτ' ἔχων
βάκχευε, πολλῶν γραμμάτων τιμῶν καπνούς·
ἐπεί γ' ἐλήφθης. τοὺς δὲ τοιούτους ἐγὼ
φεύγειν προφωνῶ πᾶσι· θηρεύουσι γὰρ
σεμνοῖς λόγοισιν, αἰσχρὰ μηχανώμενοι [3].

Alongside the last lines in the above passage we may set these words of Pentheus (*Bacch.* 221–225):—

πλήρεις δὲ θιάσοις ἐν μέσοισιν ἑστάναι
κρατῆρας, ἄλλην δ' ἄλλοσ' εἰς ἐρημίαν
πτώσσουσαν εὐναῖς ἀρσένων ὑπηρετεῖν,
πρόφασιν μὲν ὡς δὴ μαινάδας θυοσκόους,
τὴν δ' 'Αφροδίτην πρόσθ' ἄγειν τοῦ Βακχίου.

But, in ll. 73 ff. of the same play, the Chorus sing of the blessedness of the man who is initiated and pure of life:—

ὦ μάκαρ, ὅστις εὐδαί-
μων τελετὰς θεῶν

---

[1] Cf. Aristoph. *Frogs*, 1032:
    'Ορφεὺς μὲν γὰρ τελετάς θ' ἡμῖν κατέδειξε φόνων τ' ἀπέχεσθαι:
Horace, *Ars Poetica*, 391–392:—
      'Silvestres homines sacer interpresque deorum
      Caedibus et victu foedo deterruit Orpheus.'

[2] See Paley's note *ad loc.*

[3] See Paley's note *ad loc.* It was at the celebration of the mysteries that Phaedra first saw Hippolytus (*Hipp.* 24–28). There is a reference to Dionysus and the Eleusinian mysteries in *Ion*, 1074 ff.:—αἰσχύνομαι τὸν πολύυμνον θεόν κ.τ.λ. See also *Her. Fur.* 613 (with Paley's and Gray & Hutchinson's notes); *Alc.* 966 ff. (with Jerram's note); and Appendix B to Hadley's edition of *Hippolytus.*

εἰδὼς βιοτὰν ἁγιστεύει
καὶ θιασεύεται ψυ-
χάν, ἐν ὄρεσσι βακχεύ-
ων ὁσίοις καθαρμοῖσιν·
τά τε ματρὸς μεγάλας ὄργια Κυβέλας θεμιτεύων,
ἀνὰ θύρσον τε τινάσσων κισσῷ τε στεφανωθεὶς
Διόνυσον θεραπεύει.

The clean hands and pure heart we find again in *Frag.* 472 (ll. 9-19):—

ἀγνὸν δὲ βίον τείνων ἐξ οὗ
Διὸς Ἰδαίου μύστης γενόμην,
καὶ νυκτιπόλου Ζαγρέως βροντὰς
τοὺς ὠμοφάγους δαῖτας τελέσας
μητρί τ' ὀρείῳ δᾷδας ἀνασχὼν
καὶ κουρήτων
βάκχος ἐκλήθην ὁσιωθείς.
πάλλευκα δ' ἔχων εἵματα φεύγω
γένεσίν τε βροτῶν καὶ νεκροθήκης
οὐ χριμπτόμενος τήν τ' ἐμψύχων
βρῶσιν ἐδεστῶν πεφύλαγμαι.

In the speech *Against Andocides* (§§ 4-5) Lysias (?) asks the Athenians to consider what the initiated will think if a man like Andocides is ἄρχων βασιλεύς, and in that capacity performs the vows and sacrifices at the mysteries:—

φέρε γάρ, ἂν νυνὶ Ἀνδοκίδης ἀθῷος ἀπαλλαγῇ δι' ἡμᾶς ἐκ τοῦδε τοῦ ἀγῶνος καὶ ἔλθῃ κληρωσόμενος τῶν ἐννέα ἀρχόντων καὶ λάχῃ βασιλεύς, ἄλλο τι ἢ ὑπὲρ ἡμῶν καὶ θυσίας θύσει καὶ εὐχὰς εὔξεται κατὰ τὰ πάτρια, τὰ μὲν ἐν τῷ ἐνθάδε Ἐλευσινίῳ, τὰ δὲ ἐν τῷ Ἐλευσῖνι ἱερῷ, καὶ τῆς ἑορτῆς ἐπιμελήσεται μυστηρίοις, ὅπως ἂν μηδεὶς ἀδικῇ μηδὲ ἀσεβῇ περὶ τὰ ἱερά; καὶ τίνα γνώμην οἴεσθε ἕξειν τοὺς μύστας τοὺς ἀφικνουμένους, ἐπειδὰν ἴδωσι τὸν βασιλέα ὅστις ἐστὶ καὶ ἀναμνησθῶσι πάντα τὰ ἠσεβημένα αὐτῷ, ἢ τοὺς ἄλλους Ἕλληνας, οἳ ἕνεκα ταύτης τῆς ἑορτῆς . . . . ἢ θύειν εἰς ταύτην τὴν πανήγυριν βουλόμενοι ἢ θεωρεῖν; οὐδὲ γὰρ ἁγνὸς ὁ Ἀνδοκίδης οὔτε τοῖς ἔξω οὔτε τοῖς ἐνθάδε διὰ τὰ ἠσεβημένα.

Initiation, says Isocrates, is one of the two best gifts ever granted to men. In the *Panegyric* (§§ 28-29) he relates the legend (μυθώδης λόγος) of how Demeter had kindness shown her at Athens, and how she repaid that kindness by instructing the Athenians in the cultivation of the ground and initiating them in the mysteries:—

Δήμητρος γὰρ ἀφικομένης εἰς τὴν χώραν, ὅτ' ἐπλανήθη τῆς Κόρης ἁρπασθείσης, καὶ πρὸς τοὺς προγόνους ἡμῶν εὐμενῶς διατεθείσης ἐκ τῶν εὐεργεσιῶν, ἃς οὐχ οἷόν τ' ἄλλοις ἢ τοῖς μεμυημένοις ἀκούειν, καὶ δούσης δωρεὰς διττάς, αἵπερ μέγισται τυγχάνουσιν οὖσαι, τούς τε καρπούς, οἳ τοῦ μὴ θηριώδως ζῆν ἡμᾶς αἴτιοι γεγόνασι, καὶ τὴν τελετήν, ἧς οἱ μετασχόντες περί τε τῆς τοῦ βίου τελευτῆς καὶ τοῦ σύμπαντος αἰῶνος ἡδίους τὰς ἐλπίδας ἔχουσιν, κ.τ.λ.

Barbarians and murderers are excluded from the mysteries (*ibid.* § 157):—

Εὐμολπίδαι δὲ καὶ Κήρυκες ἐν τῇ τελετῇ τῶν μυστηρίων διὰ τὸ τούτων (sc. τῶν Περσῶν) μῖσος καὶ τοῖς ἄλλοις βαρβάροις εἴργεσθαι τῶν ἱερῶν ὥσπερ τοῖς ἀνδροφόνοις προαγορεύουσιν.

Violation of the mysteries occasioned strong resentment (Isocr. xvi. § 6):—

εἰδότες δὲ τὴν πόλιν τῶν μὲν περὶ τοὺς θεοὺς μάλιστ' ἂν ὀργισθεῖσαν, εἴ τις εἰς τὰ μυστήρια φαίνοιτ' ἐξαμαρτάνων, τῶν δ' ἄλλων εἴ τις τὴν δημοκρατίαν τολμῴη καταλύειν, κ.τ.λ.[1].

§ 3. An interesting set of passages is that relating to bloodguiltiness and pollution, and to the treatment of the murderer. The words found in this connexion are such as these:—μίασμα, προστρόπαιος, ἀλιτήριος, καθαρός, &c. The pollution affects all with whom the murderer comes into

[1] The secrecy observed and the exclusion of aliens is mentioned also by the author of the speech *Against Neaera* (§ 73) in an interesting passage where we learn something of the special privileges of the wife of the βασιλεύς. Andocides (*On the Mysteries*, § 11) speaks of Alcibiades' having performed the mysteries in a private house and before men who were not initiated. In an interesting passage (*Agst. Andocides*, §§ 51-53) Andocides is himself accused by Lysias (?) of a similar offence. The following passages have reference to special laws dealing with the mysteries:—Andocides, *On the Mysteries*, § 115: Demosthenes, *Against Midias*, § 158. 'Lycurgus the orator caused a law to be enacted that the women should not drive to Eleusis, that the poorer classes might not feel the distinction' (Becker, *Charicles*). For various instances of punishment for violation of the mysteries see Demosthenes, *Against Midias*, §§ 175-180.

contact, and he himself is an outcast. He has no part in religious rites; he cannot sit at the same table with the innocent, or even speak to them; no temple or city will receive him. From many similar passages in Euripides we select the following:—

τί μοι προσείων χεῖρα σημαίνεις φόνον ;
ὡς μὴ μύσος με σῶν βάλῃ προσφθεγμάτων ;
(*Her. Fur.* 1218–1219).
οὔτ' ἐμαῖς φίλαις
Θήβαις ἐνοικεῖν ὅσιον· ἦν δὲ καὶ μένω,
ἐς ποῖον ἱρὸν ἢ πανήγυριν φίλων
εἶμ' ; οὐ γὰρ ἄτας εὐπροσηγόρους ἔχω
(*ibid.* 1281–1284)[1].
ἐλθὼν δ' ἐκεῖσε, πρῶτα μέν μ' οὐδεὶς ξένων
ἑκὼν ἐδέξαθ', ὡς θεοῖς στυγούμενον·
οἱ δ' ἔσχον αἰδῶ, ξένια μονοτράπεζά μοι
παρέσχον, οἴκων ὄντες ἐν ταὐτῷ στέγει,
σιγῇ δ' ἐτεκτήναντ' ἀπόφθεγκτόν μ', ὅπως
δαιτὸς γενοίμην πώματός τ' αὐτῶν δίχα,
ἐς δ' ἄγγος ἴδιον ἴσον ἅπασι Βακχίου
μέτρημα πληρώσαντες εἶχον ἡδονήν.
κἀγὼ 'ξελέγξαι μὲν ξένους οὐκ ἠξίουν,
ἤλγουν δὲ σιγῇ κἀδόκουν οὐκ εἰδέναι,
μέγα στενάζων, οὕνεκ' ἦν μητρὸς φονεύς
(*Iph. Taur.* 947–957)[2].
ἔδοξε δ' Ἄργει τῷδε μήθ' ἡμᾶς στέγαις,
μὴ πυρὶ δέχεσθαι, μήτε προσφωνεῖν τινα
μητροκτονοῦντας (*Orestes*, 46–48).

Passages to the same effect are not infrequent in the Orators. The following may be instanced:—

ἀσύμφορόν θ' ὑμῖν ἐστι τόνδε μιαρὸν καὶ ἄναγνον ὄντα εἴς ⟨τε⟩ τὰ τεμένη τῶν θεῶν εἰσιόντα μιαίνειν τὴν ἁγνείαν αὐτῶν, ἐπί τε τὰς αὐτὰς τραπέζας ἰόντα συγκαταπιμπλάναι τοὺς ἀναιτίους (*Antiphon*, τετρ. A. a. § 10)[3].

---

[1] See Paley's note *ad loc.*
[2] See Paley's note *ad loc.*
[3] Cf. τετρ. A. β. § 11.

E

καθαρὰν τὴν πόλιν καταστῆσαι (*ibid.* § 11)[1].

εἰ δὲ δὴ θεία κηλὶς τῷ δράσαντι προσπίπτει ἀσεβοῦντι, οὐ δίκαιον τὰς θείας προσβολὰς διακωλύειν γίγνεσθαι (τετρ. Β. γ. § 8)[2].

ἔτι δὲ παρελθὼν τὸν νόμον ὃν ὑμεῖς ἔθεσθε, εἴργεσθαι τῶν ἱερῶν αὐτὸν ὡς ἀλιτήριον ὄντα, ταῦτα πάντα βιασάμενος εἰσελήλυθεν ἡμῶν εἰς τὴν πόλιν, καὶ ἔθυσεν ἐπὶ τῶν βωμῶν ὧν οὐκ ἐξῆν αὐτῷ, καὶ ἀπήντα τοῖς ἱεροῖς περὶ ἃ ἠσέβησεν, εἰσῆλθεν εἰς τὸ Ἐλευσίνιον, ἐχερνίψατο ἐκ τῆς ἱερᾶς χέρνι3ος. τίνα χρὴ ταῦτα ἀνασχέσθαι; ποῖον φίλον, ποῖον συγγενῆ, ποῖον δικαστὴν χρὴ τούτῳ χαρισάμενον κρύβδην φανερῶς τοῖς θεοῖς ἀπεχθέσθαι; νῦν οὖν χρὴ νομίζειν τιμωρουμένους καὶ ἀπαλλαττομένους Ἀνδοκίδου τὴν πόλιν καθαίρειν καὶ ἀποδιοπομπεῖσθαι καὶ φαρμακὸν ἀποπέμπειν καὶ ἀλιτηρίου ἀπαλλάττεσθαι, ὡς ἐν τούτων οὗτός ἐστι (Lysias(?), *Agst. Andocides,* §§ 52-53).

ὥσπερ ἀλιτηρίῳ οὐδεὶς ἀνθρώπων αὐτῷ διελέγετο (Lysias, *Agst. Agoratus,* § 79).

ἀπιέναι ἐκέλευσεν ἐς κόρακας ἐκ τῶν πολιτῶν· οὐ γὰρ ἔφη δεῖν ἀνδροφόνον αὐτὸν ὄντα συμπέμπειν τὴν πομπὴν τῇ Ἀθηνᾷ (*ibid.* § 81).

οὐδεὶς γὰρ αὐτῷ διελέγετο ὡς ἀνδροφόνῳ ὄντι (*ibid.* § 82).

καὶ τοῖς ἄλλοις βαρβάροις εἴργεσθαι τῶν ἱερῶν ὥσπερ τοῖς ἀνδροφόνοις προαγορεύουσιν (Isocrates, *Panegyr.* § 157).

ἐν τοίνυν τοῖς περὶ τούτων νόμοις ὁ Δράκων φοβερὸν κατασκευάζων καὶ δεινὸν τό τινα αὐτόχειρα ἄλλον ἄλλου γίγνεσθαι, καὶ γράφων χερνίβων εἴργεσθαι τὸν ἀνδροφόνον, σπονδῶν, κρατήρων, ἱερῶν, ἀγορᾶς, πάντα τἄλλα διελθὼν οἷς μάλιστ' ἄν τινας ᾤετο ἐπισχεῖν τοῦ τοιοῦτόν τι ποιεῖν, ὅμως οὐκ ἀφείλετο τὴν τοῦ δικαίου τάξιν, ἀλλ' ἔθηκεν ἐφ' οἷς ἐξεῖναι ἀποκτιννύναι, κἂν οὕτω τις δράσῃ, καθαρὸν διώρισεν εἶναι (Demosthenes, *Leptines,* § 158).

τοιγαροῦν οὐδεμία πόλις αὐτὸν εἴασε παρ' αὑτῇ μετοικεῖν, ἀλλὰ μᾶλλον τῶν ἀνδροφόνων ἤλαυνεν (Lycurgus, *Agst. Leocrates,* § 133)[3].

---

[1] Cf. τετρ. Α. γ. § 11 (ἀγνεύετε τὴν πόλιν); τετρ. Γ. γ. § 7.

[2] Cf. Euripides, *Iph. Taur.* 1200:—εἴπερ γε κηλὶς ἔβαλέ νιν μητροκτόνος: τετρ. Γ. α. §§ 3-5; *ibid.* δ. §§ 10-11.

[3] For the pollution arising to a deity from seeing or touching a corpse see Euripides, *Alcestis,* 22 (with Jerram's note); *Hipp.* 1437-1438.

CHAPTER IV

DEATH AND FUTURE LIFE—SUICIDE—BURIAL AND MOURNING CUSTOMS

§ 1. BETWEEN the ninth and fifth centuries B.C. Greek ideas on the subject of death had undergone a considerable change[1]. In Homer the dead are mere εἴδωλα or phantoms; ἀτὰρ φρένες οὐκ ἔνι πάμπαν (Il. xxiii. 104). The life in the next world is by no means a thing to be desired. Achilles would rather work for hire and live on ground with a landless man than rule among the dead that are departed (Od. xi. 489 ff.). Special crimes are visited by special punishment (Od. xi. 576–600). The dead pursue in the next world the vocations they had followed in this. Heracles—αὐτός as contrasted with εἴδωλον—dwells with the gods (Od. xi. 601 ff.), and Menelaus is transported to the Elysian plain (Od. iv. 561–569)[2], but in both cases this is due to divine relationship[3].

Sophocles, in a fragment[4] preserved by Plutarch (Mor. p. 21), speaks of the better fortune of the initiated[5], but elsewhere

---

[1] For an able and interesting discussion on ancient beliefs regarding the soul and death see Coulanges, La Cité Antique, Livre I. cc. i, ii. pp. 7–20. He points out that the Indo-European race had from the earliest times believed in a future existence. See also ibid. pp. 416–417.

[2] Cf. Euripides, Hel. 1676–1677 :—

καὶ τῷ πλανήτῃ Μενέλεῳ θεῶν πάρα
μακάρων κατοικεῖν νῆσόν ἐστι μόρσιμον:

Demosthenes (?), Epitaph. § 34. The 'Isles of the Blest' are unknown to Homer.

[3] See Jebb's Homer, pp. 71–72.

[4] 753 (Nauck).

[5] This belief is often alluded to by Aristophanes (e. g., Peace, 375; Frogs, 158).

(e. g. *Oed. Col.* 955; *Trach.* 1173; *El.* 1166, 1170) he speaks of the dead as having no share in anything.

In Aeschylus the dead are not deprived of understanding: they are cognisant of human things and aid their friends (*Choeph.* 139, 323–326, 456–457; *Eum.* 598–599).

So far the poets. Let us turn our attention to the philosophers. The Pythagorean theory—borrowed perhaps from the Egyptians, perhaps from the Orphic mysteries—was that the soul had fallen from a higher existence, and was in this life shut up in the body as in a prison, whence it escaped at death and passed into the bodies of animals. This theory was accepted by Empedocles and extended by Plato.

Heraclitus held that what we call life is really death, and that death is life.

The physicists—Epicharmus, Democritus, &c.—explained death by physical laws.

Socrates consistently declared that he was ignorant of the nature of death: his opinion seems to have been merely that it was a separation of soul and body (*Apol.* 29 A; *Gorg.* 524 B; *Phaed.* 64 C).

Here, as in the matter of religion, Euripides wavers between various opinions, expressing at one time the vulgar belief, at another that of the physicists, at another that of the philosophers[1]. He is deeply impressed with the uncertainty of the whole matter. In *Frag.* 638 he says:—

τίς δ' οἶδεν εἰ τὸ ζῆν μέν ἐστι κατθανεῖν,
τὸ κατθανεῖν δὲ ζῆν κάτω νομίζεται[2];

These lines recall forcibly such passages in the philosophers as those alluded to above—Plato, *Gorg.* 492 E–493 A, &c.—, but it is uncertain whether they are to be directly referred to Pythagoras, to whom the idea is attributed by Plato (*Phaed.* 61 D, 62 B; cf. *Cratyl.* 400 C). Berlage (pp. 204–205) prefers

---

[1] For the conflicting thoughts of Euripides on death see Decharme, *Euripide, &c.,* pp. 124–132.

[2] Cf. *Frag.* 833 :—

τίς δ' οἶδεν εἰ ζῆν τοῦθ' ὃ κέκληται θανεῖν,
τὸ ζῆν δὲ θνήσκειν ἐστί; πλὴν ὅμως βροτῶν
νοσοῦσιν οἱ βλέποντες, οἱ δ' ὀλωλότες
οὐδὲν νοσοῦσιν οὐδὲ κέκτηνται κακά.

to set them alongside this passage from the περὶ φύσεως of Heraclitus:—

ἀθάνατοι θνητοί, θνητοὶ ἀθάνατοι, ζῶντες τὸν ἐκείνων θάνατον, τὸν δὲ ἐκείνων βίον τεθνεῶτες [1].

As for physical explanations we may compare specially the second part of *Frag.* 839:—χωρεῖ δ' ὀπίσω κ.τ.λ. (See above, p. 16.) Everything returns to the place whence it came: body and soul are separated by death: the latter returns to aether, the former to earth [2].

We have a reminiscence of Anaxagoras in *Hel.* 1014–1016:—

ὁ νοῦς
τῶν κατθανόντων ζῇ μὲν οὔ, γνώμην δ' ἔχει
ἀθάνατον, εἰς ἀθάνατον αἰθέρ' ἐμπεσών [3].

The following passages may also be noted as conflicting with current opinions:—

οὐδέν ἐσθ' ὁ κατθανών (*Alc.* 381).

οὐ ταὐτόν, ὦ παῖ, τῷ βλέπειν τὸ κατθανεῖν·
τὸ μὲν γὰρ οὐδέν, τῷ δ' ἔνεισιν ἐλπίδες
(*Tro.* 628–629).

τὸ μὴ γενέσθαι τῷ θανεῖν ἴσον λέγω (*ibid.* 631) [4].

τὸ φῶς τόδ' ἀνθρώποισιν ἥδιστον βλέπειν,
τὰ νέρθε δ' οὐδέν· μαίνεται δ' ὃς εὔχεται
θανεῖν· κακῶς ζῆν κρεῖσσον ἢ θανεῖν καλῶς
(*Iph. Aul.* 1250–1252).

τοὺς ζῶντας εὖ δρᾶν· κατθανὼν δὲ πᾶς ἀνὴρ
γῆ καὶ σκιά· τὸ μηδὲν εἰς οὐδὲν ῥέπει (*Frag.* 532).

Frag. 450 recalls the νεκύων ἀμενηνὰ κάρηνα of Homer, and is perhaps due to the Epic tradition in tragedy:—

εἰ μὲν γὰρ οἰκεῖ νερτέρας ὑπὸ χθονός,
ἐν τοῖσιν οὐκέτ' οὖσιν, οὐδὲν ἂν σθένοι.

In several places we find the belief that the dead are able

---

[1] *Frag.* 60. See Zeller, *Pre-Socratic Philosophy*, vol. ii. p. 84 (English Translation).

[2] Cf. *Frag.* 195:—ἅπαντα τίκτει χθὼν πάλιν τε λαμβάνει.

[3] There we find also the idea of the future punishment of sin. See Jerram's and Paley's notes *ad loc.*; and cf. *Suppl.* 532.

[4] Cf. Hyperides, *Epitaph. ad fin.*:—εἰ μέν ἐστι τὸ ἀποθανεῖν ὅμοιον τῷ μὴ γενέσθαι, κ.τ.λ.

to hear and answer prayers (*Hel.* 64, 961–968; *Her. Fur.* 490; *El.* 677–684; *Or.* 1225 ff. [1]). They can aid friends and injure foes (*Heracl.* 1032–1044; *Tro.* 1234).

Sometimes death is spoken of as an evil, sometimes as a blessing:—

$$\text{ὁ θάνατος δεινὸν κακόν} \quad (Iph. \ Aul. \ 1416).$$

$$\text{τὸ γὰρ θανεῖν}$$
$$\text{κακῶν μέγιστον φάρμακον νομίζεται}$$
$$(Heracl. \ 595–596)\,[2].$$

$$\text{ἐχρῆν γὰρ ἡμᾶς σύλλογον ποιουμένους}$$
$$\text{τὸν φύντα θρηνεῖν εἰς ὅσ' ἔρχεται κακά,}$$
$$\text{τὸν δ' αὖ θανόντα καὶ πόνων πεπαυμένον}$$
$$\text{χαίροντας εὐφημοῦντας ἐκπέμπειν δόμων} \quad (Frag. \ 449).$$

Macaria prays that there may be nothing beneath the earth (*Heracl.* 593):—

$$\ldots \ldots \text{εἴ τι δὴ κατὰ χθονός·}$$
$$\text{εἴη γε μέντοι μηδέν}\,[3].$$

There are, besides numerous commonplaces about death. All must die (*Alc.* 419, &c.): all shrink from death (*ibid.* 671, &c.). Death is better than a life of shame (*Hec.* 377, &c.).

It is such commonplaces as these that are most frequent in the Orators [4]. Of philosophic discussion as to death and a future life there is, naturally, little or nothing. In a few passages we find a reference, usually introduced by an εἰ, to the idea that after death knowledge may yet remain. But this εἰ is a mere form of language, and not meant to give rise to doubt or questioning. It is not the sceptical εἰ of Euripides:—

$$\text{εἴ τις ἐστὶν αἴσθησις τοῖς τετελευτηκόσι περὶ τῶν ἐνθάδε γιγνο-}$$
$$\text{μένων} \quad (\text{Isocrates, ix. § 2: cf. xiv. § 61}).$$

---

[1] See above, p. 52.

[2] Cf. *Alc.* 937; *Hipp.* 599; *Or.* 1522; Hyperides, *Epitaph. ad fin.*

[3] See Paley's note *ad loc.* For other passages relating to a future state see *Alc.* 364, 437 (τὸν ἀνάλιον οἶκον), 745, 1092 (with Paley's and Jerram's notes); *Her. Fur.* 607.

[4] Cf. Andocides, *On the Mysteries*, §§ 57, 125: Lysias, *Frag.* xxxiv. 53, § 4: Isocrates, *Ad Nic.* § 36; *Ad Demon.* § 43; *Evag.* §§ 1–5; *Archid.* § 108; *Panegyr.* §§ 77, 95: Aeschines, *On the Embassy*, § 181: Demosth. *Crown*, §§ 97, 205; *Lept.* § 82: Lycurgus, *Agst. Leocrates*, § 81.

εἰ δ' ἔστιν αἴσθησις ἐν "Αιδου καὶ ἐπιμέλεια παρὰ τοῦ δαιμονίου, ὥσπερ ὑπολαμβάνομεν, κ.τ.λ. (Hyperides, *Epitaph. ad fin.*).

ἡγοῦμαι δ' ἔγωγε καὶ τὸν πατέρα αὐτῷ τὸν τετελευτηκότα, εἴ τις ἄρα ἔστιν αἴσθησις τοῖς ἐκεῖ περὶ τῶν ἐνθάδε γιγνομένων, ἁπάντων ἂν χαλεπώτατον γενέσθαι δικαστήν, κ.τ.λ. (Lycurgus, *Agst. Leocrates*, § 136).

In a striking passage in the speech *Against Leptines* (§ 64), Demosthenes affirms that a man may die, but his deeds never:—

ἠκούσατε μὲν τῶν ψηφισμάτων, ὦ ἄνδρες δικασταί, τούτων δ' ἴσως ἔνιοι τῶν ἀνδρῶν οὐκέτ' εἰσίν. ἀλλὰ τὰ ἔργα τὰ πραχθέντ' ἔστιν, ἐπειδήπερ ἅπαξ ἐπράχθη.

Though the idea is different, the language recalls that of George Eliot:—'Our deeds are like children that are born to us; they live and act apart from our will: nay, children may be strangled, but deeds never; they have an indestructible life both in and out of our consciousness [1].'

§ 2. Suicide is rarely mentioned. In one passage (*Hel.* 96-97) Euripides says that only a madman would commit suicide:—

ΤΕ. οἰκεῖον αὐτὸν ὤλεσ' ἅλμ' ἐπὶ ξίφος.

ΕΛ. μανέντ'; ἐπεὶ τίς σωφρονῶν τλαίη τάδ' ἄν;

In another passage he speaks of it as ἀνόσιον (*Her. Fur.* 1210-1212):—

ἰὼ παῖ, κατάσχεθε λέοντος ἀγρίου θυμόν, ὡς
δρόμον ἐπὶ φόνιον, ἀνόσιον ἐξάγει,
κακὰ θέλων κακοῖς συνάψαι, τέκνον [2].

But there are circumstances which render it noble (*Tro.* 1012-1014):—

ποῦ δῆτ' ἐλήφθης ἢ βρόχους ἀρτωμένη,
ἢ φάσγανον θήγουσ', ἃ γενναία γυνὴ
δράσειεν ἂν ποθοῦσα τὸν πάρος πόσιν [3];

---

[1] The passage is quoted by Prof. Butcher, *Some Aspects of the Greek Genius*, p. 114.

[2] Cf. *ibid.* 1248 (with Paley's note, ; Or. 415.

[3] See Paley's note *ad loc.*

In *Hel.* 298-302, suicide is regarded as a virtue, but suffocation is deprecated [1] :—

> θανεῖν κράτιστον· πῶς θάνοιμ' ἂν οὖν καλῶς ;
> ἀσχήμονες μὲν ἀγχόναι μετάρσιοι,
> κἂν τοῖσι δούλοις δυσπρεπὲς νομίζεται,
> σφαγαὶ δ' ἔχουσιν εὐγενές τι καὶ καλόν,
> σμικρὸν δ' ὁ καιρὸς κάρτ' ἀπαλλάξαι βίου [2].

I have found only one passage in the Orators where suicide is mentioned. Andocides speaks of a case of attempted suicide by hanging :—

> ἡ δὲ τοῦ Ἰσχομάχου θυγάτηρ τεθνάναι νομίσασα λυσιτελεῖν ἢ ζῆν ὁρῶσα τὰ γιγνόμενα ἀπαγχομένη μεταξὺ κατεκωλύθη (*On the Mysteries*, § 125).

§ 3. There was no observance in which the Greeks were more punctilious than in the burial of the dead and mourning ceremonies [3]. A strong religious feeling attached to this observance. It was, besides, the universal usage among the Greeks, and to deprive one of burial was to be guilty of a deed peculiarly horrible. The usual ceremonies are duly described by Becker,—the washing and arraying of the dead body, the cutting of the hair, the lacerating of the cheeks, &c. The phrase most frequently employed in speaking of these burial and mourning customs is τὰ νομιζόμενα (or its equivalent). So we find in Euripides, *Alc.* 609, ὡς νομίζεται; *Suppl.* 19, νόμιμ' ἀτίζοντες θεῶν: Antiphon, περὶ τοῦ χορευτοῦ, § 37, τὰ νομιζόμενα ποιῆσαι [4].

---

[1] Because it was regarded as preventing the free escape of the ψυχή.   See Jerram's note *ad loc.*, and Paley's notes on this passage and on *Andr.* 811-813. For Euripides on suicide see Decharme, *Euripide, &c.*, pp. 122-123.

[2] Cf. Hamlet's soliloquy.

[3] See Becker, *Charicles*, Excursus to Scene ix : Mahaffy, *Old Greek Life*, pp. 59-60 : Coulanges, *La Cité Antique*, Livre I. c. i.

[4] Cf. also Euripides, *Suppl.* 561 : Isocrates, xix. § 33 : Isaeus, ii. §§ 4, 10 ; vi. § 65 ; vii. § 30 ; ix. §§ 4, 7, 32 : Aeschines, *Agst. Timarchus*, § 13 ; *Agst. Ctesiphon*, § 77 : Demosthenes, *On the Crown*, § 243 ; *Agst. Timocrates*, § 107 : Dinarchus, *Agst. Aristogeiton*, §§ 8, 18.   And see Coulanges, *La Cité Antique*, p. 33.

Especially may we compare a passage in the *Supplices* with one in Lysias:—

> νεκροὺς δὲ τοὺς θανόντας, οὐ βλάπτων πόλιν,
> οὐδ' ἀνδροκμῆτας προσφέρων ἀγωνίας,
> θάψαι δικαιῶ, τὸν Πανελλήνων νόμον
> σώζων (*Suppl.* 524–527).

Ἑλληνικοῦ νόμου στερηθέντες (Lysias, *Epitaph.* § 9).

Even a slain enemy, as we see from these passages, was not deprived of the rites of burial[1].

For the anxiety as to the discharge of these rites we may adduce a passage from Isaeus (vii. § 30):—

> πάντες γὰρ οἱ τελευτήσειν μέλλοντες πρόνοιαν ποιοῦνται σφῶν αὐτῶν, ὅπως μὴ ἐξερημώσουσι τοὺς σφετέρους αὐτῶν οἴκους, ἀλλ' ἔσται τις καὶ ὁ ἐναγιῶν καὶ πάντα τὰ νομιζόμενα αὐτοῖς ποιήσων· διὸ κἂν ἄπαιδες τελευτήσωσιν, ἀλλ' οὖν υἱὸν ποιησάμενοι καταλείπουσι.

As to the religious feeling the following passages may be instanced:—

> τοῖς γὰρ θανοῦσι χρὴ τὸν οὐ τεθνηκότα
> τιμὰς διδόντα χθόνιον εὖ σέβειν θεόν
>
> (Euripides, *Phoen.* 1320–1321).

ἵνα μηκέτι εἰς τοὺς τεθνεῶτας ἐξαμαρτάνοντες πλείω περὶ τοὺς θεοὺς ἐξυβρίσωσιν (Lysias, *Epitaph.* § 9. See the whole passage, §§ 7–9).

. . . . ἐδεῖτο μὴ περιιδεῖν τοιούτους ἄνδρας ἀτάφους γενομένους μηδὲ παλαιὸν ἔθος καὶ πάτριον νόμον καταλυόμενον, ᾧ πάντες ἄνθρωποι χρώμενοι διατελοῦσιν οὐχ ὡς ὑπ' ἀνθρωπίνης κειμένῳ φύσεως ἀλλ' ὡς ὑπὸ δαιμονίας προστεταγμένῳ δυνάμεως (Isocrates, *Panath.* § 169).

τελευτήσαντα δ' αὐτόν, ἡνίκα ὁ μὲν εὐεργετούμενος οὐκ αἰσθάνεται ὧν εὖ πάσχει, τιμᾶται δὲ ὁ νόμος καὶ τὸ θεῖον, θάπτειν ἤδη κελεύει καὶ τἄλλα ποιεῖν τὰ νομιζόμενα (Aeschines, *Agst. Timarchus*, § 14)[2].

---

[1] Cf. also Lysias, x. § 7; xii. § 96. To deprive a criminal of the rites of burial was the most terrible punishment that could be inflicted on him. Cf. Aesch. *Septem contra Thebas*, 1013 ff.; Soph. *Antig.* 198 ff.; Eur. *Phoen.* 1627–1634; Lysias, *Epitaph.* §§ 7–9.

[2] Cf. Coulanges, *La Cité Antique*, Livre I. c. i. p. 10:—'Toute l'antiquité a été persuadée que sans la sépulture l'âme était misérable, et que par la sépulture

In illustration of the mourning ceremonies—the κόσμος of the dead, &c.—the following passages may be quoted:—

> ἐκ δ᾽ ἑλοῦσα κεδρίνων δόμων
> ἐσθῆτα κόσμον τ᾽ εὐπρεπῶς ἠσκήσατο
>
> (Eur. *Alc.* 160–161)[1].

> πυλῶν πάροιθε δ᾽ οὐχ ὁρῶ
> πηγαῖον ὡς νομίζεται
> χέρνιβ᾽ ἐπὶ φθιτῶν πύλαις,
> χαῖτα τ᾽ οὔτις ἐπὶ προθύροις
> τομαῖος, ἃ δὴ νεκύων
> πένθει πίτνει, οὐδὲ νεαλῆς
> δουπεῖ χεὶρ γυναικῶν (*ibid.* 98–104).

τίς γὰρ οὐκ ἀπεκείρατο, ἐπειδὴ τὼ δύο ταλάντω ἐξ ᾽Ακῆς ἤλθετον; ἢ τίς οὐ μέλαν ἱμάτιον ἐφόρησεν, ὡς διὰ τὸ πένθος κληρονομήσων τῆς οὐσίας; (Isaeus, iv. § 7).

αἱ μὲν οὖν γυναῖκες, οἷον εἰκός, περὶ τὸν τετελευτηκότα ἦσαν (Isaeus, vi. § 41)[2].

But Euripides reminds us that costly obsequies matter nothing to the dead, that mourning is useless, that grief ought to be kept within due limits:—

> δοκῶ δὲ τοῖς θανοῦσι διαφέρειν βραχύ,
> εἰ πλουσίων τις τεύξεται κτερισμάτων.
> κενὸν δὲ γαύρωμ᾽ ἐστὶ τῶν ζώντων τόδε
>
> (*Tro.* 1248–1250)[3].
> τί δ᾽ ἂν προκόπτοις, εἰ θέλεις ἀεὶ στένειν;
>
> (*Alc.* 1079).

---

elle devenait à jamais heureuse.' And again (p. 11):—'On peut voir dans les écrivains anciens combien l'homme était tourmenté par la crainte qu'après sa mort les rites ne fussent pas observés à son égard. C'était une source de poignantes inquiétudes. On craignait moins la mort que la privation de sépulture. C'est qu'il y allait du repos et du bonheur éternel.' He goes on to explain on this ground the conduct of the Athenians in the trial of the generals after Arginusae.

[1] See Paley's note *ad loc.* And cf. *Alc.* 149, 613, 663 (with Jerram's notes); *Hel.* 1062, 1186, 1279; *Tro.* 1147, 1200; *Hec.* 578, 615; *El.* 90, 146, 509; *Iph. Taur.* 156, 632; *Or.* 96, 112, 457; *Phoen.* 322; *Heracl.* 568.

[2] Cf. Eur. *Tro.* 381, 480; *El.* 323; *Alc.* 425, 818, 827; *Hec.* 653; *Her. Fur.* 1389; *Andr.* 1209; *Suppl.* 50, 73, 826, 983. And see Coulanges, *La Cité Antique*, Livre I. c. 1.

[3] Cf. *Hel.* 1421; *Frag.* 640.

παῦσαι δὲ λύπης τῶν τεθνηκότων ὕπερ·
πᾶσιν γὰρ ἀνθρώποισιν ἥδε πρὸς θεῶν
ψῆφος κέκραιται, κατθανεῖν ὀφείλεται
(*Andr.* 1270–1272).

πάντων τὸ θανεῖν· τὸ δὲ κοινὸν ἄχος
μετρίως ἀλγεῖν σοφία μελετᾷ (*Frag.* 46)[1].

γίγνωσκε τἀνθρώπεια μηδ' ὑπερμέτρως
ἄλγει· κακοῖς γὰρ οὐ σὺ πρόσκεισαι μόνη (*Frag.* 418).

Very similar are the words of Lysias (?) (II. § 77):—

ἀλλὰ γὰρ οὐκ οἶδ' ὅ τι δεῖ τοιαῦτα ὀλοφύρεσθαι· οὐ γὰρ ἐλανθάνομεν ἡμᾶς αὐτοὺς ὄντες θνητοί· ὥστε τί δεῖ, ἃ πάλαι προσεδοκῶμεν πείσεσθαι, ὑπὲρ τούτων νῦν ἄχθεσθαι, ἢ λίαν οὕτω βαρέως φέρειν ἐπὶ ταῖς τῆς φύσεως συμφοραῖς, ἐπισταμένους ὅτι ὁ θάνατος κοινὸς καὶ τοῖς χειρίστοις καὶ τοῖς βελτίστοις ; κ.τ.λ.

---

[1] Cf. *Hec.* 960; *Tro.* 693; *Andr.* 1234; *Frag.* 332.

CHAPTER V

LIFE IN ITS GENERAL ASPECTS

A MAN'S way of looking at death is closely connected with his ideas of life; and we may now proceed to consider how Euripides and the Orators regarded life—I mean life as a whole, life in its general and universal aspect. In such a matter individual temperament is always a prominent factor,—a fact of which Euripides is a striking example. He was naturally gloomy and morose, lived the life of a retired student, and took little or no part in the pleasures of public life. His sceptical doubts in the matter of religion also exercised, doubtless, a strong reflex action on his judgment of life generally. Further—at least in the latter part of his life—times had changed : life had become sadder, Greece had been torn by long wars and civil discord, and the ancient morality had been undermined. New opinions, aided greatly by Socrates and his disciples—and not least by Euripides himself—had begun to prevail. If, then, Euripides regards life as difficult, sad, gloomy, it is only what we should have expected. His plays abound everywhere with reflections on the evils of existence, on the difficulty of attaining to happiness, on the fleeting, unstable nature of human things [1].

There are, no doubt, some passages of a different cast.

Alcestis declares that nothing is more precious than life (*Alc.* 301):—

$$\psi\upsilon\chi\hat{\eta}s \ \gamma\grave{\alpha}\rho \ o\dot{\upsilon}\delta\acute{\epsilon}\nu \ \dot{\epsilon}\sigma\tau\iota \ \tau\iota\mu\iota\acute{\omega}\tau\epsilon\rho o\nu.$$

---

[1] Cf. Decharme, *Euripide, &c.*, p. 105 :—'Un des caractères essentiels de la morale d'Euripide est le pessimisme.'

Iphigenia exclaims (*Iph. Aul.* 1250-1252):—

> τὸ φῶς τόδ' ἀνθρώποισιν ἥδιστον βλέπειν,
> τὰ νέρθε δ' οὐδέν· μαίνεται δ' ὃς εὔχεται
> θανεῖν· κακῶς ζῆν κρεῖσσον ἢ καλῶς θανεῖν.

In *Troades*, 628-629, we have these words:—

> οὐ ταὐτόν, ὦ παῖ, τῷ βλέπειν τὸ κατθανεῖν·
> τὸ μὲν γὰρ οὐδέν, τῷ δ' ἔνεισιν ἐλπίδες.

But such sentiments are peculiarly appropriate to the characters to whom they are assigned; for, in each case, death is to them the greatest of evils. They are, therefore, no proof of inconsistency in Euripides. One passage (*Suppl.* 195-218) Berlage (p. 135) singles out for special consideration. It is a panegyric on human life, the growth of civilisation, and the beneficence of the deity. The poet seems to express a belief even in divination (ll. 211-213), though elsewhere he speaks of it with deep distrust and hatred. Berlage is right, I think, in regarding this passage as a rhetorical exercise or ἐπίδειξις, especially as it is introduced by these words:—

> ἄλλοισι δὴ 'πόνησ' ἁμιλληθεὶς λόγῳ
> τοιῷδ'.

Besides, the play of the *Supplices* is entirely free from religious scepticism; and, in any case, such passages are as scarce as those of an opposite nature are plentiful. It is true that Euripides was not the first Greek writer to express gloomy thoughts about life [1]. The dark side of human experience cannot remain unnoticed by any man who thinks.

In Homer (*Il.* xvii. 446-447) we have these words:—

> οὐ μὲν γάρ τί πού ἐστιν ὀιζυρώτερον ἀνδρὸς
> πάντων, ὅσσα τε γαῖαν ἔπι πνείει τε καὶ ἕρπει [2].

Similar sentiments are to be found in Hesiod. Pindar speaks of man as a σκιᾶς ὄναρ [3]. In Herodotus, Solon's speech

---

[1] For the melancholy of the Greeks see Butcher, *Some Aspects of the Greek Genius*, pp. 130-165: Campbell, *Greek Tragedy*, pp. 103 ff.: Berlage, *De Euripide Philosopho*, pp. 135 138: Decharme, *Euripide, &c.*, pp. 105-108. M. Decharme says (p. 105):—'Dès le temps des poèmes homériques, l'humanité grecque a conscience de sa misère.'

[2] Cf. *Il.* vi. 146 ff.; *Od.* xx. 201-203.

[3] *Pyth.* viii. 95.

to Croesus is of a similar tenor.   Such passages abound also
in Aeschylus and Sophocles.   In *Ajax*, 126, Odysseus speaks
of men as εἴδωλα ἢ κούφην σκιάν; and, in the *Oed. Col.*
(1225 ff.), the Chorus declare that it is better never to be
born :—

> μὴ φῦναι τὸν ἅπαντα νικᾷ λόγον· τὸ δ᾽, ἐπεὶ φανῇ,
> βῆναι κεῖθεν ὅθεν περ ἥκει
> πολὺ δεύτερον ὡς τάχιστα [1].

But in no writer do we find such a continual iteration of
these thoughts as in Euripides [2].

Life is a shadow, a wrestling: there is no music to heal
sorrow, no rest from trouble: all must suffer: mortals are
fed on trouble: no man is fortunate: woes are numerous,
happiness is scarce: none is altogether happy: human ills are
infinite.

> τὰ θνητὰ δ᾽ οὐ νῦν πρῶτον ἡγοῦμαι σκιάν (*Med.* 1224).
> παλαίσμαθ᾽ ἡμῶν ὁ βίος (*Suppl.* 550).
> στυγίους δὲ βροτῶν οὐδεὶς λύπας
> ηὕρετο μούσῃ καὶ πολυχόρδοις
> ᾠδαῖς παύειν, ἐξ ὧν θάνατοι
> δειναί τε τύχαι σφάλλουσι δόμους (*Med.* 195–198).
> πᾶς δ᾽ ὀδυνηρὸς βίος ἀνθρώπων
> κοὐκ ἔστι πόνων ἀνάπαυσις (*Hipp.* 190–191).
> μοχθεῖν δὲ βροτοῖσιν ἀνάγκη (*ibid.* 207).
> ὦ πόνοι τρέφοντες βροτούς (*ibid.* 367).
> οὐκ οἶδ᾽ ὅπως εἴποιμ᾽ ἂν εὐτυχεῖν τινα
> θνητῶν (*ibid.* 981).
> πολλαί γε πολλοῖς εἰσι συμφοραὶ βροτῶν,
> μορφαὶ δὲ διαφέρουσιν. ἐν δ᾽ ἂν εὐτυχὲς
> μόλις ποτ᾽ ἐξεύροι τις ἀνθρώπων βίῳ (*Ion*, 381–383).
> θνητῶν δ᾽ ὄλβιος ἐς τέλος οὐδεὶς
> οὐδ᾽ εὐδαίμων·
> οὔπω γὰρ ἔφυ τις ἄλυπος (*Iph. Aul.* 161–163).
> ὥστ᾽ οὔ τις ἀνδρῶν εἰς ἅπαντ᾽ εὐδαιμονεῖ (*Frag.* 45).

---

[1] See Jebb's note *ad loc.* Cf. Theognis, 425–428 ; and see Butcher, *loc. cit.*
(p. 142) ; Decharme, *Euripide, &c*, p. 119.
[2] Theognis comes nearest to Euripides in this respect.

. . . κοὐδεὶς διὰ τέλους εὐδαιμονεῖ (*Frag.* 273).
οὐκ ἔστιν ὅστις πάντ' ἀνὴρ εὐδαιμονεῖ κ.τ.λ. (*Frag.* 661).
πόλλ' ἔστιν ἀνθρώποισιν, ὦ ξένοι, κακά (*Frag.* 204).
φεῦ φεῦ, βροτείων πημάτων ὅσαι τύχαι
ὅσαι τε μορφαί· τέρμα δ' οὐκ εἴποι τις ἄν (*Frag.* 211).
οὐ θαῦμ' ἔλεξας θνητὸν ὄντα δυστυχεῖν (*Frag.* 651).
ἄρασσα, πολλοῖς ἔστιν ἀνθρώπων κακά,
τοῖς δ' ἄρτι λήγει, τοῖς δὲ κίνδυνος μολεῖν.
κύκλος γὰρ αὐτὸς καρπίμοις τε γῆς φυτοῖς
θνητῶν τε γενεᾷ· τῶν μὲν αὔξεται βίος,
τῶν δὲ φθίνει τε καὶ θερίζεται πάλιν (*Frag.* 415)[1].
θνητὸς γὰρ ὢν καὶ θνητὰ πείσεσθαι δόκει·
⟨ἢ⟩ θεοῦ βίον ζῆν ἀξιοῖς ἄνθρωπος ὤν; (*Frag.* 1075).

Joy and sorrow are mingled in human life: he is most
blessed whom day by day no ill befalls:—

> δεῖ δέ σε χαίρειν καὶ λυπεῖσθαι·
> θνητὸς γὰρ ἔφυς (*Iph. Aul.* 31–32)[2].
> τοιόσδε θνητῶν τῶν ταλαιπώρων βίος·
> οὔτ' εὐτυχεῖ τὸ πάμπαν οὔτε δυστυχεῖ.
> [εὐδαιμονεῖ τε καὖθις οὐκ εὐδαιμονεῖ] (*Frag.* 196).
>   κεῖνος ὀλβιώτατος,
> ὅτῳ κατ' ἦμαρ τυγχάνει μηδὲν κακόν (*Hec.* 627–628).

Fortune is capricious and changeful: all things are fleeting:
the future is uncertain:—

> οὐκ ἔστιν οὐδὲν πιστὸν οὔτ' εὐδοξία
> οὔτ' αὖ καλῶς πράσσοιτα μὴ πράξειν κακῶς.
> φύρουσι δ' αὐτὰ θεοὶ πάλιν τε καὶ πρόσω, κ.τ.λ.
>   (*Hec.* 956–958).
> τὰ θνητὰ τοιαῦτ'· οὐδὲν ἐν ταὐτῷ μένει (*Ion,* 969).
> κοὐκ ἔστι θνητῶν ὅστις ἐξεπίσταται
> τὴν αὔριον μέλλουσαν εἰ βιώσεται (*Alc.* 783–784).
> ποῦ δὴ τὸ σαφὲς θνατοῖσι βιοτᾶς;
> θοαῖσι μὲν ναυσὶ πόρον πνοαὶ κατὰ βένθος ἅλιον
> ἰθύνουσι· τύχας δὲ θνητῶν

---

[1] Cf. Homer's well-known lines, *Il.* vi. 146 ff.:—
> οἵη περ φύλλων γενεή, τοίη δὲ καὶ ἀνδρῶν· κ.τ.λ.

[2] Cf. *Suppl.* 196.

τὸ μὲν μέγ' εἰς οὐδὲν ὁ πολὺς χρόνος
μεθίστησι, τὸ δὲ μεῖον αὔξων (*Frag.* 304).
. . . βέβαιον οὐδὲν τῆς ἀεὶ τύχης ἔχων (*Hel.* 715).
ἰὼ ἰώ, πανδάκρυτ' ἐφαμέρων
ἔθνη πολύπονα, λεύσσεθ', ὡς παρ' ἐλπίδας
μοῖρα βαίνει·
ἕτερα δ' ἕτερος ἀμείβεται
πήματ' ἐν χρόνῳ μακρῷ·
βροτῶν δ' ὁ πᾶς ἀστάθμητος αἰών (*Or.* 976–981)[1].

'A sorrow's crown of sorrow is remembering happier things'
(*Frag.* 285, esp. ll. 18–20):—

οὕτως ἄριστον μὴ πεπειρᾶσθαι καλῶν.
ἐκεῖνο γὰρ μεμνήμεθ'· οἷος ἦν ποτε
κἀγὼ μετ' ἀνδρῶν ἡνίκ' ηὐτύχουν βίῳ[2].

Moral inequalities exist and perplex (*Hipp.* 1102–1110):—

ἦ μέγα μοι τὰ θεῶν μελεδήμαθ', ὅταν φρένας ἔλθῃ,
λύπας παραιρεῖ· ξύνεσιν δέ τιν' ἐλπίδι κεύθων
λείπομαι ἔν τε τύχαις θνατῶν καὶ ἐν ἔργμασι λεύσσων·
ἄλλα γὰρ ἄλλοθεν ἀμείβεται,
μετὰ δ' ἵσταται ἀνδράσιν αἰὼν
πολυπλάνητος ἀεί[3].

Every man must bear his own burden (*Iph. Taur.* 687):—

τἀμὰ δεῖ φέρειν ἐμέ.

The future terrifies: 'carpe diem':—

ἦ που τὸ μέλλον ἐκφοβεῖ καθ' ἡμέραν·
ὡς τοῦ γε πάσχειν τοὐπιὸν μεῖζον κακόν (*Frag.* 135).
ταῦτ' οὖν ἀκούσας καὶ μαθὼν ἐμοῦ πάρα,
εὔφραινε σαυτόν, πῖνε, τὸν καθ' ἡμέραν
βίον λογίζου σόν, τὰ δ' ἄλλα τῆς τύχης (*Alc.* 787–789)[4].

---

[1] Cf. *Hipp.* 1109; *Hec.* 55, 60, 283, 492, 846; *Andr.* 5, 462; *Her. Fur.* 101, 216, 735, 1291; *Suppl.* 331, 552, 608; *Ion,* 1504, 1512; *Tro.* 472, 610, 634, 1203; *Hel.* 510, 713, 1140; *El.* 183, 304; *Iph. Taur.* 721, 1121; *Or.* 340; *Iph. Aul.* 1610; *Phoen.* 1758; *Heracl.* 610, 863; *Rhesus,* 317, 332, 882; *Frag.* 157, 158, 262, 330, 420, 536, 549, 554, 684, 1074.

[2] Cf. *Tro.* 147 ff.

[3] See above, p. 27, and cf. *Suppl.* 226; *Frag.* 286, 832.

[4] Cf. *Her. Fur.* 503–505; *Bacch.* 395.

Amid all the uncertainties of life it is best to trust ever in hope :—

> οὗτος δ' ἀνὴρ ἄριστος ὅστις ἐλπίσι
> πέποιθεν ἀεί· τὸ δ' ἀπορεῖν ἀνδρὸς κακοῦ
> (*Her. Fur.* 105-106).
> ἐν ἐλπίσιν χρὴ τοὺς σοφοὺς ἄγειν βίον (*Frag.* 408).
> μήτ' εὐτυχοῦσα πᾶσαν ἡνίαν χάλα
> κακῶς τε πράσσουσ' ἐλπίδος κεδνῆς ἔχου (*Frag.* 409) [1].

And Euripides, as we might expect, wonders what is the origin and explanation of evil (*Frag.* 912, ll. 9-13):—

> πέμψον δ' ἐς φῶς ψυχὰς ἑτέρων
> τοῖς βουλομένοις ἄθλους προμαθεῖν
> πόθεν ἔβλαστον, τίς ῥίζα κακῶν,
> τίνα δεῖ μακάρων ἐκθυσαμένους
> εὑρεῖν μόχθων ἀνάπαυλαν.

It is seldom that the Orators linger to indulge in such reflections. They are, as might be expected, most numerous in the essayist Isocrates.

The following are, I think, most of the passages bearing on the subject :—

> ἐμοὶ δέ, ὦ ἄνδρες, καὶ τῷ πρώτῳ τοῦτο εἰπόντι ὀρθῶς δοκεῖ εἰρῆσθαι, ὅτι πάντες ἄνθρωποι γίγνονται ἐπὶ τῷ εὖ καὶ κακῶς πράττειν [2], μεγάλη δὲ δήπου καὶ τὸ ἐξαμαρτεῖν δυσπραξία ἐστί, καὶ εἰσὶν εὐτυχέστατοι μὲν οἱ ἐλάχιστα ἐξαμαρτάνοντες, σωφρονέστατοι δὲ οἱ ἂν τάχιστα μεταγιγνώσκωσι. καὶ ταῦτα οὐ διακέκριται τοῖς μὲν γίγνεσθαι τοῖς δὲ μή, ἀλλ' ἔστιν ἐν τῷ κοινῷ πᾶσιν ἀνθρώποις καὶ ἐξαμαρτεῖν τι καὶ κακῶς πρᾶξαι (Andocides, περὶ τῆς ἑαυτοῦ καθ-όδου, §§ 5-6).
> κοινὴ γὰρ ἡ τύχη καὶ τὸ μέλλον ἀόρατον (Isocrates, *Ad Demon.* § 29).
> νόμιζε μηδὲν εἶναι τῶν ἀνθρωπίνων βέβαιον (*ibid.* § 42).
> ... ὁρῶσα δὲ περὶ μὲν τὰς ἄλλας πράξεις οὕτω ταραχώδεις οὔσας

---

[1] For this happier aspect of Hope cf. *Tro* 676 ; *Frag.* 761, 826. Hope was more usually regarded as vain, deceitful, winged. See *Iph. Taur.* 414-418 ; *Suppl.* 479 ; *Her. Fur.* 460 ; *Frag.* 391, 650. And cf. Butcher, *Some Aspects of the Greek Genius*, pp. 133-136.
[2] Cf. above, p. 63.

F

τὰς τύχας ὥστε πολλάκις ἐν αὐταῖς καὶ τοὺς φρονίμους ἀτυχεῖν καὶ τοὺς ἀνοήτους κατορθοῦν, κ.τ.λ. (Isocr. Panegyr. § 48).

αἴτιον δὲ τούτων ἐστίν, ὅτι τῶν ἀγαθῶν καὶ τῶν κακῶν οὐδὲν αὐτὸ καθ' αὑτὸ παραγίγνεται τοῖς ἀνθρώποις, κ.τ.λ. (Isocr. Areop. § 4).

καὶ κυβερνήτης ἀγαθὸς ἐνίοτε ναυαγεῖ καὶ ἀνὴρ σπουδαῖος ἀτυχεῖ (Isocr. Frag. iii. (δ'.) 3).

ὁ μεμνημένος τί ἐστιν ἄνθρωπος, ἐπ' οὐδενὶ τῶν συμβάντων δυσχερανεῖ (ibid. 5).

τῆς εὐτυχίας ὥσπερ ὀπώρας παρούσης ἀπολαύειν δεῖ (ibid. 7).

In the speech *Against Ctesiphon*, §§ 132 ff., Aeschines gives a list of sudden and unexpected changes of fortune.

The following passages are also in point :—

ἐπειδήπερ ἄδηλον τὸ μέλλον ἅπασιν ἀνθρώποις (Demosthenes, *For the Liberty of the Rhodians*, § 21).

ἦν γὰρ (sc. τύχην) ὁ βέλτιστα πράττειν νομίζων καὶ ἀρίστην ἔχειν οἰόμενος, οὐκ οἶδεν εἰ [τοιαύτη] μενεῖ μέχρι τῆς ἑσπέρας, κ.τ.λ. (Demosth. *On the Crown*, § 252).

. . . πάντα δ' ἀνθρώπινα ἡγεῖσθαι (Demosth. *Lept.* § 161).

ἀλλ', οἶμαι, τὸ μέλλον ἄδηλον πᾶσιν ἀνθρώποις, καὶ μικροὶ καιροὶ μεγάλων πραγμάτων αἴτιοι γίγνονται (ibid. § 162).

ἐγίνωσκον ἀκριβῶς τὸν μὲν τῶν πολιτευομένων βίον εὐκίνητον ὄντα, τὸ δὲ μέλλον ἀόρατον, ποικίλας δὲ τὰς τῆς τύχης μεταβολάς, ἀκρίτους δὲ τοὺς τὴν Ἑλλάδα κατέχοντας καιρούς (Demades (?), *Frag.* 34).

ὀλισθηραὶ δὲ καὶ συνεχεῖς αἱ παρὰ τῶν πραγμάτων γινόμεναι μεταβολαί (Demades (?), *Frag.* 47).

CHAPTER VI

ETHICS

WE have already remarked (Introd. p. 7) that the dramas of Euripides reflect faithfully the circumstances which in Greece distinguished the close of the fifth century B.C.—the struggle between the old and the new, the spirit of restless inquiry, the growing rationalism and scepticism in matters of philosophy and religion. Hence such a prayer as that of *Frag.* 912 (quoted above, p. 65), with which we may compare *Frag.* 376 :—

οὐκ οἶδ' ὅτῳ χρὴ κανόνι τὰς βροτῶν τύχας
ὀρθῶς σταθμήσαντ' εἰδέναι τὸ δραστέον[1].

There is, I think, nothing like this to be found in the Orators.

It does not concern us here to inquire how much truth there is in the indictment brought by Aristophanes against Euripides—a pupil of the sophists—and against the sophists themselves. There are certainly many things in Euripides which might tend to corrupt Athenian morality, just as there is much which might tend to improve it. But it is neither profitable nor fair to isolate these passages and consider them apart from the context and the dramatic proprieties[2]. Besides, in this respect a comparison with

---

[1] See Berlage, p. 140.

[2] For a discussion of these questions see Berlage, pp. 144 ff. There are many passages in Euripides which breathe a high morality—'l'élévation des sentences morales dont son théâtre est semé' (Decharme, *Euripide, &c.,* p. 22)— and go to prove that, as the influence of religion decayed, the influence of the human conscience increased,—that Greek morality was purer than Greek

the Orators would be singularly barren. What they have in common with Euripides is rather the commonplace maxims of morality.

It is probable, I think, that the highest virtue was regarded by Euripides not in the way in which it had been commonly regarded in Greece. The ἀρετή of the Greeks consisted in the union of wise thought with noble action, and each of these was as important as the other. That man only was possessed of true 'excellence' who was a good citizen. This civil and political side of ἀρετή was by Euripides less emphasised than that side of it which looked to moral purity. He himself chose a life of seclusion in preference to a life of publicity. In this, as in much else, he showed himself more modern than his contemporaries.

Nowhere has he stated definitely his idea of the highest virtue.

In *Frag.* 853 we have not so much a definition of virtue as a whole as an enumeration of individual virtues:—

τρεῖς εἰσὶν ἀρεταὶ τὰς χρεών σ' ἀσκεῖν, τέκνον,
θεούς τε τιμᾶν τούς τε φύσαντας γονῆς
νόμους τε κοινοὺς Ἑλλάδος· καὶ ταῦτα δρῶν
κάλλιστον ἕξεις στέφανον εὐκλείας ἀεί.

Very similar is the passage in Isocrates, *Ad. Demon.* § 16:—

τοὺς μὲν θεοὺς φοβοῦ, τοὺς δὲ γονεῖς τίμα, τοὺς δὲ φίλους αἰσχύνου, τοῖς δὲ νόμοις πείθου.

Passages are numerous in which Euripides commends and extols virtue.—Wealth without virtue is worthless (*Frag.* 163):—

ἀνδρὸς φίλου δὲ χρυσὸς ἀμαθίας μέτα
ἄχρηστος, εἰ μὴ κἀρετὴν ἔχων τύχοι [1].

religion. With a passage in Demosthenes (*On the Embassy*, § 21) we might compare *Hipp.* 317:—χεῖρες μὲν ἀγναί, φρὴν δ' ἔχει μίασμά τι: and *Or.* 1604 :—
ME. ἀγνὸς γάρ εἰμι χεῖρας. OP. ἀλλ' οὐ τὰς φρένας.
Berlage (p. 165) compares these words of Democritus:—ἀγαθὸν οὐ τὸ μὴ ἀδικέειν ἀλλὰ τὸ μηδὲ θέλειν. We may add the words of Isocrates (*Ad Demon.* § 15):—ἃ ποιεῖν αἰσχρόν, ταῦτα νόμιζε μηδὲ λέγειν εἶναι καλόν.
[1] Cf. *Andr.* 639-641 ; *Frag.* 405.

Virtue is not to be bought (*Frag.* 527):—

> μόνον δ' ἂν ἀντὶ χρημάτων οὐκ ἂν λάβοις
> γενναιότητα κἀρετήν.

' 'Tis only noble to be good ' (*Frag.* 336):—

> εἰς δ' εὐγένειαν ὀλίγ' ἔχω φράσαι καλά·
> ὁ μὲν γὰρ ἐσθλὸς εὐγενὴς ἔμοιγ' ἀνήρ,
> ὁ δ' οὐ δίκαιος, κἂν ἀμείνονος πατρὸς
> Ζηνὸς πεφύκῃ, δυσγενὴς εἶναι δοκεῖ[1].

Nothing has greater power than virtue (*Frag.* 446):—

> . . . . οὔποτε θνητοῖς
> ἀρετῆς ἄλλη δύναμις μείζων.

Virtue is the highest good (*Frag.* 1030):—

> ἀρετὴ μέγιστον τῶν ἐν ἀνθρώποις καλόν[2].

Isocrates has much of a similar tendency[3]. With him, as with Euripides, virtue is the highest good (*Nicocles*, § 47):—

> μέγιστόν ἐστι τῶν ἀγαθῶν ἀρετή.

It is better than wealth, beauty, strength, high birth (*Ad Demon.* §§ 5–7):—

> . . . . τῆς ἀρετῆς . . . . ἧς οὐδὲν κτῆμα σεμνότερον οὐδὲ βεβαιότερόν
> ἐστι. . . . . ἡ δὲ τῆς ἀρετῆς κτῆσις οἷς ἂν ἀκιβδήλως ταῖς διανοίαις
> συναυξηθῇ, μόνη μὲν συγγηράσκει, πλούτου δὲ κρείττων, χρησιμωτέρα
> δ' εὐγενείας ἐστί, κ.τ.λ.

It is the salvation of humanity (*Archid.* § 36):—

> . . . . ὅλως δὲ τὸν βίον τὸν τῶν ἀνθρώπων διὰ μὲν κακίαν ἀπολ-
> λύμενον, δι' ἀρετὴν δὲ σωζόμενον.

A good name is better than wealth: it cannot be bought with money: it never dies (*Ad Nicocl.* § 32);—

> περὶ πλείονος ποιοῦ δόξαν καλὴν ἢ πλοῦτον μέγαν τοῖς παισὶ

---

[1] Cf. *Frag.* 53:— οὐκ ἔστιν ἐν κακοῖσιν εὐγένεια,
 παρ' ἀγαθοῖσι δ' ἀνδρῶν.

[2] Cf. *Frag.* 1029:— οὐκ ἔστιν ἀρετῆς κτῆμα τιμιώτερον.

[3] See Schandau, *De Isocratis doctrina rhetorica et ethica*, p. 15. Prof. Jebb discusses the high moral tone of Isocrates in *Attic Orators*, ii. pp. 44-45.

καταλιπεῖν· ὁ μὲν γὰρ θνητός, ἡ δ' ἀθάνατος [1], καὶ δόξῃ μὲν χρήματα κτητά, δόξα δὲ χρημάτων οὐκ ὠνητή [2].

Not wealth but a clear conscience is to be envied (*Nicocl.* § 59):—

ζηλοῦτε μὴ τοὺς πλεῖστα κεκτημένους ἀλλὰ τοὺς μηδὲν κακὸν σφίσιν αὐτοῖς συνειδότας.

Virtue is the true source of all happiness (*De Pace*, § 32):—

.... ὡς οὔτε πρὸς χρηματισμὸν οὔτε πρὸς δόξαν οὔτε πρὸς ἃ δεῖ πράττειν οὔθ' ὅλως πρὸς εὐδαιμονίαν οὐδὲν ἂν συμβάλοιτο τηλικαύτην δύναμιν, ὅσην περ ἀρετὴ καὶ τὰ μέρη ταύτης [3].

Better a noble death than an ignoble life (*Ad Nicocl.* § 36):—

ἢν δ' ἀνασκασθῇς κινδυνεύειν, αἱροῦ τεθνάναι καλῶς μᾶλλον ἢ ζῆν αἰσχρῶς [4].

Aeschines says that it is better to lose one's life than virtue (*Agst. Ctesiphon*, § 160):—

... αἵματός ἐστιν ἡ ἀρετὴ ὠνία.

Demosthenes speaks of virtue as better than wealth (*For Phormio*, § 52):—

πολλῶν χρημάτων τὸ χρηστὸν εἶναι λυσιτελέστερόν ἐστι [5].

What Euripides regarded as the source of virtue, and whether or not he considered virtue as capable of being taught, is a question which cannot be definitely settled. The Socratic dictum that knowledge is virtue—implying that virtue can be imparted by instruction—was no doubt familiar to him. He was a friend of Socrates. And there are certainly some passages in Euripides which bear a strong

---

[1] Cf. Eur. *Frag.* 734 :—

       ἀρετὴ δὲ κἂν θάνῃ τις οὐκ ἀπόλλυται,
       ζῇ δ' οὐκέτ' ὄντος σώματος.

[2] Cf. Isocr. *Phil.* §§ 133 ff. ; *Epist.* vii. § 1.

[3] Cf. *Nicocl.* §§ 29-30, 36 ; *Panath.* § 32.

[4] Cf. *Ad Dem.* § 43 ; *Evag.* §§ 1-4 ; *Panegyr.* § 95 ; *Phil.* §§ 133-136 ; *Archid.* § 108.

[5] Cp. *Lept.* § 10.

resemblance to the Socratic teaching. The herald in the *Supplices* says (l. 510):—

καὶ τοῦτό τοι τἀνδρεῖον, ἡ προμηθία:

and τἀνδρεῖον is a virtue.

Again (*ibid.* 913–915):—

ἡ δ' εὐανδρία
διδακτόν, εἴπερ καὶ βρέφος διδάσκεται
λέγειν ἀκούειν θ' ὧν μάθησιν οὐκ ἔχει.

In the *Medea* (844–845) we find these words:—

τᾷ σοφίᾳ παρέδρους πέμπειν ἔρωτας,
παντοίας ἀρετᾶς ξυνεργούς.

Of a similar tenor is *Frag.* 897:—

παίδευμα δ' Ἔρως σοφίας ἀρετῆς
πλεῖστον ὑπάρχει.

Here ἀρετή is plainly said to be διδακτόν, and the chief teacher of it is Ἔρως[1].

These passages are, however, very few indeed as compared with those in which Euripides affirms that a man's nature is, if not the only, at least far the greatest factor in virtue. A few of these may here be quoted:—

καὶ μανθάνω μὲν οἷα δρᾶν μέλλω κακά,
θυμὸς δὲ κρείσσων τῶν ἐμῶν βουλευμάτων
(*Med.* 1078–1079).

τὰ χρήστ' ἐπιστάμεσθα καὶ γιγνώσκομεν,
οὐκ ἐκπονοῦμεν δ' οἱ μὲν ἀργίας ὕπο,
οἱ δ' ἡδονὴν προθέντες ἀντὶ τοῦ καλοῦ
ἄλλην τιν' (*Hipp.* 380–383).

In the *Supplices* (481 ff.) the herald says that men choose war in preference to peace, the evil in preference to the good[2]:—

καίτοι δυοῖν γε πάντες ἄνθρωποι λόγοιν

---

[1] Euripides may here have in his mind the Socratic—or rather, Platonic—ἔρως (see Plato, *Sympos.*, *passim*; but it is not at all certain. See Berlage, p. 168: Decharme, *Euripide, &c.*, pp. 44-45. Cf. also Paley's notes on *Ion*, 642; *Iph. Aul.* 562 ff.

[2] Cf. Isocrates, *De Pace*, § 106: Demosthenes, *Agst. Androtion*, § 62 *ad fin.*

τὸν κρείσσον' ἴσμεν καὶ τὰ χρηστὰ καὶ κακά,
ὅσῳ τε πολέμου κρεῖσσον εἰρήνη βροτοῖς.

Chastity depends on one's nature (*Bacch.* 314–316):—

οὐχ ὁ Διόνυσος σωφρονεῖν ἀναγκάσει
γυναῖκας ἐς τὴν Κύπριν, ἀλλ' ἐν τῇ φύσει
τὸ σωφρονεῖν ἔνεστιν ἐς τὰ πάντ' ἀεί.

Men know the good, but do it not (*Frag.* 840, 841):—

λέληθεν οὐδὲν τῶνδέ μ' ὧν σὺ νουθετεῖς,
γνώμην δ' ἔχοντά μ' ἡ φύσις βιάζεται.

. . . .

αἰαῖ, τόδ' ἤδη θεῖον ἀνθρώποις κακόν,
ὅταν τις εἰδῇ τἀγαθόν, χρῆται δὲ μή.

Education will never make bad good (*Frag.* 810):—

μέγιστον ἄρ' ἦν ἡ φύσις· τὸ γὰρ κακὸν
οὐδεὶς τρέφων εὖ χρηστὸν ἂν θείη ποτέ.

It is clear from these passages, I think, that Euripides put less value on education as promoting virtue than he did on natural tendency[1].

There is in the Orators very little bearing on this question. Isocrates, as might be expected, lays all the stress on education:—

ἄξιον μὲν οὖν καὶ τοὺς φύσει κοσμίους ὄντας ἐπαινεῖν καὶ θαυμάζειν, ἔτι δὲ μᾶλλον τοὺς καὶ μετὰ λογισμοῦ τοιούτους ὄντας (*Nicocl.* § 46).

... τοὺς γὰρ πολλοὺς ὁμοίους τοῖς ἤθεσιν ἀποβαίνειν, ἐν οἷς ἂν ἕκαστοι παιδευθῶσιν (*Areop.* § 40).

Ἰσοκράτης ὁ ῥήτωρ παρήνει τοῖς γνωρίμοις προτιμᾶν τῶν γονέων τοὺς διδασκάλους, ὅτι οἱ μὲν τοῦ ζῆν μόνον, οἱ δὲ διδάσκαλοι καὶ τοῦ καλῶς ζῆν αἴτιοι γεγόνασιν (*Frag.* iii. (β'.) 9).

According to Demosthenes (?), the beginning of all ἀρετή is σύνεσις (*Epitaph.* § 17):—

ἔστι γὰρ ἔστιν ἁπάσης ἀρετῆς ἀρχὴ μὲν σύνεσις, πέρας δ' ἀνδρεία.

---

[1] See Berlage, pp. 167-169: and cf. Wilamowitz-Moellendorff, *Herakles,* Einleitung, p. 30:—' Das hauptprincip seiner ethik, die macht der φύσις, &c.'

Hyperides holds the view that virtue is to be taught (*Epitaph.* iv. 19-22) :—

ἀλλ' οἶμαι πάντας εἰδέναι ὅτι τούτου ἕνεκα τοὺς παῖδας παιδεύομεν,
ἵνα ἄνδρες ἀγαθοὶ γένωνται.

Compare *Fray.* 209 :—Ὑπ. ὁ ῥήτωρ ἔφη μὴ δύνασθαι καλῶς
ζῆν, μὴ μαθὼν τὰ καλὰ τὰ ἐν τῷ βίῳ.

It is a commonplace to speak of the reasonableness of the Greeks. Nothing is more distinctive of the race than the μηδὲν ἄγαν, the golden mean. And so, in matters of conduct, the highest virtue was σωφροσύνη. In both Euripides and the Orators—as, in fact, in all Greek writers—is found frequent commendation of this σωφροσύνη, this μετριότης. Hippolytus had sought to exceed the bounds of human nature, and so had transgressed σωφροσύνη. To this he owed his fate[1]. There are in Euripides numerous passages expressive of the same idea. Some of these may here be quoted:—

τῶν γὰρ μετρίων πρῶτα μὲν εἰπεῖν
τοὔνομα νικᾷ, χρῆσθαί τε μακρῷ
λῷστα βροτοῖσιν (*Med.* 125-127).
στέργοι δέ με σωφροσύνα, δώρημα κάλλιστον θεῶν
(*ibid.* 635).
χρῆν γὰρ μετρίας εἰς ἀλλήλους
φιλίας θνητοὺς ἀνακίρνασθαι, κ.τ.λ. (*Hipp.* 253 ff.)[2].
οὕτω τὸ λίαν ἧσσον ἐπαινῶ
τοῦ μηδὲν ἄγαν (*ibid.* 264-265).
φεῦ φεῦ. τὸ σῶφρον ὡς ἁπανταχῇ καλόν,
καὶ δόξαν ἐσθλὴν ἐν βροτοῖς καρπίζεται
(*ibid.* 431-432).
πρὸς σοφοῦ γὰρ ἀνδρὸς ἀσκεῖν σῶφρον' εὐοργησίαν
(*Bacch.* 641).
τὸ σωφρονεῖν δὲ καὶ σέβειν τὰ τῶν θεῶν
κάλλιστον οἶμαι τοῦτο καὶ σοφώτατον
θνητοῖσιν εἶναι χρῆμα τοῖσι χρωμένοις
(*ibid.* 1150-1152).

---

[1] See above, p. 26. Cf. Pentheus in the *Bacchae*, Adrastus in the *Supplices*, &c.

[2] Cf. Sophocles, *Ajax*, 678-682 : Demosth. *Agst. Aristocrates*, § 122. Both passages are quoted below, c. ix *ad fin.*

αἰνῶ δ' ὅτι σέβεις τὸ σωφρονεῖν (Iph. Aul. 824).

μέθετον τὸ λίαν, μέθετον (Phoen. 584).

οὐ σωφρονίζειν ἔμαθον· αἰδεῖσθαι δὲ χρή,
γύναι, τὸ λίαν καὶ φυλάσσεσθαι φθόνον (Frag. 209).

ἐγὼ δ'
οὐδὲν πρεσβύτερον νομί-
ζω τᾶς σωφροσύνας, ἐπεὶ
τοῖς ἀγαθοῖς ἀεὶ ξύνεστιν (Frag. 959)[1].

Andocides says that the greatness and prosperity of the state depend on σωφροσύνη and ὁμόνοια (On the Mysteries, § 109):—

... ἡ πόλις ... μεγάλη καὶ εὐδαίμων ἐγένετο. ἃ νῦν αὐτῇ ὑπάρχει, εἰ ἐθέλοιμεν οἱ πολῖται σωφρονεῖν τε καὶ ὁμονοεῖν ἀλλήλοις[2].

Lysias, in testifying to a man's good character, frequently uses the word σώφρων:—

... διὰ τέλους τὸν πάντα χρόνον κόσμιον εἶναι καὶ σώφρονα, κ.τ.λ. (xxi. § 19).

ἄλλως δὲ κόσμιοί εἰσι καὶ σωφρόνως βεβιώκασιν (xiv. § 41).

οἳ ἂν καὶ σιωπῶντες ἐν ἅπαντι τῷ βίῳ παρέχωσι σώφρονας σφᾶς αὐτοὺς καὶ δικαίους (xix. § 54)[3].

Passages in praise of σωφροσύνη abound in Isocrates;—

ἡγοῦ μάλιστα σεαυτῷ πρέπειν [κόσμον] αἰσχύνην, δικαιοσύνην, σωφροσύνην (Ad Demon. § 15).

ἀγάπα τῶν ὑπαρχόντων ἀγαθῶν μὴ τὴν ὑπερβάλλουσαν κτῆσιν ἀλλὰ τὴν μετρίαν ἀπόλαυσιν (ibid. § 27)[4].

... λυποῦ δὲ μετρίως ἐπὶ τοῖς γιγνομένοις τῶν κακῶν (ibid. § 42).

ἐν μὲν γὰρ τῷ ῥᾳθυμεῖν καὶ τὰς πλησμονὰς ἀγαπᾶν εὐθὺς αἱ λῦπαι ταῖς ἡδοναῖς παραπεπήγασι, τὸ δὲ περὶ τὴν ἀρετὴν φιλοπονεῖν

---

[1] Cf. Ion, 632 ; Electra, 295-296 ; Or. 708, 1161-1162 ; Bacch. 395, 427-431 (where there is special reference to the sophists. See Paley's note ad loc.) ; Iph. Aul. 544, 924, 977 ; Heracl. 202 ; Frag. 46, 79, 799, 893, 928.

[2] Ibid. § 145, he combines τὸ σωφρονεῖν with τὸ ὀρθῶς βουλεύεσθαι.

[3] Cf. following quotations ; and Hyperides, Frag. 121:—οὗτος ἐβίω μὲν σωφρόνως, κ.τ.λ.

[4] Cf. ibid. §§ 32 (ἐὰν δέ ποτέ σοι συμπέσῃ καιρός, ἐξανίστασο πρὸ μέθης), 28.

καὶ σωφρόνως τὸν αὑτοῦ βίον οἰκονομεῖν ἀεὶ τὰς τέρψεις εἰλικρινεῖς καὶ βεβαιοτέρας ἀποδίδωσι (ibid. § 46).

σοφοὺς νόμιζε ... τοὺς καλῶς καὶ μετρίως καὶ τὰς συμφορὰς καὶ τὰς εὐτυχίας φέρειν ἐπισταμένους (Ad Nicocl. § 39).

οἶμαι γὰρ ἐγὼ πάντας ἂν ὁμολογῆσαι πλείστου τῶν ἀρετῶν ἀξίας εἶναι τήν τε σωφροσύνην καὶ τὴν δικαιοσύνην (Nicocl. § 29).

... πρὸς δὲ ταύτῃ τὸ καλῶς πολιτεύεσθαι καὶ σωφρόνως ζῆν κ.τ.λ. (Archid. § 59).

καίτοι τὰς εὐπραγίας ἅπαντες ἴσμεν καὶ παραγιγνομένας καὶ παραμενούσας ... τοῖς ἄριστα καὶ σωφρονέστατα τὴν αὑτῶν πόλιν διοικοῦσιν (Areop. § 13).

.... εὑρήσετε τὴν μὲν ἀκολασίαν καὶ τὴν ὕβριν τῶν κακῶν αἰτίαν γιγνομένην, τὴν δὲ σωφροσύνην τῶν ἀγαθῶν (De Pace, § 119)[1].

I will add only one or two passages from Aeschines and Demosthenes:—

.. ὅσον κεχωρίσθαι ἐνόμισαν τοὺς σώφρονας καὶ τῶν ὁμοίων ἐρῶντας καὶ τοὺς ἀκρατεῖς ὧν οὐ χρὴ καὶ τοὺς ὑβριστάς (Aeschin. Agst. Timarchus, § 141).

... καὶ περὶ πλείστου τῶν τέκνων τὴν σωφροσύνην ἐποιοῦντο (ibid. § 182)[2].

διὸ δεῖ μετριάζειν ἐν ταῖς εὐπραξίαις καὶ προορωμένους τὸ μέλλον φαίνεσθαι (Demosth. Lept. § 162).

σπουδαίων τοίνυν ἐστὶν ἀνθρώπων, ὅταν βελτίστῃ τῇ παρούσῃ τύχῃ χρῶνται, τότε πλείστην σπουδὴν πρὸς τὸ σωφρονεῖν ἔχειν (Demosth. Prooem. xliii. § 2).

Very frequently, as can be seen from these passages, σωφροσύνη is contrasted with ὕβρις[3]. A few further passages relating to ὕβρις may here be adduced:—

> ἀλλ', ὦ φίλη παῖ, λῆγε μὲν κακῶν φρενῶν,
> λῆξον δ' ὑβρίζουσ'· οὐ γὰρ ἄλλο πλὴν ὕβρις
> τάδ' ἐστί, κρείσσω δαιμόνων εἶναι θέλειν.
> τόλμα δ' ἐρῶσα· θεὸς ἐβουλήθη τάδε
> (Eurip. Hipp. 473-476).

---

[1] Cf. Ad Nicocl. §§ 26, 31 ; Archid. § 36; Areop. § 4; Evag. § 22.
[2] Cf. Agst. Ctesiphon, § 218.
[3] Cf. Eur. Phoen. 1110-1112 (with Paley's note).

οὐ γὰρ ὁ θάνατος δεινόν, ἀλλ' ἡ περὶ τὴν τελευτὴν ὕβρις φοβερά (Aeschin. *On the Embassy*, § 181).

οὐ γὰρ ἔστιν, οὐκ ἔστιν, ὦ ἄνδρες Ἀθηναῖοι, τῶν πάντων οὐδὲν ὕβρεως ἀφορητότερον, οὐδ' ἐφ' ὅτῳ μᾶλλον ὑμῖν ὀργίζεσθαι προσήκει (Demosth. *Agst. Midias*, § 46).

This ὕβρις is often the result of wealth and prosperity:—

> ὁ χρυσὸς ἅ τ' εὐτυχία
> φρενῶν βροτοὺς ἐξάγεται,
> δύνασιν [ἄδικον] ἐφέλκων (Eurip. *Her. Fur.* 774-776).
> ὁρῶ δὲ τοῖς πολλοῖσιν ἀνθρώποις ἐγὼ
> τίκτουσαν ὕβριν τὴν πάροιθ' εὐπραξίαν (*Frag.* 437).
> ὕβριν τε τίκτει πλοῦτος, ἢ φειδὼ βίου (*Frag.* 438)[1].

οὐ γὰρ πενομένους καὶ λίαν ἀπόρως διακειμένους ὑβρίζειν εἰκός, ἀλλὰ τοὺς πολλῷ πλείω τῶν ἀναγκαίων κεκτημένους· οὐδὲ τοὺς ἀδυνάτους τοῖς σώμασιν ὄντας, ἀλλὰ τοὺς μάλιστα πιστεύοντας ταῖς αὐτῶν ῥώμαις· οὐδὲ τοὺς ἤδη προβεβηκότας τῇ ἡλικίᾳ, ἀλλὰ τοὺς ἔτι νέους καὶ νέαις ταῖς διανοίαις χρωμένους (Lysias, xxiv. § 16)[2].

That perception of human weakness and human limits to which σωφροσύνη owes it origin is also the best safeguard in prosperity and the best solace in adversity. Endurance —τέτλαθι δή, κραδίη—is continually enjoined. 'Why should a living man complain?'—

> κούφως φέρειν χρὴ θνητὸν ὄντα συμφοράς
> (Eurip. *Med.* 1018).
> οὐ σοὶ τάδ', ὦναξ, ἦλθε δὴ μόνῳ κακά,
> πολλῶν μετ' ἄλλων δ' ὤλεσας κεδνὸν λέχος
> (*Hipp.* 834-835).
> ἔχεις μὲν ἀλγεῖν', οἶδα· σύμφορον δέ τοι
> ὡς ῥᾷστα τἀναγκαῖα τοῦ βίου φέρειν (*Hel.* 253-254).
> οὐκ ἔστιν οὐδὲν δεινὸν ὧδ' εἰπεῖν ἔπος,
> οὐδὲ πάθος, οὐδὲ συμφορὰ θεήλατος,
> ἧς οὐκ ἂν ἄραιτ' ἄχθος ἀνθρώπου φύσις (*Or.* 1-3).

---

[1] 'πλοῦτος, οὐ φειδὼ βίου scribendum suspicor' (Nauck). This conjecture is surely right.
[2] Cf. Isocr. *Panath.* § 196.

τὴν δ' ἀναγκαίως ἔχει
δούλοισιν εἶναι τοῖς σοφοῖσι τῆς τύχης (*ibid.* 715-716).
μοχθεῖν ἀνάγκη· τὰς δὲ δαιμόνων τύχας
ὅστις φέρει κάλλιστ', ἀνὴρ οὗτος σοφός (*Frag.* 37).
ἀλλ' εὖ φέρειν χρὴ συμφορὰς τὸν εὐγενῆ (*Frag.* 98).
οἴμοι· τί δ' οἴμοι; θνητά τοι πεπόνθαμεν (*Frag.* 300).
. . . . τί ταῦτα δεῖ
στέγειν, ἅπερ δεῖ κατὰ φύσιν διεκπερᾶν;
δεινὸν γὰρ οὐδὲν τῶν ἀναγκαίων βροτοῖς (*Frag.* 757)[1].
μήτε αὐτοὶ ταῖς τούτων ἀτυχίαις βοηθοῦντες ἐναντία τοῦ δαίμονος
γνῶτε (Antiphon, τετρ. Β. δ. § 10).
. . . στέργειν ἂν ἦν ἀνάγκη τὴν τύχην (Lysias, xxxiii. § 4).
ἀλλὰ δεῖ καρτερεῖν ἐπὶ τοῖς παροῦσι καὶ θαρρεῖν περὶ τῶν μελ-
λόντων (Isocr. *Archid.* § 48).
ὁ μεμιημένος τί ἐστὶν ἄνθρωπος, ἐπ' οὐδενὶ τῶν συμβάντων
δυσχερανεῖ (Isocr. *Frag.* iii. (δ'.) 5).
ἀλλὰ χρή γε ἀνθρώπους ὄντας . . . πάντα ἀνθρώπινα ἡγεῖσθαι
(Demosth. *Leptines*, § 161).

In no respect are Euripides and the Orators more at one
in the matter of ethics than in their adherence to the principle—so frequently met with in Greek literature—of Retaliation. 'Love your enemies' is a maxim never found in them.
In no instance do they rise to the high level of the Socratic
or Platonic dictum that it is better to suffer than to do
wrong[2]: their law is 'An eye for an eye, and a tooth for
a tooth,'—ἀδικούμενον ἀδικεῖν, δράσαντα παθεῖν—the received
opinion, as Socrates says, of the many[3]. It is well expressed
in Solon's prayer to the Muses (*Frag.* 13. 5-6):—

εἶναι δὲ γλυκὺν ὧδε φίλοις, ἐχθροῖσι δὲ πικρόν,
τοῖσι μὲν αἰδοῖον, τοῖσι δὲ δεινὸν ἰδεῖν[4].

---

[1] Cf. *Hipp.* 205-207; *Her. Fur.* 1227, 1348; *Hel.* 267; *Iph. Taur.* 484; *Or.* 1023;
Phoen. 382. 1762; *Frag.* 175, 302, 454, 505, 572, 702.

[2] See *Crito,* 49 B:—οὐδὲ ἀδικούμενον ἄρα ἀνταδικεῖν, ὡς οἱ πολλοὶ οἴονται,
ἐπειδή γε οὐδαμῶς δεῖ ἀδικεῖν. Cf. also *Gorg.* 469 B, 508 D-E. Contrast with
this Isocr. *Panath.* § 117.

[3] See preceding note; and cf. Xen. *Mem.* ii. 3. 14:—καὶ μὴν πλείστου
γε δοκεῖ ἀνὴρ ἐπαίνου ἄξιος εἶναι, ὃς ἂν φθάνῃ τοὺς μὲν πολεμίους κακῶς ποιῶν, τοὺς
δὲ φίλους εὐεργετῶν.

[4] Cf. Hesiod, *Works and Days*, 340-351: Aesch. *Prom. Vinct.* 1041-1042;
Choeph. 123: Soph. *Antig.* 643-644: Simonides, in Plato, *Republic*, 332 A.

There is only one passage in Euripides where vengeance on a captured foe is deprecated [1], and in the Orators there is not even one. The ordinary view, on the other hand, is frequently found. A few passages may here be quoted in illustration:—

βαρεῖαν ἐχθροῖς καὶ φίλοισιν εὐμενῆ

(Euripides, *Med.* 809).

ἐσθλοῦ γὰρ ἀνδρὸς τῇ δίκῃ θ' ὑπηρετεῖν,
καὶ τοὺς κακοὺς δρᾶν πανταχοῦ κακῶς ἀεί

(*Hec.* 844–845).

οὐ γάρ με χαίρειν χρή σε τιμωρουμένην; (*ibid.* 1258).

AN. ἢ ταῦτ' ἐν ὑμῖν τοῖς παρ' Εὐρώτᾳ σοφά;
ME. καὶ τοῖς γε Τροίᾳ, τοὺς παθόντας αἰτιδρᾶν

(*Andr.* 437–438).

πρὸς σοῦ μὲν, ὦ παῖ, τοῖς φίλοις εἶναι φίλον
τά τ' ἐχθρὰ μισεῖν (*Her. Fur.* 585–586).

ὅταν δὲ πολεμίους δρᾶσαι κακῶς
θέλῃ τις, οὐδεὶς ἐμποδὼν κεῖται νόμος

(*Ion,* 1046–1047).

οὐ δεινὰ πάσχειν δεινὰ τοὺς εἰργασμένους (*Or.* 413) [2].

ἀνέχου πάσχων· δρῶν γὰρ ἔχαιρες (*Frag.* 1090).

νόμου τὸν ἐχθρὸν δρᾶν, ὅπου λάβῃς, κακῶς

(*Frag.* 1091).

ἐχθροὺς κακῶς δρᾶν ἀνδρὸς ἡγοῦμαι μέρος

(*Frag.* 1092).

οὗτος δὲ ἢ πάντων εὐτυχέστατός ἐστιν ἢ πλεῖστον γνώμῃ διαφέρει τῶν ἄλλων, ὃς μόνος τῶν συγγενομένων Ἀνδοκίδῃ οὐκ ἐξηπατήθη ὑπ' ἀνδρὸς τοιούτου, ὃς τέχνην ταύτην ἔχει, τοὺς μὲν ἐχθροὺς μηδὲν ποιεῖν κακόν, τοὺς δὲ φίλους ὅ τι ἂν δύνηται κακόν (Lysias, vi. § 7).

ἐγὼ μὲν οὖν καὶ φίλῳ ὄντι Ἀρχεστρατίδῃ βοηθῶν, καὶ Ἀλκιβιάδην ἐχθρὸν ὄντα ἐμαυτοῦ τιμωρούμενος, δέομαι τὰ δίκαια ψηφίσασθαι (Lys. xv. § 12).

---

[1] The passage referred to is in *Heracl.*, ad fin. See esp. ll. 965–966:—

ΑΛ. τί δὴ τόδ'; ἐχθροὺς τοισίδ' οὐ καλὸν κτανεῖν;
ΑΓ. οὐχ ὄντιν' ἄν γε ζῶνθ' ἕλωσιν ἐν μάχῃ.

But Alcmena's question shows her surprise at the bare idea of such a thing; and Berlage (p. 144, note) is perhaps right in thinking that a reference is intended to the case of the Thebans (Thuc. iii. 58).

[2] Cf. *ibid.* 646 ff. (with Paley's note).

... ἡγούμενος τετάχθαι τοὺς μὲν ἐχθροὺς κακῶς ποιεῖν, τοὺς δὲ φίλους εὖ (Lys. ix. § 20).

εἰ δ' ἐκεῖνοι δοκοῦσι βελτίους εἶναι σώζοντες τοὺς φίλους, δῆλον ὅτι καὶ ὑμεῖς ἀμείνους δόξετε εἶναι τιμωρούμενοι τοὺς ἐχθρούς (Lys. xiv. § 19).

χρὴ τοίνυν, ὥσπερ ἂν τούτους ὁρᾶτε προθύμως σώζοντας τοὺς φίλους, οὕτως καὶ ὑμᾶς τοὺς ἐχθροὺς τιμωρεῖσθαι (Lys. xxx. § 33)[1].

ὁμοίως αἰσχρὸν εἶναι νόμιζε τῶν ἐχθρῶν νικᾶσθαι ταῖς κακοποιίαις καὶ τῶν φίλων ἡττᾶσθαι ταῖς εὐεργεσίαις (Isocrates, *Ad Demon.* § 26).

.... τὸ δὲ τιμωρεῖσθαι καὶ ἐπεξιέναι τοῖς πεπονθόσι καὶ τοῖς ἐχθροῖς παραλείπεται (Demosthenes, *Agst. Midias*, § 118)[2].

We need not linger over the many wise and true *sententiae* concerning morality and life generally which are frequent in the Orators and abound in Euripides[3]. They are just such as we find in the conversation of all who have the seeing eye, and in the literature of every age. Many parallels to those we meet in Euripides and the Attic Orators might be found in the proverbs alike of Solomon and of Sancho Panza. I will therefore refer here to only a very few of them.

It seems to have been a proverbial expression that one should not 'sail in the same boat with the guilty.' So in Euripides (*Electra*, 1354-1355), we have the words:—

οὕτως ἀδικεῖν μηδεὶς θελέτω,
μηδ' ἐπιόρκων μέτα συμπλείτω.

Similarly Antiphon (περὶ τοῦ Ἡρῴδου φόνου, § 82):—

οἶμαι γὰρ ὑμᾶς ἐπίστασθαι ὅτι πολλοὶ ἤδη ἄνθρωποι μὴ καθαροὶ χεῖρας ἢ ἄλλο τι μίασμα ἔχοντες συνεισβάντες εἰς τὸ πλοῖον συναπώλεσαν μετὰ τῆς αὑτῶν ψυχῆς τοὺς ὁσίως διακειμένους τὰ πρὸς τοὺς θεούς.

In the speech *Against Timarchus* (§§ 154 ff.) Aeschines

---

[1] See also *Epitaph.* § 8.
[2] See also Antiphon, τετρ. Α. α. § 8; Γ. β. § 2; Γ. δ. § 5.
[3] For the gnomic, rhetorical, and analytic character of Euripides' poetry see Symonds, *Greek Poets* (Second Series), p. 280.

quotes and applies the following lines from Euripides, to
the effect that a man is known by the company he keeps:—

> ὅστις δ' ὁμιλῶν ἥδεται κακοῖς ἀνήρ,
> οὐ πώποτ' ἠρώτησα, γιγνώσκων, ὅτι
> τοιοῦτός ἐστιν οἷσπερ ἥδεται ξυνών[1].

'Fight with your equals' is an advice found both in
Euripides and in Lysias. In the one case it is folly to fight
with those who are stronger: in the other, it is wrong to
take advantage of the weaker:—

> τοῖς κρατοῦσι μὴ μάχου (Eur. *Hec.* 404)[2].

. . . οὗτος δὲ τοῦ λοιποῦ μαθήσεται μὴ τοῖς ἀσθενεστέροις ἐπι-
βουλεύειν ἀλλὰ τῶν ὁμοίων αὐτῷ περιγενέσθαι (Lys. xxiv. § 27).

'To err is human':—

> σύγγνωθ'· ἁμαρτεῖν εἰκὸς ἀνθρώπους, τέκνον (Eur. *Hipp.* 615).

. . . ἐν οἷς ἅπαντες πεφύκαμεν ἁμαρτάνειν (Isaeus, i. § 13).

But I will refrain from a multiplication of such parallel
passages. They can be reduced to no definite principle, and
the comparison is one which is more interesting than profitable[3].

---

[1] Cf. Isocrates, *Frag.* (*Apophthegmata*) (β'.) 1:—πρὸς τὸν εἰπόντα πατέρα, ὡς
οὐδὲν ἀλλ' ἢ ἀνδράποδον συνέπεμψε τῷ παιδίῳ, τοιγαροῦν, ἔφη, ἄπιθι, δύο γὰρ ἀνθ'
ἑνὸς ἕξεις ἀνδράποδα.

[2] Cf. *Frag.* 337:—μὴ νεῖκος, ὦ γεραιέ, κοιράνοις τίθου,
    σέβειν δὲ τοὺς κρατοῦντας ἀρχαῖος νόμος.

[3] It ought to be remembered, however, that these γνῶμαι had never before
been codified as they now were by Euripides, and that to the Athenians of
the time they would not appear to be mere commonplaces (see Campbell,
Greek Tragedy, p. 247). One might compare the position of Pope in the
English literature of the eighteenth century.

CHAPTER VII

§ 1. THE aim of education in ancient Greece[1] was to develop
a sound and beautiful mind in a sound and beautiful body,
and neither of these to the exclusion of the other. They
aimed at making the man καλοκἀγαθός: the highest result of
education was καλοκἀγαθία. And so, naturally, the education
of the young Greek consisted of μουσική and γυμναστική[2].
The latter was cultivated with an ardour which we can
understand only if we appreciate the Greek's instinctive love
of the beautiful and hatred of the ugly. Beauty of the
outward form alone had on the Greek mind an influence
which we can hardly realise[3].

[1] For a full treatment of Greek education see Wilkins, *National Education in
Greece* : Becker, *Charicles*, Excursus on Scene i. For the Gymnasia see Becker,
Excursus on Scene v.

[2] Cf. Plato, *Rep.* ii. 376 E :—ἔστι δέ που ἡ μὲν (sc. παιδεία) ἐπὶ σώμασι γυμναστική, ἡ δ' ἐπὶ ψυχῇ μουσική. Isocrates (*Antid.* §§ 180 181) says that a man is
composed of the two, body and soul, the former being inferior to, and servant
of, the latter, and proceeds thus :—οὕτω δὲ τούτων ἐχόντων ὁρῶντές τινες τῶν
πολὺ πρὸ ἡμῶν γεγονότων περὶ μὲν τῶν ἄλλων πολλὰς τέχνας συνεστηκυίας, περὶ δὲ
τὸ σῶμα καὶ τὴν ψυχὴν οὐδὲν τοιοῦτον συντεταγμένον, εὑρόντες διττὰς ἐπιμελείας
κατέλιπον ἡμῖν, περὶ μὲν τὰ σώματα τὴν παιδοτριβικήν, ἧς ἡ γυμναστικὴ μέρος ἐστί,
περὶ δὲ τὰς ψυχὰς τὴν φιλοσοφίαν. For a description of Spartan education see
Panath. §§ 209 ff. 'The Greek education laid its hands on the entire citizen,
and, within the range that it recognised, moulded all his powers into a
finished unity' (Wilkins, *op. cit.*, p. 164). See also Coulanges, *La Cité Antique*,
p. 267.

[3] Cf. Mahaffy, *Old Greek Life*, pp. 8-9, 54-56: Isocrates, *Hel.* §§ 54-60 :—
κάλλους γὰρ πλεῖστον μέρος μετέσχεν, ὃ σεμνότατον καὶ τιμιώτατον καὶ θειότατον
τῶν ὄντων ἐστίν. κ.τ.λ. Elsewhere Isocrates speaks of virtue as superior to
beauty (*Ad Demon.* §§ 6-7; *Evag.* § 74 .

Andocides mentions with disapprobation that the youth spend their time in the lawcourt instead of the gymnasium (*Agst. Alcibiades*, § 22):—

τοιγάρτοι τῶν νέων αἱ διατριβαὶ οὐκ ἐν τοῖς γυμνασίοις ἀλλ' ἐν τοῖς δικαστηρίοις εἰσί, καὶ στρατεύονται μὲν οἱ πρεσβύτεροι, δημηγοροῦσι δὲ οἱ νεώτεροι, κ.τ.λ.

Isocrates thus describes the education of the rich (*Areop.* § 45):—

τοὺς δὲ βίον ἱκανὸν κεκτημένους περί τε τὴν ἱππικὴν καὶ τὰ γυμνάσια καὶ τὰ κυνηγέσια καὶ τὴν φιλοσοφίαν ἠνάγκασαν διατρίβειν, ὁρῶντες ἐκ τούτων τοὺς μὲν διαφέροντας γιγνομένους, τοὺς δὲ τῶν πλείστων κακῶν ἀπεχομένους [1].

The practise of gymnastics, however, he commends with a reservation (*Ad Demon.* § 14):—

ἄσκει τῶν περὶ τὸ σῶμα γυμνασίων μὴ τὰ πρὸς τὴν ῥώμην ἀλλὰ τὰ πρὸς τὴν ὑγίειαν· τούτου δ' ἂν ἐπιτύχοις, εἰ λήγοις τῶν πόνων ἔτι πονεῖν δυνάμενος.

To none was more extravagant honour paid than to the victorious gymnast. So Demosthenes says (*Lept.* § 141):—

εἶτα μεγίστας δίδοτε ἐκ παντὸς τοῦ χρόνου δωρεὰς τοῖς τοὺς γυμνικοὺς νικῶσιν ἀγῶνας τοὺς στεφανίτας . . . [2].

Gymnastic training was, however, frequently carried to excess, and a degrading 'professionalism' in athletics seems to have gained ground. Euripides was among the first to try to bring it down to a lower level [3]. 'Of the countless evils that exist in Greece,' he says, 'there is none worse than the athlete.' The whole passage (*Frag.* 282) is worth quoting:—

κακῶν γὰρ ὄντων μυρίων καθ' Ἑλλάδα,
οὐδὲν κάκιόν ἐστιν ἀθλητῶν γένους·
οἳ πρῶτα μὲν ζῆν οὔτε μανθάνουσιν εὖ,
οὔτ' ἂν δύναιτο· πῶς γὰρ ὅστις ἔστ' ἀνὴρ

---

[1] Cf. *Ad Nicocl.* §§ 12-13.
[2] Cf. Isocrates, xvi. § 32.
[3] Berlago (p. 170) quotes from Xenophanes and Sophocles praises of wisdom as against bodily strength similar to those we find in Euripides. But neither of these presses the point with the energy and elaboration of Euripides.

γνάθου τε δοῦλος νηδύος θ' ἡσσημένος
κτήσαιτ' ἂν ὄλβον εἰς ὑπερβολὴν πατρός ;
οὐδ' αὖ πένεσθαι κἀξυπηρετεῖν τύχαις
οἷοί τ'· ἔθη γὰρ οὐκ ἐθισθέντες καλά,
σκληρῶς μεταλλάσσουσιν εἰς τἀμήχανον.
λαμπροὶ δ' ἐν ἥβῃ καὶ πόλεως ἀγάλματα
φοιτῶσ'· ὅταν δὲ προσπέσῃ γῆρας πικρόν,
τρίβωνες ἐκβαλόντες οἴχονται κρόκας.
ἐμεμψάμην δὲ καὶ τὸν Ἑλλήνων νόμον,
οἳ τῶνδ' ἕκατι σύλλογον ποιούμενοι
τιμῶσ' ἀχρείους ἡδονὰς δαιτὸς χάριν.
τίς γὰρ παλαίσας εὖ, τίς ὠκύπους ἀνὴρ
ἢ δίσκον ἄρας ἢ γνάθον παίσας καλῶς
πόλει πατρῴᾳ στέφανον ἤρκεσεν λαβών ;
πότερα μαχοῦνται πολεμίοισιν ἐν χεροῖν
δίσκους ἔχοντες ἢ δι' ἀσπίδων χερὶ
θείνοντες ἐκβαλοῦσι πολεμίους πάτρας ;
οὐδεὶς σιδήρου ταῦτα μωραίνει πέλας
†στάς. ἄνδρας χρὴ σοφούς τε κἀγαθοὺς
φύλλοις στέφεσθαι, χὥστις ἡγεῖται πόλει
κάλλιστα σώφρων καὶ δίκαιος ὢν ἀνήρ,
ὅστις τε μύθοις ἔργ' ἀπαλλάσσει κακὰ
μάχας τ' ἀφαιρῶν καὶ στάσεις· τοιαῦτα γὰρ
πόλει τε πάσῃ πᾶσί θ' Ἕλλησιν καλά[1].

Ideas like these we find also in the Orators. For example,
Isocrates says (*Panegyr.* §§ 1-2):—

πολλάκις ἐθαύμασα τῶν τὰς πανηγύρεις συναγαγόντων καὶ τοὺς
γυμνικοὺς ἀγῶνας καταστησάντων, ὅτι τὰς μὲν τῶν σωμάτων εὐτυχίας
οὕτω μεγάλων δωρεῶν ἠξίωσαν, τοῖς δ' ὑπὲρ τῶν κοινῶν ἰδίᾳ
πονήσασι καὶ τὰς αὐτῶν ψυχὰς οὕτω παρασκευάσασιν ὥστε καὶ τοὺς
ἄλλους ὠφελεῖν δύνασθαι, τούτοις δ' οὐδεμίαν τιμὴν ἀπένειμαν, ὧν
εἰκὸς ἦν αὐτοὺς μᾶλλον ποιήσασθαι πρόνοιαν· τῶν μὲν γὰρ ἀθλητῶν
δὶς τοσαύτην ῥώμην λαβόντων οὐδὲν ἂν πλέον γένοιτο τοῖς ἄλλοις,
ἑνὸς δ' ἀνδρὸς εὖ φρονήσαντος ἅπαντες ἂν ἀπολαύσειαν οἱ βουλόμενοι
κοινωνεῖν τῆς ἐκείνου διανοίας.

---

[1] Cf. *Electra*, 386-390.

This resembles so closely the words of Euripides above, that one is inclined to think that here the orator has borrowed from the poet [1].

In another place (xvi. § 33) Isocrates speaks of the athletes as being often low-born and uneducated:—

... τοὺς μὲν γυμνικοὺς ἀγῶνας ὑπερεῖδεν, εἰδὼς ἐνίους τῶν ἀθλητῶν καὶ κακῶς γεγονότας καὶ μικρὰς πόλεις οἰκοῦντας καὶ ταπεινῶς πεπαιδευμένους ....

The idea that wisdom is better than beauty or strength, that knowledge is power, we find, in its more general form, both in Euripides and in the Orators.   In the *Electra* (386–390) Orestes, praising the Autourgos, speaks thus:—

> οἱ γὰρ τοιοῦτοι τὰς πόλεις οἰκοῦσιν εὖ
> καὶ δώμαθ', αἱ δὲ σάρκες αἱ κεναὶ φρενῶν
> ἀγάλματ' ἀγορᾶς εἰσιν.   οὐδὲ γὰρ δόρυ
> μᾶλλον βραχίων σθεναρὸς ἀσθενοῦς μένει·
> ἐν τῇ φύσει δὲ τοῦτο κἀν εὐψυχίᾳ.

Similar passages are the following:—

> τὸ δ' ἀσθενές μου καὶ τὸ θῆλυ σώματος
> κακῶς ἐμέμφθης· καὶ γὰρ εἰ φρονεῖν ἔχω,
> κρεῖσσον τόδ' ἐστὶ καρτεροῦ βραχίονος (*Frag.* 199).
> γνώμαις γὰρ ἀνδρὸς εὖ μὲν οἰκοῦνται πόλεις,
> εὖ δ' οἶκος, εἴς τ' αὖ πόλεμον ἰσχύει μέγα·
> σοφὸν γὰρ ἐν βούλευμα τὰς πολλὰς χέρας
> νικᾷ, σὺν ὄχλῳ δ' ἀμαθία πλεῖστον κακόν (*Frag.* 200).
> νοῦν χρὴ θεᾶσθαι, νοῦν· τί τῆς εὐμορφίας
> ὄφελος, ὅταν τις μὴ φρένας καλὰς ἔχῃ ; (*Frag.* 548).
> ῥώμη δέ τ' ἀμαθὴς πολλάκις τίκτει βλάβην
>   (*Frag.* 732)[2].

καίτοι πῶς οὐκ ἄλογον τοὺς τοῦ φαυλοτέρου ποιουμένους τὴν ἐπιμέλειαν ἐπαινεῖν μᾶλλον ἢ τοὺς τοῦ σπουδαιοτέρου ; καὶ ταῦτα

---

[1] For another passage in disparagement of the ordinary (professional) gymnastics, boxing, &c. see Demosth. (?) *Erot.* §§ 23–24.

[2] Cf. also the fragment from the *Antiopa* in Plato, *Gorg.* 485 E (185, Nauck); *Iph. Aul.* 374–375 (with Paley's note).   But even in education of the intellect, the proper limits must not be exceeded (*Med.* 295–296):—

> χρὴ δ' οὔποθ' ὅστις ἀρτίφρων πέφυκ' ἀνὴρ
> παῖδας περισσῶς ἐκδιδάσκεσθαι σοφούς.

πάντων εἰδότων διὰ μὲν εὐεξίαν σώματος οὐδὲν πώποτε τὴν πόλιν τῶν ἐλλογίμων ἔργων διαπραξαμένην, διὰ δὲ φρόνησιν ἀνδρὸς εὐδαιμονεστάτην καὶ μεγίστην τῶν Ἑλληνίδων πόλεων γενομένην; (Isocrates, *Antid.* § 250)[1].

βίᾳ μὲν οὐδὲ τῶν ἐλαχίστων δύναται κρατεῖν ἄνθρωπος, ἐπινοίᾳ δὲ καὶ μεθόδῳ ὑπέζευξε μὲν ἀρότρῳ βοῦν πρὸς τὴν ἐργασίαν τῆς χώρας, ἐχαλίνωσε δὲ τὸν ἵππον, ἐλέφαντι δὲ παρέστησεν ἐπιβάτην καὶ ξύλῳ τὴν ἀμέτρητον θάλασσαν διεπέρασεν. τούτων δὲ πάντων ἀρχιτέκτων καὶ δημιουργός ἐστιν ὁ νοῦς, κ.τ.λ. (Demades (?), ὑπὲρ τῆς δωδεκαετίας, § 42)[2].

§ 2. I have already (p. 76) quoted from Euripides and Lysias passages expressive of the idea that ὕβρις is the result of wealth and prosperity. In Euripides we find only a few passages where wealth is not spoken of in a disparaging way.

In the *Electra* (426-429) wealth is praised as giving one the means of benefiting friends and curing sickness:—

ἐν τοῖς τοιούτοις δ' ἡνίκ' ἂν γνώμη πέσῃ,
σκοπῶ τὰ χρήμαθ' ὡς ἔχει μέγα σθένος,
ξένοις τε δοῦναι, σῶμά τ' ἐς νόσον πεσὸν
δαπάναισι σῶσαι[3].

So, in *Frag.* 407, the poet says it is an ill thing that the wealthy man should not be helpful:—

ἀμουσία τοι μηδ' ἐπ' οἰκτροῖσιν δάκρυ
στάζειν· κακὸν δέ, χρημάτων ὄντων ἅλις,
φειδοῖ πονηρᾷ μηδέν' εὖ ποιεῖν βροτῶν.

There is a right kind of gain,—that which brings with it no sorrow (*Frag.* 459):—

κέρδη τοιαῦτα χρή τινα κτᾶσθαι βροτῶν,
ἐφ' οἷσι μέλλει μήποθ' ὕστερον στένειν[4].

---

[1] See also *Ad Demon.* § 40; *Epist.* viii. § 5.   [2] Cf. *ibid.* § 40.
[3] See Paley's note ad loc.
[4] As Berlage points out (p. 172, note), *Frag.* 326 (cf. *Cycl.* 316) does not express the true opinion of Euripides, and *Frag.* 142 is ironical. For the power of wealth, and advantages which it brings, or is supposed to bring, see *Heracl.* 745; *Iph. Aul.* 597; *Andr.* 332; *Phoen.* 438·440; *Frag.* 249, 324, 462, 580, 1017.

Those passages are numerous, on the other hand, where wealth is despised[1]. Several of them may here be quoted. The wealthy are covetous and useless (*Suppl.* 238-239):—

> τρεῖς γὰρ πολιτῶν μερίδες· οἱ μὲν ὄλβιοι
> ἀνωφελεῖς τε πλειόνων τ' ἐρῶσ' ἀεί.

Wealth is fleeting (*Her. Fur.* 511-512):—

> ὁ δ' ὄλβος ὁ μέγας ἥ τε δόξ' οὐκ οἶδ' ὅτῳ
> βέβαιός ἐστι[2].

The car of wealth is a black car (*ibid.* 780):—

> ἔθραυσε δ' ὄλβου κελαινὸν ἅρμα.

Wealth brings trouble, and is a mere name (*Phoen.* 552-554):—

> ἢ πολλὰ μοχθεῖν πόλλ' ἔχων ἐν δώμασι
> βούλει; τί δ' ἔστι τὸ πλέον; ὄνομ' ἔχει μόνον·
> ἐπεὶ τά γ' ἀρκοῦνθ' ἱκανὰ τοῖς γε σώφροσιν[3].

It causes cowardice (*ibid.* 597):—

> δειλὸν δ' ὁ πλοῦτος καὶ φιλόψυχον κακόν[4].

It may be acquired even by the vilest (*Frag.* 20):—

> μὴ πλοῦτον εἴπῃς· οὐχὶ θαυμάζω θεὸν
> ὃν χὢ κάκιστος ῥᾳδίως ἐκτήσατο[5].

It is ἄδικον (*Frag.* 55):—

> ἄδικον ὁ πλοῦτος, πολλὰ δ' οὐκ ὀρθῶς ποιεῖ.

It is σκαιόν (*Frag.* 96):—

> σκαιόν τι χρῆμα πλοῦτος ἥ τ' ἀπειρία[6].

There is a certain φαυλότης in wealth (*Frag.* 641):—

> πλουτεῖς, τὰ δ' ἄλλα μὴ δόκει ξυνιέναι·
> ἐν τῷ γὰρ ὄλβῳ φαυλότης ἔνεστί τις,
> πενία δὲ σοφίαν ἔλαχε διὰ τὸ συγγενές.

---

[1] It is true that other Greek poets besides Euripides speak disparagingly of wealth, but none before him so frequently or with such a deep hatred of it. A more elaborate attack on wealth was afterwards made by Aristophanes in the *Plutus.*

[2] Cf. *El.* 941; *Phoen.* 558; *Frag.* 354, 420, 518, 618.

[3] Cf. *Frag.* 813.

[4] Cf. *Frag.* 54, 235.

[5] Cf. *Frag.* 95.

[6] Cf. *Frag.* 776, 1069.

Ill-gotten wealth yields a bitter harvest (*Frag.* 419):—

> βίᾳ νυν ἕλκετ' ὦ κακοὶ τιμὰς βροτοί,
> καὶ κτᾶσθε πλοῦτον πάντοθεν θηρώμενοι,
> σύμμικτα μὴ δίκαια καὶ δίκαι' ὁμοῦ·
> ἔπειτ' ἀμᾶσθε τῶνδε δύστηνον θέρος[1].

Wealth is inferior to health (*Frag.* 714), to reputation (*Frag.* 405)[2], to good society (*Frag.* 7), to virtue (*Frag.* 163).

Poverty, again, is an evil thing (*Phoen.* 405):—

> κακὸν τὸ μὴ 'χειν· τὸ γένος οὐκ ἔβοσκέ με[3].

It is grievous (*Her. Fur.* 303–304):—

> ἀλλὰ καὶ τόδ' ἄθλιον
> πενίᾳ σὺν οἰκτρᾷ περιβαλεῖν σωτηρίαν.

The poor man is friendless (*Med.* 561):—

> πένητα φεύγει πᾶς τις ἐκποδὼν φίλος[4].

Poverty destroys nobility (*El.* 37–38):—

> λαμπροὶ γὰρ ἐς γένος γε, χρημάτων δὲ δὴ
> πένητες, ἔνθεν ηὐγένει' ἀπόλλυται.

Poverty has no shrine: it is θεὸς αἰσχίστη (*Frag.* 248):—

> οὐκ ἔστι πενίας ἱερὸν αἰσχίστης θεοῦ.

Frag. 326—κακὸς δ' ὁ μὴ 'χων, οἱ δ' ἔχοντες ὄλβιοι—is ironical[5].

Ill-repute and infamy attend on poverty (*Frag.* 362, ll. 16–17):—

> ἐν τῷ πένεσθαι δ' ἐστὶν ἥ τ' ἀδοξία
> κἂν ᾖ σοφός τις, ἥ τ' ἀτιμία βίου.

But one may be noble though poor (*El.* 362–363):—

> καὶ γὰρ εἰ πένης ἔφυν,
> οὔτοι τό γ' ἦθος δυσγενὲς παρέξομαι[6].

---

[1] Cf. *Hel.* 905.
[2] Cf. *Med.* 542–544; *Andr.* 639–641.
[3] Cf. *Frag.* 230.
[4] Cf. *El.* 1131.
[5] See p. 85, note 4.
[6] For the respect of Euripides for the poor, and especially his conception of the Autourgos in the *Electra* see Mahaffy, *Social Greece*, pp. 191–195: Decharme, *Euripide*, &c., pp. 164–167. M. Decharme says (p. 167, :—'Ce poète à l'âme si tendre est plein de pitié pour les pauvres gens.'

And poverty has good effects (*Frag.* 54):—

> πενία δὲ δύστηνον μέν, ἀλλ᾽ ὅμως τρέφει
> μοχθεῖν τ᾽ ἀμείνω τέκνα καὶ δραστήρια[1].

Isocrates and Demosthenes are the orators in whom we find most parallels to Euripides on this point.

Isocrates tells us that wealth is fleeting, wisdom abides (*Ad Demon.* § 19):—

> ἡγοῦ τῶν ἀκουσμάτων πολλὰ πολλῶν εἶναι χρημάτων κρείττω· τὰ μὲν γὰρ ταχέως ἀπολείπει, τὰ δὲ πάντα τὸν χρόνον παραμένει· σοφία γὰρ μόνον τῶν κτημάτων ἀθάνατον.

A good name is better than wealth [2].

Just poverty is better than unjust wealth (*Ad Demon.* §§ 38–39):—

> μᾶλλον ἀποδέχου δικαίαν πενίαν ἢ πλοῦτον ἄδικον· κ.τ.λ. [3].

Ill-gotten gain is dangerous (*Nicocl.* § 50):—

> τοὺς χρηματισμοὺς τοὺς παρὰ τὸ δίκαιον γιγνομένους ἡγεῖσθε μὴ πλοῦτον ἀλλὰ κίνδυνον ποιήσειν.

He mentions, however, the power of wealth (*Phil.* § 15), and the advantages in education which the wealthy enjoy (*Areop.* § 45). But wealth is inferior to honour (*Epist.* vii. § 1):—

> ..... ἔπειθ᾽ ὅτι προαιρεῖ δόξαν καλὴν κτήσασθαι μᾶλλον ἢ πλοῦτον μέγαν συναγαγεῖν.

One of the evils of poverty is that it begets evil deeds (*Areop.* § 44):—

> .... εἰδότες τὰς ἀπορίας μὲν διὰ τὰς ἀργίας γιγνομένας, τὰς δὲ κακουργίας διὰ τὰς ἀπορίας.

Demosthenes declares that poverty is no disgrace, and wealth no reason for pride (*On the Crown,* § 256):—

> ἐγὼ γὰρ οὔτ᾽ εἴ τις πενίαν προπηλακίζει νοῦν ἔχειν ἡγοῦμαι, οὔτ᾽ εἴ τις ἐν ἀφθόνοις τραφεὶς ἐπὶ τούτῳ σεμνύνεται [4].

---

[1] Cf. *Frag.* 641.   [2] See passages quoted above, pp. 69–70.
[3] Cf. *De Pace,* § 93.
[4] Cf. Demades (?), ὑπὲρ τῆς δωδεκαετίας, § 8 :—ἡ πενία δ᾽ ἴσως δύσχρηστον μὲν ἔχει τι καὶ χαλεπόν, κεχώρισται δ᾽ αἰσχύνης, ὡς ἂν οἶμαι τῆς ἀπορίας ἐπὶ πολλῶν οὐ τρόπου κακίαν ἀλλὰ τύχης ἀγνωμοσύνην ἐλεγχούσης.

Good fame is better than wealth (*Lept.* § 10): —

οὐ γὰρ εἰ μὴ χρήματ' ἀπόλλυτε μόνον σκεπτέον, ἀλλ' εἰ καὶ δόξον
χρηστήν, περὶ ἧς μᾶλλον σπουδάζετε ἢ περὶ χρημάτων [1].

So, in the speech *For Phormio* (§ 52), we have these words: —

.... πολλῶν χρημάτων τὸ χρηστὸν εἶναι λυσιτελέστερόν ἐστι.

Wealth is inferior to γένος (*ibid.* § 30): —

ὑμῖν μὲν γάρ, ὦ ἄνδρες Ἀθηναῖοι, τοῖς γένει πολίταις οὐδὲ ἐν
πλῆθος χρημάτων ἀντὶ τοῦ γένους καλόν ἐστιν ἑλέσθαι [2].

§ 3. In the opinion of Euripides, nobility of birth (τὸ
εὐγενές) was of more importance than wealth (*Frag.* 739): —

> φεῦ φεῦ, τὸ φῦναι πατρὸς εὐγενοῦς ἄπο
> ὅσην ἔχει φρόνησιν ἀξίωμά τε.
> κἂν γὰρ πένης ὢν τυγχάνῃ, χρηστὸς γεγὼς
> τιμὴν ἔχει τιν', ἀναμετρούμενος δέ πως
> τὸ τοῦ πατρὸς γενναῖον ὠφελεῖ τρόπῳ [3].

It is with the noble, not with the merely wealthy, that one
should marry and give in marriage (*Andr.* 1279-1283): —

> κᾆτ' οὐ γαμεῖν δῆτ' ἔκ τε γενναίων χρεών,
> δοῦναί τ' ἐς ἐσθλούς, ὅστις εὖ βουλεύεται ;
> κακῶν δὲ λέκτρων μὴ 'πιθυμίαν ἔχειν,
> μηδ' εἰ ζαπλούτους οἴσεται φερνὰς δόμοις·
> οὐ γάρ ποτ' ἂν πράξειαν ἐκ θεῶν κακῶς [4].

Τὸ εὐγενές has other advantages also (*Alc.* 601-603): —

> τὸ γὰρ εὐγενὲς ἐκφέρεται πρὸς αἰδῶ.
> ἐν τοῖς ἀγαθοῖσι δὲ πάντ' ἔνεστιν σοφίας.

It is a δεινὸς χαρακτὴρ κἀπίσημος upon men (*Hec.* 379-381): —

> δεινὸς χαρακτὴρ κἀπίσημος ἐν βροτοῖς
> ἐσθλῶν γενέσθαι, κἀπὶ μεῖζον ἔρχεται
> τῆς εὐγενείας ὄνομα τοῖσιν ἀξίοις [5].

---

[1] Cf. *ibid.* § 25.
[2] The right and the wrong use of wealth are contrasted in the speech *Against Midias*, § 109.
[3] Cf. *Frag.* 1066.
[4] Cf. *Frag.* 232.
[5] See Paley's note *ad loc.*

The gods hate not the noble (*Hel.* 1678):—

> τοὺς εὐγενεῖς γὰρ οὐ στυγοῦσι δαίμονες.

Nobility is a defence against misfortune (*Heracl.* 302–303):—

> τὸ δυστυχὲς γὰρ ηὐγένει᾽ ἀμύνεται
> τῆς δυσγενείας μᾶλλον.

The ignoble man cannot hide his nature (*Frag.* 617):—

> οὐκ ἔστιν ἀνθρώποισι τοιοῦτο σκότος,
> οὐ χῶμα γαίας κλῃστόν, ἔνθα τὴν φύσιν
> ὁ δυσγενὴς κρύψας ἂν †εἴη σοφός.

But Euripides frequently declares that high or low birth matters little[1]. All men are originally and naturally equal: praise of noble birth is περισσόμυθον (*Frag.* 52):—

> περισσόμυθος ὁ λόγος, εὐγένειαν εἰ
> βρότειον εὐλογήσομεν.
> τὸ γὰρ πάλαι καὶ πρῶτον ὅτ᾽ ἐγενόμεθα,
> διὰ δ᾽ ἔκρινεν ἁ τεκοῦσα γᾶ βροτούς,
> ὁμοίαν χθὼν ἅπασιν ἐξεπαίδευσεν ὄψιν.
> ἴδιον οὐδὲν ἔσχομεν· μία δὲ γονὰ
> τό τ᾽ εὐγενὲς καὶ τὸ δυσγενές.

' 'Tis only noble to be good' (*Frag.* 336):—

> εἰς δ᾽ εὐγένειαν ὀλίγ᾽ ἔχω φράσαι καλά·
> ὁ μὲν γὰρ ἐσθλὸς εὐγενὴς ἔμοιγ᾽ ἀνήρ,
> ὁ δ᾽ οὐ δίκαιος κἂν ἀμείνονος πατρὸς
> Ζηνὸς πεφύκῃ, δυσγενὴς εἶναι δοκεῖ[2].

In one place (*Frag.* 22) Euripides says that nobility depends only on wealth. But this is spoken with bitter irony:—

> τὴν δ᾽ εὐγένειαν πρὸς θεῶν μή μοι λέγε·
> ἐν χρήμασιν τόδ᾽ ἐστί, μὴ γαυροῦ, πάτερ·
> κύκλῳ γὰρ ἕρπει· τῷ μὲν ἔσθ᾽, ὁ δ᾽ οὐκ ἔχει·
> κοινοῖσι δ᾽ αὐτοῖς χρώμεθ᾽· ᾧ δ᾽ ἂν ἐν δόμοις
> χρόνον συνοικῇ πλεῖστον, οὗτος εὐγενής[3].

---

[1] M. Decharme says (*Euripide*, &c., p. 162):—'Euripide prend résolument parti pour les seconds (δυσγενεῖς) contre les premiers (εὐγενεῖς).'

[2] Cf. *El.* 383-385; *Frag.* 53, 377.

[3] Cf. *Frag.* 9.

There is no criterion of nobility (*El.* 550-551):—

ἀλλ' εὐγενεῖς μέν, ἐν δὲ κιβδήλῳ τόδε.
πολλοὶ γὰρ ὄντες εὐγενεῖς εἰσιν κακοί[1].

It is destroyed by poverty (*ibid.* 37-38):—

λαμπροὶ γὰρ ἐς γένος γε, χρημάτων δὲ δὴ
πένητες, ἔνθεν ηὐγένει' ἀπόλλυται.

There are in the Orators only one or two passages bearing on this question. Isocrates says that virtue is of more advantage than noble birth (*Ad Demon.* § 7):—

ἡ δὲ τῆς ἀρετῆς κτῆσις οἷς ἂν ἀκιβδήλως ταῖς διανοίας συναυξηθῇ, μόνη μὲν συγγηράσκει, πλούτου δὲ κρείττων, χρησιμωτέρα δ' εὐγενείας ἐστί, κ.τ.λ.

But nobility is never lost (*Hel.* § 44):—

ἠπίστατο γὰρ τὰς μὲν ἄλλας εὐτυχίας ταχέως μεταπιπτούσας, τὴν δ' εὐγένειαν ἀεὶ τοῖς αὐτοῖς παραμένουσαν, κ.τ.λ.

Isaeus implies that ἀνδραγαθία is more deserving of honour than γένος (v. § 47):—

ἔτι δὲ ὁ Ἀριστογείτων ἐκεῖνος καὶ Ἁρμόδιος οὐ διὰ τὸ γένος ἐτιμήθησαν ἀλλὰ διὰ τὴν ἀνδραγαθίαν, ἧς σοὶ οὐδὲν μέτεστιν, ὦ Δικαιόγενες[2].

Berlage (pp. 173-174) points out that Euripides was not the first Greek writer to maintain that noble birth is inferior to mental endowment. Democritus, Epicharmus, and Sophocles had all made this observation. The words of Euripides, *Frag.* 52 (see p. 90), are recalled by those of Sophocles, *Frag.* 532 (Nauck):—

ἓν φῦλον ἀνθρώπων μί' ἔδειξε πατρὸς
καὶ ματρὸς ἡμᾶς ἁμέρα τοὺς πάντας· οὐδεὶς
ἔξοχος ἄλλος ἔβλαστεν ἄλλου.
βόσκει δὲ τοὺς μὲν μοῖρα δυσαμερίας,
τοὺς δ' ὄλβος ἡμῶν, τοὺς δὲ δουλείας ◡ – –
– ◡ ◡ – ζυγὸν ἔσχ' ἀνάγκας.

---

[1] Cf. *ibid.* 367 ff. ; *Hec.* 592-598 (with Paley's notes).
[2] Cf. Demosthenes, *For Phormio*, § 30 (quoted above, p. 89).

But the sophist Lycophron alone had said plainly that the advantage of nobility was in appearance only, and that in reality there was no difference between gentle and simple [1],—a conclusion to which he may have come by applying the sophistic doctrine concerning νόμος and φύσις [2]. Berlage admits that Euripides also may have reasoned from this doctrine, but is of opinion that his views are rather to be ascribed to the social and political changes which had occurred in Athens. In the early history of a state, the noble are the wealthy, and the noble and wealthy are really the best men in the state. This is true of the early history of Athens. But, with the defeat of the Persians and the steady growth of democracy, a change came. It was not, perhaps, so apparent in the generation which actually drove back the Persian invaders. But it *was* apparent in the next generation. A youth who had not known the hardships of their fathers, and had become accustomed to the idea of oriental softness and luxury, gradually became more haughty, dissipated, effeminate. On the other hand the common people had done their part in the wars, and had proved themselves in no way inferior to the rest of the citizens. The numbers, wealth and importance of the ναυτικὸς ὄχλος had steadily increased, and they could no longer be disregarded. Men began to see that the wealthy and highborn were not always the ablest men, and that it was not just that all the honours should go to them. Hence the idea arose that the position of the highborn—which originally had rested upon a certain *natural* difference—was unjustifiable; that wealth and rank and noble birth, by which men were now distinguished, were nothing; that all men were originally equal; and that the only superiority which one man could possess over another was the superiority of body or of mind.

§ 4. The most interesting question here is, whether this

---

[1] Berlage (p. 174) quotes from Pseudo-Plut. *de nobilit.* 18. 2:—ἐκεῖνος γὰρ (sc. Lycophron) ἀντιπαραβάλλων ἑτέροις ἀγαθοῖς αὐτήν, εὐγενείας μὲν οὖν, φησίν, ἀφανὲς τὸ κάλλος, ἐν λόγῳ δὲ τὸ σεμνόν, ὡς πρὸς δόξαν οὖσαν τὴν αἵρεσιν αὐτῆς· κατὰ δ' ἀλήθειαν οὐδὲν διαφέροντας τοὺς ἀγενεῖς τῶν εὐγενῶν.

[2] See Zeller, *Pre-Socratic Philosophy*, ii. p. 477 (English Translation).

idea of the equality of all men—this distinction between
νόμος and φύσις—was carried to its logical limits, and whether
it was held to apply to the slaves who, numerically, formed
so large a proportion of the Athenian state, though politically
they were mere ciphers.

Slaves, generally, were in evil repute with the ancients.
Homer says that slavery takes away half a man's virtue
(*Od.* xvii. 322-323):—

> ἥμισυ γάρ τ' ἀρετῆς ἀποαίνυται εὐρύοπα Ζεὺς
> ἀνέρος, εὖτ' ἄν μιν κατὰ δούλιον ἦμαρ ἕλησιν.

This, the ordinary view, is what we find frequently in the
Orators. Lysias says they are evilly-disposed to their masters
(vii. § 35):—

> . . . περὶ δὲ τῶν δεσποτῶν, οἷς πεφύκασι κακονούστατοι . . .

It is a reproach to be δοῦλος καὶ ἐκ δούλων (xiii. §§ 18, 64).

Demosthenes tells us that to the Greeks of a former age
freedom was the ὅρος and κανών of all good (*On the Crown*,
§ 296):—

> . . . τὴν δ' ἐλευθερίαν καὶ τὸ μηδέν' ἔχειν δεσπότην αὐτῶν, ἃ
> τοῖς προτέροις Ἕλλησιν ὅροι τῶν ἀγαθῶν ἦσαν καὶ κανόνες, ἀνατε-
> τροφότες.

In one place (*Lept.* § 131) he has the combination δοῦλοι καὶ
μαστιγίαι.

In the speech *Against Timocrates* (§ 124) there is an interesting comparison drawn between rhetors and depraved
and thankless slaves:—

> εἶτα προπηλακίζουσιν ὑμᾶς ἰδίᾳ τοῖς λόγοις, ὡς αὐτοὶ καλοὶ
> κἀγαθοί, πονηρῶν καὶ ἀχαρίστων οἰκετῶν τρόπους ἔχοντες. καὶ
> γὰρ ἐκείνων, ὦ ἄνδρες δικασταί, ὅσοι ἂν ἐλεύθεροι γένωνται, οὐ τῆς
> ἐλευθερίας χάριν ἔχουσι τοῖς δεσπόταις, ἀλλὰ μισοῦσι μάλιστα
> πάντων ἀνθρώπων, ὅτι συνίσασιν αὐτοῖς δουλεύσασιν. οὕτω δὴ
> καὶ οὗτοι οἱ ῥήτορες οὐκ ἀγαπῶσιν ἐκ πενήτων πλούσιοι ἀπὸ τῆς
> πόλεως γιγνόμενοι, ἀλλὰ καὶ προπηλακίζουσι τὸ πλῆθος, ὅτι σύνοιδεν
> αὐτῶν ἑκάστοις τὰ ἐν τῇ πενίᾳ καὶ νεότητι ἐπιτηδεύματα.

A freeman could not be tortured in giving evidence, a slave

might (*Aphobus*, § 39):—διόπερ τοὺς ὁμολογουμένως δούλους παραβὰς τὸν ἐλεύθερον ἠξίου βασανίζειν, ὃν οὐδ᾽ ὅσιον παραδοῦναι[1].

Slaves had, however, a right to a trial in murder cases (Antiphon, περὶ τοῦ Ἡρῴδου φόνου, § 48):—

καίτοι οὐδὲ οἱ τοὺς δεσπότας ἀποκτείναντες, ἐὰν ἐπ᾽ αὐτοφώρῳ ληφθῶσιν, οὐδ᾽ οὗτοι ἀποθνήσκουσιν ὑπ᾽ αὐτῶν τῶν προσηκόντων, ἀλλὰ παραδιδόασιν αὐτοὺς τῇ ἀρχῇ κατὰ νόμους ὑμετέρους πατρίους. κ.τ.λ.[2].

At Athens, as we learn from Isocrates and Demosthenes, slaves were treated with great kindness. It was perhaps due to this fact, and to their presuming on the indulgence shown them, that they frequently exhibited such impudence as they did. Specimens of this impudence are numerous in Aristophanes; and, though they are doubtless exaggerated, doubtless also they contain some truth.

Isocrates tells us that the Athenians treated their slaves better than the Spartans did their freemen (*Panegyr.* § 123):—

οὐδεὶς γὰρ ἡμῶν οὕτως αἰκίζεται τοὺς οἰκέτας ὡς ἐκεῖνοι τοὺς ἐλευθέρους κολάζουσιν[3].

And from Demosthenes we learn that the law relating to ὕβρις protected slaves no less than freemen (*Agst. Midias*, §§ 47–50).

But in the Orators there is not, so far as I can find, a single passage which so much as suggests that the slave is the equal of the freeman, or that slavery is in opposition to natural right.

Let us see what Euripides has to say on the subject. As we might expect, there is much both of blame and of praise.

Not all slaves are loyal to their masters (*Alc.* 210–211):—

οὐ γάρ τι πάντες εὖ φρονοῦσι κοιράνοις,
ὥστ᾽ ἐν κακοῖσιν εὐμενεῖς παρεστάναι.

---

[1] Cf. *Agst. Timocrates*, § 167.

[2] Cf. (with Paley's note) Euripides, *Hecuba*, 291–292:—
νόμος δ᾽ ἐν ὑμῖν τοῖς τ᾽ ἐλευθέροις ἴσος
καὶ τοῖσι δούλοις αἵματος κεῖται πέρι.

[3] See Mahaffy, *Euripides*, p. 9; *Old Greek Life*, p. 40: Fowler, *The City-State of the Greeks and Romans*, p. 179.

Τὸ δοῦλον is always κακόν (*Hec.* 332–333):—

> αἰαῖ· τὸ δοῦλον ὡς κακὸν πέφυκ' ἀεί,
> τολμᾷ θ' ἃ μὴ χρή, τῇ βίᾳ κρατούμενον[1].

Slaves are friendly to the strongest (*El.* 632–633):—

> OP. ἡμῖν δ' ἂν εἶεν, εἰ κρατοῖμεν, εὐμενεῖς ;
> ΠΡ. δούλων γὰρ ἴδιον τοῦτο, σοὶ δὲ σύμφορον.

Their god is their belly (*Frag.* 49):—

> ἤλεγχον· οὕτω γὰρ κακὸν δοῦλον γένος·
> γαστὴρ ἅπαντα, τοὐπίσω δ' οὐδὲν σκοπεῖ.

A slave with too high thoughts is a grievous burden (*Frag.* 48):—

> . . . δούλου φρονοῦντος μᾶλλον ἢ φρονεῖν χρεὼν
> οὐκ ἔστιν ἄχθος μεῖζον οὐδὲ δώμασιν
> κτῆσις κακίων οὐδ' ἀνωφελεστέρα.

He is a fool who trusts a slave (*Frag.* 86):—

> ὅστις δὲ δούλῳ φωτὶ πιστεύει βροτῶν,
> πολλὴν παρ' ἡμῖν μωρίαν ὀφλισκάνει.

Death with freedom is better than life with slavery (*Frag.* 245):—

> ἐν δέ σοι μόνον προφωνῶ, μὴ ἐπὶ δουλείαν ποτὲ
> ζῶν ἑκὼν ἔλθῃς, παρὸν σοὶ κατθανεῖν ἐλευθέρῳ.

But there are good slaves, who are concerned at their masters' woes (*Alc.* 813):—

> χαίρων ἴθ'· ἡμῖν δεσποτῶν μέλει κακά[2].

Their only disgrace is their name (*Ion,* 854–856):—

> ἐν γάρ τι τοῖς δούλοισιν αἰσχύνην φέρει,
> τοὔνομα· τὰ δ' ἄλλα πάντα τῶν ἐλευθέρων
> οὐδεὶς κακίων δοῦλος, ὅστις ἐσθλὸς ᾖ[3].

---

[1] For various renderings of this passage see Paley's note *ad loc.* Cf. *Frag.* 217.

[2] Cf. *Medea,* 54–55:—

> χρηστοῖσι δούλοις ξυμφορὰ τὰ δεσποτῶν
> κακῶς πίτνοντα καὶ φρενῶν ἀνθάπτεται.

See also *ibid.* 1138; *Hel.* 1641; *Bacch.* 1028; *Frag.* 85.

[3] Cf. *Frag.* 511.

The messenger in the *Helena* prays that he may be in the number of good slaves, and that his mind may be free if his name is not (*Hel.* 726-733):—

> κακὸς γὰρ ὅστις μὴ σέβει τὰ δεσποτῶν
> καὶ ξυγγέγηθε καὶ ξυνωδίνει κακοῖς.
> ἐγὼ μὲν εἴην, κεἰ πέφυχ' ὅμως λάτρις,
> ἐν τοῖσι γενναίοισιν ἠριθμημένος
> δούλοισι, τοὔνομ' οὐκ ἔχων ἐλεύθερον,
> τὸν νοῦν δέ. κρεῖσσον γὰρ τόδ' ἢ δυοῖν κακοῖν
> ἕν' ὄντα χρῆσθαι, τὰς φρένας τ' ἔχειν κακὰς
> ἄλλων τ' ἀκούειν δοῦλον ὄντα τῶν πέλας.

A similar idea we find in *Frag.* 831 :—

> πολλοῖσι δούλοις τοὔνομ' αἰσχρόν, ἡ δὲ φρὴν
> τῶν οὐχὶ δούλων ἐστ' ἐλευθερωτέρα.

In no Greek author do we find the case of the slave so often and so ably pleaded as we do in Euripides[1]. In this, as in much else, he has a great deal more of the modern mind than his contemporaries or his immediate successors. Yet even Euripides nowhere says clearly and plainly that slavery violates nature,—unless indeed he means to extend to slaves the idea expressed in *Frag.* 52 (quoted above, p. 90). Alcidamas, a pupil of Gorgias, declared that by nature all men were born free. Aristotle, too, in one or two passages (e. g. *Ethics*, viii. 11. 7) would draw a distinction between the slave as slave and the slave as man. But this, though he does not seem to see it, is inconsistent with his whole position in regard to slavery[2]. And Aristotle's position was that of ancient Greece[3].

---

[1] Cf. Decharme, *Euripide, &c.*, pp. 168-171: Mahaffy, *Social Life in Greece*, pp. 188-191: Paley, *Euripides*, i. Preface, xiii-xiv, and note on *Andr.* 56: Jerram, notes on *Hel.* 728; *Alc.* 194.

[2] Aristotle had no high opinion of the character of slaves. See *Poetics*, 1454 a.

[3] Cf. Mahaffy, *Euripides*, p. 9; *Greek Antiquities*, pp. 39, 58. See also, for some account of slavery at Athens, Becker, *Charicles*, Excursus on Scene vii: Abbott, *Pericles and the Golden Age of Athens*, pp. 342-344: and, for the growth of humanity, Campbell, *Greek Tragedy*, p. 250.

CHAPTER VIII

POLITICS : ABSTENTION FROM PUBLIC LIFE—PATRIOTISM
—EXILE—GREEKS AND BARBARIANS—ATHENS AND
SPARTA—TYRANNY, OLIGARCHY, AND DEMOCRACY—
DEMAGOGUES—COSMOPOLITANISM.

IT would be superfluous in this place to trace the history
of Greece from the Persian Wars to the victory of Philip,
and to show how Athens gradually reached the summit of
her power under Pericles; how that power began to decline
about the time of Pericles' death, and received its downfall
at Aegospotami[1]; how Sparta succeeded Athens, and Thebes
Sparta; how Greek disunion became a disease past remedy,
and how Greek liberty was finally crushed at Chaeronea[2].

---

[1] For the social and political decay of Athens,—the effect of the loss of
Pericles, of the great plague, of the war, &c. see Abbott, *Pericles, &c.*,
pp. 235-236, 351-354. The effects of the plague are of more importance,
I think, than is sometimes assigned to them by historians. It was un-
doubtedly one of the causes which gave Athens her first great impulse on
her downward career. The careful calculations of Pericles were overturned;
the people were disheartened and their strength reduced; worst of all, there
were sown those seeds of moral and social disorder which were afterwards to
yield so bitter a fruit. If the physical disease was bad, infinitely worse was
the moral disease which it engendered. The plague shook the material
power of Athens more than Sparta had yet been able to do, but it did more:
it introduced evils which would make Sparta's work easier in time to come.
There was neither fear of the gods nor regard for men : the sensual pleasures
of the moment were all that was craved. See Thuc. ii. 53 : Lloyd, *Age of
Pericles*, ii. pp. 400-401. Grote (c. lxvii) denies any such moral (or political)
corruption, but his account, as it seems to me, is exaggerated and one-sided.
For the evil effects of internal στάσις as one of the causes of the decay of the
city-state see Fowler, *The City-State of the Greeks and Romans*, c. ix : Thuc. iii.
82-83.

[2] i. e. Liberty or political freedom in the old Greek sense : see Jebb, *Attic

II

If the external condition of things was bad, the internal was
no better. During the period of disintegration which began
with the Peloponnesian War, the severance of each state
from its neighbours and from the whole national life of
Greece was reflected in the severance of the individual from
the particular state of which he was a member. Formerly
the individual had hardly viewed himself as apart from the
state, but now private needs and private interests assumed
an ever increasing importance [1]. This movement is best seen
in the case of Athens. There was a great fall from Pericles
to Cleon and Hyperbolus, and a still greater fall to the
demagogue of the fourth century B.C. as painted for us by
the Orators. Politics had fallen into disrepute, and many
of the noblest citizens held aloof from public life. The
government thus fell into inferior hands. The people became distrustful of themselves, and political leaders were
everything. The citizens could not bring themselves to
undergo personal hardship and personal service for the good
of the state: they preferred to be amused, and to leave the
fighting to mercenaries. In the earlier history of Greece the
political and military departments had been united; and
much of the splendour of that earlier history is no doubt
due to this fact. But later came specialisation; and, though
one might now find men who were better generals and
men who were better speakers, there were not to be found

Orators, ii. p. 23. And cf. Coulanges, *La Cité Antique*, pp. 265-269 (Livre III.
c. xviii.—*De l'omnipotence de l'État ; les anciens n'ont pas connu la liberté individuelle*):—'Dans une société établie sur de tels principes, la liberté individuelle ne pouvait pas exister. ... Il n'y avait rien dans l'homme qui fût
indépendant.... Les anciens ne connaissaient ni la liberté de la vie privée,
ni la liberté de l'éducation, ni la liberté religieuse.... La funeste maxime
que le salut de l'État est la loi suprême, a été formulée par l'antiquité. On
pensait que le droit, la justice, la morale, tout devait céder devant l'intérêt
de la patrie. ... Le gouvernement s'appela tour à tour monarchie, aristocratie,
démocratie ; mais aucune de ces révolutions ne donna aux hommes la vraie
liberté, la liberté individuelle. Avoir des droits politiques, voter, nommer
des magistrats, pouvoir être archonte, voilà ce qu'on appelait la liberté ; mais
l'homme n'en était pas moins asservi à l'État. Les anciens, et surtout les
Grecs, s'exagérèrent toujours l'importance et les droits de la société.'

[1] The great peril of Hellas was the selfish blindness of political leaders.
See Lloyd, *Age of Pericles*, ii. c. xli, and c. lxiv (p. 401).

better statesmen who were at once generals and speakers [1]. The view of public affairs was narrower, and the government in consequence became worse. The political and military as well as the moral character of the people had become degraded [2].

To the political life of his time Euripides did not stand in any very close relation. In him the Greek idea that every citizen should be a politician was not realised. He lived the retired life of a student [3], and cultivated no companionship so sedulously as that of books, of which his collection was famous in Athens. Yet, though he never played an active part in politics, he was by no means indifferent to public

---

[1] See Macaulay, *On the Athenian Orators*: Jebb, *Attic Orators*, ii. pp. 371-372.

[2] See Butcher, *Demosthenes*, c. i: Jebb, *Attic Orators*, ii. pp. 14-17: Kennedy's Translation of Demosthenes, *Agst. Timocrates, &c.*, Appendix X (*The Empire of Athens*).

[3] See Decharme, *Euripide, &c.*, p. 9 ('C'était un mélancolique, un méditatif passionné pour la solitude. . . . Ce solitaire dédaigneux de la vie active,' &c.): Lloyd, *Age of Pericles*, ii. c. lxii: Aristoph. *Frogs*, 1498. Cf. also *Alc.* 962 ff., where Euripides seems to speak of his own literary researches (see Paley's note *ad loc.*) :—

ἐγὼ καὶ διὰ μούσας
καὶ μετάρσιος ᾖξα, καὶ
πλείστων ἁψάμενος λόγων
κρεῖσσον οὐδὲν ἀνάγκας
ηὗρον, κ.τ.λ.

But Euripides saw that he that increaseth knowledge increaseth sorrow (*El.* 295-296) :—   οὐ γὰρ οὐδ' ἄζημον
γνώμην ἐνεῖναι τοῖς σοφοῖς λίαν σοφήν.

And there is the passage in the *Medea* (295-305), where Euripides seems to have his own case in view :—

χρὴ δ' οὔποθ' ὅστις ἀρτίφρων πέφυκ' ἀνὴρ
παῖδας περισσῶς ἐκδιδάσκεσθαι σοφούς·
χωρὶς γὰρ ἄλλης ἧς ἔχουσιν ἀργίας
φθόνον πρὸς ἀστῶν ἀλφάνουσι δυσμενῆ.
σκαιοῖσι μὲν γὰρ καινὰ προσφέρων σοφὰ
δόξεις ἀχρεῖος κοὐ σοφὸς πεφυκέναι·
τῶν δ' αὖ δοκούντων εἰδέναι τι ποικίλον
κρείσσων νομισθεὶς λυπρὸς ἐν πόλει φανεῖ.
ἐγὼ δὲ καὐτὴ τῆσδε κοινωνῶ τύχης.
σοφὴ γὰρ οὖσα τοῖς μέν εἰμ' ἐπίφθονος,
[τοῖς δ' ἡσυχαία, τοῖς δὲ θατέρου τρόπου,]
τοῖς δ' αὖ προσάντης· εἰμὶ δ' οὐκ ἄγαν σοφή.

For a passage on the cultivation of the Muses see *Her. Fur.* 673 ff.

H 2

interest[1]. The *Medea*, for example, exhibited in 431 r.c., has a distinct bearing on the relations of Athens to Corinth and Megara. Nor was Euripides the only prominent Athenian citizen who sinned—if sin it was—by thus withdrawing from public life. Anaxagoras had set the example: it was followed by Socrates[2], Plato, Aristotle, Isocrates, and others.

In the *Antiopa* the rival advantages of a life of publicity and a life of retirement are put forward by Zethus and Amphion. There can be little doubt that, in the person of Amphion, Euripides is pleading his own cause. Zethus is the mouthpiece of orthodox opinion. The fragment is thus restored by Nauck (185):—

. . . . ἀμελεῖς ὧν [σε φροντίζειν ἐχρῆν·]
ψυχῆς φύσιν [γὰρ] ὧδε γενναίαν [λαχὼν]
γυναικομίμῳ διαπρέπεις μορφώματι
. . . . κοῦτ' ἂν ἀσπίδος κύτει
[καλῶς] ὁμιλήσειας, οὔτ' ἄλλων ὕπερ
γεανικὸν βούλευμα βουλεύσαιό [τι][3].

With the arguments of Zethus we may compare *Suppl.* 881–887,—lines in which the active duties of a citizen are set forth, and Euripides accuses his own mode of life:—

ὁ δ' αὖ τρίτος τῶνδ' Ἱππομέδων τοιόσδ' ἔφυ·
παῖς ὢν ἐτόλμησ' εὐθὺς οὐ πρὸς ἡδονὰς
μουσῶν τραπέσθαι, πρὸς τὸ μαλθακὸν βίου,
ἀγροὺς δὲ ναίων, σκληρὰ τῇ φύσει διδοὺς
ἔχαιρε πρὸς τἀνδρεῖον, ἔς τ' ἄγρας ἰὼν
ἵπποις τε χαίρων τόξα τ' ἐντείνων χεροῖν
πόλει παρασχεῖν σῶμα χρήσιμον θέλων[4].

---

[1] For an excellent discussion on the relation of many of the dramas of Euripides to the political events of the time at which they were written see Wilamowitz-M., *Herakles*, Einleitung, pp. 13-15. See also Decharme, *Euripide, &c.*, pp. 172-206: Lloyd, *Age of Pericles*, ii. c. lxii (the play with which he deals specially being the *Medea*): Jerram's *Heracl.* Introd. pp. 4-5: Beck's *Heracl.* Introd. p. xi: Mahaffy, *Hist. of Gr. Lit.* (1883) I. p. 341. For a special treatment of the *Heracl.* and *Suppl.* as 'drames de circonstance' see Decharme, *Euripide, &c.*, pp. 191-204.

[2] Cf. Plato, *Apol.* 23 B:—καὶ ὑπὸ ταύτης τῆς ἀσχολίας οὔτε τι τῶν τῆς πόλεως πρᾶξαί μοι σχολὴ γέγονεν ἄξιον λόγου οὔτε τῶν οἰκείων.

[3] See the fragment in Plato, *Gorg.* 485 E, and the whole speech of Callicles in that passage.

[4] Cf. *Frag.* 512.

It is the quiet, retired life, however, that is the life of the good and wise (*Ion*, 598-601):—

> ὅσοι δὲ χρηστοὶ δυνάμενοί τ' εἶναι σοφοὶ
> σιγῶσι κοὐ σπεύδουσιν ἐς τὰ πράγματα,
> γέλωτ' ἐν αὐτοῖς μωρίαν τε λήψομαι
> οὐχ ἡσυχάζων ἐν πόλει φόβου πλέᾳ.

(*Ibid.* 634):—

> τὴν φιλτάτην μὲν πρῶτον ἀνθρώποις σχολήν.

And we may again quote the famous lines (*Frag.* 910):—

> ὄλβιος ὅστις τῆς ἱστορίας
> ἔσχε μάθησιν,
> μήτε πολιτῶν ἐπὶ πημοσύνην
> μήτ' εἰς ἀδίκους πράξεις ὁρμῶν,
> ἀλλ' ἀθανάτου καθορῶν φύσεως
> κόσμον ἀγήρων, πῇ τε συνέστη
> καὶ ὅπῃ καὶ ὅπως.
> τοῖς δὲ τοιούτοις οὐδέποτ' αἰσχρῶν
> ἔργων μελέδημα προσίζει.

The busybody is a fool (*Frag.* 193):—

> ὅστις δὲ πράσσει πολλὰ μὴ πράσσειν παρόν,
> μῶρος, παρὸν ζῆν ἡδέως ἀπράγμονα[1].

He who is busiest makes most mistakes (*Frag.* 576):—

> ὁ πλεῖστα πράσσων πλεῖσθ' ἁμαρτάνει βροτῶν.

The ideal life, to Euripides' way of thinking, is that of the αὐτουργός described in the *Orestes* (917-922):—

> ἄλλος δ' ἀναστὰς ἔλεγε τῷδ' ἐναντία,
> μορφῇ μὲν οὐκ εὐωπός, ἀνδρεῖος δ' ἀνήρ,
> ὀλιγάκις ἄστυ κἀγορᾶς χραίνων κύκλον,
> αὐτουργός, οἵπερ καὶ μόνοι σώζουσι γῆν,
> ξυνετὸς δὲ χωρεῖν ὁμόσε τοῖς λόγοις θέλων,
> ἀκέραιος, ἀνεπίληπτον ἠσκηκὼς βίον[2].

---

[1] Cf. *Hipp.* 785; *Frag.* 787, 788.
[2] Euripides was friendly to the agricultural interest: see Paley's note *ad loc.* Isaeus says that a good life is the best λειτουργία (*Frag.* 30 :—ἡγοῦμαι μεγίστην εἶναι τῶν λειτουργιῶν τὸν καθ' ἡμέραν βίον κόσμιον καὶ σώφρονα παρέχειν.

During the Peloponnesian war, when Athens was a prey to civil strife, and when selfish interests were so large a factor in the motives of her leaders, it was little wonder that a man like Euripides, whose natural bent was not towards action, but towards thought and study, should have preferred to leave politics alone.

Not on this account, however, are we to think that Euripides cared nothing for his country. Again and again we meet with the thought that nothing is dearer than one's native land, nothing more wretched than exile.

It is only in one's native land that one can live a life of happiness and joy (*Alc.* 168-169):—

> . . . . ἀλλ' εὐδαίμονας
> ἐν γῇ πατρῴᾳ τερπνὸν ἐκπλῆσαι βίον.

One *must* love one's country (*Phoen.* 358-359):—

> ἀλλ' ἀναγκαίως ἔχει
> πατρίδος ἐρᾶν ἅπαντας.

Nothing else is so dear to mortals (*ibid.* 406):—

> ἡ πατρίς, ὡς ἔοικε, φίλτατον βροτοῖς[1].

It is an impious thing to invade one's country (*ibid.* 432-434):—

> ἐπὶ γὰρ τὴν ἐμὴν στρατεύομαι
> πόλιν. θεοὺς δ' ἐπώμοσ' ὡς ἀκουσίως
> τοῖς φιλτάτοις τοκεῦσιν ἠράμην δόρυ[2].

It is a glorious thing to die for one's country (*Tro.* 386-387):—

> Τρῶες δὲ πρῶτον μέν, τὸ κάλλιστον κλέος,
> ὑπὲρ πάτρας ἔθνησκον[3].

---

[1] Cf. *Frag.* 6, 817.

[2] Cf. *ibid.* 994-996.

[3] Cf. *ibid.* 1168-1170; *Phoen.* 997 ff. For the feeling for country cf. also *Med.* 35; *Tro.* 375, 378, 386, 389, 458, 599, 1275 ff., 1302, 1311, 1316, 1331; *Frag.* 347, 360 (ll. 5-8), 729. For the religious side of this patriotism see Coulanges, *La Cité Antique*, p. 234:—'L'amour de la patrie, c'est la piété des anciens.' The whole chapter is interesting (Livre III. c. xiii.—*Le Patriotisme; L'Exil*).

Exile brings many evils in its train (*Med.* 461-462):—

> πόλλ' ἐφέλκεται φυγὴ
> κακὰ ξὺν αὐτῇ.

A life of exile is a bitter life (*Hipp.* 1048-1049):—

> ἀλλ' ἐκ πατρῴας φυγὰς ἀλητεύων χθονὸς
> ξένην ἐπ' αἶαν λυπρὸν ἀντλήσεις βίον[1].

It is the last and worst of Hecuba's miseries (*Tro.* 1272-1274):—

> οἲ 'γὼ τάλαινα· τοῦτο δὴ τὸ λοίσθιον
> καὶ τέρμα πάντων τῶν ἐμῶν ἤδη κακῶν·
> ἔξειμι πατρίδος, πόλις ὑφάπτεται πυρί.

There is no woe like exile (*El.* 1314-1315):—

> καὶ τίνες ἄλλαι στοναχαὶ μείζους
> ἢ γῆς πατρίας ὅρον ἐκλείπειν;

Some of the evils of exile are described in the *Phoen.* (388-397):—

> IO. τί τὸ στέρεσθαι πατρίδος; ἦ κακὸν μέγα;
> ΠΟ. μέγιστον· ἔργῳ δ' ἐστὶ μεῖζον ἢ λόγῳ.
> IO. τίς ὁ τρόπος αὐτοῦ; τί φυγάσιν τὸ δυσχερές;
> ΠΟ. ἓν μὲν μέγιστον, οὐκ ἔχει παρρησίαν.
> IO. δούλου τόδ' εἶπας, μὴ λέγειν ἅ τις φρονεῖ.
> ΠΟ. τὰς τῶν κρατούντων ἀμαθίας φέρειν χρεών.
> IO. καὶ τοῦτο λυπρόν, ξυνασοφεῖν τοῖς μὴ σοφοῖς.
> ΠΟ. ἀλλ' ἐς τὸ κέρδος παρὰ φύσιν δουλευτέον.
> IO. αἱ δ' ἐλπίδες βόσκουσι φυγάδας, ὡς λόγος.
> ΠΟ. καλοῖς βλέπουσί γ' ὄμμασιν, μέλλουσι δέ[2].

---

[1] Cf. ibid. 897-898.

[2] For other passages bearing on the misery of exile see *Med.* 34, 643; *Hec.* 480, 913; *Tro.* 375-378; *Hel.* 273-275; *El.* 236, 352; *Bacch.* 1350, 1353-1355, 1382; *Phoen.* 369-370, 378, 417 418, 1621, 1710, 1723. Cf. also Plato, *Crito*, 52 C: and see Coulanges, *La Cité Antique*, pp. 234-236:—'Il fallait que la possession de la patrie fût bien précieuse; car les anciens n'imaginaient guère de châtiment plus cruel d'en priver l'homme. La punition ordinaire des grands crimes était l'exil. ... Il contenait ce que les modernes ont appelé l'excommunication. ... L'exil mettait un homme hors de la religion. ... Il n'est pas surprenant que les républiques anciennes aient presque toujours permis au coupable d'échapper à la mort par la fuite. L'exil ne semblait pas un supplice plus doux que la mort.'

Passages abound in which Euripides asserts that the Greek is superior to the Barbarian [1].

In Greece justice and law are observed: with the barbarian might is right (*Med.* 536–538):—

πρῶτον μὲν 'Ελλάδ' ἀντὶ βαρβάρου χθονὸς
γαῖαν κατοικεῖς, καὶ δίκην ἐπίστασαι
νόμοις τε χρῆσθαι, μὴ πρὸς ἰσχύος χάριν.

We have a picture of barbarian lawlessness and outrage in *Andr.* 173–176:—

τοιοῦτον πᾶν τὸ βάρβαρον γένος·
πατήρ τε θυγατρὶ παῖς τε μητρὶ μίγνυται
κόρη τ' ἀδελφῷ, διὰ φόνου δ' οἱ φίλτατοι
χωροῦσι, καὶ τῶνδ' οὐδὲν ἐξείργει νόμος.

Greeks should rule barbarians. The barbarian is a slave, the Greek is free (*Iph. Aul.* 1400–1401):—

βαρβάρων δ' "Ελληνας ἄρχειν εἰκός, ἀλλ' οὐ βαρβάρους,
μῆτερ, 'Ελλήνων· τὸ μὲν γὰρ δοῦλον, οἱ δ' ἐλεύθεροι [2].

The Phrygians are described as soft, luxurious, cowardly (*Or.* 1111–1112):—

ΠΥ. τίνας ; Φρυγῶν γὰρ οὐδέν' ἂν τρέσαιμ' ἐγώ.
ΟΡ. οἵους ἐνόπτρων καὶ μύρων ἐπιστάτας.

And again (*ibid.* 1351–1352):—

. . . οὕνεκ' ἄνδρας, οὐ Φρύγας κακούς,
εὑρὼν ἔπραξεν οἷα χρὴ πράσσειν κακούς.

It is a reproach that Greeks should act like barbarians (*Tro.* 759–760):—

ὦ βάρβαρ' ἐξευρόντες "Ελληνες κακά,
τί τόνδε παῖδα κτείνετ' οὐδὲν αἴτιον [3] ;

---

[1] 'The Greeks were, in their own view, something even more than a chosen people ; they were, as they conceived, a race primarily and lineally distinct from all the races of men, the very children of the gods, whose holy separation was attested by that deep instinct of their nature which taught them to loathe the alien' (Jebb, *Attic Orators*, ii. p. 417). Cf. Coulanges, *La Cité Antique*, p. 228 :—' C'est ainsi que la religion établissait entre le citoyen et l'étranger une distinction profonde et ineffaçable.' See the whole chapter (Livre III. c. xii.—*Le Citoyen et l'Étranger*).

[2] See Paley's note *ad loc.*

[3] See also *Med.* 1339 ff. ; *Hec.* 1129–1131 ; *Hel.* 276 ; *Bacch.* 483 ; *Heracl.* 130–131 ; *Or.* 485–487, 1426 ff., 1483–1485 ; *Iph. Aul.* 74 ; *Frag.* 719.

Praise of Athens was a commonplace with the dramatists as it was later with the orators. But none speaks with more pride and affection of Athens than does Euripides: he was deeply conscious of the proud position of being an Athenian citizen[1]. Passages in praise of Athens are abundant—in fact, too abundant—in his plays[2]. For, as he himself says (*Heracl.* 202-203):—καὶ γὰρ οὖν ἐπίφθονον λίαν ἐπαινεῖν ἐστι.

Most famous of all is that eulogy of Athens in the *Medea* (824-845), which has been compared with the celebrated ode in the *Oedipus Coloneus* of Sophocles:—

Ἐρεχθεῖδαι τὸ παλαιὸν ὄλβιοι
καὶ θεῶν παῖδες μακάρων, ἱερᾶς
χώρας ἀπορθήτου τ' ἀποφερβόμενοι
κλεινοτάταν σοφίαν, ἀεὶ διὰ λαμπροτάτου
βαίνοντες ἁβρῶς αἰθέρος, ἔνθα ποθ' ἁγνὰς
ἐννέα Πιερίδας Μούσας λέγουσι
ξανθὰν Ἁρμονίαν φυτεῦσαι·
τοῦ καλλινάου τ' ἀπὸ Κηφισοῦ ῥοὰς
τὰν Κύπριν κλῄζουσιν ἀφυσσαμέναν
χώρας καταπνεῦσαι μετρίας ἀνέμων
ἡδυπνόους αὔρας· ἀεὶ δ' ἐπιβαλλομέναν
χαίταισιν εὐώδη ῥοδέων πλόκον ἀνθέων
τᾷ σοφίᾳ παρέδρους πέμπειν ἔρωτας,
παντοίας ἀρετᾶς ξυνεργούς[3].

Athens is renowned for piety and justice (*Heracl.* 901-903):—

ἔχεις ὁδόν τιν', ὦ πόλις, δίκαιον·
οὐ χρή ποτε τόδ' ἀφελέσθαι,
τιμᾶν θεούς[4].

---

[1] Cf. Wilamowitz-M., *Herakles*, Einleitung, p. 5 :—'Athen, die hauptstadt von Hellas, das attische Reich berufen zur vormacht aller Hellenen, das ist die voraussetzung seines politischen denkens, wie sie es sein musste.'

[2] For this 'almost vulgar patriotism' see Mahaffy, *Euripides*, p. 36. Κλεινός and λιπαρός are adjectives continually used to describe Athens. As to Athenian invention of legends for the glorification of Athens see Holm, i. pp. 111, 132; Jerram's *Heracl.* Introd. pp. 7 8; Beck's *Heracl.* Introd. p. xii. M. Decharme says (*Euripide, &c.*, p. 206) :—'La tragédie grecque est encore chez Euripide ce qu'elle était chez Eschyle : une école de patriotisme.'

[3] For the thought that the Muses honour Athens see *Rhesus*, 941 ff.

[4] See Paley's note *ad loc.*, and cf. *Heracl.* 770-783, 1012-1013; *Med.* 846 ff.

Athens is free (*Heracl.* 61-62):—

> οὐ δῆτ'· ἐπεί μοι βωμὸς ἀρκέσει θεοῦ
> ἐλευθέρα τε γαῖ', ἐν ᾗ βεβήκαμεν[1].

Athens is the champion of the weak (*Suppl.* 379-380):—

> σύ τοι σέβεις δίκαν, τὸ δ' ἧσσον ἀδικίᾳ
> νέμεις, τόν τε δυστυχῆ πάντα ῥύει[2].

The Athenian citizen enjoys παρρησία and ἰσηγορία (*Heracl.* 181-182):—

> ἄναξ, ὑπάρχει μὲν τόδ' ἐν τῇ σῇ χθονί,
> εἰπεῖν ἀκοῦσαί τ' ἐν μέρει πάρεστί μοι,
> κοὐδείς μ' ἀπώσει πρόσθεν, ὥσπερ ἄλλοθεν[3].

The Athenians are αὐτόχθονες (*Ion,* 589-590):—

> εἶναί φασι τὰς αὐτόχθονας
> κλεινὰς Ἀθήνας οὐκ ἐπείσακτον γένος[4].

This boast, as we shall see, is a commonplace with the Orators.

The obverse to Euripides' love of Athens is his hatred of Sparta.

Athens and Sparta are contrasted in the *Supplices* (187-190):—

> Σπάρτη μὲν ὠμὴ καὶ πεποίκιλται τρόπους·
> τὰ δ' ἄλλα μικρὰ κἀσθενῆ. πόλις δὲ σὴ
> μόνη δύναιτ' ἂν τόνδ' ὑποστῆναι πόνον·
> τά τ' οἰκτρὰ γὰρ δέδορκε κ.τ.λ.

---

[1] Cf. *Heracl.* 113, 197-200, 244, 287, 957; *Suppl.* 403-408, 477, 518-521. The play of the *Supplices*—like the *Heraclidae*—is filled with praise of Athens. To quote the argument, τὸ δὲ δρᾶμα ἐγκώμιον Ἀθηνῶν.

[2] Cf. *Med.* 759 ff.; *Her. Fur.* 1334-1335; *Heracl.* 176-178. For the humanity of the Athenians and their protection of strangers see Holm, i. pp. 111, 121, 377-378; and cf. Thuc. i. 2. Of the *Heraclidae* M. Decharme says (*Euripide, &c.,* p. 197):—'Cette tragédie a pour objet principal la glorification d'Athènes, vengeresse des faibles contre le fort, protectrice des droits saints de l'hospitalité.'

[3] Cf. *Hipp.* 421-423.

[4] Cf. *Frag.* 360 (ll. 5-8); and see Holm, i. p. 377. For other passages in praise of Athens see *Alc.* 452; *Hipp.* 759, 1094; *Suppl.* 187 ff., 353, 575-577; *Ion,* 29, 262, 737, 1038; *Tro.* 800; *El.* 1320; *Iph. Taur.* 1130; *Heracl.* 306, 423-424.

And there is a fierce invective against Sparta in the *Andromache* (445-453):—

ὦ πᾶσιν ἀνθρώποισιν ἔχθιστοι βροτῶν,
Σπάρτης ἔνοικοι, δόλια βουλευτήρια,
ψευδῶν ἄνακτες, μηχανορράφοι κακῶν,
ἑλικτὰ κοὐδὲν ὑγιές, ἀλλὰ πᾶν πέριξ
φρονοῦντες, ἀδίκως εὐτυχεῖτ' ἀν' Ἑλλάδα.
τί δ' οὐκ ἐν ὑμῖν ἐστιν; οὐ πλεῖστοι φόνοι;
οὐκ αἰσχροκερδεῖς; οὐ λέγοντες ἄλλα μὲν
γλώσσῃ, φρονοῦντες δ' ἄλλ' ἐφευρίσκεσθ' ἀεί;
ὄλοισθ'[1].

The cause of this hatred is not far to seek. The Spartan system[2], with its secrecy and restraints, and, above all, its care of the body to the neglect of the mind, could be regarded by Euripides only with disfavour.

Euripides was not the kind of man to be the devoted adherent of any political party,—at least in an active, public way. There was too much indecision in his character for that[3]. He inveighs bitterly against tyranny, but no less bitterly against demagogues, the bane of democracy. On the whole, his theory of government—if theory it can be called—seems to resemble that of Carlyle. He would have a democracy, but it must be led by the 'Kanning man[4].' Here

---

[1] See Paley's note *ad loc.*, and cf. *Andr.* 724-726; *Tro.* 210 ff. So Euripides always depicts Menelaus in a bad light: see *Iph. Aul.* 360 (with Paley's note). See also Paley's notes on *Andr.* 445, 595 ff.: Decharme, *Euripide, &c.*, pp. 189 ff.

[2] See Pericles' Funeral Oration in Thuc. ii: Lloyd, *Age of Pericles*, ii. c. xl.

[3] This indecision has been already noticed in his treatment of religion and the myths.

[4] See Mahaffy, *Euripides*, p. 37:—'He was precisely that sort of broadminded sympathetic thinker who refuses to adopt the views of any party, but holds sometimes with the one and sometimes with the other. Thus in matters of education and of general enlightenment, he certainly stood with the advanced Radicals and Freethinkers, with Anaxagoras, with the sophists and rhetoricians, who were breaking down the old barriers of thought. But in politics his plays produce a strong conviction that he opposed this very party, and held with the old Conservatives and the peace policy, represented by a section of the nobility and the stout farmers of Attica.' M. Decharme says (*Euripide, &c.*, p. 187):—'Euripide est donc partisan de la paix. . . . Il aime la paix parceque la guerre lui fait naturellement horreur, parceque son âme est

we may with safety regard the opinions of Euripides as expressed by the words he puts in the mouths of his characters. He is careless of anachronisms. Theseus (*Suppl.* 232 ff.) speaks like an Athenian of the Periclean age: Hecuba (*Her.* 291-292) refers to a law passed in the time of the democracy.

Euripides has much to say against tyrants [1]. They are inexorable (*Med.* 119-121):—

> δεινὰ τυράννων λήματα, καί πως
> ὀλίγ' ἀρχόμενοι, πολλὰ κρατοῦντες,
> χαλεπῶς ὀργὰς μεταβάλλουσιν.

Tyranny is a prosperous wrong (*Phoen.* 549-551):—

> τί τὴν τυραννίδ', ἀδικίαν εὐδαίμονα,
> τιμᾷς ὑπέρφευ, καὶ μέγ' ἥγησαι τόδε,
> περιβλέπεσθαι τίμιον ; κενὸν μὲν οὖν.

It is the most wretched of all things (*Frag.* 605):—

> τὸ δ' ἔσχατον δὴ τοῦτο θαυμαστὸν βροτοῖς,
> τυραννίς, οὐχ εὕροις ἂν ἀθλιώτερον.

The tyrant lives a life of alarm: he hates the good, and makes friends of the evil: he is in constant fear of death (*Ion*, 621-628):—

> τυραννίδος δὲ τῆς μάτην αἰνουμένης
> τὸ μὲν πρόσωπον ἡδύ, τἀν δόμοισι δὲ
> λυπηρά· τίς γὰρ μακάριος, τίς εὐτυχής,
> ὅστις δεδοικὼς καὶ παραβλέπων βίαν
> αἰῶνα τείνει ; δημότης ἂν εὐτυχὴς
> ζῆν ἂν θέλοιμι μᾶλλον ἢ τύραννος ὤν,
> ᾧ τοὺς πονηροὺς ἡδονὴ φίλους ἔχειν,
> ἐσθλοὺς δὲ μισεῖ κατθανεῖν φοβούμενος [2].

---

largement ouverte à la pitié pour tous les maux de l'humanité.' See also Paley's and Jerram's notes on *Hel.* 1151; and Paley's notes on *El.* 1347; *Or.* 1682; *Bacch.* 420.

[1] The typical tyrant in Euripides is Lycus in the *Her. Fur.* For the manner in which the Greeks regarded tyranny see Holm, i. p. 429: Fowler, *The City-State of the Greeks and Romans*, pp. 140 ff. And cf. Herodotus, iii. 80; v. 90 93: Aristotle, *Pol.* iii. 7. 5; vi. iv. 10 (1295 a).

[2] See Paley's note *ad loc.*, and cf. *Frag.* 605, ll. 3-4.

A state has no greater enemy than a tyrant: he acts not by law, but by caprice (*Suppl.* 429-432):—

οὐδὲν τυράννου δυσμενέστερον πόλει,
ὅπου τὸ μὲν πρώτιστον οὐκ εἰσὶν νόμοι
κοινοί, κρατεῖ δ' εἰς τὸν νόμον κεκτημένος
αὐτὸς παρ' αὑτῷ, καὶ τόδ' οὐκέτ' ἔστ' ἴσον[1].

Tyranny and freedom are contrasted in *Frag.* 275:—

κακῶς δ' ὄλοιντο πάντες οἱ τυραννίδι
χαίρουσιν ὀλίγῃ τ' ἐν πόλει μοναρχίᾳ·
τοὐλεύθερον γὰρ ὄνομα παντὸς ἄξιον,
κἂν σμίκρ' ἔχῃ τις, μεγάλ' ἔχειν νομιζέτω[2].

But, if the tyrant be a good man, even tyranny may be good (*Frag.* 8):—

ἀνδρὸς δ' ὑπ' ἐσθλοῦ καὶ τυραννεῖσθαι καλόν.

Euripides sees, however, that the δῆμος may be led astray by passion (*Iph. Aul.* 1357)[3]:—

ΑΧ. ἀλλ' ἐνικώμην κεκραγμοῦ. ΚΛ. τὸ πολὺ γὰρ δεινὸν κακόν.

Its moods change readily: it is quick to anger, but also magnanimous and compassionate (*Or.* 696-703):—

ὅταν γὰρ ἡβᾷ δῆμος, εἰς ὀργὴν πεσών,
ὅμοιον ὥστε πῦρ κατασβέσαι λάβρον·
εἰ δ' ἡσύχως τις αὐτὸς ἐντείνοντι μὲν
χαλῶν ὑπείκοι, καιρὸν εὐλαβούμενος,
ἴσως ἂν ἐκπνεύσει'· ὅταν δ' ἀνῇ πνοάς,
τύχοις ἂν αὐτοῦ ῥᾳδίως ὅσον θέλεις.
ἔνεστι δ' οἶκτος, ἔνι δὲ καὶ θυμὸς μέγας,
καραδοκοῦντι κτῆμα τιμιώτατον.

The δῆμος is often wiser than they who sit in office (*Andr.* 699-702):—

σεμνοὶ δ' ἐν ἀρχαῖς ἥμενοι κατὰ πτόλιν
φρονοῦσι δήμου μεῖζον, ὄντες οὐδένες·
οἱ δ' εἰσὶν αὐτῶν μυρίῳ σοφώτεροι,
εἰ τόλμα προσγένοιτο βούλησίς θ' ἅμα.

---

[1] See the whole speech of Theseus *ad loc.*
[2] Cf. *Hipp.* 1013-1020; *Tro.* 1170; *Phoen.* 506; *Frag.* 171, 172, 250, 774, 850.
[3] 'Il n'adule pas la foule' (Decharme, *Euripide*, &c., p. 178).

It is foolish to seek to hold the δῆμος in check (*Frag.* 92):—

> ἴστω τ' ἄφρων ὢν ὅστις ἄνθρωπος γεγὼς
> δῆμον κολούει χρήμασιν γαυρούμενος.

Yet it must not have unlimited power (*Frag.* 626):—

> δήμῳ δὲ μήτε πᾶν ἀναρτήσῃς κράτος,
> μήτ' αὖ κακώσῃς, πλοῦτον ἔντιμον τιθείς,
> μηδ' ἄνδρα δήμῳ πιστὸν ἐκβάλῃς ποτὲ
> μηδ' αὖξε καιροῦ μείζον', οὐ γὰρ ἀσφαλές,
> μή σοι τύραννος λαμπρὸς ἐξ ἀστοῦ φανῇ.
> κόλουε δ' ἄνδρα παρὰ δίκην τιμώμενον·
> πόλει γὰρ εὐτυχοῦντες οἱ κακοὶ νόσος.

Nor must one stand too much in fear of the ὄχλος (*Iph. Aul.* 517):—

> οὔτοι χρὴ λίαν ταρβεῖν ὄχλον.

The better should rule the worse (*Frag.* 1107):—

> ἄρχεσθαι χρεὼν
> κακοὺς ὑπ' ἐσθλῶν καὶ κλύειν τῶν κρεισσόνων.

Whether the many will act wisely or the reverse all depends on the character of their leaders (*Or.* 772–773):—

> ΟΡ. δεινὸν οἱ πολλοί, κακούργους ὅταν ἔχωσι προστάτας.
> ΠΥ. ἀλλ' ὅταν χρηστοὺς λάβωσι, χρηστὰ βουλεύουσ' ἀεί.

Athens under Pericles would correspond to the description in line 773; Athens after Pericles to that in line 772. Euripides has no hatred for the δῆμος; only he sees that it needs to be well led.

Of no class has Euripides more bitter things to say than of the demagogues,—the men who lead the people astray[1]. It is they who are attacked when he speaks thus of specious words (*Hipp.* 486–489):—

> τοῦτ' ἔσθ' ὃ θνητῶν εὖ πόλεις οἰκουμένας
> δόμους τ' ἀπόλλυσ', οἱ καλοὶ λίαν λόγοι.
> οὐ γάρ τι τοῖσιν ὠσὶ τερπνὰ δεῖ λέγειν,
> ἀλλ' ἐξ ὅτου τις εὐκλεὴς γενήσεται.

---

[1] 'Euripide n'est pas suspect de tendresse à l'égard des démagogues' (Decharme, *Euripide, &c.*, p. 180).

The demagogue who catches the popular ear is of no account
among wise men (*ibid.* 988-989):—

οἱ γὰρ ἐν σοφοῖς
φαῦλοι παρ' ὄχλῳ μουσικώτεροι λέγειν.

The class is fiercely attacked in the *Hecuba* (254-257):—

ἀχάριστον ὑμῶν σπέρμ', ὅσοι δημηγόρους
ζηλοῦτε τιμάς· μηδὲ γιγνώσκοισθέ μοι,
οἱ τοὺς φίλους βλάπτοντες οὐ φροντίζετε,
ἢν τοῖσι πολλοῖς πρὸς χάριν λέγητέ τι [1].

And more elaborate is the attack made by the Theban
herald on democracies under the sway of demagogues (*Suppl.*
409-425):—

ἐν μὲν τόδ' ἡμῖν, ὥσπερ ἐν πεσσοῖς, δίδως
κρεῖσσον· πόλις γὰρ ἧς ἐγὼ πάρειμ' ἄπο
ἑνὸς πρὸς ἀνδρός, οὐκ ὄχλῳ κρατύνεται·
οὐδ' ἔστιν αὐτὴν ὅστις ἐκχαυνῶν λόγοις
πρὸς κέρδος ἴδιον ἄλλος ἄλλοσε στρέφει.
ὁ δ' αὐτίχ' ἡδὺς καὶ διδοὺς πολλὴν χάριν
εἰσαῦθις ἔβλαψ', εἶτα διαβολαῖς νέαις
κλέψας τὰ πρόσθε σφάλματ' ἐξέδυ δίκης.
ἄλλως τε πῶς ἂν μὴ διορθεύων λόγους
ὀρθῶς δύναιτ' ἂν δῆμος εὐθύνειν πόλιν;
ὁ γὰρ χρόνος μάθησιν ἀντὶ τοῦ τάχους
κρείσσω δίδωσι. γαπόνος δ' ἀνὴρ πένης,
εἰ καὶ γένοιτο μὴ ἀμαθής, ἔργων ὕπο
οὐκ ἂν δύναιτο πρὸς τὰ κοίν' ἀποβλέπειν.
ἦ δὴ νοσῶδες τοῦτο τοῖς ἀμείνοσιν,
ὅταν πονηρὸς ἀξίωμ' ἀνὴρ ἔχῃ,
γλώσσῃ κατασχὼν δῆμον οὐδὲν ὢν τὸ πρίν [2].

The smooth-tongued, foolish demagogue is contrasted with
the prudent counsellor (*Or.* 902-911):—

κἀπὶ τῷδ' ἀνίσταται
ἀνήρ τις ἀθυρόγλωσσος, ἰσχύων θράσει,
Ἀργεῖος οὐκ Ἀργεῖος, ἠναγκασμένος,

---

[1] See Paley's note *ad loc.*, and his Preface to *Euripides*, vol. i. p. xviii. Cf.
also *Hec.* 1187 ff.; *Bacch.* 270-271 (with Paley's notes).
[2] Cf. *Tro.* 967; *Suppl.* 878-880; *Frag.* 597.

θορύβῳ τε πίσυνος κἀμαθεῖ παρρησίᾳ,
πιθανὸς ἔτ' αὐτοὺς περιβαλεῖν κακῷ τινι.
ὅταν γὰρ ἡδὺς τοῖς λόγοις, φρονῶν κακῶς,
πείθῃ τὸ πλῆθος, τῇ πόλει κακὸν μέγα·
ὅσοι δὲ σὺν νῷ χρηστὰ βουλεύουσ' ἀεί,
κἂν μὴ παραυτίκ', αὖθίς εἰσι χρήσιμοι
πόλει [1].

Then, as always, candidates for office were frequently humble
and fawning (*Iph. Aul.* 337–345):—

οἶσθ' ὅτ' ἐσπούδαζες ἄρχειν Δαναΐδαις πρὸς Ἴλιον,
τῷ δοκεῖν μὲν οὐχὶ χρῄζων, τῷ δὲ βούλεσθαι θέλων,
ὡς ταπεινὸς ἦσθα πάσης δεξιᾶς προσθιγγάνων,
καὶ θύρας ἔχων ἀκλῄστους τῷ θέλοντι δημοτῶν,
καὶ διδοὺς πρόσρησιν ἐξῆς πᾶσι, κεἰ μή τις θέλοι,
τοῖς τρόποις ζητῶν πρίασθαι τὸ φιλότιμον ἐκ μέσου,
κᾆτ' ἐπεὶ κατέσχες ἀρχάς, μεταβαλὼν ἄλλους τρόπους
τοῖς φίλοισιν οὐκέτ' ἦσθα τοῖς πρὶν ὡς πρόσθεν φίλος,
δυσπρόσιτος, ἔσω τε κλῄθρων σπάνιος.

It is the μέσοι πολῖται [2] who, in Euripides' opinion, are the
salvation of the state (*Suppl.* 238–245):—

τρεῖς γὰρ πολιτῶν μερίδες· οἱ μὲν ὄλβιοι
ἀνωφελεῖς τε πλειόνων τ' ἐρῶσ' ἀεί·
οἱ δ' οὐκ ἔχοντες καὶ σπανίζοντες βίου,
δεινοί, νέμοντες τῷ φθόνῳ πλεῖον μέρος,
ἐς τοὺς ἔχοντας κέντρ' ἀφιᾶσιν κακά,
γλώσσαις πονηρῶν προστατῶν φηλούμενοι·
τριῶν δὲ μοιρῶν ἡ 'ν μέσῳ σώζει πόλεις,
κόσμον φυλάσσουσ' ὅντιν' ἂν τάξῃ πόλις [3].

In one or two passages we have glimpses of a cosmopolitanism

---

[1] See Paley's note on l. 903; and cf. *Bacch.* 270–271; *Iph. Aul.* 526 (where
Odysseus is painted as a wily demagogue).

[2] I. e., moderates in politics as well as in wealth, position, &c.: cf. Arist.
Pol. iv. 11: Thuc. viii. 75. 1.   See Goodhart's *Thuc. VIII.* Introd. p. xvi: Paley,
Euripides, i. Pref. p. xvi: Gray and Hutchinson's note on *Her. Fur.* 588.   Cf.
also Decharme, *Euripide, &c.,* p. 181 :—' Dans le déchaînement de la violence des
partis, Euripide imagine donc un régime de juste équilibre et d'équitable
pondération; il appartient en politique à l'honnête famille des modérés.'

[3] Cf. *Or.* 920.

which remind us of the '*κόσμιος*' which was Socrates' answer when one asked him of what country he was [1].

In *Frag.* 777 we have these words:—

ὡς παιταχοῦ γε πατρὶς ἡ βόσκοισα γῆ:

and in *Frag.* 1047 these:—

ἅπας μὲν ἀὴρ ἀετῷ περάσιμος,
ἅπασα δὲ χθὼν ἀνδρὶ γενναίῳ πατρίς.

We have already seen (p. 98) that in the early history of Greece the individual hardly viewed himself apart from the state, and that it was not till decay and disintegration set in that individual citizens began to hold aloof from public life, and private interests became dominant. The Greek theory was that the state is everything, the individual nothing; and there is no thought so frequent in Demosthenes as this. He felt that, if only the Athenians could be persuaded to put once again into practice what even then they held in theory, Athens and Greece might yet be saved.— I will here adduce some passages from the Orators in illustration of this idea.

Andocides commends the sacrifice of personal feelings to the welfare of the state (*On the Mysteries*, § 81):—

ἐπειδὴ δ' ἐπανήλθετε ἐκ Πειραιέως, γενόμενον ἐφ' ὑμῖν τιμωρεῖσθαι ἔγνωτε ἐᾶν τὰ γεγενημένα, καὶ περὶ πλείονος ἐποιήσασθε σῴζειν τὴν πόλιν ἢ τὰς ἰδίας τιμωρίας [2].

It is a great virtue, he says elsewhere (*On his Return*, § 18), to benefit the state in any way whatever:—

μεγάλη γάρ ἐστιν ἀρετή, ὅστις τὴν ἑαυτοῦ πόλιν ὁτῳοῦν δύναται τρόπῳ ἀγαθόν τι ἐργάζεσθαι.

Self-sacrifice for the state is urged as a defence by Lysias (xxi. § 16):—

τοιοῦτον γὰρ ἐμαυτὸν τῇ πόλει παρέχω, ὥστ' ἰδίᾳ μὲν τῶν [ὄντων]

---

[1] Cf. Decharme, *Euripide, &c.*, p. 188:—'Il n'en est pas moins vrai qu'on rencontre chez lui, comme chez Socrate, les traces d'une sorte de cosmopolitisme qui alors était chose nouvelle : pareille chimère ne pouvait hanter qu'un grand esprit.'

[2] So Demosthenes says that a good citizen must stifle private hatred for the good of the state (*Prooem.* xii. § 1).

1

φείδομαι, δημοσίᾳ δὲ λειτουργῶν ἥδομαι, καὶ οὐκ ἐπὶ τοῖς περιοῦσι μέγα φρονῶ, ἀλλ᾽ ἐπὶ τοῖς εἰς ὑμᾶς ἀνηλωμένοις [1].

So Isocrates says (*Antid.* § 124):—

οὐ γὰρ τούτῳ προσεῖχε τὸν νοῦν, ὅπως ἐκ τῶν τοιούτων αὐτὸς εὐδοκιμήσει παρὰ τοῖς στρατιώταις, ἀλλ᾽ ὅπως ἡ πόλις παρὰ τοῖς Ἕλλησιν.

Demosthenes declares that country must rank even above parents (*On the Crown,* § 205):—

ἡγεῖτο γὰρ αὐτῶν ἕκαστος, οὐχὶ τῷ πατρὶ καὶ τῇ μητρὶ μόνον γεγενῆσθαι, ἀλλὰ καὶ τῇ πατρίδι [2].

He bewails the fact that old things have passed away, when the citizen looked to the splendour of the state alone (*Agst. Aristocrates,* § 206):—

καὶ γάρ τοι τότε τὰ μὲν τῆς πόλεως ἦν εὔπορα καὶ λαμπρὰ δημοσίᾳ, ἰδίᾳ δὲ οὐδεὶς ὑπερεῖχε τῶν πολλῶν.

The interests of the state, he says again, must be consulted, private interests forgotten (*Epist.* i. § 9):—

μεγαλοψύχως τοίνυν καὶ πολιτικῶς τὰ κοινῇ συμφέροντα πράττετε, καὶ τῶν ἰδίων μὴ μέμνησθε.

Similarly Lycurgus (*Agst. Leocrates,* § 67):—

τοῦτον μέντοι [ἡγοῦμαι] διὰ τοῦτο μείζονος τιμωρίας ἄξιον εἶναι τυχεῖν, ὅτι μόνος τῶν ἄλλων πολιτῶν οὐ κοινὴν ἀλλ᾽ ἰδίαν τὴν σωτηρίαν ἐζήτησεν [3].

There are in Lysias two passages illustrative of the discredit attaching to indifference to public business:—

οὑτοσὶ γάρ μοι δοκεῖ ὑπὸ ῥαθυμίας καὶ μαλακίας οὐδ᾽ εἰς Ἄρειον πάγον ἀναβεβηκέναι (x. § 11).

---

[1] Cf. vi. § 47; xv. § 10; xvi. § 13; xxvi. § 22; xxxi. § 6. It is, in fact, a commonplace with the Orators. Cf. Isaeus, vii. § 40; x. § 25: Demosthenes, *On the Chersonese,* §§ 70-72.

[2] In the speech *On the Embassy,* § 247, Demosthenes quotes from the *Antigone* of Sophocles a passage to the effect that everything is to be counted secondary to one's country. Cf. Plato, *Crito,* 50 D-51 C, especially 51 A-B :—ἢ οὕτως εἶ σοφός, ὥστε λέληθέν σε, ὅτι μητρός τε καὶ πατρὸς καὶ τῶν ἄλλων προγόνων ἁπάντων τιμιώτερόν ἐστιν ἡ πατρὶς καὶ σεμνότερον καὶ ἁγιώτερον καὶ ἐν μείζονι μοίρᾳ καὶ παρὰ θεοῖς καὶ παρ᾽ ἀνθρώποις τοῖς νοῦν ἔχουσι, κ.τ.λ. For the Greek idea of the state see Butcher, *Some Aspects of the Greek Genius,* pp. 46-82. See also above, p. 97, note 2.

[3] Cf. *ibid.* § 20.

ἤδη δέ τινων ἠσθόμην, ὦ βουλή, καὶ διὰ ταῦτα ἀχθομένων μοι,
ὅτι νεώτερος ὢν ἐπεχείρησα λέγειν ἐν τῷ δήμῳ. ἐγὼ δὲ τὸ μὲν
πρῶτον ἠναγκάσθην ὑπὲρ τῶν ἐμαυτοῦ πραγμάτων δημηγορῆσαι,
ἔπειτα μέντοι καὶ ἐμαυτῷ δοκῶ φιλοτιμότερον διατεθῆναι τοῦ δέοντος,
ἅμα μὲν τῶν προγόνων ἐνθυμούμενος, ὅτι οὐδὲν πέπαυται τῶν τῆς
πόλεως πράττοντες, ἅμα δὲ ὑμᾶς ὁρῶν (τὰ γὰρ ἀληθῆ χρὴ λέγειν)
τούτους μόνους ἀξίους νομίζοντας εἶναι. ὥστε ὁρῶν ὑμᾶς ταύτην τὴν
γνώμην ἔχοντας τίς οὐκ ἂν ἐπαρθείη πράττειν καὶ λέγειν ὑπὲρ τῆς
πόλεως ; (xvi. §§ 20-21).

It is, says Demosthenes (?), ridiculous to be wholly unin-
structed in the science which relates to practical and political
questions (*Erot.* § 44):—

νόμιζε δὲ πᾶσαν μὲν τὴν φιλοσοφίαν μεγάλα τοὺς χρωμένους
ὠφελεῖν, πολὺ δὲ μάλιστα τὴν περὶ τὰς πράξεις καὶ τοὺς πολιτικοὺς
λόγους ἐπιστήμην. τῆς γὰρ γεωμετρίας καὶ τῆς ἄλλης τῆς τοιαύτης
παιδείας ἀπείρως μὲν ἔχειν αἰσχρόν, ἄκρον δ' ἀγωνιστὴν γενέσθαι
ταπεινότερον τῆς σῆς ἀξίας· ἐν ἐκείνῃ δὲ τὸ μὲν διενεγκεῖν ζηλωτόν,
τὸ δ' ἄμοιρον γενέσθαι παντελῶς καταγέλαστον [1].

We have seen (p. 100) that Isocrates, like Euripides, held
aloof from public life, but he feels the necessity of apologising
for his action. It was due, he says, to a weak voice and lack
of confidence (*Phil.* §§ 81-82):—

καὶ μὴ θαυμάσῃς, ἅπερ ἐπέστειλα καὶ πρὸς Διονύσιον τὸν τὴν
τυραννίδα κτησάμενον, εἰ μήτε στρατηγὸς ὢν μήτε ῥήτωρ μήτ'
ἄλλως δυνάστης θρασύτερόν σοι διείλεγμαι τῶν ἄλλων. ἐγὼ γὰρ
πρὸς μὲν τὸ πολιτεύεσθαι πάντων ἀφιέστατος ἐγενόμην τῶν πολιτῶν,
οὔτε γὰρ φωνὴν ἔσχον ἱκανὴν οὔτε τόλμαν δυναμένην ὄχλῳ χρῆσθαι
καὶ μολύνεσθαι καὶ λοιδορεῖσθαι τοῖς ἐπὶ τοῦ βήματος καλινδου-
μένοις, τοῦ δὲ φρονεῖν εὖ καὶ πεπαιδεῦσθαι καλῶς, εἰ καί τις
ἀγροικότερον εἶναι φήσει τὸ ῥηθέν, ἀμφισβητῶ, καὶ θείην ἂν ἐμαυτὸν
οὐκ ἐν τοῖς ἀπολελειμμένοις ἀλλ' ἐν τοῖς προέχουσι τῶν ἄλλων.
διόπερ ἐπιχειρῶ συμβουλεύειν τὸν τρόπον τοῦτον, ὃν ἐγὼ πέφυκα
καὶ δύναμαι, καὶ τῇ πόλει καὶ τοῖς Ἕλλησι καὶ τῶν ἀνδρῶν τοῖς
ἐνδοξοτάτοις [2].

---

[1] See the whole passage '§§ 44-50).
[2] He employs almost the same language in *Epist.* viii. § 7.

The love of country and horror of exile which were illustrated from Euripides are no less prominent in the Orators.

Antiphon thus enumerates what men value most highly (περὶ τοῦ χορευτοῦ, § 4):—

ἀνάγκη γάρ, ἐὰν ὑμεῖς καταψηφίσησθε, καὶ μὴ ὄντα φονέα μηδὲ ἔνοχον τῷ ἔργῳ χρήσασθαι τῇ δίκῃ, καὶ νόμῳ εἴργεσθαι πόλεως ἱερῶν ἀγώνων θυσιῶν, ἅπερ μέγιστα καὶ παλαιότατα τοῖς ἀνθρώποις [1].

It is a great crime to betray one's country (περὶ τοῦ Ἡρῴδου φόνου, § 10):—

φασὶ δὲ αὐτό γε ⟨τὸ⟩ ἀποκτείνειν μέγα κακούργημα εἶναι, καὶ ἐγὼ ὁμολογῶ μέγιστόν γε, καὶ τὸ ἱεροσυλεῖν καὶ τὸ προδιδόναι τὴν πόλιν.

He seeks in one place to arouse pity by the picture of an old man in beggary and exile (Τετρ. Α. β. § 9):—

ἐὰν δὲ νῦν καταληφθεὶς ἀποθάνω, ἀνόσια ὀνείδη τοῖς παισὶν ὑπολείψω, ἢ φυγὼν γέρων καὶ ἄπολις ὢν ἐπὶ ξενίας πτωχεύσω.

Andocides declares that he would rather live at Athens than in any other country, even though there he might enjoy every blessing (*On the Mysteries*, § 5):—

ἄλλοθί τε γὰρ ὢν πάντα τὰ ἀγαθὰ ἔχειν στερόμενος τῆς πατρίδος οὐκ ἂν δεξαίμην.

Better death, he says, than exile (*On his Return*, § 10):—

ἔγνων λυσιτελεῖν μοι ἢ τοῦ βίου ἀπηλλάχθαι, ἢ τὴν πόλιν ταύτην ἀγαθόν τι τοσοῦτον ἐργάσασθαι, ὥστε ὑμῶν ἑκόντων εἶναί ποτέ μοι πολιτεύσασθαι μεθ' ὑμῶν.

To the same effect Lysias (*Epitaph.* § 62):—

. . . . μᾶλλον βουληθέντες ἐν τῇ αὑτῶν ἀποθνήσκειν ἢ ζῆν τὴν ἀλλοτρίαν οἰκοῦντες [2].

Death for one's country, he says elsewhere, is better than a life of shame (xxi. § 24):—

οὐδ' εἴ ποτε κινδυνεύσειν ἐν ταῖς ναυμαχίαις μέλλοιμι, οὐδεπώποτ'

---

[1] Cf. περὶ τοῦ Ἡρῴδου φόνου, § 62.   [2] Cf. vii. § 25.

ἠλέησα οὐδ᾽ ἐδάκρυσα οὐδ᾽ ἐμνήσθην γυναικὸς οὐδὲ παίδων τῶν
ἐμαυτοῦ, οὐδ᾽ ἡγούμην δεινὸν εἶναι εἰ τελευτήσας ὑπὲρ τῆς πατρίδος
τὸν βίον ὀρφανοὺς καὶ πατρὸς ἀπεστερημένους αὐτοὺς καταλείψω,
ἀλλὰ πολὺ μᾶλλον εἰ σωθεὶς αἰσχρῶς ὀνείδη καὶ ἐμαυτῷ καὶ ἐκείνοις
περιάψω.

Isocrates asserts that a man should be patriotic (*Ad
Nicocl.* § 15):—

.... πρὸς δὲ τούτοις φιλάνθρωπον εἶναι δεῖ καὶ φιλόπολιν[1].

Country should be as dear as parents (*Phil.* § 32):—

Ἄργος μὲν γάρ ἐστί σοι πατρίς, ἧς δίκαιον τοσαύτην σε ποιεῖσθαι
πρόνοιαν, ὅσην περ τῶν γονέων τῶν σαυτοῦ.

He, too, declares that death is preferable to exile (*Archid.*
§ 25):—

εἰ δὲ μηδεὶς ἂν ὑμῶν ἀξιώσειε ζῆν ἀποστερούμενος τῆς πατρίδος,
κ.τ.λ.[2]

No man, Aeschines maintains, should set more store on
ἀλλοτρία εὔνοια than on his native land (*Agst. Ctesiphon,*
§ 46):—

ἀλλ᾽, οἶμαι, διὰ τὸ ξενικὸν εἶναι τὸν στέφανον καὶ ἡ καθιέρωσις
γίγνεται, ἵνα μηδεὶς ἀλλοτρίαν εὔνοιαν περὶ πλείονος ποιούμενος
τῆς πατρίδος χείρων γένηται τὴν ψυχήν.

In several other passages (*Epist.* ii. § 2 ; ix. § 2 ; xii. §§ 12 ff.)
Aeschines(?) speaks of the miseries of exile[3].

The feeling for country is well illustrated also in Demosthenes, *Agst. Eubulides,* § 70. The speaker beseeches his
judges not to make him an outcast (ἄπολις), and declares that,
rather than abandon his relatives, he will kill himself, that he
may at least be buried by them in his native land:—

.... πρότερον γὰρ ἢ προλιπεῖν τούτους, εἰ μὴ δυνατὸν ὑπ᾽ αὐτῶν
εἴη σωθῆναι, ἀποκτείναιμ᾽ ἂν ἐμαυτόν, ὥστ᾽ ἐν τῇ πατρίδι γ᾽ ὑπὸ
τούτων ταφῆναι.

[1] Cf. *Archid.* § 54.
[2] Cf. *Phil.* § 55 ; xvi. § 12.
[3] On ἀτιμία, which was 'une sorte d'exil à l'intérieur,' see Aeschines, *Agst.
Timarchus,* § 21 : Andocides, *On the Mysteries,* §§ 73-80 : Coulanges, *La Cité
Antique,* p. 232.

In *Epist.* ii. § 25, Demosthenes speaks of the πατρίδος πόθος he has in exile, and (§ 20) says he has changed his abode in order that, among other things, he may every day be able to see his native land:—

.... μετελθὼν εἰς τὸ τοῦ Ποσειδῶνος ἱερὸν ἐν Καλαυρείᾳ κάθημαι, οὐ μόνον τῆς ἀσφαλείας ἕνεκα, ... ἀλλ᾿ ὅτι καὶ τὴν πατρίδ᾿ ἐντεῦθεν ἑκάστης ἡμέρας ἀφορῶ.

It is a glorious thing, says Demades (?), to sacrifice self for country, and bring about public εὔνοια by one's death (ὑπὲρ τῆς δωδεκαετίας, § 4):—

κτήσασθαι γὰρ ἰδίῳ θανάτῳ δημοσίαν εὔνοιαν καλόν, ἐὰν ἡ χρεία τῆς πατρίδος ... τὸ ζῆν ἀφαιρῆται.

Death is, according to Lycurgus, too slight a penalty for the traitor to his country (*Agst. Leocrates*, § 8):—

τί γὰρ χρὴ παθεῖν τὸν ἐκλιπόντα μὲν τὴν πατρίδα, μὴ βοηθήσαντα δὲ τοῖς πατρῴοις ἱεροῖς, ἐγκαταλιπόντα δὲ τὰς τῶν προγόνων θήκας, ἅπασαν δὲ τὴν πόλιν ὑποχείριον τοῖς πολεμίοις παραδόντα; τὸ μὲν γὰρ μέγιστον καὶ ἔσχατον τῶν τιμημάτων, θάνατος, ἀναγκαῖον μὲν ἐκ τῶν νόμων ἐπιτίμιον, ἔλαττον δὲ τῶν Λεωκράτους ἀδικημάτων καθέστηκε[1].

Lycurgus (*ibid.* § 113) quotes an interesting decree to the effect that a traitor to his country should not be buried in Attica:—

καὶ ψηφίζεται ὁ δῆμος Κριτίου εἰπόντος τὸν μὲν νεκρὸν (sc. Φρύνιχον) κρίνειν προδοσίας, κἂν δόξῃ προδότης ὢν ἐν τῇ χώρᾳ τεθάφθαι, τά τε ὀστᾶ αὐτοῦ ἀνορύξαι καὶ ἐξορίσαι ἔξω τῆς ᾿Αττικῆς, ὅπως ἂν μὴ κέηται ἐν τῇ χώρᾳ μηδὲ τὰ ὀστᾶ τοῦ τὴν χώραν καὶ τὴν πόλιν προδιδόντος.

He praises Euripides (*ibid.* § 100) for inculcating love of country (τὸ τὴν πατρίδα φιλεῖν) in the *Erechtheus*, and quotes a long passage from that play (*Frag.* 360) in illustration of his remarks. In § 103, he quotes Homer to the effect that it is glorious to die fighting for native land:—

οὐ οἱ ἀεικὲς ἀμυννομένῳ περὶ πάτρης
τεθνάμεν:

---

[1] Cf. *ibid.* §§ 5, 27.

and, in § 107, Tyrtaeus:—

> τεθνάμεναι γὰρ καλὸν ἐνὶ προμάχοισι πεσόντα
> ἄνδρ᾽ ἀγαθόν, περὶ ᾗ πατρίδι μαρνάμενον.

In his own words (§ 49):—

 εἰ δὲ δεῖ καὶ παραδοξότατον μὲν εἰπεῖν ἀληθὲς δέ, ἐκεῖνοι νικῶντες ἀπέθανον. τὰ γὰρ ἆθλα τοῦ πολέμου τοῖς ἀγαθοῖς ἀνδράσιν ἐστὶν ἐλευθερία καὶ ἀρετή· ταῦτα γὰρ ἀμφότερα τοῖς τελευτήσασιν ὑπάρχει.

The orators in whom we find most strongly expressed the Greek hatred of the barbarian are Isocrates and Demosthenes. The ruling idea of the life of the former was a war by united Greece against Persia, of the latter, against Philip.

Isocrates says (*Panegyr.* § 19):—

ἐμοὶ δ᾽ οὖν ἀμφοτέρων ἕνεκα προσήκει περὶ ταῦτα ποιήσασθαι τὴν πλείστην διατριβήν, μάλιστα μὲν ἵνα προὔργου τι γένηται καὶ παυσάμενοι τῆς πρὸς ἡμᾶς αὐτοὺς φιλονικίας κοινῇ τοῖς βαρβάροις πολεμήσωμεν, κ.τ.λ.

A united war against Persia is the only thing which will secure abiding peace in Greece (*ibid.* § 173):—

οὔτε γὰρ εἰρήνην οἷόν τε βεβαίαν ἀγαγεῖν, ἢν μὴ κοινῇ τοῖς βαρβάροις πολεμήσωμεν, κ.τ.λ. [1]

The Greeks are natural enemies of the barbarians (*ibid.* § 158):—

οὕτω δὲ φύσει πολεμικῶς πρὸς αὐτοὺς ἔχομεν [2], ὥστε καὶ τῶν μύθων ἥδιστα συνδιατρίβομεν τοῖς Τρωϊκοῖς [καὶ Περσικοῖς], δι᾽ ὧν ἔστι πυνθάνεσθαι τὰς ἐκείνων συμφοράς. κ.τ.λ.

So again (*Panath.* § 102):—

τὸ τοίνυν τελευταῖον, ὃ μόνοι καὶ καθ᾽ αὑτοὺς ἔπραξαν, τίς οὐκ οἶδεν, ὅτι κοινῆς ἡμῖν τῆς ἔχθρας ὑπαρχούσης τῆς πρὸς τοὺς βαρβάρους καὶ τοὺς βασιλέας αὐτῶν, ἡμεῖς μὲν ἐν πολέμοις πολλοῖς γιγνόμενοι καὶ μεγάλαις συμφοραῖς ἐνίοτε περιπίπτοντες καὶ τῆς χώρας ἡμῶν θαμὰ πορθουμένης καὶ τεμνομένης οὐδεπώποτ᾽ ἐβλέψαμεν πρὸς τὴν ἐκείνων φιλίαν καὶ συμμαχίαν, ἀλλ᾽ ὑπὲρ ὧν τοῖς Ἕλλησιν

[1] Cf. *Epist.* ix. § 9.
[2] Cf. *Panath.* § 163; *Antid.* § 293.

ἐπεβούλευσαν μισοῦντες αὐτοὺς διετελέσαμεν μᾶλλον ἢ τοὺς ἐν τῷ
παρόντι κακῶς ἡμᾶς ποιοῦντας.

The Persians are effeminate and cowardly (*Panegyr.* § 149):—

ὥστε μοι δοκοῦσιν ἐν ἅπασι τοῖς τόποις ἐπιδεδεῖχθαι τὴν αὐτῶν
μαλακίαν.

Similarly (*Phil.* § 137):—

. . . . καὶ τὴν τῶν βαρβάρων ἀνανδρίαν, κ.τ.λ. [1].

They are notorious for their impiety and sacrilege (*Panegyr.*
§§ 155-156):—

τί δ' οὐκ ἐχθρὸν αὐτοῖς ἐστὶ τῶν παρ' ἡμῖν, οἳ καὶ τὰ τῶν θεῶν ἕδη
καὶ τοὺς νεὼς συλᾶν ἐν τῷ προτέρῳ πολέμῳ καὶ κατακάειν ἐτόλ-
μησαν; διὸ καὶ τοὺς Ἴωνας ἄξιον ἐπαινεῖν, ὅτι τῶν ἐμπρησθέντων
ἱερῶν ἐπηράσαντ' εἴ τινες κινήσειαν ἢ πάλιν εἰς τἀρχαῖα καταστῆσαι
βουληθεῖεν, οὐκ ἀποροῦντες, πόθεν ἐπισκευάσωσιν, ἀλλ' ἵν' ὑπόμνημα
τοῖς ἐπιγιγνομένοις ᾖ τῆς τῶν βαρβάρων ἀσεβείας, καὶ μηδεὶς
πιστεύῃ τοῖς τοιαῦτ' εἰς τὰ τῶν θεῶν ἐξαμαρτεῖν τολμῶσιν, ἀλλὰ
καὶ φυλάττωνται καὶ δεδίωσιν, ὁρῶντες αὐτοὺς οὐ μόνον τοῖς σώμασιν
ἡμῶν ἀλλὰ καὶ τοῖς ἀναθήμασι πολεμήσαντας.

And there are numerous passages recalling Athens' glorious
deeds in the Persian Wars [2].

For Philip, whom Isocrates thought it possible to persuade
to lead Hellas against the barbarians [3], Demosthenes regards
even the name of barbarian as too good (*Phil.* iii. § 31):—

ἀλλ' οὐχ ὑπὲρ Φιλίππου καὶ ὧν ἐκεῖνος πράττει νῦν, οὐχ οὕτως
ἔχουσιν, οὐ μόνον οὐχ Ἕλληνος ὄντος οὐδὲ προσήκοντος οὐδὲν [τοῖς
Ἕλλησιν], ἀλλ' οὐδὲ βαρβάρων ἔντευθεν ὅθεν καλὸν εἰπεῖν, ἀλλ'
ὀλέθρου Μακεδόνος, ὅθεν οὐδ' ἀνδράποδον πρίαιτό τις ἄν ποτε [4].

Like tyrants, barbarians are regarded with distrust (*Phil.* iii.
§ 38):—

. . . . οὐδὲ τὴν πρὸς τοὺς τυράννους καὶ τοὺς βαρβάρους ἀπιστίαν,
κ.τ.λ.

---

[1] Cf. *Phil.* §§ 90, 124.
[2] See *Panegyr.* §§ 37, 68, 71, 157; *Phil.* § 139; *Archid.* §§ 42-43; *Panath.* §§ 42,
189-190.
[3] See Jebb, *Attic Orators*, ii. pp. 19 ff.   [4] Cf. *Phil.* i. § 10.

And the Greek contempt for barbarian effeminacy is brought out in another passage (*For the Liberty of the Rhodians*, § 23):—

εἶτ' οὐκ αἰσχρόν, ὦ ἄνδρες Ἀθηναῖοι, εἰ τὸ μὲν Ἀργείων πλῆθος οὐκ ἐφοβήθη τὴν Λακεδαιμονίων ἀρχὴν ἐν ἐκείνοις τοῖς καιροῖς οὐδὲ τὴν ῥώμην, ὑμεῖς δ' ὄντες Ἀθηναῖοι βάρβαρον ἄνθρωπον, καὶ ταῦτα γυναῖκα, φοβήσεσθε [1] ;

Aeschines uses the word βάρβαρος as a strong term of reproach and abuse (*On the Embassy*, § 183):—

.... ἡ τύχη, ἢ συνεκλήρωσέ με ἀνθρώπῳ συκοφάντῃ βαρβάρῳ, ὃς οὔτε ἱερῶν οὔτε σπονδῶν οὔτε τραπέζης φροντίσας, κ.τ.λ.

And he tells the Athenians it is a glorious thing to fight against the barbarians, and give freedom to the Greeks (*Epist.* xi. § 6):—

οὐ γὰρ ἠγνόουν, μὰ τὸν Δία καὶ τοὺς ἄλλους θεούς, ὅτι λαμπρόν ἐστι τὸ τοῖς μὲν βαρβάροις πολεμεῖν, τοὺς δὲ Ἕλληνας ἐλευθεροῦν, καὶ ταῦτά γε καὶ τοὺς πατέρας ἡμῶν προελομένους· κ.τ.λ.

'Barbarian impiety' we find in an oath given in Lycurgus (*Agst. Leocrates*, § 81):—

.... καὶ τῶν ἱερῶν τῶν ἐμπρησθέντων καὶ καταβληθέντων ὑπὸ τῶν βαρβάρων οὐδὲν ἀνοικοδομήσω παντάπασιν, ἀλλ' ὑπόμνημα τοῖς ἐπιγινομένοις ἔασω καταλείπεσθαι τῆς τῶν βαρβάρων ἀσεβείας [2].

The praise of Athens is no less frequently sounded by the Orators than it is by Euripides.

Andocides reminds his hearers that at Marathon Athens stood forward as the champion of Hellas, and won salvation for her country (*On the Mysteries*, § 107):—

.... ἠξίουν σφᾶς αὐτοὺς προτάξαντες πρὸ τῶν Ἑλλήνων ἁπάντων ἀπαντῆσαι τοῖς βαρβάροις Μαραθῶνάδε .... μαχεσάμενοί τε ἐνίκων, καὶ τήν τε Ἑλλάδα ἠλευθέρωσαν καὶ τὴν πατρίδα ἔσωσαν.

---

[1] Cf. *Olynth.* iii. § 24 ; *On the Embassy*, § 305 ; *Agst. Midias*, § 106 ; *Agst. Stephanus*, i. § 30.

[2] Cf. Isocrates, *Panegyr.* §§ 155-156 (quoted above, p. 120).

Lysias speaks to the same effect (*Epitaph.* § 20):—

μόνοι γὰρ ὑπὲρ ἁπάσης τῆς Ἑλλάδος πρὸς πολλὰς μυριάδας τῶν βαρβάρων διεκινδύνευσαν [1].

Isocrates, speaking of Athens as the saviour of Hellas from Persia, says (*Panath.* § 52):—

τίς δ᾽ ἂν εὐεργεσίαν εἰπεῖν ἔχοι ταύτης μείζω τῆς ἅπασαν τὴν Ἑλλάδα σῶσαι δυνηθείσης ;

Aeschines (?) speaks of Themistocles as the liberator of Greece (*Epist.* iii. § 2):—

. . . . ἐξ ἧς πόλεως ὁ Θεμιστοκλῆς ὁ τὴν Ἑλλάδα ἐλευθερώσας ἐξηλάθη, κ.τ.λ.

Demosthenes is continually recurring to the former glory of Athens, and recalling the time when she saved Hellas. One passage may be quoted (*Agst. Androtion,* § 13):—

. . . . ἴστε δήπου τοῦτο ἀκοῇ, ὅτι τὴν πόλιν ἐκλιπόντες καὶ κατακλεισθέντες εἰς Σαλαμῖνα, ἐκ τοῦ τριήρεις ἔχειν πάντα μὲν τὰ σφέτερα αὐτῶν καὶ τὴν πόλιν, τῇ ναυμαχίᾳ νικήσαντες, ἔσωσαν, πολλῶν δὲ καὶ μεγάλων ἀγαθῶν τοῖς ἄλλοις Ἕλλησι κατέστησαν αἴτιοι, ὧν οὐδ᾽ ὁ χρόνος τὴν μνήμην ἀφελέσθαι δύναται.

And so Lycurgus (*Agst. Leocrates,* § 70):—

ἐγκαταλειπόμενοι δὲ οἱ πρόγονοι ὑπὸ πάντων τῶν Ἑλλήνων βίᾳ καὶ τοὺς ἄλλους ἠλευθέρωσαν, ἀναγκάσαντες ἐν Σαλαμῖνι μετ᾽ αὐτῶν πρὸς τοὺς βαρβάρους ναυμαχεῖν [2].

Athens is free and the champion of freedom:—

. . . . ὑμεῖς δ᾽ ὅμως καὶ οὕτω διακείμενοι ἐθορυβεῖτε ὡς οὐ ποιήσοντες ταῦτα· ἐγιγνώσκετε γὰρ ὅτι περὶ δουλείας καὶ ἐλευθερίας ἐν ἐκείνῃ τῇ ἡμέρᾳ ἐξεκλησιάζετε (Lysias, xii. § 73).

οἱ δ᾽ Ἀθηναῖοι, τῆς ἐλευθερωτάτης πόλεως, πρέσβεις ταχθέντες, κ.τ.λ. (Demosthenes, *On the Embassy,* § 69) [3].

---

[1] See the whole passage there.

[2] Cf. Andocides, *On the Mysteries,* § 142 ; *On the Peace with Sparta,* § 5 : Lysias, *Epitaph. passim*: Isocrates, *Panegyr.* §§ 52, 83 ; *Phil.* §§ 129, 147 ; *Archid.* § 83 ; *Areop.* §§ 51-52 ; *De Pace,* § 42 ; *Plat.* § 60 ; xvi. § 27 : Demosthenes, *On the Symmories,* §§ 29-30 ; *On the Crown,* §§ 204, 208 ; *On the Embassy,* § 312 ; *Agst. Aristocrates,* § 124 ; *Epist.* iv. § 9 ; *Epitaph.* § 10 : Hyperides, *Epitaph.* v-vii : Lycurgus, *Agst. Leocrates,* §§ 50, 82, 104.

[3] Cf. Lysias, *Epitaph.* §§ 19, 20, 33 ; *Olymp.* § 6 ; *On the Constitution,* §§ 10-11 :

There are in the Orators a few passages which may be compared with the famous eulogy of Athens (*Med.* 824-845: see above, p. 105), in which Euripides declares that it is the home of wisdom and of the muses.

Athens, says Isocrates, is a perpetual πανήγυρις (*Panegyr.* § 46):—

χωρὶς δὲ τούτων αἱ μὲν ἄλλαι πανηγύρεις διὰ πολλοῦ χρόνου συλλεγεῖσαι ταχέως διελύθησαν, ἡ δ' ἡμετέρα πόλις ἅπαντα τὸν αἰῶνα τοῖς ἀφικνουμένοις πανήγυρίς ἐστιν.

It is the school of Hellas (*Antid.* § 295):—

χρὴ γὰρ μηδὲ τοῦτο λανθάνειν ὑμᾶς, ὅτι πάντων τῶν δυναμένων λέγειν ἢ παιδεύειν ἡ πόλις ἡμῶν δοκεῖ γεγενῆσθαι διδάσκαλος, κ.τ.λ.

Demosthenes (?) speaks of Athens as celebrated in prose and poetry (*Epitaph.* § 9):—

τῶν μὲν οὖν εἰς μύθους ἀνενηνεγμένων ἔργων πολλὰ παραλιπὼν τούτων ἐπεμνήσθην, ὧν οὕτως ἕκαστον εὐσχήμονας καὶ πολλοὺς ἔχει λόγους, ὥστε καὶ τοὺς ἐμμέτρους καὶ τοὺς τῶν ᾀδομένων ποιητὰς καὶ πολλοὺς τῶν συγγραφέων ὑποθέσεις τἀκείνων ἔργα τῆς αὑτῶν μουσικῆς πεποιῆσθαι.

Athens stands preeminent in understanding and education (*Epist.* iii. § 11):—

θαυμάζω δ' εἰ μηδεὶς ὑμῶν ἐννοεῖ, ὅτι τῶν αἰσχρῶν ἐστι τὸν δῆμον τὸν Ἀθηναίων, συνέσει καὶ παιδείᾳ πάντων προέχειν δοκοῦντα, ὃς καὶ τοῖς ἀτυχήσασιν ἀεὶ κοινὴν ἔχει καταφυγήν, ἀγνωμονέστερον φαίνεσθαι Φιλίππου, κ.τ.λ.

Aeschines testifies to the political wisdom of Athens (*On the Embassy*, § 176):—

πάλιν δὲ σωφρόνως πολιτευθέντες, καὶ τοῦ δήμου κατελθόντος ἀπὸ Φυλῆς, Ἀρχίνου καὶ Θρασυβούλου προστάντων τοῦ δήμου καὶ τὸ μὴ μνησικακεῖν πρὸς ἀλλήλους ἔνορκον ἡμῖν καταστησάντων, ὅθεν σοφωτάτην πάντες τὴν πόλιν ἡγήσαντο εἶναι, κ.τ.λ.[1]

Demosthenes, *On the Crown*, §§ 68, 72, 99, 100, 183, 204-205; *On the Chersonese*, §§ 42, 49, 60; *On the Symmories*, § 6; *Epist.* i. § 16, ii. § 5. See also preceding note.

[1] In another passage (*ibid.* § 104) Aeschines speaks of foresight as a characteristic of all Hellenes:—ἅπαντες δὲ οἱ Ἕλληνες πρὸς τὸ μέλλον ἔσεσθαι βλέπουσιν.

And Demosthenes also speaks of the reputation of Athens in this respect (*Agst. Aristocrates,* § 109):—

εἶτ' Ὀλύνθιοι μὲν ἴσασι τὸ μέλλον προορᾶν, ὑμεῖς δὲ ὄντες Ἀθηναῖοι ταὐτὸ τοῦτ' οὐχὶ ποιήσετε ; ἀλλ' αἰσχρὸν τοὺς τῷ περὶ πραγμάτων ἐπίστασθαι βουλεύσασθαι δοκοῦντας προέχειν ἧττον Ὀλυνθίων τὸ συμφέρον εἰδότας ὀφθῆναι.

The piety and justice of Athens are also favourite themes with the Orators.

Isocrates speaks of the city as dear to the gods (*Panegyr.* § 29):—

... οὕτως ἡ πόλις ἡμῶν οὐ μόνον θεοφιλῶς ἀλλὰ καὶ φιλανθρώπως ἔσχεν, κ.τ.λ.

It is preeminent both in arts and in piety (*ibid.* § 33):—

οὐ τοὺς ὑπὸ πάντων ὁμολογουμένως καὶ πρώτους γενομένους καὶ πρός τε τὰς τέχνας εὐφυεστάτους ὄντας καὶ πρὸς τὰ τῶν θεῶν εὐσεβέστατα διακειμένους ;

Its piety and justice are again mentioned in a eulogy of Athens (*Panath.* §§ 124-125):—

οὕτω γὰρ ὁσίως καὶ καλῶς καὶ τὰ περὶ τὴν πόλιν καὶ τὰ περὶ σφᾶς αὐτοὺς διῴκησαν, ὥσπερ προσῆκον ἦν τοὺς ἀπὸ θεῶν μὲν γεγονότας, πρώτους δὲ καὶ πόλιν οἰκήσαντας καὶ νόμοις χρησαμένους, ἅπαντα δὲ τὸν χρόνον ἠσκηκότας εὐσέβειαν μὲν περὶ τοὺς θεούς, δικαιοσύνην δὲ περὶ τοὺς ἀνθρώπους, ὄντας δὲ μήτε μιγάδας μήτ' ἐπήλυδας ἀλλὰ μόνους αὐτόχθονας τῶν Ἑλλήνων, καὶ ταύτην ἔχοντας τὴν χώραν τροφόν, ἐξ ἧσπερ ἔφυσαν, καὶ στέργοντας αὐτὴν ὁμοίως ὥσπερ οἱ βέλτιστοι τοὺς πατέρας καὶ τὰς μητέρας τὰς αὐτῶν, πρὸς δὲ τούτοις οὕτω θεοφιλεῖς ὄντας, ὥσθ' ὃ δοκεῖ χαλεπώτατον εἶναι καὶ σπανιώτατον, εὑρεῖν τινὰς τῶν οἴκων τῶν τυραννικῶν καὶ βασιλικῶν ἐπὶ τέτταρας ἢ πέντε γενεὰς διαμείναντας, καὶ τοῦτο συμβῆναι μόνοις ἐκείνοις.

Demosthenes speaks of the glory and piety of Athens (*On the Crown,* § 1):—

... ὅπερ ἐστὶ μάλισθ' ὑπὲρ ὑμῶν καὶ τῆς ὑμετέρας εὐσεβείας τε καὶ δόξης, κ.τ.λ.

And so again (*Prooem.* liv.):—

καὶ δίκαιον ὦ ἄνδρες 'Αθηναῖοι καὶ καλὸν καὶ σπουδαῖον, ὅπερ ὑμεῖς εἰώθατε, καὶ ἡμᾶς προνοεῖν, ὅπως τὰ πρὸς τοὺς θεοὺς εὐσεβῶς ἕξει [1].

The Athenians love justice (*Prooem.* xxiv. § 4):—

ἡμῖν δὲ προσήκει .... σπουδάσαι δεῖξαι πᾶσιν ἀνθρώποις ὅτι καὶ πρότερον καὶ νῦν καὶ ἀεὶ ἡμεῖς μὲν τὰ δίκαια προαιρούμεθα πράττειν, κ.τ.λ. [2].

According to Lycurgus, the chief points in which the Athenians excel other men are piety, filial duty, patriotism (*Agst. Leucrates*, § 15):—

εὖ γὰρ ἴστε, ὦ 'Αθηναῖοι, ὅτι ᾧ πλεῖστον διαφέρετε τῶν ἄλλων ἀνθρώπων, τῷ πρός τε τοὺς θεοὺς εὐσεβῶς καὶ πρὸς τοὺς γονεῖς ὁσίως καὶ πρὸς τὴν πατρίδα φιλοτίμως ἔχειν, τούτων πλεῖστον ἀμελεῖν δόξειτ' ἄν, εἰ τὴν παρ' ὑμῶν οὗτος διαφύγοι τιμωρίαν.

Frequent allusion is made by the Orators to Athens' championship of the weak and the wronged. It is a policy which she sometimes pursues even to her own detriment.

Andocides calls this policy τὸ εἰθισμένον κακόν (*On the Peace with Sparta*, § 28):—

ἐγὼ μὲν οὖν ἐκεῖνο δέδοικα μάλιστα, ὦ 'Αθηναῖοι, τὸ εἰθισμένον κακόν, ὅτι τοὺς κρείττους φίλους ἀφιέντες ἀεὶ τοὺς ἥττους αἱρούμεθα, καὶ πόλεμον ποιούμεθα δι' ἑτέρους, ἐξὸν δι' ἡμᾶς αὐτοὺς εἰρήνην ἄγειν [3].

Lysias instances the case of the Heraclidae [4] (*Epitaph.* § 12):—

.... ἐξαιτουμένου δὲ αὐτοὺς Εὐρυσθέως 'Αθηναῖοι οὐκ ἠθέλησαν ἐκδοῦναι, ἀλλὰ τὴν 'Ηρακλέους ἀρετὴν μᾶλλον ᾐδοῦντο ἢ τὸν κίνδυνον τὸν ἑαυτῶν ἐφοβοῦντο, καὶ ἠξίουν ὑπὲρ τῶν ἀσθενεστέρων μετὰ τοῦ δικαίου διαμάχεσθαι μᾶλλον ἢ τοῖς δυναμένοις χαριζόμενοι τοὺς ὑπ' ἐκείνων ἀδικουμένους ἐκδοῦναι [5].

---

[1] Cf *Agst. Midias*, § 12; *Agst. Neaera*, § 76.
[2] Cf. *On the Embassy*, § 272; *Lept.* § 142; *Prooem.* xxxiii. § 2.
[3] In the sections which follow he quotes examples from Athenian history. See also *ibid.* § 13.
[4] Cf. Euripides, *Herad.*
[5] Cf. *ibid.* §§ 7-9, 16, 22.

Similarly Isocrates (*Panegyr.* § 52):—

.... ἄπαντα γὰρ τὸν χρόνον διετέλεσαν κοινὴν τὴν πόλιν παρέχοντες καὶ τοῖς ἀδικουμένοις ἀεὶ τῶν Ἑλλήνων ἐπαμύνουσαν [1].

Athens, says Aeschines, is the common refuge of the Hellenes (*Agst. Ctesiphon*, § 134):—

ἡ δὲ ἡμετέρα πόλις, ἡ κοινὴ καταφυγὴ τῶν Ἑλλήνων, κ.τ.λ.

Demosthenes speaks of Athens as having the reputation of always ensuring the safety of the unfortunate (*For the Liberty of the Rhodians*, § 22):—

οὐ γὰρ ἂν ὑμᾶς βουλοίμην, δόξαν ἔχοντας τοῦ σῴζειν τοὺς ἀτυχήσαντας ἀεί, χείρους Ἀργείων ἐν ταύτῃ τῇ πράξει φανῆναι [2].

According to Hyperides, Athens punishes the wicked and protects the just (*Epitaph.* iii):—

.... οὕτως καὶ ἡ πόλις ἡμῶν διατελεῖ τοὺς μὲν κακοὺς κολάζουσα, τοὺς δὲ δικαίους ῥυομένη, τὸ δὲ ἴσον ἀντὶ τῆς πλεονεξίας ἅπασιν φυλάττουσα, τοῖς δὲ ἰδίοις κινδύνοις καὶ δαπάναις κοινὴν ἄδειαν τοῖς Ἕλλησιν παρασκευάζουσα [3].

Παρρησία and ἰσηγορία are words frequently employed by the Orators. Demosthenes tells us that at Athens not only citizens but even foreigners and slaves enjoyed the privilege of παρρησία (*Phil.* iii. § 3):—

ὑμεῖς τὴν παρρησίαν ἐπὶ μὲν τῶν ἄλλων οὕτω κοινὴν οἴεσθε δεῖν εἶναι πᾶσι τοῖς ἐν τῇ πόλει, ὥστε καὶ τοῖς ξένοις καὶ τοῖς δούλοις αὐτῆς μεταδεδώκατε, κ.τ.λ.

And he speaks of the ἰσηγορία enjoyed by democracies (*For the Liberty of the Rhodians*, § 18):—

οὐ γὰρ ἔσθ' ὅπως [ὀλίγοι πολλοῖς καὶ] ζητοῦντες ἄρχειν τοῖς μετ' ἰσηγορίας ζῆν ᾑρημένοις εὖνοι γένοιντ' ἄν [4].

---

[1] In the following sections he instances several examples, the case of the Heraclidae among others. See also *ibid.* § 41; *Phil.* §§ 33-34; *Panath.* §§ 168 ff., 194; *Plat.* §§ 1, 52-53.

[2] Cf. *Olynth.* ii. § 24; *Crown*, § 186 (cases of Oedipus and of the Heraclidae); *Agst. Timocrates*, § 171 (ἦθος of Athens); *Agst. Aristocrates*, § 156; *Epitaph.* § 8.

[3] Cf. *For Euxenippus*, xliii, xlvii: Dinarchus, *Agst. Demosthenes*, § 39.

[4] Cf. Aeschines, *Agst. Timarchus*, §§ 172-173: Demosthenes, *Agst. Midias*, § 124; *Agst. Stephanus*, i. § 79; *Epitaph.* § 28 (where Theseus is said to have been the first to establish ἰσηγορία in Athens).

The following phrase is used by Demades(?) (ὑπὲρ τῆς δωδεκαετίας, § 43):—

ἄρρενα λόγου καὶ τοῦ τῶν Ἀθηναίων ὀνόματος ἀξίαν παρρησίαν.

In actual experience, however, it was sometimes difficult to obtain free speech. Μὴ θορυβεῖτε is a phrase of frequent recurrence. Demosthenes often craves παρρησία from his audience, and there are frequent appeals for a fair hearing.

For example, in the speech *On the Chersonese*, § 32, we have a parenthesis to this effect:—

καί μοι πρὸς θεῶν, ὅταν εἵνεκα τοῦ βελτίστου λέγω, ἔστω παρρησία.

And in one passage he says plainly, that not in all cases was παρρησία enjoyed at Athens (*Olynth.* iii. § 32):—

οὐδὲ γὰρ παρρησία περὶ πάντων ἀεὶ παρ' ὑμῖν ἐστιν, ἀλλ' ἔγωγ' ὅτι καὶ νῦν γέγονεν θαυμάζω.

Isocrates uses even stronger language (*De Pace*, § 14):—

ἐγὼ δ' οἶδα μέν, ὅτι πρόσαντές ἐστιν ἐναντιοῦσθαι ταῖς ὑμετέραις διανοίαις, καὶ ὅτι δημοκρατίας οὔσης οὐκ ἔστι παρρησία, πλὴν ἐνθάδε μὲν τοῖς ἀφρονεστάτοις καὶ μηδὲν ὑμῶν φροντίζουσιν, ἐν δὲ τῷ θεάτρῳ τοῖς κωμῳδοδιδασκάλοις[1].

I remarked in a former place (p. 106) that we should find that the boast that the Athenians were autochthonous was a commonplace with the Orators. I will here adduce a few passages in illustration.

Lysias (*Epitaph.* § 17) has these words:—

οὐ γὰρ ὥσπερ οἱ πολλοί, πανταχόθεν συνειλεγμένοι καὶ ἑτέρους ἐκβαλόντες τὴν ἀλλοτρίαν ᾤκησαν, ἀλλ' αὐτόχθονες ὄντες τὴν αὐτὴν ἐκέκτηντο καὶ μητέρα καὶ πατρίδα.

Isocrates employs almost the same language (*Panegyr.* §§ 24-25):—

ταύτην γὰρ οἰκοῦμεν οὐχ ἑτέρους ἐκβαλόντες οὐδ' ἐρήμην καταλαβόντες οὐδ' ἐκ πολλῶν ἐθνῶν μιγάδες συλλεγέντες, ἀλλ' οὕτω καλῶς καὶ γνησίως γεγόναμεν, ὥστ' ἐξ ἧσπερ ἔφυμεν, ταύτην ἔχοντες ἅπαντα τὸν χρόνον διατελοῦμεν, αὐτόχθονες ὄντες καὶ τῶν ὀνομάτων

---

[1] For some effects of παρρησία see Demades (?), ὑπὲρ τῆς δωδεκαετίας, § 8.

τοῖς αὐτοῖς οἷσπερ τοὺς οἰκειοτάτους τὴν πόλιν ἔχοντες προσειπεῖν·
μόνοις γὰρ ἡμῖν τῶν Ἑλλήνων τὴν αὐτὴν τροφὸν καὶ πατρίδα καὶ
μητέρα καλέσαι προσήκει [1].

Demosthenes speaks of the Athenians and the Arcadians
as the only Greeks who were αὐτόχθονες (*On the Embassy*,
§ 261):—

. . . . μόνοι γὰρ πάντων αὐτόχθονες ὑμεῖς ἐστε κἀκεῖνοι [2].

We find the boast also in Hyperides (*Epitaph.* iv):—

περὶ δὲ Ἀθηναίων ἀνδρῶν τοὺς λόγους ποιούμενον, οἷς ἡ κοινὴ
γένεσις αὐτόχθοσιν οὖσιν ἀνυπέρβλητον τὴν εὐγένειαν ἔχει, περίεργον
ἡγοῦμαι εἶναι ἰδίᾳ τὰ γένη ἐγκωμιάζειν:

and in Lycurgus (*Agst. Leocrates*, § 41):—

. . . . ὃς (sc. Ἀθηναῖος ὢν) πρότερον ἐπὶ τῷ αὐτόχθων εἶναι καὶ
ἐλεύθερος ἐσεμνύνετο.

The hatred of Sparta—the other side to the love of
Athens—is no less prominent in the Orators than in Euripides.
But, on the whole, they speak with less bitterness and
rancour than Euripides does. Athenian feelings against
Sparta were not, in the fourth century B.C., at the same white
heat as they had been during the Peloponnesian War. Other
things demanded their attention. Isocrates the theorist
dreamed of a war against Persia: Demosthenes had to face
the machinations of Philip.

Andocides speaks of Spartan treachery (*On the Peace with
Sparta*, § 2):—

. . . . εἰκότως ἂν ἐφοβούμεθα αὐτὸ διά τε τὴν ἀπειρίαν τοῦ ἔργου
διά τε τὴν ἐκείνων ἀπιστίαν.

Lysias, referring to Athenian jealousy of Sparta, says (xviii.
§ 15):—

. . . . καὶ τοῖς μὲν ἄλλοις Ἕλλησιν ὀργίζεσθε (Cobet's reading
for the MS. ὀργίζοισθε), εἴ τις Λακεδαιμονίους ὑμῶν περὶ πλείονος
ποιεῖται, ὑμεῖς δ᾽ αὐτοὶ φανήσεσθε πιστότερον πρὸς ἐκείνους ἢ πρὸς
ὑμᾶς αὐτοὺς διακείμενοι;

---

[1] Cf. *De Pace*, § 49; *Panath.* §§ 124-125.
[2] Cf. *Epitaph.* § 4.

In *Epitaph.* §§ 44-45, he contrasts the conduct of the Athenians with that of the Spartans in the Persian Wars. In *Olymp.* § 7, there is mingled praise and blame of Sparta.

Isocrates speaks of Spartan ἀργία and πλεονεξία (*Busiris*, § 20):—

εἰ μὲν γὰρ ἅπαντες μιμησαίμεθα τὴν Λακεδαιμονίων ἀργίαν καὶ πλεονεξίαν, εὐθὺς ἂν ἀπολοίμεθα καὶ διὰ τὴν ἔνδειαν τῶν καθ᾿ ἡμέραν καὶ διὰ τὸν πόλεμον τὸν πρὸς ἡμᾶς αὐτούς.

He blames the conduct of Sparta in her hegemony in no mild terms (*Panegyr.* § 113):—

... αὐτοὶ (sc. οἱ Λακεδαιμόνιοι) πλείους ἐν τρισὶ μησὶν ἀκρίτους ἀποκτείναντες ὧν ἡ πόλις ἐπὶ τῆς ἀρχῆς ἁπάσης ἔκρινεν.

And again (*ibid.* §§ 122-123):—

ὧν ἄξιον ἐνθυμηθέντας ἀγανακτῆσαι μὲν ἐπὶ τοῖς παροῦσι, ποθέσαι δὲ τὴν ἡγεμονίαν τὴν ἡμετέραν, μέμψασθαι δὲ Λακεδαιμονίοις, ὅτι τὴν μὲν ἀρχὴν εἰς τὸν πόλεμον κατέστησαν ὡς ἐλευθερώσοντες τοὺς Ἕλληνας, ἐπὶ δὲ τελευτῆς οὕτω πολλοὺς αὐτῶν ἐκδότους ἐποίησαν, καὶ τῆς μὲν ἡμετέρας πόλεως τοὺς Ἴωνας ἀπέστησαν, ἐξ ἧς ἀπῴκησαν καὶ δι᾿ ἣν πολλάκις ἐσώθησαν, τοῖς δὲ βαρβάροις αὐτοὺς ἐξέδοσαν, ὧν ἀκόντων τὴν χώραν ἔχουσι καὶ πρὸς οὓς οὐδὲ πώποτ᾿ ἐπαύσαντο πολεμοῦντες. ... οὐδεὶς γὰρ ἡμῶν οὕτως αἰκίζεται τοὺς οἰκέτας ὡς ἐκεῖνοι τοὺς ἐλευθέρους κολάζουσιν [1].

But, as the object of Isocrates was to effect the unity of Greece, he frequently has words of praise for Sparta.

He testifies to Spartan prowess (xvi. § 11):—

... καί φασι παρ᾿ ἐκείνου μαθεῖν Λακεδαιμονίους, ὡς χρὴ πολεμεῖν, οἳ καὶ τοὺς ἄλλους διδάσκειν τέχνην ἔχουσιν [2].

Again (*Epist.* ix. § 4):—

τίς δ᾿ ἂν ἠπόρησε, διεξιέναι βουληθεὶς τὴν ἀνδρίαν ὅλης τῆς πόλεως καὶ σωφροσύνην καὶ πολιτείαν τὴν ὑπὸ τῶν προγόνων τῶν ὑμετέρων συνταχθεῖσαν;

[1] See the whole passage (§§ 122-128); and Butcher, *Demosthenes*, p. 2. Cf. also, for similar passages, *De Pace*, §§ 96-101; *Areop.* § 7.

[2] Cf. *Epist.* ii. § 6; and for a discussion on Spartan education, prowess, virtues, &c. see the whole of the *Panath.* Most men's praise of Sparta, he says, is moderate (§ 41):—ἣν sc. Sparta) οἱ πολλοὶ μετρίως ἐπαινοῦσιν. For an anticipated contrast between the σωφροσύνη and πειθαρχία of Sparta and the ὀλιγωρίαι of Athens see § 111.

The Spartan polity is good (*Busiris*, § 17):—

> ... καὶ Λακεδαιμονίους μέρος τι τῶν ἐκεῖθεν (sc. the Egyptians) μιμουμένους ἄριστα διοικεῖν τὴν αὐτῶν πόλιν.

There was a strong rivalry, Isocrates tells us, between Athens and Sparta in the earliest times, but then it was περὶ καλλίστων (*Panegyr.* § 85). He would fain have the two cities to sink their differences and unite against Persia (*ibid.* §§ 187–189)[1]. He recalls the prowess of the Spartans at Thermopylae (*Archid.* §§ 99-100)[2]. Empire had made the Spartans too proud, and involved them in the same perils as it had the Athenians before them, but they had acquired that empire διὰ τὸ σωφρόνως ζῆν καὶ στρατιωτικῶς (*Areop.* § 7).

Aeschines, after paying a compliment to Spartan judges, and declaring that they, unlike the Athenians, have regard to a good life more than to words (*Agst. Timarchus*, §§ 179–181), seems to think an apology necessary (§ 182):—

> ἵνα δὲ μὴ δοκῶ Λακεδαιμονίους θεραπεύειν, καὶ τῶν ἡμετέρων προγόνων μνησθήσομαι.

From a phrase used by Demosthenes, we gather that he did not think φιλανθρωπία a Spartan characteristic (*For the Megalopolitans*, § 16):—

> ὀψὲ γὰρ ἂν φιλάνθρωποι γένοιντο.

The empire of Sparta was a tyranny (*Lept.* § 70):—

> ἡγοῦντο γὰρ οὐ μικρὰν τυραννίδα καὶ τοῦτον (sc. Conon), τὴν Λακεδαιμονίων ἀρχὴν καταλύσαντα, πεπαυκέναι.

Their behaviour to the Asiatic Greeks was shameful (*Agst. Aristocrates*, § 140):—

> πῶς γὰρ οὐκ αἰσχρὸν Λακεδαιμονίοις μὲν ἐγκαλεῖν ὅτι τοὺς μὲν Ἀσίαν οἰκοῦντας Ἕλληνας ἔγραψαν ἐξεῖναι δρᾶσαι πᾶν ὅ τι ἂν ἐθέλῃ βασιλεύς, κ.τ.λ.

---

[1] It was Athens and Sparta that first occurred to Isocrates as the possible leaders of the invasion of Asia; and hence 'he calls upon Athens and Sparta to forego their jealousies, and to take the joint leadership of an expedition to Asia' (Jebb, *Attic Orators*, ii. p. 18).

[2] For Spartan energy and endurance see *Archid.* § 56; and, for some advantages of the Spartan system of government, *ibid.* § 81. The whole of the *Archidamus* is interesting in connexion with Sparta.

There is one point, however, in which the Spartans contrast favourably with the Athenians,—that in Spartan politics the minority fall in and loyally support the decision arrived at (*Prooem.* xxxv)[1].

If Sparta is not always blamed, neither is Athens always praised.

Andocides tells the Athenians that they are suspicious and perverse (*On the Peace with Sparta*, § 35):—

ὑμεῖς γὰρ περὶ μὲν τῶν ἑτοίμων ὑμῖν ὑπονοεῖν εἰώθατε καὶ δυσχεραίνειν, τὰ δ' οὐκ ὄντα λογοποιεῖν ὡς ἔστιν ὑμῖν ἕτοιμα· κἂν μὲν πολεμεῖν δέῃ, τῆς εἰρήνης ἐπιθυμεῖτε, ἐὰν δέ τις ὑμῖν τὴν εἰρήνην πράττῃ, λογίζεσθε τὸν πόλεμον ὅσα ἀγαθὰ ὑμῖν κατειργάσατο.

Isocrates and Demosthenes frequently contrast the degenerate Athens of their own time with the Athens of former days.

Good men, says Isocrates, are oppressed: full licence is given to evildoers (*Antid.* § 164):—

οὕτω γὰρ ἡ πόλις ἐν τῷ παρόντι χαίρει τοὺς μὲν ἐπιεικεῖς πιέζουσα καὶ ταπεινοὺς ποιοῦσα, τοῖς δὲ πονηροῖς ἐξουσίαν διδοῦσα καὶ λέγειν καὶ ποιεῖν ὅ τι ἂν βουληθῶσιν. ὥστε Λυσίμαχος μὲν ὁ προῃρημένος ζῆν ἐκ τοῦ συκοφαντεῖν καὶ κακῶς ἀεί τινα ποιεῖν τῶν πολιτῶν κατηγορήσων ἡμῶν ἀναβέβηκεν, κ.τ.λ.

Athens lends a ready ear to calumny (*Epist.* ii. § 15):—

ῥᾳδίως πείθεται τοῖς διαβάλλουσιν.

In a fragment (iii (a'). 1) Isocrates compares Athens to ἑταῖραι.

In the *Antid.* §§ 316–319, he gives an account of the misgovernment at Athens after the death of Pericles.

The city is going from bad to worse (*Areop.* § 18):—

καίτοι πῶς χρὴ ταύτην τὴν πολιτείαν ἐπαινεῖν ἢ στέργειν τὴν τοσούτων μὲν κακῶν αἰτίαν πρότερον γενομένην, νῦν δὲ καθ' ἕκαστον τὸν ἐνιαυτὸν ἐπὶ τὸ χεῖρον φερομένην ;

The Athens of former days is eulogised (*ibid.* §§ 20–27).

---

[1] For a comparison of the Athenian with the Spartan and Theban governments see *Lept.* §§ 105-111.

There was a ὁμόνοια in ancient Athens which has ceased to exist (*Areop.* § 31).

The Athenian youth are degenerate (*ibid.* §§ 48–49).

Athens is not now regarded as she formerly was either by Greeks or by barbarians (*ibid.* §§ 79–81)[1].

Both the state and individuals, according to Aeschines, have degenerated (*Agst. Ctesiphon*, § 178):—

εἰ γάρ τις ὑμᾶς ἐρωτήσειε, πότερον ὑμῖν ἐνδοξοτέρα δοκεῖ ἡ πόλις ἡμῶν εἶναι ἐπὶ τῶν νυνὶ καιρῶν ἢ ἐπὶ τῶν προγόνων, ἅπαντες ἂν ὁμολογήσαιτε, ἐπὶ τῶν προγόνων. ἄνδρες δὲ πότερον τότε ἀμείνους ἦσαν ἢ νυνί; τότε μὲν διαφέροντες, νυνὶ δὲ πολλῷ καταδεέστεροι[2].

The Athenian δῆμος, says Demosthenes, is unstable and shifting as the sea (*On the Embassy*, §§ 135–136):—

... ἃ καὶ πρότερόν ποτ' εἶπον ἐγὼ πρὸς ὑμᾶς ἐν τῷ δήμῳ καὶ τούτων οὐδεὶς ἀντεῖπεν, ὡς ὁ μὲν δῆμός ἐστιν ἀσταθμητότατον πρᾶγμα τῶν πάντων καὶ ἀσυνθετώτατον, ὥσπερ θάλαττ' ἀκατάστατον, ὡς ἂν τύχῃ κινούμενον.

Demosthenes had a hard task to rouse his countrymen to individual and personal effort,—a thing which in his time they shirked on every possible occasion[3].

The Athenians, he says, are easily taught what is best, but slow to act (*For the Liberty of the Rhodians*, § 1):—

ἐγὼ δ' οὐδεπώποθ' ἡγησάμην χαλεπὸν τὸ διδάξαι τὰ βέλτισθ' ὑμᾶς, ἀλλὰ τὸ πεῖσαι πράττειν ταῦτα.

So again (*Agst. Aristocrates*, § 145):—

ὅτι, ὦ ἄνδρες Ἀθηναῖοι, πολλὰ γιγνώσκοντες ὀρθῶς ὑμεῖς οὐ διὰ τέλους αὐτοῖς χρῆσθε.

The δῆμος is easily deceived (*Lept.* § 3):—

διὰ τὸ ῥᾳδίως ἐξαπατᾶσθαι τὸν δῆμον.

In a passage where he contrasts the poverty of Aristides with the wealth and self-aggrandisement of those in office in his

---

[1] See the whole passage, §§ 71–84; and cf. *De Pace*, §§ 43–44, 75. For praise of ancestors see *Areop.* §§ 20 ff.

[2] Cf. *ibid.* § 154; *Epist.* xi. § 9.

[3] See the *Philippics* and *Olynthiacs*, *passim*.

own day, he says that then the δῆμος was master, whereas now it is the servant (*Agst. Aristocrates*, § 2c9):—

τότε μὲν γὰρ ὁ δῆμος ἦν δεσπότης τῶν πολιτευομένων, νῦν δ' ὑπηρέτης.

Athens does not now punish evildoers as she once did (*ibid.* § 204):—

οὐδὲ γὰρ δίκην ἔτι λαμβάνειν ἐθέλετε παρὰ τῶν ἀδικούντων, ἀλλὰ καὶ τοῦτ' ἐξελήλυθεν ἐκ τῆς πόλεως.

The Athenians are inferior in counsel, not only to their ancestors, but to all other men (*ibid.* § 211):—

ἀλλ' οὐ τοῦτ' ἐστι τὸ δεινόν, εἰ τῶν προγόνων, οἱ διενηνόχασιν ἁπάντων ἀρετῇ, χεῖρον βουλευόμεθα, ἀλλ' ὅτι καὶ πάντων ἀνθρώπων [1].

'Quantum mutatus ab illo,'—that describes the Athenian δῆμος in the time of the Orators.

Two only of the Orators resemble Euripides in not being party-politicians. These are Isaeus and Isocrates. Of the life of Isaeus practically nothing is known. He neither took nor pretended to take any part in political life. Isocrates, as we have seen, also held aloof from public life, and conjured up the dream of a victorious Pan-Hellenism [2]. Theoretically, however, he regarded democracy as the best form of government. The rest of the Orators were all party-politicians. Antiphon was an oligarch, and one of the leaders of the Four Hundred. Andocides, a democrat, played an important part at the time of the mutilation of the Hermae, and was lucky to escape with his life when the Four Hundred were in power. Lysias, though he always remained a μέτοικος, rendered valuable aid to the democracy at and after the time of the Thirty [3]. The others belonged either to the Macedonian or to the anti-Macedonian party.

---

[1] Cf. *Agst. Timocrates*, § 186; *Agst. Aristocrates*, §§ 145-147; *On the Trierarchic Crown*, §§ 21-22; *Prooem.* xiv. §§ 2-3. lv; *Epist.* iii. § 21.

[2] Cf. Perrot, *L'Eloquence, &c.*, p. 348.

[3] For the relation of Lysias to political life see Jebb, *Attic Orators*, i. p. 156. Cf. also *ibid.* ii. p. 2:—'As Antiphon breathes the spirit of the elder common-

I will not attempt, however, to illustrate their respective party-feelings by quotation. These feelings dominated their whole life and work. But it may be interesting to observe the way in which they regarded the various forms of government; to note which they thought best, and why; and to see what, in their view, constituted a country's salvation. It is an all-important question what sort of constitution a state shall have; for, in the words of Isocrates (*Areop.* § 14) the πολιτεία is the soul of the state:—ἔστι γὰρ ψυχὴ πόλεως οὐδὲν ἕτερον ἢ πολιτεία [1].

The polity which any man will favour is, according to Lysias, dependent on the principle of utility (xxv. § 8):—

πρῶτον μὲν οὖν ἐνθυμηθῆναι χρὴ ὅτι οὐδείς ἐστιν ἀνθρώπων φύσει οὔτε ὀλιγαρχικὸς οὔτε δημοκρατικός, ἀλλ᾽ ἥτις ἂν ἑκάστῳ πολιτεία συμφέρῃ, ταύτην προθυμεῖται καθιστάναι.

The evils incident to oligarchy will cause a revolution in favour of democracy, and *vice versa* (*ibid.* § 27):—

πᾶσι γὰρ ἤδη φανερόν ἐστιν ὅτι διὰ τοὺς μὲν ἀδίκως πολιτευομένους ἐν τῇ ὀλιγαρχίᾳ δημοκρατία [2] γίνεται, διὰ δὲ τοὺς ἐν τῇ δημοκρατίᾳ συκοφαντοῦντας ὀλιγαρχία δὶς κατέστη.

Aeschines, in enumerating the three forms of government, says that tyrannies and oligarchies are managed according to the individual tempers of the tyrant or oligarchs, democracies by existing laws (*Agst. Timarchus*, § 4):—

ὁμολογοῦνται γὰρ τρεῖς εἶναι πολιτεῖαι παρὰ πᾶσιν ἀνθρώποις, τυραννὶς καὶ ὀλιγαρχία καὶ δημοκρατία· διοικοῦνται δ᾽ αἱ μὲν τυραννίδες καὶ ὀλιγαρχίαι τοῖς τρόποις τῶν ἐφεστηκότων, αἱ δὲ πόλεις αἱ δημοκρατούμεναι τοῖς νόμοις τοῖς κειμένοις [3].

---

wealth, as Andokides is associated with the troubled politics of Athens in the second half of the Peloponnesian War, as Lysias expresses the ordinary citizen-life of the restored democracy, so Isokrates is distinctively the man of the decadence—an Athenian, still more a Greek, of the age of declining independence.'

[1] Cf. *Panath.* § 138, where almost the same words are employed.

[2] For the meaning of δημοκρατία as compared with our word ' democracy ' see Fowler, *The City-State of the Greeks and Romans*, pp. 162-163.

[3] He uses the same words, *Agst. Ctesiphon*, § 6.

Isocrates reminds Nicocles that in all governments attention must be paid to the many (*Ad Nicocl.* §§ 15-16):—

μελέτω σοι τοῦ πλήθους, καὶ περὶ παντὸς ποιοῦ κεχαρισμένως αὐτοῖς ἄρχειν, γιγνώσκων, ὅτι καὶ τῶν ὀλιγαρχιῶν καὶ τῶν ἄλλων πολιτειῶν αὗται πλεῖστον χρόνον διαμένουσιν, αἵτινες ἂν ἄριστα τὸ πλῆθος θεραπεύωσιν[1].

He goes on to enumerate the first and most important elements of a good polity:—

καλῶς δὲ δημαγωγήσεις, ἢν μήθ' ὑβρίζειν τὸν ὄχλον ἐᾷς μήθ' ὑβριζόμενον περιορᾷς, ἀλλὰ σκοπῇς, ὅπως οἱ βέλτιστοι μὲν τὰς τιμὰς ἕξουσιν, οἱ δ' ἄλλοι μηδὲν ἀδικήσονται· ταῦτα γὰρ στοιχεῖα πρῶτα καὶ μέγιστα χρηστῆς πολιτείας ἐστίν.

In the *Areop.* § 55, he gives us his idea of what the best polity should effect:—

ὧν οὐδὲν ἦν ἐπ' ἐκείνης τῆς βουλῆς· ἀπήλλαξε γὰρ τοὺς μὲν πένητας τῶν ἀποριῶν ταῖς ἐργασίαις καὶ ταῖς παρὰ τῶν ἐχόντων ὠφελείαις, τοὺς δὲ νεωτέρους τῶν ἀκολασιῶν τοῖς ἐπιτηδεύμασι καὶ ταῖς αὑτῶν ἐπιμελείαις, τοὺς δὲ πολιτευομένους τῶν πλεονεξιῶν ταῖς τιμωρίαις καὶ τῷ μὴ λανθάνειν τοὺς ἀδικοῦντας, τοὺς δὲ πρεσβυτέρους τῶν ἀθυμιῶν ταῖς τιμαῖς ταῖς πολιτικαῖς καὶ ταῖς παρὰ τῶν νεωτέρων θεραπείαις. καίτοι πῶς ἂν γένοιτο ταύτης πλείονος ἀξία πολιτεία, τῆς οὕτω καλῶς ἁπάντων τῶν πραγμάτων ἐπιμεληθείσης;

Democracy, Isocrates maintains, is a better form of government than oligarchy; and he compares the Athenian democracy with the oligarchy of the Thirty (*Areop.* § 62):—

τῶν τοίνυν ἄλλων πόλεων ταῖς ἐπιφανεστάταις καὶ μεγίσταις, ἢν ἐξετάζειν βουληθῶμεν, εὑρήσομεν τὰς δημοκρατίας μᾶλλον ἢ τὰς ὀλιγαρχίας συμφερούσας· ἐπεὶ καὶ τὴν ἡμετέραν πολιτείαν, ἣ πάντες ἐπιτιμῶσιν, ἢν παραβάλωμεν αὐτὴν μὴ πρὸς τὴν ὑπ' ἐμοῦ ῥηθεῖσαν ἀλλὰ πρὸς τὴν ὑπὸ τῶν τριάκοντα καταστᾶσαν, οὐδεὶς ὅστις οὐκ ἂν θεοποίητον εἶναι νομίσειεν[2].

---

[1] Cf. *Philippus*, § 79.

[2] For another comparison of the democracy with the Thirty see *ibid.* § 69. The advantages of a monarchy over an oligarchy or democracy are set forth in the *Nicocles*, §§ 14-26.

Of the best kind of democracy we have a description also in the *Areop.* §§ 26-27:—

ὡς δὲ συντόμως εἰπεῖν, ἐκεῖνοι διεγνωκότες ἦσαν, ὅτι δεῖ τὸν μὲν δῆμον ὥσπερ τύραννον καθιστάναι τὰς ἀρχὰς καὶ κολάζειν τοὺς ἐξαμαρτάνοντας καὶ κρίνειν περὶ τῶν ἀμφισβητουμένων, τοὺς δὲ σχολὴν ἄγειν δυναμένους καὶ βίον ἱκανὸν κεκτημένους ἐπιμελεῖσθαι τῶν κοινῶν ὥσπερ οἰκέτας, καὶ δικαίους μὲν γενομένους ἐπαινεῖσθαι καὶ στέργειν ταύτῃ τῇ τιμῇ, κακῶς δὲ διοικήσαντας μηδεμιᾶς συγγνώμης τυγχάνειν ἀλλὰ ταῖς μεγίσταις ζημίαις περιπίπτειν. καίτοι πῶς ἄν τις εὕροι ταύτης βεβαιοτέραν ἢ δικαιοτέραν δημοκρατίαν, τῆς τοὺς μὲν δυνατωτάτους ἐπὶ τὰς πράξεις καθιστάσης, αὐτῶν δὲ τούτων τὸν δῆμον κύριον ποιούσης[1];

Demosthenes speaks of the equality and justice which all men enjoy in a democracy (*Agst. Midias*, § 67):—

... ὅτι τῶν ἴσων καὶ τῶν δικαίων ἕκαστος ἡγεῖται ἑαυτῷ μετεῖναι ἐν δημοκρατίᾳ.

Democracy, he says elsewhere, is the form of government most unfavourable to men of infamous lives (*Agst. Androtion*, § 31):—

ᾔδει γάρ, ᾔδει τοῖς αἰσχρῶς βεβιωκόσιν ἁπασῶν οὖσαν ἐναντιωτάτην πολιτείαν ἐν ᾗ πᾶσιν ἔξεστι λέγειν κἀκείνων ὀνείδη. ἔστι δ' αὕτη τίς; δημοκρατία.

We have already seen (p. 135) how Isocrates regarded the actions of the Thirty. Similar passages are to be met with in Demosthenes. For example, in the speech *Agst. Timocrates*, § 163, he says:—

ἀλλὰ παρ' ἡμῖν πότε πώποτε δεινότατα ἐν τῇ πόλει γέγονεν; εὖ οἶδ' ὅτι ἐπὶ τῶν τριάκονθ' ἅπαντες ἂν εἴποιτε[2].

There is more clemency in a democracy (*Agst. Androtion*, § 51):—

εἰ γὰρ ἐθέλοιτ' ἐξετάσαι τίνος ἕνεκα μᾶλλον ἄν τις ἕλοιτο ἐν δημοκρατίᾳ ζῆν ἢ ἐν ὀλιγαρχίᾳ, τοῦτ' ἂν εὕροιτε προχειρότατον, ὅτι πάντα πραότερ' ἐστὶν ἐν δημοκρατίᾳ[3].

[1] Cf. *Panath.* §§ 130-131, where a good and a bad democracy are contrasted.
[2] Cf. *ibid.* §§ 56-57, 90.
[3] The same words are employed in the speech *Agst. Timocrates*, § 163. For a passage bearing on the greater honour and security attaching to favours

In an oligarchy there is no freedom of speech: one cannot criticise those in power (*ibid.* § 32):—

ἐν γὰρ ταῖς ὀλιγαρχίαις, οὐδ᾽ ἂν ὦσιν ἔτ᾽ Ἀνδροτίωνός τινες αἴσχιον βεβιωκότες, οὐκ ἔστι λέγειν κακῶς τοὺς ἄρχοντας.

An oligarchy is the foe of freedom (*For the Liberty of the Rhodians,* § 20):—

τοὺς δὲ τὰς πολιτείας καταλύοντας καὶ μεθιστάντας εἰς ὀλιγαρχίαν. κοινοὺς ἐχθροὺς παραινῶ νομίζειν πάντων τῶν ἐλευθερίας ἐπιθυμούντων[1].

The things on which the safety of a state depends are ὁμόνοια, σωφροσύνη, εὐκοσμία, observance of laws, oaths, and covenants.

If the laws are guarded, says Aeschines, the democracy is preserved (*Agst. Ctesiphon,* § 6):—

διόπερ καὶ ὁ νομοθέτης τοῦτο πρῶτον ἔταξεν ἐν τῷ τῶν δικαστῶν ὅρκῳ, "ψηφιοῦμαι κατὰ τοὺς νόμους," ἐκεῖνό γε εὖ εἰδώς, ὅτι, ὅταν διατηρηθῶσιν οἱ νόμοι τῇ πόλει, σώζεται καὶ ἡ δημοκρατία[2].

Similarly Lycurgus (*Agst. Leocrates,* §§ 3–4):—

τρία γάρ ἐστι τὰ μέγιστα, ἃ διαφυλάττει καὶ διασώζει τὴν δημοκρατίαν καὶ τὴν τῆς πόλεως εὐδαιμονίαν, πρῶτον μὲν ἡ τῶν νόμων τάξις, δεύτερον δ᾽ ἡ τῶν δικαστῶν ψῆφος, τρίτον δ᾽ ἡ τούτοις τἀδικήματα παραδιδοῦσα κρίσις.

In a democracy, says Hyperides, the laws must be κύριοι (*For Euxenippus,* xxi):—

... οὔτε πλείους οἶμαι δεῖν λόγους ποιεῖσθαι περὶ ἄλλου τινὸς ἢ ὅπως ἐν δημοκρατίᾳ κύριοι οἱ νόμοι ἔσονται, κ.τ.λ.

And, according to Lysias, the safeguard of a democracy is to abide by oaths and covenants (xxv. § 28):—

... πολλάκις ἤδη τῷ ὑμετέρῳ πλήθει διεκελεύσαντο τοῖς ὅρκοις καὶ ταῖς συνθήκαις ἐμμένειν, ἡγούμενοι ταύτην δημοκρατίας εἶναι φυλακήν.

shown by a democracy than to those coming from a tyranny or oligarchy see *Lept.* §§ 15-16.

[1] In the *Epitaph.* §§ 25-26, a contrast is drawn between oligarchy and democracy, all in favour of the latter.

[2] Cf. *ibid.* §§ 23, 196.

Conversely, as Demosthenes says, the δῆμος is the only sure safeguard of the laws (*Agst. Timocrates*, § 37):—

τίς οὖν μόνη φυλακὴ καὶ δικαία καὶ βέβαιος τῶν νόμων ; ὑμεῖς οἱ πολλοί· κ.τ.λ.

According to Aeschines, that city will be best governed where there is σωφροσύνη and εὐκοσμία (*Agst. Timarchus*, § 48):—

καὶ πόθεν ἄρχεται ; νόμοι, φησί, περὶ εὐκοσμίας. ἀπὸ σωφροσύνης πρῶτον ἤρξατο, ὡς, ὅπου πλείστη εὐκοσμία ἐστί, ταύτην ἄριστα τὴν πόλιν οἰκησομένην.

Ὁμόνοια, says Lysias, is the greatest blessing a state can enjoy ; στάσις is the root of all evil (xviii. § 17):—

νυνὶ δὲ πάντες ἂν ὁμολογήσαιτε ὁμόνοιαν μέγιστον ἀγαθὸν εἶναι πόλει, στάσιν δὲ πάντων κακῶν αἰτίαν, κ.τ.λ.

To the same effect Isocrates (xviii. § 44):—

καὶ μὴν οὐ δεῖ γ᾽ ὑμᾶς παρ᾽ ἑτέρων μαθεῖν, ὅσον ἐστὶν ὁμόνοια ἀγαθὸν ἢ στάσις κακόν [1].

Demosthenes reminds the Athenians that ὁμόνοια is an absolute necessity (*Epist.* i. § 5):—

δεῖ δ᾽ ὑμᾶς, ὦ ἄνδρες Ἀθηναῖοι, πρῶτον μὲν ἁπάντων πρὸς ὑμᾶς αὐτοὺς ὁμόνοιαν εἰς τὸ κοινῇ συμφέρον τῇ πόλει παρασχέσθαι, καὶ τὰς ἐκ τῶν προτέρων ἐκκλησιῶν ἀμφισβητήσεις ἐᾶσαι, δεύτερον δὲ πάντας ἐκ μιᾶς γνώμης τοῖς δόξασι προθύμως συναγωνίζεσθαι· ὡς τὸ μήθ᾽ ἐν μήθ᾽ ἁπλῶς πράττειν οὐ μόνον ἐστὶν ἀνάξιον ὑμῶν καὶ ἀγεννές, ἀλλὰ καὶ τοὺς μεγίστους κινδύνους ἔχει.

So Dinarchus (*Agst. Philocles*, § 19):—

... εἰδότας ὅτι μετὰ μὲν δικαιοσύνης καὶ τῆς πρὸς ἀλλήλους ὁμονοίας ῥᾳδίως ἀμυνούμεθα, θεῶν ἵλεων ὄντων, ἐάν τινες ἡμῖν ἀδίκως ἐπιτίθωνται, κ.τ.λ. [2]

Andocides, Isocrates, and Demosthenes are the orators who make the most frequent attacks upon tyrants,—Isocrates in a theorising, unimpassioned manner, Andocides and Demo-

---

[1] For Isocrates' opinion as to what constitutes the true safety of the state (δεῖν δὲ τοὺς ὀρθῶς πολιτευομένους . . . ἐν ταῖς ψυχαῖς ἔχειν τὸ δίκαιον) see *Areop.* §§ 39 ff.

[2] For Socrates' views on a citizen's duty see Plato, *Crito* (esp. cc. xi ff.).

sthenes with real feeling, the former as seeing a possible tyrant in every prominent oligarch, the latter with Philip always before him.

Andocides quotes an interesting law of Solon relating to the punishment of any man who should subvert the democracy and establish a tyranny (*On the Mysteries*, §§ 96–98):—

… ὁ δὲ ὅρκος ἔστω ὅδε· "κτενῶ καὶ λόγῳ καὶ ἔργῳ καὶ ψήφῳ καὶ τῇ ἐμαυτοῦ χειρί, ἂν δυνατὸς ὦ, ὃς ἂν καταλύσῃ τὴν δημοκρατίαν τὴν Ἀθήνησι, καὶ ἐάν τις ἄρξῃ τινὰ ἀρχὴν καταλελυμένης τῆς δημοκρατίας τὸ λοιπόν, καὶ ἐάν τις τυραννεῖν ἐπαναστῇ ἢ τὸν τύραννον συγκαταστήσῃ. καὶ ἐάν τις ἄλλος ἀποκτείνῃ, ὅσιον αὐτὸν νομιῶ εἶναι καὶ πρὸς θεῶν καὶ δαιμόνων, ὡς πολέμιον κτείναντα τὸν Ἀθηναίων, καὶ τὰ κτήματα τοῦ ἀποθανόντος πάντα ἀποδόμενος ἀποδώσω τὰ ἡμίσεα τῷ ἀποκτείναντι, καὶ οὐκ ἀποστερήσω οὐδέν. ἐὰν δέ τις κτείνων τινὰ τούτων ἀποθάνῃ ἢ ἐπιχειρῶν, εὖ ποιήσω αὐτόν τε καὶ τοὺς παῖδας τοὺς ἐκείνου καθάπερ Ἁρμόδιόν τε καὶ Ἀριστογείτονα καὶ τοὺς ἀπογόνους αὐτῶν. …"

Again he says (*ibid.* § 106):—

… γενομένων τῇ πόλει κακῶν μεγάλων, ὅτε οἱ τύραννοι μὲν εἶχον τὴν πόλιν, ὁ δὲ δῆμος ἔφευγε, κ.τ.λ.

The author of the speech *Agst. Alcibiades* says that discreet men should beware of over-prominent citizens, who often establish tyrannies (§ 24):—

ἔστι δὲ σωφρόνων ἀνδρῶν φυλάττεσθαι τῶν πολιτῶν τοὺς ὑπεραυξανομένους, ἐνθυμουμένους ὑπὸ τῶν τοιούτων τὰς τυραννίδας καθισταμένας.

People regard it as absurd that one man should have more power than the whole state (*ibid.* § 29):—

ὅσοι δὲ ἢ παρὰ τῶν πολιτῶν ἤκουον ἢ καὶ ἐπεγίγνωσκον τὰ τούτου, κατεγέλων ἡμῶν, ὁρῶντες ἕνα ἄνδρα μεῖζον ἁπάσης τῆς πόλεως δυνάμενον [1].

Distrust, say Demosthenes, is the right safeguard against tyrants (*Phil.* ii. § 24):—

ἐν δέ τι κοινὸν ἡ φύσις τῶν εὖ φρονούντων ἐν αὑτῇ κέκτηται

---

[1] Cf. Demosthenes, *On the Embassy*, § 296.

φυλακτήριον, ὃ πᾶσι μέν ἐστ' ἀγαθὸν καὶ σωτήριον, μάλιστα δὲ τοῖς πλήθεσιν πρὸς τοὺς τυράννους.   τί οὖν ἐστι τοῦτο ; ἀπιστία [1].

It is dangerous to associate too intimately with tyrants (*Phil.* ii. § 21):—

οὐ γὰρ ἀσφαλεῖς ταῖς πολιτείαις αἱ πρὸς τοὺς τυράννους αὗται λίαν ὁμιλίαι.

Kings and tyrants are foes to freedom and law (*ibid.* § 25):—

βασιλεὺς γὰρ καὶ τύραννος ἅπας ἐχθρὸν ἐλευθερίᾳ καὶ νόμοις ἐναντίον.

And in the speech *Agst. Aristocrates,* § 142, we see how tyrants were regarded at Athens:—

ἐν δὴ Λαμψάκῳ τινὲς ἄνθρωποι γίγνονται δύο . . . οἱ παραπλήσια τοῖς παρ' ἡμῖν γνόντες περὶ τῶν τυράννων ἀποκτιννύασι τὸν Φιλίσκον δικαίως, τὴν αὑτῶν πατρίδα οἰόμενοι δεῖν ἐλευθεροῦν [2].

But in one thing tyrannies are better than democracies—in swiftness of action (*On the Embassy,* §§ 184–186).

Ordinary citizens, says Isocrates (*Ad Nicocl.* §§ 2–6), have many things to teach them,—the absence of luxury, the laws, freedom of speech, liability to reproof from friends and attack from foes.   None of these advantages does the tyrant possess. He who most needs advisers gets no advice.   Most men shun him: those who do associate with him humour him.   Which life is better?   When men look to the honour, wealth, and power which a tyrant enjoys, they think his life like that of the gods; but, when they consider the perpetual terror in which he lives and the dangers to which he is exposed, and that, in order to escape death himself, he is frequently compelled to put to death his nearest friends, they come to think that even the humblest life is preferable [3].

The best safeguard for a tyrant is the virtue of his friends, the goodwill of his subjects, and his own prudence (*ibid.* § 21):—

φυλακὴν ἀσφαλεστάτην ἡγοῦ τοῦ σώματος εἶναι τήν τε τῶν φίλων

---

[1] Cf. *Olynth.* i. § 5; *Phil.* iii. § 38.
[2] Cf. the law quoted above, p. 139.
[3] Cf. *Hel.* §§ 32-34; *Epist.* vi. § 11: Euripides, *Ion,* 621-628 (quoted above, p. 108).

ἀρετὴν καὶ τὴν τῶν πολιτῶν εὔνοιαν καὶ τὴν σαυτοῦ φρόνησιν·
διὰ γὰρ τούτων καὶ κτᾶσθαι καὶ σώζειν τὰς τυραννίδας μάλιστ' ἂν
τις δύναιτο [1].

The tyrant's pleasure depends on other people's pain, and in
the end he must pay the penalty. There is a difference
between ἄρχειν and τυραννεῖν (*De Pace*, § 91):—

ὧν ἀμελήσαντες οἱ γενόμενοι μετ' ἐκείνους οὐκ ἄρχειν ἀλλὰ
τυραννεῖν ἐπεθύμησαν, ἃ δοκεῖ μὲν τὴν αὐτὴν ἔχειν δύναμιν, πλεῖστον
δ' ἀλλήλων κεχώρισται· τῶν μὲν γὰρ ἀρχόντων ἔργον ἐστὶ τοὺς
ἀρχομένους ταῖς αὑτῶν ἐπιμελείαις ποιεῖν εὐδαιμονεστέρους, τοῖς δὲ
τυράννοις ἔθος καθέστηκε τοῖς τῶν ἄλλων πόνοις καὶ κακοῖς αὑτοῖς
ἡδονὰς παρασκευάζειν. ἀνάγκη δὲ τοὺς τοιούτοις ἔργοις ἐπιχειροῦντας
τυραννικαῖς καὶ ταῖς συμφοραῖς περιπίπτειν, καὶ τοιαῦτα πάσχειν,
οἷά περ ἂν καὶ τοὺς ἄλλους δράσωσιν.

In the same speech (§ 143) he draws a contrast between king-
ship in Sparta and tyranny based on force:—

ἐκείνοις (sc. the Spartan kings) γὰρ ἀδικεῖν μὲν ἧττον ἔξεστιν ἢ
τοῖς ἰδιώταις, τοσούτῳ δὲ μακαριστότεροι τυγχάνουσιν ὄντες τῶν
βίᾳ τὰς τυραννίδας κατεχόντων, ὅσον οἱ μὲν τοὺς τοιούτους ἀποκτείναντες τὰς μεγίστας δωρεὰς παρὰ τῶν συμπολιτευομένων λαμ-
βάνουσιν, ὑπὲρ ἐκείνων δ' οἱ μὴ τολμῶντες ἐν ταῖς μάχαις
ἀποθνῄσκειν ἀτιμότεροι γίγνονται τῶν τὰς τάξεις λειπόντων καὶ τὰς
ἀσπίδας ἀποβαλλόντων [2].

But a good tyranny is possible (*Hel.* § 34):—

. . . ἐπέδειξεν (sc. ὁ Θησεύς), ὅτι ῥᾴδιόν ἐστιν ἅμα τυραννεῖν
καὶ μηδὲν χεῖρον διακεῖσθαι τῶν ἐξ ἴσου πολιτευομένων [3].

The Orators, however, see no less clearly than did Euripides
that the δῆμος is not immaculate. Some passages illustrating
this statement have been already referred to or quoted [4]. I
will here add a few more.

---

[1] Cf. *Ep st.* vii. §§ 3-5, where he tells Timotheus how a tyrant should live
and act.

[2] For the contrast between βασιλικῶς and τυραννικῶς see also *Phil.* § 154.

[3] Isocrates here contrasts Theseus with the ordinary tyrant. See the
whole passage (§§ 31-37); and cf. Euripides, *Frag.* 8 (quoted above, p. 109).

[4] See pp. 131-133.

In Isocrates we are told that the many prefer those who please to those who benefit (*Antid.* § 133):—

"ὁρᾷς δὲ τὴν φύσιν τὴν τῶν πολλῶν ὡς διάκειται πρὸς τὰς ἡδονάς, καὶ διότι μᾶλλον φιλοῦσι τοὺς πρὸς χάριν ὁμιλοῦντας ἢ τοὺς εὖ ποιοῦντας, καὶ τοὺς μετὰ φαιδρότητος καὶ φιλανθρωπίας φενακίζοντας ἢ τοὺς μετ᾽ ὄγκου καὶ σεμνότητος ὠφελοῦντας. . . ."

The δῆμος, says Aeschines, loves flattery (*Agst. Ctesiphon,* § 234):—

ἔχαιρε γὰρ (sc. ὁ δῆμος) κολακευόμενος.

Athens treated her benefactors badly (*Epist.* iii. § 2):—

οὐ γὰρ οὕτως ἔγωγε ἠλίθιός εἰμι, ὥστε, ἐξ ἧς πόλεως ὁ Θεμιστοκλῆς ὁ τὴν Ἑλλάδα ἐλευθερώσας ἐξηλάθη, καὶ ὅπου Μιλτιάδης, ὅτι μικρὸν ὦφλε τῷ δημοσίῳ, γέρων ἐν τῷ δεσμωτηρίῳ ἀπέθανε, ταύτῃ τῇ πόλει Αἰσχίνην τὸν Ἀτρομήτου φεύγοντα ἀγανακτεῖν οἴεσθαι δεῖν, εἴ τι τῶν εἰωθότων Ἀθήνησιν ἔπαθεν.

In *Epist.* xii. § 14, we are told that the Athenians are quick to anger, but quick again to show kindness:—

καὶ γὰρ ὀργίζεσθαι ῥᾳδίως ὑμῖν ἔθος ἐστὶ καὶ χαρίζεσθαι πάλιν[1].

But we are reminded, as we were by Euripides[2], that the character and actions of the many will depend on those who lead them.

Like ruler, like people, says Isocrates (*Ad Nicocl.* § 31):—

τὸ τῆς πόλεως ὅλης ἦθος ὁμοιοῦται τοῖς ἄρχουσιν[3].

Dinarchus also declares that the salvation or ruin of states depends on their counsellors and leaders (*Agst. Demosthenes,* § 72):—

ὦ Ἀθηναῖοι, παρὰ τί οἴεσθε τὰς πόλεις τοτὲ μὲν εὖ τοτὲ δὲ φαύλως πράττειν; οὐδὲν εὑρήσετ᾽ ἄλλο πλὴν παρὰ τοὺς συμβούλους καὶ τοὺς ἡγεμόνας.

So again (*ibid.* § 74):—

οὐ γὰρ ψεῦδός ἐστιν ἀλλὰ καὶ λίαν ἀληθές, τὸ τοὺς ἡγεμόνας

---

[1] Cf. Euripides, *Orestes,* 696-703 (quoted above, p. 109).
[2] *Orestes,* 772-773 (quoted above, p. 110).
[3] Cf. *ibid.* § 10; *Nicocl.* § 37; *Areop.* § 22; *Panath.* §§ 132-133.

αἰτίους ἀπάιτων γίγνεσθαι καὶ τῶν ἀγαθῶν καὶ τῶν ἐναντίων τοῖς πολίταις.

And again (*ibid.* § 76):—

μία γὰρ αὕτη σωτηρία καὶ πόλεως καὶ ἔθνους ἐστί, τὸ προστατῶν ἀνδρῶν ἀγαθῶν καὶ συμβούλων σπουδαίων τυχεῖν.

We have seen (pp. 110 ff.) that Euripides had much to say against demagogues, the deceivers of the δῆμος. And if the demagogue was an evil in the time of Euripides, he was a still greater evil in the following century, when paid hirelings consulted only their own material interests without any public spirit or regard for their country's fortunes. Against the ῥήτωρ, the δημαγωγός, the συκοφάντης—the men who impudently flattered and hoodwinked the δῆμος, who tried only to say what would please their hearers, with self-interest as their only motive—almost all of the Orators join in hurling their fiercest denunciations.

Andocides(?) speaks of the πονηρὸς προστάτης who regards the present moment only, and gives not the best but the most pleasant counsel (*Agst. Alcibiades*, § 12):—

ἐγὼ δὲ νομίζω τὸν τοιοῦτον πονηρὸν εἶναι προστάτην, ὅστις τοῦ παρόντος χρόνου (μόνον) ἐπιμελεῖται, ἀλλὰ μὴ καὶ τοῦ μέλλοντος προνοεῖται, καὶ τὰ ἥδιστα τῷ πλήθει, παραλιπὼν τὰ βέλτιστα, συμβουλεύει.

Lysias accuses the ῥήτορες of having no motive save personal gain (xviii. § 16):—

ἄξιον δὲ μάλιστα φθονῆσαι ὅτι οὕτως ἤδη [οἱ] τὰ τῆς πόλεως [πράττοντες] διάκειται, ὥστ' οὐχ ὅ τι ἂν τῇ πόλει βέλτιστον ᾖ, τοῦτο οἱ ῥήτορες λέγουσιν, ἀλλ' ἀφ' ὧν ἂν αὐτοὶ κερδαίνειν μέλλωσι, ταῦτα ὑμεῖς ψηφίζεσθε.

Evil ῥήτορες and δημαγωγοί are, says Isocrates, the class who are worst-affected to the state, and who would gladly see one and all of the citizens reduced to a state of poverty (*De Pace*, §§ 129–131):—

θαυμάζω δ' εἰ μὴ δύνασθε συνιδεῖν, ὅτι γένος οὐδέν ἐστι κακονούστερον τῷ πλήθει πονηρῶν ῥητόρων καὶ δημαγωγῶν· πρὸς γὰρ τοῖς ἄλλοις κακοῖς καὶ τῶν κατὰ τὴν ἡμέραν ἑκάστην ἀναγκαίων οὗτοι μάλιστα βούλονται σπανίζειν ὑμᾶς. . . . . ἐν οὖν ταῖς ἀπορίαις, ἐν αἷς δυναστεύουσιν, ἐν ταύταις ἥδιστ᾽ ἂν ἴδοιεν ἅπαντας ὄντας τοὺς πολίτας. κ.τ.λ.

They are mere impostors and charlatans (*De Pace*, § 36):—

διεφθάρμεθα γὰρ πολὺν ἤδη χρόνον ὑπ᾽ ἀνθρώπων οὐδὲν ἀλλ᾽ ἢ φενακίζειν δυναμένων, κ.τ.λ.

They pander to the popular wish (*Phil.* § 3):—

οὗτοι μὲν γὰρ (sc. οἱ ῥήτορες) παρώξυνον ἐπὶ τὸν πόλεμον, συναγορεύοντες ταῖς ἐπιθυμίαις ὑμῶν.

All their advice is given *ad captandum vulgus* (*De Pace*, § 10):—

καίτοι προσῆκεν ὑμᾶς, εἴπερ ἠβούλεσθε ζητεῖν τὸ τῇ πόλει συμφέρον, μᾶλλον τοῖς ἐναντιουμένοις ταῖς ὑμετέραις γνώμαις προσέχειν τὸν νοῦν ἢ τοῖς καταχαριζομένοις, εἰδότας, ὅτι τῶν ἐνθάδε παριόντων οἱ μὲν ἃ βούλεσθε λέγοντες ῥᾳδίως ἐξαπατᾶν δύνανται, τὸ γὰρ πρὸς χάριν ῥηθὲν ἐπισκοτεῖ τῷ καθορᾶν ὑμᾶς τὸ βέλτιστον, ὑπὸ δὲ τῶν μὴ πρὸς ἡδονὴν συμβουλευόντων οὐδὲν ἂν πάθοιτε τοιοῦτον.

Their selfish motives are exposed in *Panath.* § 12:—

καίτοι πάντες ἴσασι τῶν μὲν ῥητόρων τοὺς πολλοὺς οὐχ ὑπὲρ τῶν τῇ πόλει συμφερόντων, ἀλλ᾽ ὑπὲρ ὧν αὐτοὶ λήψεσθαι προσδοκῶσι, δημηγορεῖν τολμῶντας, κ.τ.λ.

And a punning fragment is worth quoting (*Frag.* iii. (δ´.) 1):—

Ἰσοκράτης, εἰπόντος αὐτῷ τινος, ὅτι ὁ δῆμος ὑπὸ τῶν ῥητόρων ἁρπάζεται, τί θαυμαστόν, εἰ Κόρακος ἐφευρόντος τὴν ῥητορικὴν οἱ ἀπ᾽ ἐκείνου κόρακές εἰσιν [1].

Aeschines speaks of the ἀκοσμία τῶν ῥητόρων (*Agst. Ctesiphon*, § 4):—

. . . τῆς δὲ τῶν ῥητόρων ἀκοσμίας οὐκέτι κρατεῖν δύνανται οὔθ᾽ οἱ

---

[1] Cf. *Phil.* § 129; *De Pace*, §§ 5, 75. 108, 122-123; *Contra Soph.* § 20; *Antid.* §§ 136-137; *Panath.* § 133. And see Schandau, *op. cit.* p. 15:—'Pro enim, qua praeditus erat, virtute ac patriae amore, sophisticas omnes et demagogicas agitationes perosus, eloquentia sua id egit, ut consilia daret, quae essent non omnium civitatum, verum patriae, sociorum, regum, singulorum summae saluti.'

νόμοι οὔθ' οἱ πρυτάνεις οὔθ' οἱ πρόεδροι οὔθ' ἡ προεδρεύουσα φυλή, τὸ δέκατον μέρος τῆς πόλεως.

Athens is saved by the gods, ruined by ῥήτορες (*ibid.* § 130):—

οὐδεμίαν τοι πώποτε ἔγωγε μᾶλλον πόλιν ἑώρακα ὑπὸ μὲν τῶν θεῶν σωζομένην, ὑπὸ δὲ τῶν ῥητόρων ἐνίων ἀπολλυμένην.

And Hesiod is quoted on the subject of πονηροὶ δημαγωγοί (*ibid.* §§ 134-135):—

εὖ γὰρ περὶ τῶν τοιούτων Ἡσίοδος ὁ ποιητὴς ἀποφαίνεται. λέγει γάρ που, παιδεύων τὰ πλήθη καὶ συμβουλεύων ταῖς πόλεσι τοὺς πονηροὺς τῶν δημαγωγῶν μὴ προσδέχεσθαι. λέξω δὲ κἀγὼ τὰ ἔπη· . . .

> πολλάκι δὴ ξύμπασα πόλις κακοῦ ἀνδρὸς ἀπηύρα,
> ὅς κεν ἀλιτραίνῃ καὶ ἀτάσθαλα μηχανάαται.
> τοῖσιν δ' οὐρανόθεν μέγ' ἐπήγαγε πῆμα Κρονίων,
> λιμὸν ὁμοῦ καὶ λοιμόν, ἀποφθινύθουσι δὲ λαοί·
> ἢ τῶν γε στρατὸν εὐρὺν ἀπώλεσεν ἢ ὅ γε τεῖχος,
> ἢ νέας ἐν πόντῳ ἀποτίνινται εὐρύοπα Ζεύς[1].

In no one is the hatred of the ῥήτωρ and δημαγωγός so intense as in Demosthenes. Speaking of the changed way in which Athenian citizenship has come to be regarded, he attacks in no mild terms the πονηρία and αἰσχροκέρδεια of the ῥήτορες (*Agst. Aristocrates,* § 201):—

οὐ μόνον δ' αὕτη τῆς πόλεως ἡ δωρεὰ προπεπηλάκισται καὶ φαύλη γέγονεν, ἀλλὰ καὶ πᾶσαι διὰ τὴν τῶν καταράτων καὶ θεοῖς ἐχθρῶν ῥητόρων, τῶν τὰ τοιαῦτα γραφόντων ἑτοίμως, πονηρίαν, οἳ τοσαύτην ὑπερβολὴν πεποίηνται τῆς αὐτῶν αἰσχροκερδίας ὥστε τὰς τιμὰς καὶ τὰς παρ' ὑμῶν δωρεάς, ὥσπερ οἱ τὰ μικρὰ καὶ κομιδῇ φαῦλα ἀποκηρύττοντες, οὕτω πωλοῦσιν ἐπευωνίζοντες καὶ πολλοῖς ἀπὸ τῶν αὐτῶν λημμάτων γράφοντες πᾶν ὅ τι ἂν βούλωνται.

They abolish the old laws of the Solonian constitution, and make new laws to their own advantage: the people will

---

[1] Cf. *ibid.* §§ 20, 148, 231; *Epist.* xi. § 4; and, for a description of agitators, *On the Embassy,* §§ 176-177.

soon be the slaves of these monsters (*Agst. Timocrates*, §§ 142–143):—

οἱ δὲ παρ' ἡμῖν ῥήτορες, ὦ ἄνδρες δικασταί, πρῶτον μὲν ὅσοι μῆνες μικροῦ δέουσι νομοθετεῖν τὰ αὑτοῖς συμφέροντα, ἔπειτ' αὐτοὶ μὲν τοὺς ἰδιώτας εἰς τὸ δεσμωτήριον ἄγουσιν, ὅταν ἄρχωσιν, ἐφ' ἑαυτοῖς δ' οὐκ οἴονται δεῖν ταὐτὸ δίκαιον τοῦτ' εἶναι· ἔπειτα τοὺς μὲν τοῦ Σόλωνος νόμους, τοὺς πάλαι δεδοκιμασμένους, οὓς οἱ πρόγονοι ἔθεντο, λύουσιν αὐτοί, τοῖς δ' ἑαυτῶν, οὓς ἐπ' ἀδικίᾳ τῆς πόλεως τιθέασι, χρῆσθαι ὑμᾶς οἴονται δεῖν. εἰ οὖν μὴ τιμωρήσεσθε τούτους, οὐκ ἂν φθάνοι τὸ πλῆθος τούτοις τοῖς θηρίοις δουλεῦον.

The συκοφάντης is a wicked thing, spiteful and faultfinding (*On the Crown*, § 242):—

πονηρὸν ἄνδρες Ἀθηναῖοι πονηρὸν ὁ συκοφάντης καὶ πανταχόθεν βάσκανον καὶ φιλαίτιον.

The motive of the ῥήτωρ is self-interest alone (*Prooem.* liii. § 1):—

. . . ἴσως γὰρ ὀργῇ καὶ φιλονικίᾳ ταῦτα πράττουσι, καὶ τὸ μέγιστον ἁπάντων, ὅτι συμφέρει ταῦτα ποιεῖν αὐτοῖς . . .

And again (*ibid.* §§ 3–4):—

ὅτι φασὶ μὲν ὦ ἄνδρες Ἀθηναῖοι φιλεῖν ὑμᾶς, φιλοῦσι δ' οὐχ ὑμᾶς, ἀλλ' αὐτούς. καὶ γελάσαι καὶ θορυβῆσαι καί ποτ' ἐλπίσαι μετέδωκαν ὑμῖν, λαβεῖν δ' ἢ κτήσασθαι τῇ πόλει κυρίως ἀγαθὸν οὐδὲν ἂν βούλοιντο.

The source of the whole evil is τὸ πρὸς χάριν δημηγορεῖν (*Olynth.* iii. § 3):—

ὁρᾶτε γάρ, ὡς ἐκ τοῦ πρὸς χάριν δημηγορεῖν ἐνίους, εἰς πᾶν προελήλυθεν μοχθηρίας τὰ παρόντα.

Again (*On the Chersonese*, § 34):—

νῦν δὲ δημαγωγοῦντες ὑμᾶς καὶ χαριζόμενοι καθ' ὑπερβολήν, οὕτω διατεθείκασιν, ὥστ' ἐν μὲν ταῖς ἐκκλησίαις τρυφᾶν καὶ κολακεύεσθαι πάντα πρὸς ἡδονὴν ἀκούοντας, ἐν δὲ τοῖς πράγμασι καὶ τοῖς γιγνομένοις περὶ τῶν ἐσχάτων ἤδη κινδυνεύειν.

And again (*Prooem.* xli. § 2):—

ἡ μὲν οὖν ἀρχὴ τοῦ ταῦθ' οὕτως ἔχειν ἐκεῖθεν ἤρτηται, ἐκ τοῦ τῆς παραχρῆμα πρὸς ὑμᾶς ἕνεκα χάριτος ἐνίους τῶν λεγόντων ἐνταυθοῖ δημηγορεῖν, ὡς οὔτ᾽ εἰσφέρειν οὔτε στρατεύεσθαι δεῖ, πάντα δ᾽ αὐτόματ᾽ ἔσται[1].

In a fragment of Hyperides, the ῥήτορες are compared to serpents (xv. 83):—

εἶναι δὲ τοὺς ῥήτορας ὁμοίους τοῖς ὄφεσι· τούς τε γὰρ ὄφεις μισητοὺς μὲν εἶναι πάντας, τῶν δὲ ὄφεων αὐτῶν τοὺς μὲν ἔχεις τοὺς ἀνθρώπους ἀδικεῖν, τοὺς δὲ παρείας αὐτοὺς τοὺς ἔχεις κατεσθίειν.

The δημαγωγοί, says Dinarchus, sacrifice their country's interest for bribes, and play into each other's hands (*Agst. Demosthenes*, § 99):—

πῶς οὖν μίαν γνώμην ἕξομεν ὦ ᾽Αθηναῖοι, πῶς ὁμονοήσομεν ἅπαντες ὑπὲρ τῶν κοινῇ συμφερόντων, ὅταν οἱ ἡγεμόνες καὶ οἱ δημαγωγοὶ χρήματα λαμβάνοντες προῶνται τὰ τῆς πατρίδος συμφέροντα, καὶ ὑμεῖς μὲν καὶ ὁ δῆμος ἅπας κινδυνεύῃ περὶ τοῦ ἐδάφους τοῦ τῆς πόλεως καὶ τῶν ἱερῶν τῶν πατρῴων καὶ παίδων καὶ γυναικῶν, οἱ δὲ διηλλαγμένοι πρὸς αὐτοὺς ἐν μὲν ταῖς ἐκκλησίαις λοιδορῶνται καὶ προσκρούωσιν ἀλλήλοις ἐξεπίτηδες, ἰδίᾳ δὲ ταὐτὰ πράττωσιν ἐξαπατῶντες ὑμᾶς τοὺς ῥᾷστα πειθομένους τοῖς τούτων λόγοις[2];

To Euripides' statement that the μέσοι πολῖται are the state's salvation[3] I have found no parallel in the Orators.

There is one passage (Lysias, xxxi. § 6) which recalls to us the cosmopolitanism which we noticed in Euripides[4]. But the cosmopolitanism mentioned in Lysias is of quite another kind than that of Euripides, and reminds us of Aristophanes' line, πατρὶς γάρ ἐστι πᾶσ᾽ ἵν᾽ ἂν πράττῃ τις εὖ[5]— 'ubi bene, ibi patria.' Lysias is speaking of those who are

---

[1] Cf. *Olynth.* ii. § 29; iii. §§ 30-31; *Phil.* i. §§ 38, 49; iii. §§ 2, 4, 63; *On the Chersonese*, §§ 1, 69; *On the Crown*, §§ 189 190; *Agst. Aristocrates*, §§ 146-147; *Agst. Timocrates*, §§ 123-124; *On the Trierarchic Crown*, §§ 21 22; *Prooem.* ix. § 2; xiii; *Epist.* ii. § 11.

[2] Cf. *ibid.* §§ 3-4, 88; and, for a former law relating to public speaking, *Agst. Aristogeiton*, § 16. See also Demades (?), ὑπὲρ τῆς δωδεκαετίας, §§ 2, 16.

[3] See above, p. 112.   [4] See above, pp. 112-113.

[5] *Plutus*, 1151.

naturally citizens, but act on the idea that every land is their country where they can get the necessaries of life. These men, he says, evidently would sacrifice the public good for the sake of their own private advantage, because they think that not their city but their property is their country :—

καὶ γὰρ οἳ φύσει μὲν πολῖταί εἰσι, γνώμῃ δὲ χρῶνται ὡς πᾶσα γῆ πατρὶς αὐτοῖς ἐστιν ἐν ᾗ ἂν τὰ ἐπιτήδεια ἔχωσιν, οὗτοι δῆλοί εἰσιν ὅτι ἂν παρέντες τὸ τῆς πόλεως κοινὸν ἀγαθὸν ἐπὶ τὸ ἑαυτῶν ἴδιον κέρδος ἔλθοιεν διὰ τὸ μὴ τὴν πόλιν ἀλλὰ τὴν οὐσίαν πατρίδα ἑαυτοῖς ἡγεῖσθαι[1].

---

[1] The idea of cosmopolitanism, though we find traces of it as early as Democritus (*Frag.* 225 : see Zeller, *Pre-Socratic Philosophy*, ii. p. 283', in the doctrines of the Cynical School, and occasionally in Aristotle, was not properly developed till the time of the later Stoics under the Roman Empire. See an interesting passage in Coulanges, *La Cité Antique*, pp. 422-423.

CHAPTER IX

PRIVATE LIFE : WOMEN—LOVE—MARRIAGE— KINSHIP—FRIENDSHIP

§ 1. In the Homeric society the conjugal tie is of the utmost sacredness and purity[1]. One need only instance the pictures of Hector and Andromache in the *Iliad*, and of Odysseus and Penelope in the *Odyssey*. Nowhere in the *Iliad* are evil words spoken of woman. If Agamemnon in the *Odyssey* (xi. 427) exclaims

ὡς οὐκ αἰνότερον καὶ κύντερον ἄλλο γυναικός,

it is no wonder.

Hesiod (*Theog.* 591) calls woman ὀλώϊον γένος: they are 'a grievous bane among mortal men' (πῆμα μέγα θνητοῖσι μετ' ἀνδράσι ναιετάουσιν)[2].

Archilochus and Hipponax make women the object of much of their satire. For example, Hipponax, *Frag.* 28 (Bergk):—

δύ' ἡμέραι γυναικός εἰσιν ἥδισται,
ὅταν γαμῇ τις κἀκφέρῃ τεθνηκυῖαν.

---

[1] See Jebb, *Homer*, p. 53: Berlage, Part iv. c. iv. For a discussion on Women and Marriage in ancient Greece see Becker, *Charicles*, Excursus on Scene xii; and for the Hetaerae see *ibid*. Excursus on Scene ii. See also Kennedy's Translation of Demosthenes, *Agst. Timocrates*, &c., Appendix iii (*Husband and Wife*).

[2] *Ibid.* 592. See Symonds, *Greek Poets* (First Series), c. iv: Decharme, *Euripide*, &c., pp. 133-135. M. Decharme says (p. 134):—'La critique des imperfections féminines était en Grèce un thème banal, une sorte de lieu commun poétique. Euripide lui-même nous dit que c'était "un vieux refrain" (παλαιγενὴς ου παλίμφαμος ἀοιδή—*Med.* 421 ; *Ion*, 1096).'

Susarion begins his poem thus:—

'Hear, O ye people! These are the words of Susarion of Tripodiscus, Philinus' son, of Megara: Woman is a curse!¹'

Aeschylus speaks sometimes of women with no great respect. In the *Supplices* (474–477) the king doubts whether it is worth while to fight for the sake of women:—

εἰ δ' αὖθ' ὁμαίμοις παισὶν Αἰγύπτου σέθεν
σταθεὶς πρὸ τειχέων διὰ μάχης ἥξω τέλους,
πῶς οὐχὶ τἀνάλωμα γίγνεται πικρόν,
ἄνδρας γυναικῶν οὕνεχ' αἱμάξαι πέδον ;

Nor does Sophocles, gentle though he was, refrain from saying hard words of women. The following fragments illustrate this:—

κάκιον ἀλλ' οὐκ ἔστιν οὐδ' ἔσται ποτὲ
γυναικός, εἴ τι πῆμα γίγνεται βροτοῖς (187, Nauck):

and the famous

ὅρκους ἐγὼ γυναικὸς εἰς ὕδωρ γράφω (742, Nauck).

When Xanthippe visits Socrates in the prison, and when she has indulged in 'a woman's usual talk' (ἀνευφήμησέ τε καὶ τοιαῦτ' ἄττα εἶπεν, οἷα δὴ εἰώθασιν αἱ γυναῖκες), Socrates merely looks to Crito and says, ἀπαγέτω τις ταύτην οἴκαδε. Then, when the disturbing element is removed, he proceeds calmly to converse with his friends (*Phaedo*, 60)².

We may end this list of references with the following lines from Aristophanes (*Thesm.* 786–788):—

καίτοι πᾶς τις τὸ γυναικεῖον φῦλον κακὰ πόλλ' ἀγορεύει,
ὡς πᾶν ἐσμεν κακὸν ἀνθρώποις κἀξ ἡμῶν ἐστιν ἄπαντα,
ἔριδες, νείκη, στάσις ἀργαλέα, λύπη, πόλεμος.

From these quotations it is clear that the position of women, high in the time of Homer, had sunk to a much

---

¹ See Symonds, *Greek Poets* (First Series), p. 106.

² In theory, indeed, Plato held 'that women had the same faculties and capacities as men, but in an inferior degree, and hampered by the inconveniences of child-bearing' (Mahaffy, *Social Greece*, p. 281). Cf. Aristotle, *Poetics*, 1454 a:—καὶ γὰρ γυνή ἐστιν χρηστὴ καὶ δοῦλος, καίτοι γε ἴσως τούτων τὸ μὲν χεῖρον, τὸ δὲ ὅλως φαῦλόν ἐστιν. See also Verrall, *Euripides the Rationalist*, p. 111.

lower level by the fifth century B.C. The Greeks had come
to regard women as in every way inferior to men [1]. They
were mere instruments of pleasure or utility, not fit to be
either the companions of men or the objects of chivalrous
affection. Rather they were considered merely as necessary
evils; and the treatment to which they were subjected was
to be kept as secluded as possible, lest they should become
corrupted by experience as well as by nature. Even the
greater freedom allowed to Spartan as compared with Athenian women had for its object only the rearing of brave
and healthy children.

In Euripides and the Orators there are numerous passages
pointing to the secluded life which Greek women were forced
to lead.

In the *Andromache*, 872–874, the nurse says to Her-
mione —

ἀλλ᾽ εἴσιθ᾽ εἴσω, μηδὲ φαντάζου δόμων
πάροιθε τῶνδε, μή τιν᾽ αἰσχύνην λάβῃς
πρόσθεν μελάθρων τῶνδ᾽ ὁρωμένη, τέκνον.

In the *Her. Fur.*, 525–528, Heracles on his return exclaims:—

ἴα· τί χρῆμα; τέκν᾽ ὁρῶ πρὸ δωμάτων
στολμοῖσι νεκρῶν κρᾶτας ἐξεστεμμένα,
ὄχλῳ τ᾽ ἐν ἀνδρῶν τὴν ἐμὴν ξυνάορον
πετέρα τε δακρύοντα συμφορᾶς τινος.

It is a disgrace for a woman to be in the company of young
men (*El.* 343–344):—

γυναικί τοι
αἰσχρὸν μετ᾽ ἀνδρῶν ἑστάναι νεανιῶν.

Maidens should not mingle in a crowd (*Or.* 108):—

εἰς ὄχλον ἕρπειν παρθένοισιν οὐ καλόν.

Neither should married women. Agamemnon says to Cly-
taemnestra (*Iph. Aul.* 735):—

οὐ καλὸν ἐν ὄχλῳ σ᾽ ἐξομιλεῖσθαι στρατοῦ.

---

[1] The social recognition of the female sex was one of the aims of Pericles.
See Holm, ii. pp. 344-345; and cf. Lloyd. *Age of Pericles*, ii. c. xlv. For the
legal disabilities of women see Coulanges, *La Cité Antique*, pp. 94-95, 99.

A good woman should remain within doors (*Frag.* 521):—

> ἔνδον μένουσαν τὴν γυναῖκ' εἶναι χρεὼν
> ἐσθλήν, θύρασι δ' ἀξίαν τοῦ μηδενός.

Macaria apologises for coming out of the house (*Heracl.* 474-477):—

> ξένοι, θράσος μοι μηδὲν ἐξόδοις ἐμαῖς
> προσθῆτε· πρῶτον γὰρ τόδ' ἐξαιτήσομαι·
> γυναικὶ γὰρ σιγή τε καὶ τὸ σωφρονεῖν
> κάλλιστον, εἴσω θ' ἥσυχον μένειν δόμων[1].

Lysias speaks of women who were so proper that they were ashamed to be seen even by their relatives (iii. § 6):—

> ... ἐκκόψας τὰς θύρας εἰσῆλθεν εἰς τὴν γυναικωνῖτιν, ἔδον
> οὐσῶν τῆς τε ἀδελφῆς τῆς ἐμῆς καὶ τῶν ἀδελφιδῶν, αἳ οὕτω κοσμίως
> βεβιώκασιν ὥστε καὶ ὑπὸ τῶν οἰκείων ὁρώμεναι αἰσχύνεσθαι[2].

Isocrates also refers to the seclusion of women (*Epist.* ix. § 10):—

> ... ἔτι δὲ παῖδας καὶ γυναῖκας ὑβρίζοντες, καὶ τὰς μὲν εὐπρεπε-
> στάτας καταισχύνοιτες, τῶν δ' ἄλλων ἃ περὶ τοῖς σώμασιν ἔχουσι
> περισπῶντες, ὥσθ' ἃς πρότερον οὐδὲ κεκοσμημένας ἦν ἰδεῖν τοῖς
> ἀλλοτρίοις, ταύτας ὑπὸ πολλῶν ὁρᾶσθαι γυμνάς, κ.τ.λ.

Isaeus tells us that married women did not dine with men (iii. § 14):—

> καίτοι οὐ δή πού γε ἐπὶ γαμετὰς γυναῖκας οὐδεὶς ἐν κωμάζειν

---

[1] See also *Hec.* 974-975; *Andr.* 364-365, 943-953; *Tro.* 644-645; *Iph. Aul.* 825-826, 830, 913-914, 998-999; *Phoen.* 88-95. 1276; *Heracl.* 43-44; *Frag.* 319, 927, 1061.

For other examples of maidenly modesty see *Hec.* 568; *Or.* 26; *Iph. Aul.* 993, 1340; *Phoen.* 1487; *Heracl.* 561.

The general upbringing of Spartan women is reprehended as contributing to unchastity (*Andr.* 595-601):—

> οὐδ' ἂν εἰ βούλοιτό τις
> σώφρων γένοιτο Σπαρτιατίδων κόρη,
> αἳ ξὺν νέοισιν ἐξερημοῦσαι δόμους
> γυμνοῖσι μηροῖς καὶ πέπλοις ἀνειμένοις
> δρόμους παλαίστρας τ' οὐκ ἀνασχετοὺς ἐμοὶ
> κοινὰς ἔχουσι. κᾆτα θαυμάζειν χρεὼν
> εἰ μὴ γυναῖκας σώφρονας παιδεύετε;

See Paley's note *ad loc.*

[2] Cf. xxxii. § 11.

τολμήσειεν· οὐδὲ αἱ γαμεταὶ γυναῖκες ἔρχονται μετὰ τῶν ἀνδρῶν ἐπὶ τὰ δεῖπνα, οὐδὲ συνδειπνεῖν ἀξιοῦσι μετὰ τῶν ἀλλοτρίων, καὶ ταῦτα μετὰ τῶν ἐπιτυχόντων [1].

Similarly, from the speech *Agst. Neaera*, § 24, we learn that it was only ἑταῖραι who sat at table in the company of men :—

συνηκολούθει δὲ καὶ ἡ Νικαρέτη αὐτῇ, κατήγοντο δὲ παρὰ Κτησίππῳ τῷ Γλαυκωνίδου τῷ Κυδαντίδῃ, καὶ συνέπινε καὶ συνεδείπνει ἐναντίον πολλῶν Νέαιρα αὐτηὶ ὡς ἂν ἑταίρα οὖσα [2].

The following phrase is used by Lycurgus (*Agst. Leocrates*, § 40):—

... ἀναξίως αὐτῶν καὶ τῆς πόλεως ὁρωμένας ...

And, lastly, there is the well-known passage in Hyperides (*Frag.* 207):—

δεῖ τὴν ἐκ τῆς οἰκίας ἐκπορευομένην ἐν τοιαύτῃ καταστάσει εἶναι τῆς ἡλικίας, ὥστε τοὺς ἀπαντῶντας πυνθάνεσθαι, μὴ τίνος ἐστὶ γυνή, ἀλλὰ τίνος μήτηρ [3].

Such seclusion was naturally followed by a double result. Acting directly on the women themselves, it made them dull and uninteresting. And it had a reflex action on the men ; for, finding no solace or companionship with women, they sought it by other means, not always—at least from our point of view—the most moral.

Of women as a whole there is in the Orators very little either of praise or of blame. When women are blamed, it is only one class of women—the ἑταῖραι.

---

[1] For the disgrace of speaking with married women cf. Euripides, *Iph. Aul.* 830 :—

αἰσχρὸν δέ μοι γυναιξὶ συμβάλλειν λόγους.

[2] Cf. *ibid.* § 48.

[3] Cf. also Plato, *Republic*, ix. 579 B :—καταδεδυκὼς δὲ ἐν τῇ οἰκίᾳ τὰ πολλὰ ὡς γυνὴ ζῇ : Xenophon, *Oec.* iii. 12 :—ἔστι δὲ ὅτῳ ἐλάττονα διαλέγει ἢ τῇ γυναικί ; εἰ δὲ μή, οὐ πολλοῖς γε, ἔφη. ἔγημας δὲ αὐτὴν παῖδα νέαν μάλιστα, καὶ ὡς ἐδύνατο ἐλάχιστα ἑορακυῖαν καὶ ἀκηκουῖαν : and this fragment of Menander :—

πέρας γὰρ αὔλειος θύρα
ἐλευθέρᾳ γυναικὶ νενόμιστ' οἰκίας.

And see Mahaffy, *Old Greek Life*, p. 48.

Isocrates, in a comparison drawn between ἐξουσία and ἑταῖραι, says that ἑταῖραι ruin their lovers (*De Pace*, § 103):—

οὐ γὰρ ᾔδεσαν τὴν ἐξουσίαν, ἧς πάντες εὔχονται τυχεῖν, ὡς δύσχρηστός ἐστιν, οὐδ᾽ ὡς παραφρονεῖν ποιεῖ τοὺς ἀγαπῶντας αὐτήν, οὐδ᾽ ὅτι τὴν φύσιν ὁμοίαν ἔχει ταῖς ἑταίραις ταῖς ἐρᾶν μὲν αὐτῶν ποιούσαις, τοὺς δὲ χρωμένοις ἀπολλυούσαις.

Hyperides speaks of the power of love to beguile our reason, when it is reinforced by a woman's wiles. The thought is general, but it is suggested by the conduct of a ἑταίρα (*Agst. Athenogenes*, i. 12 ff.):—

οὕτως, ὡς ἔοικεν, ἐξίστησιν [ἡμῶν τὴν] φύσιν ἔρως προσλαβὼν γυναι[κὸς ποικιλ]ίαν. κ.τ.λ.

Isaeus, in a passage from which I have already quoted, speaks of the μάχαι καὶ κῶμοι καὶ ἀσέλγεια of ἑταῖραι (iii. §§ 13-14):—

ὡς μὲν ἑταίρα ἦν τῷ βουλομένῳ καὶ οὐ γυνὴ τοῦ ἡμετέρου θείου, ἣν οὗτος ἐγγυῆσαι ἐκείνῳ μεμαρτύρηκεν, ὑπὸ τῶν ἄλλων οἰκείων καὶ ὑπὸ τῶν γειτόνων τῶν ἐκείνου μεμαρτύρηται πρὸς ὑμᾶς· οἱ μάχας καὶ κώμους καὶ ἀσέλγειαν πολλήν, ὁπότε ἡ τούτου ἀδελφὴ εἴη παρ᾽ αὐτῷ, μεμαρτυρήκασι γίγνεσθαι περὶ αὐτῆς. καίτοι οὐ δή πού γε ἐπὶ γαμετὰς γυναῖκας οὐδεὶς ἂν κωμάζειν τολμήσειεν· κ.τ.λ. (see above, p. 152)[1].

When praise is assigned to women by any of the Orators, it is usually from a utilitarian point of view.

Lysias thus describes a good wife (i. § 7):—

ἐν μὲν οὖν τῷ πρώτῳ χρόνῳ, ὦ Ἀθηναῖοι, πασῶν ἦν βελτίστη· καὶ γὰρ οἰκονόμος δεινὴ καὶ φειδωλὸς [ἀγαθὴ] καὶ ἀκριβῶς πάντα διοικοῦσα.

---

[1] In the speech *Agst. Neaera* (§ 122) there is a *locus classicus* as to the distinction between ἑταῖραι, παλλακαί, and γυναῖκες:—τὰς μὲν γὰρ ἑταίρας ἡδονῆς ἕνεκ᾽ ἔχομεν, τὰς δὲ παλλακὰς τῆς καθ᾽ ἡμέραν θεραπείας τοῦ σώματος, τὰς δὲ γυναῖκας τοῦ παιδοποιεῖσθαι γνησίως καὶ τῶν ἔνδον φύλακα πιστὴν ἔχειν.

I may add here a passage in which Lysias speaks in strong terms of the result of unchastity in women (*Frag.* 90):—ᾗ γὰρ ἂν ἡμέρᾳ γυνὴ προδῷ τὸ σῶμα καὶ τὴν τάξιν λίπῃ τῆς αἰδοῦς, εὐθέως παραλλάττει τῶν φρενῶν, ὥστε νομίζειν τοὺς μὲν οἰκείους ἐχθρούς, τοὺς δὲ ἀλλοτρίους πιστούς, περὶ δὲ τῶν καλῶν καὶ αἰσχρῶν ἐναντίαν ἔχειν τὴν γνώμην.

The value of women as nurses is mentioned in the speech *Agst. Neaera*, § 56:—

ἴστε δήπου καὶ αὐτοί, ὅσου ἀξία ἐστὶ γυνὴ ἐν ταῖς νόσοις, παροῦσα κάμνοντι ἀνθρώπῳ [1].

All women, says Lycurgus, love their children (*Agst. Leocrates*, § 101):—

φύσει γὰρ οὐσῶν φιλοτέκνων πασῶν τῶν γυναικῶν ταύτην ἐποίησε (sc. Euripides) τὴν πατρίδα μᾶλλον τῶν παίδων φιλοῦσαν, κ.τ.λ.

But Lycurgus seems to regard this love of children in quite a passionless manner, and not to consider it as any virtue. Women are φύσει φιλότεκνοι.

If there is a dearth of opinions on women in the Orators, there is no scarcity of them in Euripides. Let us look, first, at those in which women are regarded as an evil.

We are not here concerned with the question whether Euripides was a misogynist or not. One who could create an Alcestis, an Iphigenia, a Macaria, could hardly be a thorough-paced misogynist. These creations are at least worthy of comparison with the Antigone of Sophocles, even if none of them is either so noble or so tender as she [2]. But Sophocles and Euripides in drawing such women are both idealising. They are painting women 'as they ought to be,' not 'as they are.' Women of this heroic mould would probably have been hard to find in the Athens of their time [3]. It is not in the creation of an ideal character that we are to look for a description of the women of Athens as Euripides found them, but rather in individual utterances. Nor are such lacking in Euripides. Whether or not the cause is to be found in an unhappy married life, he is far more bitter against women than either Aeschylus or Sophocles was. The following passages are here in point.

---

[1] See also *ibid.* § 122, quoted above, p. 154, note 1.

[2] See Jebb, *Attic Orators*, i. Introd. ci.

[3] This point Prof. Mahaffy fails to observe. See his *Social Greece*, pp. 198–206.

Women are worse than fire or vipers: they are an evil for which no remedy has yet been found (*Andr.* 271-273):—

> ἃ δ' ἔστ' ἐχίδνης καὶ πυρὸς περαιτέρω,
> οὐδεὶς γυναικὸς φάρμακ' ἐξηύρηκέ πω
> κακῆς· τοσοῦτόν ἐσμεν ἀνθρώποις κακόν[1].

The race of women is treacherous (*Iph. Taur.* 1298):—

> ὁρᾶτ', ἄπιστον ὡς γυναικεῖον γένος[2].

They heighten misfortunes (*Or.* 605-606):—

> ἀεὶ γυναῖκες ἐμποδὼν ταῖς ξυμφοραῖς
> ἔφυσαν ἀνδρῶν πρὸς τὸ δυστυχέστερον.

In the *Medea* (573-575) Jason says that there should be no women. Children should be got in some other way, and so men would be free from all evil:—

> χρῆν γὰρ ἄλλοθέν ποθεν βροτοὺς
> παῖδας τεκνοῦσθαι, θῆλυ δ' οὐκ εἶναι γένος·
> χοὕτως ἂν οὐκ ἦν οὐδὲν ἀνθρώποις κακόν.

In the same play (406-408) Medea herself declares that women are resourceless in good, but skilful to devise all evil:—

> πρὸς δὲ καὶ πεφύκαμεν
> γυναῖκες, ἐς μὲν ἔσθλ' ἀμηχανώταται,
> κακῶν δὲ πάντων τέκτονες σοφώταται.

Women are a ruinous evil (*Andr.* 352-354):—

> οὐ χρὴ 'πὶ μικροῖς μεγάλα πορσύνειν κακά,
> οὐδ', εἰ γυναῖκές ἐσμεν ἀτηρὸν κακόν,
> ἄνδρας γυναιξὶν ἐξομοιοῦσθαι φύσιν.

They are cowards, save when their bed is dishonoured (*Med.* 263-266):—

> γυνὴ γὰρ τἆλλα μὲν φόβου πλέα,
> κακὴ δ' ἐς ἀλκὴν καὶ σίδηρον εἰσορᾶν·
> ὅταν δ' ἐς εὐνὴν ἠδικημένη κυρῇ,
> οὐκ ἔστιν ἄλλη φρὴν μιαιφονωτέρα[3].

---

[1] Cf. *Hipp.* 616-668. In this passage, which is too long for quotation, Euripides speaks with a certain fervour, which makes one think he is expressing his real opinions.

[2] Cf. *Or.* 1103; *Frag.* 671.   [3] Cf. *Frag.* 276.

They are a specious curse, a grievous bane: children should be got otherwise [1] (*Hipp.* 616-668):—

ὦ Ζεῦ, τί δὴ κίβδηλον ἀνθρώποις κακὸν
γυναῖκας ἐς φῶς ἡλίου κατῴκισας ;

. . . .

τούτῳ δὲ δῆλον ὡς γυνὴ κακὸν μέγα· (627)

. . . .

ὄλοισθε. μισῶν δ' οὔποτ' ἐμπλησθήσομαι
γυναῖκας, οὐδ' εἴ φησί τίς μ' ἀεὶ λέγειν·
ἀεὶ γὰρ οὖν πώς εἰσι κἀκειναι κακαί.
ἤ νύν τις αὐτὰς σωφρονεῖν διδαξάτω,
ἢ κἄμ' ἐάτω ταῖσδ' ἐπεμβαίνειν ἀεί [2].

They are devoid of accomplishment (*Med.* 1087-1089):—

παῦρον δὲ γένος (μίαν ἐν πολλαῖς
εὕροις ἂν ἴσως)
οὐκ ἀπόμουσον τὸ γυναικῶν.

They are jealous (*Andr.* 181-182):—

ἐπίφθονόν τι χρῆμα θηλειῶν ἔφυ,
καὶ ξυγγάμοισι δυσμενὲς μάλιστ' ἀεί.

They are vain (*Med.* 1156-1166):—

ἡ δ' ὡς ἐσεῖδε κόσμον, οὐκ ἠνέσχετο,
ἀλλ' ἤνεσ' ἀνδρὶ πάντα· κ.τ.λ. [3].

Folly—in a special sense—is of women, not of men (*Hipp.* 966-967):—

ἀλλ' ὡς τὸ μῶρον ἀνδράσιν μὲν οὐκ ἔνι,
γυναιξὶ δ' ἐμπέφυκεν.

A noble mind is seldom found in women (*Hel.* 1686-1687):—

καὶ χαίρεθ', Ἑλένης οὕνεκ' εὐγενεστάτης
γνώμης, ὃ πολλαῖς ἐν γυναιξὶν οὐκ ἔνι.

It is hard to teach women to be chaste (*Tro.* 1055-1059):—

ἐλθοῦσα δ' Ἄργος ὥσπερ ἀξία κακῶς
κακὴ θανεῖται, καὶ γυναιξὶ σωφρονεῖν
πάσαισι θήσει. ῥᾴδιον μὲν οὐ τόδε· κ.τ.λ.

---

[1] Cf. *Med.* 573-575 (quoted above, p. 156).
[2] In these last lines Euripides seems to speak in his own defence. See above, p. 156, note 1.
[3] Cf. *El.* 1068-1075; *Or.* 128-129.

One man's life is worth the lives of a thousand women (*Iph. Aul.* 1394):—

εἷς γ' ἀνὴρ κρείσσων γυναικῶν μυρίων ὁρᾶν φάος[1].

Women are fond of slander (*Phoen.* 198-201):—

φιλόψογον δὲ χρῆμα θηλειῶν ἔφυ,
σμικρὰς τ' ἀφορμὰς ἢν λάβωσι τῶν λόγων,
πλείους ἐπεσφέρουσιν· ἡδονὴ δέ τις
γυναιξὶ μηδὲν ὑγιὲς ἀλλήλας λέγειν.

There is nothing so hard to guard as they (*Frag.* 320):—

οὐκ ἔστιν οὔτε τεῖχος οὔτε χρήματα
οὔτ' ἄλλο ἐυσφύλακτον οὐδὲν ὡς γυνή[2].

Man at his worst is better than woman at her best (*Frag.* 546):—

πᾶσα γὰρ ἀνδρὸς κακίων ἄλοχος,
κἂν ὁ κάκιστος
γήμῃ τὴν εὐδοκιμοῦσαν.

There is no evil so terrible as woman (*Frag.* 1059):

δεινὴ μὲν ἀλκὴ κυμάτων θαλασσίων,
δειναὶ δὲ ποταμῶν καὶ πυρὸς θερμοῦ πνοαί,
δεινὸν δὲ πενία, δεινὰ δ' ἄλλα μυρία,
ἀλλ' οὐδὲν οὕτω δεινὸν ὡς γυνὴ κακόν·
οὐδ' ἂν γένοιτο γράμμα τοιοῦτον γραφῇ
οὐδ' ἂν λόγος δείξειεν. εἰ δέ του θεῶν
τόδ' ἐστι πλάσμα, δημιουργὸς ὢν κακῶν
μέγιστος ἴστω καὶ βροτοῖσι δυσμενής[3].

This is not the only tone, however, in which Euripides speaks of women. There are lines, too, expressing pity for the hardness of a woman's lot.

---

[1] Cf. *Iph. Taur.* 1004-1006; and see above, p. 150. Thus, from the Greek point of view, the conduct of Admetus in the *Alcestis* needed less excuse. See Jerram's *Alcestis*, Introd. p. xv.

[2] Cf. *Frag.* 111, 1061.

[3] See also *Andr.* 93, 218, 756; *Hipp.* 406; *Hec.* 885, 1177 ff. (with Paley's note); *Ion*, 616; *Hel.* 1621; *El.* 645, 1014, 1035, 1072 ff.; *Or.* 518, 566, 935; *Bacch.* 260; *Iph. Aul.* 1162; *Frag.* 3, 36, 429, 463, 464, 497, 498, 528, 544, 808.

For passages where both good and evil is spoken of women see *Frag.* 494, 545, 1056, 1057.

Women are the most wretched of all creatures. They must marry those to whom they are given, and bear their griefs in silence and solitude. Medea declares that rather than endure once the throes of childbirth she would thrice take her stand in battle (*Med.* 230-251):—

πάντων δ' ὅσ' ἔστ' ἔμψυχα καὶ γνώμην ἔχει
γυναῖκές ἐσμεν ἀθλιώτατον φυτόν[1].

.   .   .   .   .   .

λέγουσι δ' ἡμᾶς ὡς ἀκίνδυνον βίον
ζῶμεν κατ' οἴκους, οἱ δὲ μάρνανται δορί,
κακῶς φρονοῦντες· ὡς τρὶς ἂν παρ' ἀσπίδα
στῆναι θέλοιμ' ἂν μᾶλλον ἢ τεκεῖν ἅπαξ.

In losing her husband, a woman loses all (*Andr.* 373):—

ἀνδρὸς δ' ἁμαρτάνουσ' ἁμαρτάνει βίου.

Good women must suffer for the faults of those that are bad (*Frag.* 493):—

ἄλγιστόν ἐστι θῆλυ μισηθὲν γένος·
αἱ γὰρ σφαλεῖσαι ταῖσιν οὐκ ἐσφαλμέναις
αἶσχος γυναιξὶ καὶ κεκοίνωνται ψόγον
ταῖς οὐ κακαῖσιν αἱ κακαί.

Similarly Creusa complains that men are indiscriminate in their blame (*Ion,* 398-400):—

τὰ γὰρ γυναικῶν δυσχερῆ πρὸς ἄρσενας,
κἂν ταῖς κακαῖσιν ἀγαθαὶ μεμιγμέναι
μισούμεθ'· οὕτω δυστυχεῖς πεφύκαμεν[2].

Nor are there wanting words of positive praise. Apart from the whole conception of ideal characters—such as Macaria (*Heracl.* 500 ff.), Antigone (*Phoen.* 1639 ff.), Iphigenia (*Iph. Aul.* 1368 ff.), Electra (*Or.* 1204-1206,—'a man's spirit and a woman's charm'), Andromache (*Andr.* 384-420)—there are many individual utterances which are here in point.

---

[1] Cf. *Hipp.* 669 :—τάλανες ὦ κακοτυχεῖς γυναικῶν πότμοι.
   Ion, 252 :—ὦ τλήμονες γυναῖκες.
   Frag. 401 :—ὅσῳ τὸ θῆλυ δυστυχέστερον γένος
      πέφυκεν ἀνδρῶν.

[2] Cf. *Hec.* 1183-1184.

No greater evil can befall a man than to lose a faithful wife (*Alc.* 879-880):—

> τί γὰρ ἀνδρὶ κακὸν μεῖζον ἁμαρτεῖν
> πιστῆς ἀλόχου;

Women are more chaste than men (*Ion,* 1090-1098):—

> ὁρᾶθ' ὅσοι δυσκελάδοισιν
> κατὰ μοῦσαν ἰόντες ἀείδεθ' ὕμνοις
> ἁμέτερα λέχεα καὶ γάμους
> Κύπριδος ἀθέμιτας ἀνοσίους
> ὅσον εὐσεβίᾳ κρατοῦμεν
> ἄδικον ἄροτον ἀνδρῶν.
> παλίμφαμος ἀοιδὰ
> καὶ μοῦσ' εἰς ἄνδρας ἴτω
> δυσκέλαδος ἀμφὶ λέκτρων.

Honour comes to the race of women: evil repute will no longer be theirs (*Med.* 417-419):—

> ἔρχεται τιμὰ γυναικείῳ γένει·
> οὐκέτι δυσκέλαδος φάμα γυναῖκας ἕξει.

In *Iph. Aul.* (1157-1161) we have a picture of a blameless wife:—

> οὐ σοὶ καταλλαχθεῖσα περὶ σὲ καὶ δόμους
> συμμαρτυρήσεις ὡς ἄμεμπτος ἦν γυνή,
> ἔς τ' Ἀφροδίτην σωφρονοῦσα καὶ τὸ σὸν
> μέλαθρον αὔξουσ', ὥστε σ' εἰσιόντα τε
> χαίρειν θύραζέ τ' ἐξιόντ' εὐδαιμονεῖν.

A good wife is the salvation of a house (*Frag.* 1055):—

> οἰκοφθόρον γὰρ ἄνδρα κωλύει γυνὴ
> ἐσθλὴ παραζευχθεῖσα καὶ σῴζει δόμους.

Fortunate he who is blessed with a good wife (*Frag.* 1057):—

> μακάριος ὅστις εὐτυχεῖ γάμον λαβὼν
> ἐσθλῆς γυναικός.

Not all women are bad (*Frag.* 657):—

> ὅστις δὲ πάσας συντιθεὶς ψέγει λόγῳ
> γυναῖκας ἑξῆς, σκαιός ἐστι κοὺ σοφός·

πολλῶν γὰρ οὐσῶν τὴν μὲν εὑρήσεις κακήν,
τὴν δ' ὥσπερ αὕτη λῆμ' ἔχουσαν εὐγενές [1].

Women are better than men (*Frag.* 499):—

μάτην ἄρ' εἰς γυναῖκας ἐξ ἀνδρῶν ψόγος
ψάλλει, κενὸν τόξευμα, καὶ κακῶς λέγει·
αἱ δ' εἰσ' ἀμείνους ἀρσένων, ἐγὼ λέγω.

Women are blamed, but men are to blame (*El.* 1039-1040):—

κἄπειτ' ἐν ἡμῖν ὁ ψόγος λαμπρύνεται,
οἱ δ' αἴτιοι τῶνδ' οὐ κλύουσ' ἄνδρες κακῶς [2].

Women, too, are wise (*Suppl.* 294):—

ὡς πολλά γ' ἐστὶ κἀπὸ θηλειῶν σοφά.

They are more resourceful than men (*Hipp.* 480-481):—

ἦ τἄρ' ἂν ὀψέ γ' ἄνδρες ἐξεύροιεν ἄν,
εἰ μὴ γυναῖκες μηχανὰς εὑρήσομεν.

Similarly (*Andr.* 85):—

πολλὰς ἂν εὕροις μηχανάς· γυνὴ γὰρ εἶ [3].

A daughter is the stay of an aged, widowed mother (*Hec.* 280-281):—

ἥδ' ἀντὶ πολλῶν ἐστί μοι παραψυχή,
πόλις, τιθήνη, βάκτρον, ἡγεμὼν ὁδοῦ [4].

The utilitarian point of view we have in the *Electra*, 422-423:—

πολλά τοι γυνὴ
χρῄζουσ' ἂν εὕροι δαιτὶ προσφορήματα.

A woman's soothing influence and her value as a nurse we find in *Frag.* 822:—

γυνὴ γὰρ ἐν κακοῖσι καὶ νόσοις πόσει
ἥδιστόν ἐστι, δώματ' ἢν οἰκῇ καλῶς,

---

[1] Cf. *Ion*, 398-400 (quoted above, p. 159).
[2] See Paley's note *ad loc.*
[3] Cf. *Iph. Taur.* 1032; *Frag.* 321 (here, as often, the inventiveness is of a bad kind). See Decharme, *Euripide*, &c., pp. 144-145. He compares (p. 148) the ruses of the wife of Euphiletus in Lysias' speech *On the Murder of Eratosthenes*.
[4] See also *Tro.* 640, 1013; *Alc.* 623; *Hec.* 579; *Her. Fur.* 1371-1373; *Iph. Taur.* 1061; *Bacch.* 317; *Frag.* 823, 909; and p. 158, note 3.

ὀργήν τε πραΰνουσα καὶ δυσθυμίας
ψυχὴν μεθιστᾶσ'· ἡδὺ κἀπάται φίλων[1].

There were reasons even apart from the dramatic proprieties why Euripides expressed sentiments so widely different
concerning women. On the whole, he probably had a keener
insight into woman's capabilities than either Aeschylus or
Sophocles[2]. But such an insight would only tend to increase
his dissatisfaction with what he saw actually existing around
him, and lead him to paint it in darker colours. In the words
of Berlage (p. 196):—'Inquisitionis igitur de vita domestica
haec summa est, quod poeta multo digniores partes tribuit
feminis quam scriptores superiores et aequales'—he has already
excepted Homer—'easque partim pinxit οἵας δεῖ et δυνατὸν
εἶναι, partim οἷαι ἦσαν.' It must be admitted, however, that
he generally shows us the dark side of the picture[3].

As one might expect, Euripides sets more store on virtue
than on beauty.

It is not beauty but virtue that gives delight (*Andr.* 207-
208):—

φίλτρον δὲ καὶ τόδ'· οὐ τὸ κάλλος, ὦ γύναι,
ἀλλ' ἀρεταὶ τέρπουσι τοὺς ξυνευνέτας.

It is beauty of the mind which is true beauty (*Frag.* 548):—

νοῦν χρὴ θεᾶσθαι, νοῦν· τί τῆς εὐμορφίας
ὄφελος, ὅταν τις μὴ φρένας καλὰς ἔχῃ[4];

Helena complains that beauty, which brings good fortune to
other women, has been her undoing (*Hel.* 304-305):—

αἱ μὲν γὰρ ἄλλαι διὰ τὸ κάλλος εὐτυχεῖς
γυναῖκες, ἡμᾶς δ' αὐτὸ τοῦτ' ἀπώλεσεν.

---

[1] Cf. above, pp. 154-155.
[2] Cf. Wilamowitz-Moellendorff, *Herakles*, Einleitung, p. 10:—'Euripides
mag die frauen nicht günstig beurteilt haben: aber er hat sie studiert.
Für Pindar Sokrates und die meisten Sokratiker existiren sie kaum.'
M. Decharme says (*Euripide*, &c.):—'Dans le cœur de la femme, dont il
explore les intimes profondeurs, &c.'
[3] See Decharme, *Euripide, &c.*, pp. 160-162.
[4] Cf. *Frag.* 212.

In beauty, as in other things, moderation is safest (*Frag.* 928):—

οὐ γὰρ ἀσφαλὲς
περαιτέρω τὸ κάλλος ἢ μέσον λαβεῖν.

Isocrates (*Evag.* § 22) includes beauty among the goods most becoming to the young. He is speaking, however, of a man :—

παῖς μὲν γὰρ ὢν ἔσχε κάλλος καὶ ῥώμην καὶ σωφροσύνην, ἅπερ τῶν ἀγαθῶν πρεπωδέστατα τοῖς τηλικούτοις ἐστίν.

Again, speaking of male beauty, he says that good men pride themselves more on their deeds and mind than on physical beauty (*ibid.* § 74):—

προκρίνω δὲ ταύτας πρῶτον μὲν εἰδὼς τοὺς καλοὺς κἀγαθοὺς τῶν ἀνδρῶν οὐχ οὕτως ἐπὶ τῷ κάλλει τοῦ σώματος σεμνυνομένους ὡς ἐπὶ τοῖς ἔργοις καὶ τῇ γνώμῃ φιλοτιμουμένους.

But beauty has great power: to beauty strength itself must yield (*Hel.* § 16):—

σπουδάσας δὲ μάλιστα περί τε τὸν ἐξ Ἀλκμήνης καὶ τοὺς ἐκ Λήδας, τοσούτῳ μᾶλλον Ἑλένην Ἡρακλέους προυτίμησεν, ὥστε τῷ μὲν ἰσχὺν ἔδωκεν, ἢ βίᾳ τῶν ἄλλων κρατεῖν δύναται, τῇ δὲ κάλλος ἀπένειμεν, ὃ καὶ τῆς ῥώμης αὐτῆς ἄρχειν πέφυκεν.

Beauty is the most divine of all things (*ibid.* § 54):—

κάλλους γὰρ πλεῖστον μέρος μετέσχεν, ὃ σεμνότατον καὶ τιμιώτατον καὶ θειότατον τῶν ὄντων ἐστίν.

Even Zeus and the gods are overcome by beauty (*ibid.* § 59):—

ἀλλὰ Ζεὺς ὁ κρατῶν πάντων ἐν μὲν τοῖς ἄλλοις τὴν αὐτοῦ δύναμιν ἐνδείκνυται, πρὸς δὲ τὸ κάλλος ταπεινὸς γιγνόμενος ἀξιοῖ πλησιάζειν. κ.τ.λ. [1].

Woman, says Aeschines, is the most beautiful of all things (*On the Embassy,* § 112):—

"οὐκ εἶπον, ὡς καλὸς εἶ· γυνὴ γὰρ τῶν ὄντων ἐστὶ κάλλιστον·
. . . ." [2]

---

[1] See the whole passage (§§ 54-60 .
[2] On the subject of beauty see also Demosthenes (?), *Erot.* §§ 1-16.

§ 2. On the subject of Love the Orators have not much to say. Lysias in one place declares that lovers are fools (iii. § 44):—

οὐ γὰρ τοῦ αὐτοῦ μοι δοκεῖ εἶναι ἐρᾶν τε καὶ συκοφαντεῖν, ἀλλὰ τὸ μὲν τῶν εὐηθεστέρων, τὸ δὲ τῶν πανουργοτάτων.

Euripides also speaks of the folly of love, introducing one of those etymologies of which he is so fond [1] (*Tro.* 987–990):—

ἦν οὑμὸς υἱὸς κάλλος εὐπρεπέστατος,
ὁ σὸς δ' ἰδών νιν νοῦς ἐποιήθη Κύπρις·
τὰ μῶρα γὰρ πάντ' ἐστὶν Ἀφροδίτη βροτοῖς,
καὶ τοὔνομ' ὀρθῶς ἀφροσύνης ἄρχει θεᾶς [2].

In his speech in Plato's *Phaedrus* (231 D) Lysias calls love a disease:—

καὶ γὰρ αὐτοὶ (sc. οἱ ἐρῶντες) ὁμολογοῦσι νοσεῖν μᾶλλον ἢ σωφρονεῖν, καὶ εἰδέναι ὅτι κακῶς φρονοῦσιν, ἀλλ' οὐ δύνασθαι αὐτῶν κρατεῖν.

Similarly Euripides (*Frag.* 339):—

. . . καὶ γὰρ οὐκ αὐθαίρετοι
βροτοῖς ἔρωτες οὐδ' ἑκουσία νόσος.

And again (*Frag.* 400):—

ὅσον νόσημα τὴν Κύπριν κεκτήμεθα [3].

Isocrates speaks of the disquiet and envy of lovers (*Antid.* § 245):—

. . . δυσκόλως ἔχειν καὶ ζηλοτυπεῖν καὶ τὰς ψυχὰς τεταραγμένως διακεῖσθαι καὶ πεπονθέναι παραπλήσια τοῖς ἐρῶσι.

Euripides also mentions some of the evil effects of love (*Hel.* 1102–1104):—

τί ποτ' ἄπληστος εἶ κακῶν,
ἔρωτας ἀπάτας δόλιά τ' ἐξευρήματα
ἀσκοῦσα φίλτρα θ' αἱματηρὰ δωμάτων;

---

[1] See Paley, *Euripides*, i, preface, p. xxxii; and cf. (with Paley's notes) *Bacch.* 292-294, 367; *Hec.* 650. 'Comme les sophistes encore, il se complaît aux étymologies' (Decharme, *Euripide, &c.*, p. 57. See his note there).

[2] Cf. *Frag.* 161 : ἐρῶν· τὸ μαίνεσθαι δ' ἄρ' ἦν ἔρως βροτοῖς.

[3] So, in the *Hippolytus*, Phaedra's passion is again and again termed a νόσος.

Aeschines declares that he has nothing to say against ἔρως δίκαιος (*Agst. Timarchus*, § 136):—

ἐγὼ δὲ οὔτε ἔρωτα δίκαιον ψέγω, κ.τ.λ.

He goes on to contrast τὸ ἐρᾶν τῶν καλῶν καὶ σωφρόνων with τὸ ἀσελγαίνειν (§ 137):—

ὁρίζομαι δ᾽ εἶναι τὸ μὲν ἐρᾶν τῶν καλῶν καὶ σωφρόνων φιλανθρώπου πάθος καὶ εὐγνώμονος ψυχῆς, τὸ δὲ ἀσελγαίνειν ἀργυρίου τινὰ μισθούμενον ὑβριστοῦ καὶ ἀπαιδεύτου ἀνδρὸς ἔργον εἶναι ἡγοῦμαι.

Elsewhere he says that vice is not compatible with δίκαιος ἔρως (*On the Embassy*, § 166):—

οὐ γὰρ προσδέχεται δίκαιος ἔρως ποιηρίαν[1].

In another place he quotes from Euripides a passage in praise of τὸ σωφρόνως ἐρᾶν (*Agst. Timarchus*, § 151):—

ὁ τοίνυν οὐδενὸς ἧττον σοφὸς τῶν ποιητῶν Εὐριπίδης, ἔν τι τῶν καλλίστων ὑπολαμβάνων εἶναι τὸ σωφρόνως ἐρᾶν, ἐν εὐχῆς μέρει τὸν ἔρωτα ποιούμενος λέγει που·

ὁ δ᾽ εἰς τὸ σῶφρον ἐπ᾽ ἀρετήν τ᾽ ἄγων ἔρως
ζηλωτὸς ἀνθρώποισιν, ὧν εἴην ἐγώ[2].

There are several other passages in which Euripides inculcates σωφροσύνη and μετριότης in love. The first I will quote is the well-known passage in the *Medea* (627–642):—

ἔρωτες ὑπὲρ μὲν ἄγαν ἐλθόντες οὐκ εὐδοξίαν
οὐδ᾽ ἀρετὰν παρέδωκαν ἀνδράσιν· εἰ δ᾽ ἅλις ἔλθοι
Κύπρις, οὐκ ἄλλα θεὸς εὔχαρις οὕτω.
μήποτ᾽, ὦ δέσποιν᾽, ἐπ᾽ ἐμοὶ χρυσέων τόξων ἐφείης
ἱμέρῳ χρίσασ᾽ ἄφυκτον οἰστόν[3].
στέργοι δέ με σωφροσύνα, δώρημα κάλλιστον θεῶν·
μηδέ ποτ᾽ ἀμφιλόγους ὀργὰς ἀκόρεστά τε νείκη

---

[1] Cf. Demosthenes (?), *Erot.* § 1:—ὁρῶν δ᾽ ὡς ἔπος εἰπεῖν τὰ πλεῖστα τῶν ἐρωτικῶν συνταγμάτων αἰσχύνην μᾶλλον ἢ τιμὴν περιάπτοντα τούτοις περὶ ὧν ἐστι γεγραμμένα, τοῦθ᾽ ὅπως μὴ πείσεται πεφύλακται, καὶ ὅπερ καὶ πεπεῖσθαί φησι τῇ γνώμῃ, τοῦτο καὶ γέγραφεν, ὡς δίκαιος ἐραστὴς οὔτ᾽ ἂν ποιήσειεν οὐδὲν αἰσχρὸν οὔτ᾽ ἀξιώσειεν.

[2] *Frag.* 672.

[3] Cf. *ibid.* 530-531:—   ... ὡς Ἔρως σ᾽ ἠνάγκασε
τόξοις ἀφύκτοις τοὐμὸν ἐκσῶσαι δέμας.

θυμὸν ἐκπλήξασ' ἑτέροις ἐπὶ λέκτροις
προσβάλοι δεινὰ Κύπρις, ἀπτολέμους δ' εὐνὰς σεβίζουσ'
ὀξύφρων κρίνοι λέχη γυναικῶν.

So again (*Hel.* 1105-1106):—

εἰ δ' ἦσθα μετρία, τἆλλα γ' ἡδίστη θεῶν
πέφυκας ἀνθρώποισιν· οὐκ ἄλλως λέγω.

The last passage I will quote in this connexion is from *Iph.
Aul.* (543-558):—

μάκαρες οἱ μετρίας θεοῦ
μετά τε σωφροσύνας μετέ-
σχον λέκτρων Ἀφροδίτας, κ.τ.λ. [1].

I will here add a few more sayings of Euripides on the subject
of love, although they have no parallels in the Orators.

Love is the sweetest of the gods (*Alc.* 790-791):—

τίμα δὲ καὶ τὴν πλεῖστον ἡδίστην θεῶν
Κύπριν βροτοῖσιν· εὐμενὴς γὰρ ἡ θεός [2].

But it is sometimes bitter (*Hipp.* 727):—

πικροῦ δ' ἔρωτος ἡσσηθήσομαι [3].

The sweetness and bitterness of love are sometimes mingled
(*ibid.* 347-348):—

ΦΑ. τί τοῦθ' ὃ δὴ λέγουσιν ἀνθρώπους ἐρᾶν;
ΤΡ. ἥδιστον, ὦ παῖ, ταὐτὸν ἀλγεινόν θ' ἅμα [4].

It is often an evil (*Med.* 330):—

φεῦ φεῦ· βροτοῖς ἔρωτες ὡς κακὸν μέγα [5].

The power and worship of love are universal (*Hipp.* 1-6):—

πολλὴ μὲν ἐν βροτοῖσι κοὐκ ἀνώνυμος
θεὰ κέκλημαι Κύπρις, οὐρανοῦ τ' ἔσω,
ὅσοι τε πόντου τερμόνων τ' Ἀτλαντικῶν
ναίουσιν εἴσω φῶς ὁρῶντες ἡλίου,

---

[1] Cf. *Frag.* 428, 897. For Euripides' ideas on love generally see Decharme,
Euripide, &c., pp. 112 ff.
[2] Cf. *Bacch.* 402 (θελξίφρονες Ἔρωτες).
[3] Cf. *ibid.* 775; *Andr.* 290.   [4] Cf. *Frag.* 26.
[5] Cf. *Hipp.* 762, 1400 (Κύπρις ἡ πανοῦργος), 1461; *Hel.* 238; *Iph. Aul.* 1301;
Frag. 322, 362, 524, 547.

τοὺς μὲν σέβοντας τἀμὰ πρεσβεύω κράτη,
σφάλλω δ' ὅσοι φρονοῦσιν εἰς ἡμᾶς μέγα [1].

I can here only refer to the famous ode on love in the *Hippolytus* (525 ff.), with which one may compare the still more famous ode in the *Antigone* of Sophocles (781 ff.) [2].

§ 3. Though we find in the Orators references to various laws, observances, &c. relating to marriage, there is little in the way of general sentiment [3].

Lysias tells us how adultery was universally regarded (i. §§ 2–3):—

καὶ ταῦτα οὐκ ἂν εἴη μόνον παρ' ὑμῖν οὕτως ἐγνωσμένα, ἀλλ' ἐν ἁπάσῃ τῇ Ἑλλάδι· περὶ τούτου γὰρ μόνου τοῦ ἀδικήματος καὶ ἐν δημοκρατίᾳ καὶ ὀλιγαρχίᾳ ἡ αὐτὴ τιμωρία τοῖς ἀσθενεστάτοις πρὸς τοὺς τὰ μέγιστα δυναμένους ἀποδέδοται, ὥστε τὸν χείριστον τῶν αὐτῶν τυγχάνειν τῷ βελτίστῳ· οὕτως, ὦ ἄνδρες, ταύτην τὴν ὕβριν ἅπαντες ἄνθρωποι δεινοτάτην ἡγοῦνται. περὶ μὲν οὖν τοῦ μεγέθους τῆς ζημίας ἅπαντας ὑμᾶς νομίζω τὴν αὐτὴν διάνοιαν ἔχειν, καὶ οὐδένα οὕτως ὀλιγώρως διακεῖσθαι, ὅστις οἴεται δεῖν συγγνώμης τυγχάνειν ἢ μικρᾶς ζημίας ἀξίους ἡγεῖται τοὺς τῶν τοιούτων ἔργων αἰτίους.

Its penalty was death (xiii. § 66):—

γυναῖκας τοίνυν τῶν πολιτῶν τοιοῦτος ὢν μοιχεύειν καὶ διαφθείρειν ἐλευθέρας ἐπεχείρησε, καὶ ἐλήφθη μοιχός· καὶ τούτου θάνατος ἡ ζημία ἐστίν [4].

In the speech *Against Neaera* (§§ 85–86) we are told that the woman taken in adultery was not admitted to the public

---

[1] Cf. *ibid.* 99, 358, 443, 1268 ff.; *Tro.* 945 ff.; *Frag.* 136, 269, 898; and the invocation with which Lucretius begins his poem.

[2] For other passages on Love see *Tro.* 1051; *Iph. Aul.* 569, 1304; *Frag.* 23, 138 ('He is fortunate, the object of whose love is good', 331, 388, 430, 547, 653, 665, 781, 895; and on Chastity (τὸ σωφρονεῖν see *El.* 53, 923, 1098 1099; *Bacch.* 314 ff.; *Frag.* 524.

[3] For what marriage was at Athens in the 5th cent. B.C. see Decharme, *Euripide, &c.*, pp. 139–140. The Athenian married in order to fulfil a duty to the state, a patriotic obligation. Woman was the means of perpetuating the family and of preserving the city.

[4] 'Adultery was punished by death, according to the laws of Draco. Later jurists seem to have distinguished violence and seduction, and to have punished the former by a fine, the latter by death,—a curious reversal of modern ideas' (Shuckburgh, note *ad loc.*).

sacrifices,—a penalty which is said to be a motive to chastity in women :—

ἐφ' ᾗ γὰρ ἂν μοιχὸς ἀλῷ γυναικί, οὐκ ἔξεστιν αὐτῇ ἐλθεῖν εἰς οὐδὲν τῶν ἱερῶν τῶν δημοτελῶν, εἰς ἃ καὶ τὴν ξένην καὶ τὴν δούλην ἐλθεῖν ἐξουσίαν ἔδοσαν οἱ νόμοι καὶ θεασομένην καὶ ἱκετεύσουσαν εἰσιέναι· ἀλλὰ μόναις ταύταις ἀπαγορεύουσιν οἱ νόμοι ταῖς γυναιξὶ μὴ εἰσιέναι εἰς τὰ ἱερὰ τὰ δημοτελῆ, ἐφ' ᾗ ἂν μοιχὸς ἀλῷ, ἐὰν δ' εἰσίωσι καὶ παρανομῶσι, νηποινεὶ πάσχειν ὑπὸ τοῦ βουλομένου ὅ τι ἂν πάσχῃ, πλὴν θανάτου, καὶ ἔδωκεν ὁ νόμος τὴν τιμωρίαν ὑπὲρ αὐτῶν τῷ ἐντυχόντι. διὰ τοῦτο δ' ἐποίησεν ὁ νόμος πλὴν θανάτου τἆλλα ὑβρισθεῖσαν αὐτὴν μηδαμοῦ λαβεῖν δίκην, ἵνα μὴ μιάσματα μηδ' ἀσεβήματα γίγνηται ἐν τοῖς ἱεροῖς, ἱκανὸν φόβον ταῖς γυναιξὶ παρασκευάζων τοῦ σωφρονεῖν καὶ μηδὲν ἁμαρτάνειν, ἀλλὰ δικαίως οἰκουρεῖν, διδάσκων ὡς, ἄν τι ἁμάρτῃ τοιοῦτον, ἅμα ἔκ τε τῆς οἰκίας τοῦ ἀνδρὸς ἐκβεβλημένη ἔσται καὶ ἐκ τῶν ἱερῶν τῶν τῆς πόλεως [1].

In the *Troades* (1028-1032) Hecuba advises Menelaus to punish Helena with death :—

... ἐπὶ τοῖς πρόσθεν ἡμαρτημένοις,
Μενέλα', ἵν' εἰδῇς οἷ τελευτήσω λόγον,
στεφάνωσον Ἑλλάδ', ἀξίως τήνδε κτανὼν
σαυτοῦ, νόμον δὲ τόνδε ταῖς ἄλλαισι θὲς
γυναιξί, θνήσκειν ἥτις ἂν προδῷ πόσιν.

Adultery is hated both by men and by the gods below (*Or.* 619-620) :—

... καὶ τοῦθ' ὃ μισήσειαν Αἰγίσθου λέχος
οἱ νέρτεροι θεοί, καὶ γὰρ ἐνθάδ' ἦν πικρόν, κ.τ.λ.

A woman who has once been guilty of adultery will be guilty again (*El.* 921-924) :—

ἴστω δ', ὅταν τις διολέσας δάμαρτά του
κρυπταῖσιν εὐναῖς εἶτ' ἀναγκασθῇ λαβεῖν,
δύστηνός ἐστιν, εἰ δοκεῖ τὸ σωφρονεῖν
ἐκεῖ μὲν αὐτὴν οὐκ ἔχειν, παρ' οἷ δ' ἔχειν [2].

---

[1] A law is quoted (*ibid.* § 66) as to what is done if a man, imprisoned as an adulterer, is found, after appeal, to have been unjustly imprisoned, what if justly.

[2] On the question of adultery see Coulanges, *La Cité Antique*, pp. 106-107.

There is practically nothing in the way of general opinion on divorce. Isaeus (iii. § 35), and the author of the speech *Against Neaera* (§ 52), refer to laws bearing on the subject. Medea, speaking of the hard lot of women, says that divorce is difficult to obtain and brings disgrace to them (*Med.* 236–237):—

> οὐ γὰρ εὐκλεεῖς ἀπαλλαγαὶ
> γυναιξίν, οὐδ' οἷόν τ' ἀνήνασθαι πόσιν[1].

Childlessness Isaeus regards as a misfortune (ii. § 23). He is speaking from the legal point of view of there being no heir:—

> ὄντων γὰρ αὐτῷ παίδων ἐκείνῳ ὄντι ἄπαιδι καὶ ἀτυχοῦντι φαίνεται ἐπιτιμῶν[2].

In Euripides, the Chorus in the *Ion* also speak of childlessness as a misfortune, but from a wider, human standpoint (*Ion*, 488–491):—

> τὸν ἄπαιδα δ' ἀποπτυγῶ
> βίον, ᾧ τε δοκεῖ, ψέγω·
> μετὰ δὲ κτεάνων μετρίων βιοτᾶς
> εὐπαιδὸς ἐχοίμαν.

Far more frequently, however, Euripides speaks of the happy lot of the unwedded and childless; e. g. *Alc.* 882–888:—

> ζηλῶ δ' ἀγάμους ἀτέκνους τε βροτῶν.
> μία γὰρ ψυχή· τῆς ὑπεραλγεῖν
> μέτριον ἄχθος·
> παίδων δὲ νόσους καὶ νυμφιδίους
> εὐνὰς θανάτοις κεραϊζομένας
> οὐ τλητὸν ὁρᾶν, ἐξὸν ἀτέκνους
> ἀγάμους τ' εἶναι διὰ παντός.

---

[1] Cf. *Frag.* 502 (l. 6), where the difficulty of divorce is regarded from the man's side :—

> ... αἱ γὰρ διαλύσεις ⟨οὐ⟩ ῥᾴδιαι.

· The Attic law of divorce is said to have favoured only the cause of the male claimant. Cf. *Medea*, 1375 (ῥᾴδιοι δ' ἀπαλλαγαί); Aesch. *Suppl.* 333 , Paley, note on *Medea*, 236 . See also Coulanges, *La Cité Antique*, p. 48.

[2] Cf. ii. §§ 10, 46; vii. § 30; ix. § 7,—where the anxiety concerns the discharge of τὰ νομιζόμενα. See Coulanges, *La Cité Antique*, pp. 50, 55–57.

Similarly (*Rhesus*, 980-982):—

> ὦ παιδοποιοὶ συμφοραί, πόνοι βροτῶν,
> ὡς ὅστις ὑμᾶς μὴ κακῶς λογίζεται,
> ἄπαις διοίσει κοὺ τεκὼν θάψει τέκνα[1].

Elsewhere he says he cannot determine whether it is better or not to have children (*Frag.* 571):—

> ἀμηχανῶ δ' ἔγωγε κοὐκ ἔχω μαθεῖν,
> εἴτ' οὖν ἄμεινόν ἐστι γίγνεσθαι τέκνα
> θνητοῖσιν εἴτ' ἄπαιδα καρποῦσθαι βίον.
> ὁρῶ γὰρ οἷς μὲν οὐκ ἔφυσαν, ἀθλίους·
> ὅσοισι δ' εἰσίν, οὐδὲν εὐτυχεστέρους.
> καὶ γὰρ κακοὶ γεγῶτες ἐχθίστη νόσος,
> κἂν αὖ γένωνται σώφρονες, κακὸν μέγα,
> λυποῦσι τὸν φύσαντα μὴ πάθωσί τι[2].

Marriage feasts and observances—the Thesmophoria, &c.—are referred to by Isaeus (iii. § 80; viii. §§ 18-19), and the bridal torch by Euripides (*Tro.* 308; *Iph. Aul.* 732; *Phoen.* 345). Reference is made to the Hymeneal Ode in *Iph. Aul.* 1036 ff.; and examples of it are found in *Tro.* 308 ff.; *Frag.* 781[3].

I will here add some passages from Euripides, who has much to say on the subject of marriage, and regards it sometimes as a blessing, sometimes as a curse.

A good marriage brings happiness and blessing (*Or.* 602-603):—

> γάμοι δ' ὅσοις μὲν εὖ καθεστᾶσιν βροτῶν,
> μακάριος αἰών.

A man should have a good wife or none (*Iph. Aul.* 749-750):—

> χρὴ δ' ἐν δόμοισιν ἄνδρα τὸν σοφὸν τρέφειν
> γυναῖκα χρηστὴν κἀγαθήν, ἢ μὴ τρέφειν[4].

---

[1] Cf. *Med.* 1090 ff.; *Suppl.* 787 ff., 1087-1093; *Frag.* 908. And see Decharme, *Euripide, &c.*, pp. 116-117.   [2] Cf. *Andr.* 418-420.

[3] See Coulanges, *La Cité Antique*, p. 44. Other references to marriage by the Orators are found in Isocrates (*Antid.* § 156), who speaks of the expense of keeping a wife and bringing up children; and in Isaeus (vii. § 12), who speaks of ἐπιγαμία as tending to reconciliation. On ἐπιγαμία see Coulanges, *La Cité Antique*, p. 238. See also Mahaffy, *Old Greek Life*, pp. 49-51: Coulanges, *La Cité Antique*, pp. 41-48.

[4] Cf. *Alc.* 626-627; *Heracl.* 297 ff.; *Frag.* 1055: and see above, pp. 159-162.

The Chorus in the *Medea* declare that marriage is the source of many evils (*Med.* 1291-1292):—

> ὦ γυναικῶν λέχος πολύπονον,
> ὅσα βροτοῖς ἔρεξας ἤδη κακά.

A bad marriage brings misfortune (*Or.* 603-604):—

> οἷς δὲ μὴ πίπτουσιν εὖ (sc. γάμοι),
> τά τ' ἔνδον εἰσὶ τά τε θύραζε δυστυχεῖς[1].

Marriage is a mixed blessing: it brings sorrow as well as joy, evil as well as good (*Alc.* 238-242):—

> οὔποτε φήσω γάμον εὐφραίνειν
> πλέον ἢ λυπεῖν, κ.τ.λ.

Similarly (*Frag.* 78):—

> γυναῖκα καὶ ὠφελίαν
> καὶ νόσον ἀνδρὶ φέρειν
> μεγίσταν ἐδίδαξα τὠμῷ λόγῳ[2].

Good wives are rare (*Alc.* 472-475):—

> τοιαύτης εἴη μοι κῦρσαι
> συνδυάδος φιλίας ἀλόχου· τὸ γὰρ
> ἐν βιότῳ σπάνιον μέρος· ἢ γὰρ ἔμοιγ' ἄλυπος
> δι' αἰῶνος ἂν ξυνείη[3].

The husband should be master (*El.* 932-933):—

> καίτοι τόδ' αἰσχρόν, προστατεῖν γε δωμάτων
> γυναῖκα, μὴ τὸν ἄνδρα[4].

Woman's view of marriage we have in *Medea*, 569-573. Not to have her bed dishonoured is to her everything:—

> ἀλλ' ἐς τοσοῦτον ἧκεθ' ὥστ' ὀρθουμένης
> εὐνῆς γυναῖκες πάντ' ἔχειν νομίζετε,
> ἢν δ' αὖ γένηται συμφορά τις ἐς λέχος,
> τὰ λῷστα καὶ κάλλιστα πολεμιώτατα
> τίθεσθε[5].

---

[1] Cf. *Hel.* 296; *El.* 1097; *Phœn.* 340; *Frag.* 914.
[2] Cf. *Tro.* 1170; *Frag.* 1056, 1057.
[3] Cf. *Iph. Aul.* 1162-1163.
[4] Cf. *ibid.* 1052-1053.
[5] Cf. *ibid.* 1366-1369.

Andromache hates the woman who forgets her former husband and marries again (*Tro.* 662-663):—

> ἀπέπτυσ᾽ αὐτήν, ἥτις ἄνδρα τὸν πάρος
> καινοῖσι λέκτροις ἀποβαλοῦσ᾽ ἄλλον φιλεῖ.

Unanimity is salvation in married life (*Med.* 14-15):—

> ἥπερ μεγίστη γίγνεται σωτηρία,
> ὅταν γυνὴ πρὸς ἄνδρα μὴ διχοστατῇ.

And chastity is the condition of married bliss (*El.* 1097-1099):—

> ὅστις δὲ πλοῦτον ἢ εὐγένειαν εἰσιδὼν
> γαμεῖ πονηράν, μῶρός ἐστι· μικρὰ γὰρ
> μεγάλων ἀμείνω σώφρον᾽ ἐν δόμοις λέχη.

In marriage also μετριότης and σωφροσύνη are best (*Frag.* 503):—

> μετρίων λέκτρων, μετρίων δὲ γάμων
> μετὰ σωφροσύνης
> κῦρσαι θνητοῖσιν ἄριστον[1].

§ 4. Both Euripides and the Orators have a good deal to say on the subject of kinship—its claims and blessings; on affection and duty paternal, maternal and filial; on the charm of children in a house, and the grief caused by their death; on the shame of family quarrels.

Kinsmen, says Andocides, should lend their aid in time of adversity (*On the Mysteries*, § 118):—

> ὅμως δ᾽ ἐγὼ καλέσας Λέαγρον ἐναντίον τῶν φίλων ἔλεγον ὅτι
> ταῦτ᾽ εἴη ἀνδρῶν ἀγαθῶν, ἐν τοῖς τοιούτοις δεικνύναι τὰς οἰκειότητας
> ἀλλήλοις.

---

[1] Cf. *El.* 936; *Frag.* 502; and the Greek proverb τὸ κηδεῦσαι καθ᾽ ἑαυτόν. For other passages bearing on marriage see *El.* 265, 921 ff.; *Frag.* 24, 804, 807.

There are in the *Andromache* some interesting passages on the question of monogamy. In ll. 177, 464, 469, 909 monogamy is regarded as good, bigamy as bad. In l. 215 reference is made to polygamy in Thrace: cf. *El.* 1033; *Frag.* 402.

See also Coulanges, *La Cité Antique*, p. 48 :—' Une telle religion ne pouvait pas admettre la polygamie.'

Isaeus declares that it is a reproach for a man to set more store on money than on kinship (ix. § 25):—

πολὺ γὰρ προὐργιαίτερον ἡγεῖται εἶναι τὸ χρηματίζεσθαι ἢ τὴν ἐμὴν συγγένειαν.

Similarly Demosthenes (*Agst. Stephanus*, i. § 54):—

... καὶ περὶ πλείονος ἐποιήσατο τὸν Φορμίωνος πλοῦτον ἢ τὰ τῆς συγγενείας ἀναγκαῖα ;

One ought to please parents, friends, relatives (Demosth. (?), *Epitaph.* § 16):—

... καὶ πᾶσιν ἀρέσκοντες οἷς χρή, γονεῦσι, φίλοις, οἰκείοις.

False witness against kinsmen, according to Demosthenes, is the worst. He gives his reason: such a thing is against nature (*Agst. Stephanus*, i. § 53):—

δεινὸν μὲν γάρ ἐστιν εἰ καθ' ὅτου τις οὖν τὰ ψευδῆ μαρτυρεῖ, πολλῷ δὲ δεινότερον καὶ πλείονος ὀργῆς ἄξιον, εἰ κατὰ τῶν συγγενῶν· οὐ γὰρ τοὺς γεγραμμένους νόμους ὁ τοιοῦτος ἄνθρωπος μόνους, ἀλλὰ καὶ τὰ τῆς φύσεως οἰκεῖ' ἀναιρεῖ.

All men, Andocides(?) says, have more regard for kinsmen than for strangers (*Agst. Alcibiades*, § 15):—

πάντες γὰρ ἄνθρωποι τοὺς οἰκείους τῶν ἀλλοτρίων ποιοῦνται περὶ πλείονος [1].

Strange is the power of kinship, says Euripides, it is a blessing in adversity (*Andr.* 985-986):—

τὸ συγγενὲς γὰρ δεινόν, ἔν τε τοῖς κακοῖς
οὐκ ἔστιν οὐδὲν κρεῖσσον οἰκείου φίλου.

One must share the toils of one's kinsfolk (*Or.* 684-686):—

καὶ χρὴ γὰρ οὕτω τῶν ὁμαιμόνων κακὰ
ξυνεκκομίζειν, δύναμιν ἢν διδῷ θεός,
θνήσκοντα καὶ κτείνοντα τοὺς ἐναντίους [2].

---

[1] Isaeus, speaking as usual from the legal point of view, mentions that kinsmen are most favoured in questions of inheritance iv. § 16):—

ἔπειτα οἱ νόμοι οὐ μόνον οἱ περὶ τῶν γενῶν ἀλλὰ καὶ οἱ περὶ τῶν δόσεων τοῖς συγγενέσι βοηθοῦσι.

He also speaks of the claims of kinship, i. § 39.

[2] Cf. *Iph. Taur.* 1402 ; *Heracl.* 6.

'Honour your parents' is one of the virtues inculcated by Isocrates (*Ad Demon.* § 16):—

τοὺς μὲν θεοὺς φοβοῦ, τοὺς δὲ γονεῖς τίμα, τοὺς δὲ φίλους αἰσχύνου, τοῖς δὲ νόμοις πείθου.

In the matter of filial duty the golden rule should be observed (*ibid.* § 14):—

τοιοῦτος γίγνου περὶ τοὺς γονεῖς, οἵους ἂν εὔξαιο περὶ σεαυτὸν γενέσθαι τοὺς σεαυτοῦ παῖδας.

Elsewhere, speaking of the degeneracy of Greece, he says that in his time men sinned against their parents with less hesitation than in a former age they contradicted or abused their elders (*Areop.* § 49):—

ἀντειπεῖν δὲ τοῖς πρεσβυτέροις ἢ λοιδορήσασθαι δεινότερον ἐνό-μιζον ἢ νῦν περὶ τοὺς γονέας ἐξαμαρτεῖν [1].

Parents, says Aeschines, ought to be honoured like the gods (*Agst. Timarchus*, § 28):—

οὓς (sc. τοὺς γονέας) ἐξ ἴσου δεῖ τιμᾶν τοῖς θεοῖς [2].

A son, according to Isaeus, should cherish and reverence his father (ii. § 18):—

... καὶ ἐγὼ τὸν αὐτὸν τρόπον ὥσπερ γόνῳ ὄντα πατέρα ἐμαυτοῦ ἐθεράπευόν τε καὶ ᾐσχυνόμην, κ.τ.λ. [3].

Children are bound by law to support their parents (viii. § 32):—

κελεύει γὰρ (sc. ὁ νόμος) τρέφειν τοὺς γονέας· γονεῖς δ' εἰσὶ μήτηρ καὶ πατὴρ καὶ πάππος καὶ τήθη καὶ τούτων μήτηρ καὶ πατήρ, ἐὰν ἔτι ζῶσιν· ἐκεῖνοι γὰρ ἀρχὴ τοῦ γένους εἰσί, καὶ τὰ ἐκείνων παραδίδοται τοῖς ἐκγόνοις· διόπερ ἀνάγκη τρέφειν αὐτούς ἐστι, κἂν μηδὲν καταλίπωσι.

The laws as to the maintenance and burial of parents are mentioned likewise by Demosthenes (*Agst. Timocrates*, § 107):—

... οἱ (sc. νόμοι) καὶ ζῶντας ἀναγκάζουσι τοὺς παῖδας τοὺς γονέας

---

[1] In a passage already quoted (*Frag.* iii. (β'.) 9) Isocrates declares, however, that teachers ought to receive greater honour than parents.

[2] In *Epist.* ii. § 5, Aeschines (?) says that men rear children in the expecta-tion that they will be the stay of their old age.

[3] Cf. *ibid.* § 41.

τρέφειν, καὶ ἐπειδὰν ἀποθάνωσιν, ὅπως τῶν νομιζομένων τύχωσι, παρασκευάζουσιν [1] ;

Lycurgus also speaks of the duties of children to parents (*Agst. Leocrates*, §§ 94–96):—

... παρ' ὧν γὰρ τὴν ἀρχὴν τοῦ ζῆν εἰλήφαμεν καὶ πλεῖστα ἀγαθὰ πεπόνθαμεν, εἰς τούτους μὴ ὅτι ἀμαρτεῖν ἀλλ' ὅτι μὴ εὐεργετοῦντας τὸν αὐτῶν βίον καταναλῶσαι μέγιστον ἀσέβημά ἐστι.

He goes on to tell a story illustrative of a son's affection and the favour shown by the gods.

We have a beautiful picture of an affectionate daughter in the *Supplices* of Euripides (1099–1103):—

ἀλλ' οὐκέτ' ἔστιν' ἥ γ' ἐμὴν γενειάδα
προσῆγετ' ἀεὶ στόματι, καὶ κάρα τόδε
κατεῖχε χειρί· πατρὶ δ' οὐδὲν ἥδιον
γέροντι θυγατρός· ἀρσίνων δὲ μείζονες
ψυχαί, γλυκεῖαι δ' ἧσσον ἐς θωπεύματα [2].

And there are several passages bearing on filial duty.

A son should aid a father in danger (*Frag.* 84):—

ἢ τί πλέον εἶναι παῖδας ἀνθρώποις, πάτερ,
εἰ μὴ ἐπὶ τοῖς δεινοῖσιν ὠφελήσομεν ;

'Children, obey your parents' (*Frag.* 110):—

ἐγὼ δ', ὁ μὲν μέγιστον, ἄρξομαι λέγειν
ἐκ τοῦδε πρῶτον· πατρὶ πείθεσθαι χρεὼν
παῖδας νομίζειν τ' αὐτὸ τοῦτ' εἶναι δίκην.

Due honour should be paid to parents (*Frag.* 949):—

καὶ τοῖς τεκοῦσιν ἀξίαν τιμὴν νέμειν [3].

Love for a mother is the sweetest love of all (*Frag.* 358):—

οὐκ ἔστι μητρὸς οὐδὲν ἥδιον τέκνοις·
ἐρᾶτε μητρός, παῖδες, ὡς οὐκ ἔστ' ἔρως
τοιοῦτος ἄλλος ὅστις ἡδίων ἐρᾶν [4].

---

[1] In the speech *On the Crown*, § 205, Demosthenes puts country before parents. In *Epist.* iii. § 45, he says that politicians ought to be to all the citizens as children to parents. In xxxix. § 23, he speaks of quarrels between husband and wife being often made up on account of their children.

[2] Cf. *Ion*, 1437–1438.

[3] Cf. *Suppl.* 361 ff. ; *Phoen.* 1444 ff. ; *Frag.* 234.

[4] In *Frag.* 1064, Euripides says that men honour father more than mother.

Sons are the pillars of a house (*Iph. Taur.* 57):—

στῦλοι γὰρ οἴκων εἰσὶ παῖδες ἄρσενες.

Children are better than winged wealth (*Frag.* 518):—

καὶ κτῆμα δ', ὦ τεκοῦσα, κάλλιστον τόδε,
πλούτου δὲ κρεῖσσον· τοῦ μὲν ὠκεῖα πτέρυξ,
παῖδες δὲ χρηστοί, κᾂν θάνωσι, δώμασιν
καλόν τι θησαύρισμα τοῖς τεκοῦσί τε
ἀνάθημα βιότου κοὔποτ' ἐκλείπει δόμους [1].

A wondrous charm are children (*Frag.* 103):—

δεινόν τι τέκνων φίλτρον ἐνῆκεν
θεὸς ἀνθρώποις [2].

'To strike or ill-use a parent was an offence punishable by fine, disfranchisement, or death: the suit was called γραφὴ κακώσεως γονέων. See Arist. *Av.* 1344: *Nub.* 1419–1430' [3].

So Andocides (*On the Mysteries*, § 74) speaks of (τὸ) τοὺς γονέας κακῶς ποιεῖν as one of the crimes punishable by ἀτιμία. And Lysias says (xiii. § 91):—

ὅστις οὖν τόν τε γόνῳ πατέρα τὸν αὑτοῦ ἔτυπτε καὶ οὐδὲν παρεῖχε τῶν ἐπιτηδείων, τόν τε ποιητὸν πατέρα ἀφείλετο ἃ ἦν ὑπάρχοντα ἐκείνῳ ἀγαθά, πῶς οὐ καὶ διὰ τοῦτο κατὰ τὸν τῆς κακώσεως νόμον ἄξιός ἐστι θανάτῳ ζημιωθῆναι;

In this connexion also the following passage from Aeschines may be quoted (*Agst. Timarchus*, § 28):—

τίνας δ' οὐκ ᾤετο δεῖν λέγειν; τοὺς αἰσχρῶς βεβιωκότας· τούτους οὐκ ἐᾷ δημηγορεῖν. καὶ ποῦ τοῦτο δηλοῖ; δοκιμασία, φησί, ῥητόρων· ἐάν τις λέγῃ ἐν τῷ δήμῳ τὸν πατέρα τύπτων ἢ τὴν μητέρα, ἢ μὴ τρέφων, ἢ μὴ παρέχων οἴκησιν· τοῦτον οὐκ ἐᾷ λέγειν. νὴ Δία καλῶς γε, ὡς ἐγώ φημι. κ.τ.λ. [4]

In Euripides, too, we find mention made of the sin of dishonouring a father, and of the paternal curse (*Phoen.* 874–877):—

οὔτε γὰρ γέρα πατρὶ
οὔτ' ἔξοδον διδόντες, ἄνδρα δυστυχῆ

---

[1] Cf. *Ion*, 481 ff. (with Paley's note); *Or.* 542–543; *Frag.* 543.
[2] Cf. *Andr.* 418 (with Paley's note); *Tro.* 371; *Frag.* 316, 652.
[3] Shuckburgh, note on Lysias, xiii. § 91.
[4] For an account of an unnatural son see Dinarchus, *Agst. Aristogeiton*, § 11.

ἐξηγρίωσαν· ἐκ δ' ἔπνευσ' αὐτοῖς ἀρὰς
δεινὰς νοσῶν τε καὶ πρὸς ἠτιμασμένος.

Reference is made by Isocrates to a father's affection for his children. Men, he says, love most their own children and wives (*Nicocl.* § 36):—

εἰδὼς γὰρ ἅπαντας ἀνθρώπους περὶ πλείστου ποιουμένους τοὺς παῖδας τοὺς αὐτῶν καὶ τὰς γυναῖκας, καὶ μάλιστ' ὀργιζομένους τοῖς εἰς ταῦτ' ἐξαμαρτάνουσι, καὶ τὴν ὕβριν τὴν περὶ ταῦτα μεγίστων κακῶν αἰτίαν γιγνομένην, κ.τ.λ.

Isaeus speaks of a father's forethought for his son (ii. § 18):—

κἀκεῖνός τε τὴν πρόνοιαν εἶχεν ὥσπερ εἰκός ἐστι πατέρα περὶ υἱέος ἔχειν, κ.τ.λ.

And again (viii. § 16), he speaks of a grandfather's prayers:—

. . . καὶ ηὔχετο ἡμῖν ὑγίειαν διδόναι καὶ κτῆσιν ἀγαθήν, ὥσπερ εἰκὸς ὄντα πάππον.

In the *Medea* (1206-1210), Euripides gives us a picture of a father's affection and grief:—

ᾤμωξε δ' εὐθύς, καὶ περιπτύξας δέμας
κυνεῖ προσαυδῶν τοιάδ'· ὦ δύστηνε παῖ,
τίς σ' ὧδ' ἀτίμως δαιμόνων ἀπώλεσεν;
τίς τὸν γέροντα τύμβον ὀρφανὸν σέθεν
τίθησιν; οἴμοι, ξυνθάνοιμί σοι, τέκνον.

So Theseus exclaims (*Hipp.* 1410):—

εἰ γὰρ γενοίμην, τέκνον, ἀντὶ σοῦ νεκρός [1].

All men love their children (*Her. Fur.* 633-635):—

πάντα τἀνθρώπων ἴσα.
φιλοῦσι παῖδας οἵ τ' ἀμείνονες βροτῶν
οἵ τ' οὐδὲν ὄντες [2].

A man should suffer—die, if need be—for his wife and children (*ibid.* 574-578):—

τῷ γάρ μ' ἀμύνειν μᾶλλον ἢ δάμαρτι χρὴ
καὶ παισὶ καὶ γέροντι; χαιρόντων πόνοι·
μάτην γὰρ αὐτοὺς τῶνδε μᾶλλον ἤνυσα.

---

[1] Cf. David's lament for Absalom.   [2] Cf. *Phoen.* 965-966.

καὶ δεῖ μ' ὑπὲρ τῶνδ', εἴπερ οἶδ' ὑπὲρ πατρός,
θνήσκειν ἀμύνοντ' [1].

Pheres, however, declares that paternal affection has its limits (*Alc.* 681–684):—

ἐγὼ δέ σ' οἴκων δεσπότην ἐγεινάμην
κἄθρεψ', ὀφείλω δ' οὐχ ὑπερθνήσκειν σέθεν·
οὐ γὰρ πατρῷον τόνδ' ἐδεξάμην νόμον,
παίδων προθνήσκειν πατέρας, οὐδ' Ἑλληνικόν.

A mother's long-suffering is described by Lysias (xxxi. § 22):—

καίτοι εἰ μήτηρ, ἣ πέφυκε καὶ ἀδικουμένη ὑπὸ τῶν ἑαυτῆς παίδων
μάλιστα ἀνέχεσθαι καὶ μίκρ' ὠφελουμένη μεγάλα ἔχειν ἡγεῖσθαι διὰ
τὸ εὐνοίᾳ μᾶλλον ἢ ἐλέγχῳ τὰ γιγνόμενα δοκιμάζειν, κ.τ.λ.

All women love their children, says Lycurgus (*Agst. Leocrates,* § 101) [2].

There are many passages in Euripides descriptive of a mother's love. I will quote first the well-known lines in *Iph. Aul.* (917–918):—

δεινὸν τὸ τίκτειν, καὶ φέρει φίλτρον μέγα
πᾶσίν τε κοινόν, ὥσθ' ὑπερκάμνειν τέκνων.

So Megara says (*Her. Fur.* 280–281):—

ἐγὼ φιλῶ μὲν τέκνα· πῶς γὰρ οὐ φιλῶ
ἅτικτον, ἀμόχθησα ;

So also the Chorus in the *Phoenissae* (355–356):—

δεινὸν γυναιξὶν αἱ δι' ὠδίνων γοναί,
καὶ φιλότεκνόν πως πᾶν γυναικεῖον γένος [3].

In a fragment of a cynical nature the mother's love for her children is said to be stronger than the father's (*Frag.* 1015):—

αἰεὶ δὲ μήτηρ φιλότεκνος μᾶλλον πατρός·
ἡ μὲν γὰρ αὑτῆς οἶδεν ὄνθ', ὁ δ' οἴεται.

---

[1] For mutual affection of father and daughter see *Iph. Aul.* 679 ff., 1220 ff.; and for that of grandsire and grandson *Bacch.* 1319 ff. Cf. also *Frag.* 950; and for advice to a son see *Frag.* 362.

[2] The passage is quoted above, p. 155.

[3] Cf. *Med.* 1021 ff.; *Suppl.* 1136 ff.; *Ion,* 1460-1461; *Tro.* 735 ff., 1175 ff.; *Iph. Aul.* 1256; *Phoen.* 306 ff.; *Frag.* 316, 323.

Then, as now, the hatred and envy of stepmothers was proverbial.

Isaeus speaks of the quarrels between a stepmother and children by a former wife (xii. § 5):—

... εἰώθασι δέ πως ὡς ἐπὶ τὸ πολὺ διαφέρεσθαι ἀλλήλαις αἵ τε μητρυιαὶ καὶ αἱ πρόγονοι· κ.τ.λ.

Euripides compares a stepmother to a viper (*Alc.* 309-310):—

<blockquote>
ἐχθρὰ γὰρ ἡ 'πιοῦσα μητρυιὰ τέκνοις
τοῖς πρόσθ', ἐχίδνης οὐδὲν ἠπιωτέρα [1].
</blockquote>

So also *Ion*, 1025:—

<blockquote>
φθονεῖν γάρ φασι μητρυιὰς τέκνοις [2].
</blockquote>

Of the mutual affection of brother and sister we have a striking picture in Orestes and Electra. I will quote only one passage by way of illustration (*Or.* 1047-1051):—

<blockquote>
ΟΡ. ἔκ τοί με τήξεις· καί σ' ἀμείψασθαι θέλω
φιλότητι χειρῶν. τί γὰρ ἔτ' αἰδοῦμαι τάλας ;
ὦ στέρν' ἀδελφῆς, ὦ φίλον πρόσπτυγμ' ἐμόν,
τάδ' ἀντὶ παίδων καὶ γαμηλίου λέχους
προσφθέγματ' ἀμφὶ τοῖς ταλαιπώροις πάρα [3].
</blockquote>

The greatest suffering for mortals, says Euripides, is to see their children dead (*Suppl.* 1120-1122):—

<blockquote>
τί γὰρ ἂν μεῖζον τοῦδ' ἔτι θνατοῖς
πάθος ἐξεύροις,
ἢ τέκνα θανόντ' ἐσιδέσθαι ;
</blockquote>

Similarly Lysias (*Epitaph.* § 73):—

<blockquote>
τί γὰρ ἂν τούτων ἀνιαρότερον γένοιτο, ἢ τεκεῖν μὲν καὶ θρέψαι [καὶ θάψαι] τοὺς αὑτῶν ... ;
</blockquote>

And Demosthenes (?) (*Epitaph.* § 36):—

<blockquote>
χαλεπὸν πατρὶ καὶ μητρὶ παίδων στερηθῆναι καὶ ἐρήμοις εἶναι τῶν οἰκειοτάτων γηροτρόφων.
</blockquote>

And lastly in this connexion I would refer to one or two passages bearing on family quarrels.

---

[1] Cf. *ibid.* 305-307 (with Jerram's note).
[2] Cf. *ibid.* 1270, 1330 ; *Frag.* 4, 824 : Hesiod, *Works and Days*, 825 : Aeschylus, *Prom. Vinct.* 727 : Horace, *Epod.* v. 9.
[3] Cf. *Phoen.* 166-167.

Lysias speaks of the disgrace attaching to such quarrels. One should bear and forbear (xxxii. § 1):—

. . . νομίζων αἴσχιστον εἶναι πρὸς τοὺς οἰκείους διαφέρεσθαι, εἰδώς τε ὅτι οὐ μόνον οἱ ἀδικοῦντες χείρους ὑμῖν εἶναι δοκοῦσιν, ἀλλὰ καὶ οἵτινες ἂν ἔλαττον ὑπὸ τῶν προσηκόντων ἔχοντες ἀνέχεσθαι μὴ δύνωνται.

Similarly Antiphon (κατηγορία φαρμακείας, § 1):—

νέος μὲν καὶ ἄπειρος δικῶν ἔγωγε ἔτι, δεινῶς δὲ καὶ ἀπόρως ἔχει μοι περὶ τοῦ πράγματος ὦ ἄνδρες, τοῦτο μὲν εἰ ἐπισκήψαντος τοῦ πατρὸς ἐπεξελθεῖν τοῖς αὐτοῦ φονεῦσι μὴ ἐπέξειμι, τοῦτο δὲ εἰ ἐπεξιόντι ἀναγκαίως ἔχει οἷς ἥκιστα ἐχρῆν ἐν διαφορᾷ καταστῆναι, ἀδελφοῖς ὁμοπατρίοις καὶ μητρὶ ἀδελφῶν [1].

Terrible, says Euripides, is the strife of brothers (*Iph. Aul.* 376-377):—

δεινὸν κασιγνήτοισι γίγνεσθαι λόγους
μάχας θ᾽, ὅταν ποτ᾽ ἐμπέσωσιν εἰς ἔριν [2].

Such strife is often caused by love and ambition (*ibid.* 508-510):—

ταραχή γ᾽ ἀδελφῶν τις δι᾽ ἔρωτα γίγνεται
πλεονεξίαν τε δωμάτων· ἀπέπτυσα
τοιάνδε συγγένειαν ἀλλήλων πικράν.

§ 5. If one pauses to think of the importance of human relationships, and to consider how great a part of life these relationships are, one will not be surprised to find that the subject of friendship is one which enters very largely into all literature. Euripides [3] and the Attic Orators are no exception in this respect.

In friendship the rule of like to like prevails. A man is known by the company he keeps [4]. Hence the necessity of a careful choice of friends.

---

[1] For a passage in Demosthenes on quarrels between husband and wife see above, p. 175, note 1.

[2] Cf. *Phoen.* 374-375 ; *Frag.* 975 :—χαλεποὶ πόλεμοι γὰρ ἀδελφῶν.

[3] Striking examples of friendship found in Euripides are those of Orestes and Pylades (*Electra, Orestes, Iph. Taur.*), Theseus and Heracles (*Her. Fur.*), Admetus and Heracles (*Alcestis*).

[4] Cf. *Electra*, 383-385.

'Evil communications,' says Euripides, 'corrupt good manners' (*Frag.* 1024):—

φθείρουσιν ἤθη χρήσθ' ὁμιλίαι κακαί.

One should therefore choose 'good communications' (*Frag.* 609):—

ὁ γὰρ ξυνὼν κακὸς μὲν ἦν τύχῃ γεγώς,
τοιούσδε τοὺς ξυνόντας ἐκπαιδεύεται,
χρηστοὺς δὲ χρηστός· ἀλλὰ τὰς ὁμιλίας
ἐσθλὰς διώκειν, ὦ νέοι, σπουδάζετε.

A man, says Demosthenes, is thought to be like his friends (*Agst. Androtion*, § 64):—

ὡς ἐκεῖνο εἰδόσι μὲν ἴσως, ὅμως δὲ ἐρῶ· ὁποίους τινὰς ἂν φαίνησθε ἀγαπῶντες καὶ σώζοντες, τούτοις ὅμοιοι δόξετ' εἶναι.

Like to like, says Lycurgus (*Agst. Leocrates*, § 135):—

... νῦν δὲ πᾶσι φανερὸν ὅτι τοῖς αὐτοῖς ἤθεσι χρώμενοι τὴν πρὸς τοῦτον φιλίαν διαφυλάττουσιν, κ.τ.λ.

A man like Theseus, who will stand by one whatever befall, is the kind of man to make one's friend (*Her. Fur.* 1404):—

τοιόνδ' ἄνδρα χρὴ κτᾶσθαι φίλον.

Choose pious friends, says Tyndareus (*Or.* 627-628):—

μηδὲ δυσσεβεῖς
ἕλῃ παρώσας εὐσεβεστέρους φίλους [1].

Isocrates tells Demonicus how to choose friends. One should first find out how they have treated former friends. Friendships should be slowly formed, but, once formed, should be firm and lasting (*Ad Demon.* § 24):—

μηδένα φίλον ποιοῦ, πρὶν ἂν ἐξετάσῃς, πῶς κέχρηται τοῖς πρότερον φίλοις· ἔλπιζε γὰρ αὐτὸν καὶ περὶ σὲ γενέσθαι τοιοῦτον, οἷος καὶ περὶ ἐκείνους γέγονε. βραδέως μὲν φίλος γίγνου, γενόμενος δὲ πειρῶ διαμένειν [2].

---

[1] Cf. *Hipp.* 997.
[2] Cf. the advice of Polonius to Laertes (*Hamlet*, i. 3):—
    'The friends thou hast, and their adoption tried,
      Grapple them to thy soul with hoops of steel;
    But do not dull thy palm with entertainment
      Of each new-hatch'd, unfledg'd comrade.'

Nature, character, choice, are of more consequence than convention, birth, necessity (*Ad Demon.* § 10):—

ἡγεῖτο γὰρ εἶναι πρὸς ἐταιρίαν πολλῷ κρείττω φύσιν νόμου καὶ τρόπον γένους καὶ προαίρεσιν ἀνάγκης.

Worthiness is a necessity in a friend: benefit is of more account than pleasure (*Ad Nicocl.* § 27):—

φίλους κτῶ μὴ πάντας τοὺς βουλομένους ἀλλὰ τοὺς τῆς σῆς φύσεως ἀξίους ὄντας, μηδὲ μεθ' ὧν ἥδιστα συνδιατρίψεις, ἀλλὰ μεθ' ὧν ἄριστα τὴν πόλιν διοικήσεις.

It is a good thing and pleasant to make good and trusty friends by acts of kindness (*Epist.* iv. § 9):—

... ἔπειτα νομίζων οὐκ ἀγνοεῖν ὑμᾶς, ὅτι πάντων ἥδιστόν ἐστι καὶ λυσιτελέστατον πιστοὺς ἅμα καὶ χρησίμους φίλους κτᾶσθαι ταῖς εὐεργεσίαις καὶ τοὺς τοιούτους εὖ ποιεῖν, ὑπὲρ ὧν πολλοὶ καὶ τῶν ἄλλων ὑμῖν χάριν ἕξουσιν, κ.τ.λ.

Genuine friendship seeks three things (*Frag.* iii. (δ'.) 13):—

ἡ ἀληθινὴ φιλία τρία ζητεῖ μάλιστα· τὴν ἀρετήν, ὡς καλόν· καὶ τὴν συνήθειαν, ὡς ἡδύ· καὶ τὴν χρείαν, ὡς ἀναγκαῖον. δεῖ γὰρ ἀποδέξασθαι κρίναντα καὶ χαίρειν συνόντα καὶ χρῆσθαι δεόμενον.

The friendships between men of no character endure but for a day: those between good men last for ever (*Ad Demon.* § 1):—

οἱ μὲν γὰρ τοὺς φίλους παρόντας μόνον τιμῶσιν, οἱ δὲ καὶ μακρὰν ἀπόντας ἀγαπῶσι, καὶ τὰς μὲν τῶν φαύλων συνηθείας ὀλίγος χρόνος διέλυσε, τὰς δὲ τῶν σπουδαίων φιλίας οὐδ' ἂν ὁ πᾶς αἰὼν ἐξαλείψειεν [1].

Hyperides urges the necessity of avoiding the friendship of evil men (*Frag.* 210 a):—

ὁ αὐτὸς (sc. Hyperides) ἔλεγε κακῶν ἀνθρώπων φεύγειν (δεῖν) φιλίαν καὶ ἀγαθῶν ἔχθραν.

Good friends, says Euripides, are better than wealth or power (*Her. Fur.* 1425–1426):—

ὅστις δὲ πλοῦτον ἢ σθένος μᾶλλον φίλων
ἀγαθῶν πεπᾶσθαι βούλεται, κακῶς φρονεῖ [2].

---

[1] Cf. Euripides, *Hec.* 311; *Andr.* 1051; *Iph. Taur.* 717; *Frag.* 655.
[2] Cf. *Or.* 1155–1156: Isaeus, v. § 30:—... ἀλλ' ἐπιδεικνύμενοι ὅτι οὐ περὶ πλείονος χρήματα ποιούμεθα τῶν οἰκείων.

A good friend is better than a thousand kinsmen (*Or.* 804-806):—

> τοῦτ' ἐκεῖνο, κτᾶσθ' ἑταίρους, μὴ τὸ συγγενὲς μόνον·
> ὡς ἀνήρ, ὅστις τρόποισι συντακῇ, θυραῖος ὤν,
> μυρίων κρείσσων ὁμαίμων ἀνδρὶ κεκτῆσθαι φίλος[1].

Sweet is friendship in weal and in woe (*Ion*, 730-732):—

> σὺν τοῖς φίλοις γὰρ ἡδὺ μὲν πράσσειν καλῶς,
> ὃ μὴ γένοιτο δ', εἴ τι τυγχάνοι κακόν,
> εἰς ὄμματ' εὔνου φωτὸς ἐμβλέψαι γλυκύ[2].

Misfortune is the best test of friends (*Her. Fur.* 57-59):—

> τοιοῦτον ἀνθρώποισιν ἡ δυσπραξία,
> ἧς μήποθ', ὅστις καὶ μέσως εὔνους ἐμοί,
> τύχοι, φίλων ἔλεγχον ἀψευδέστατον.

Megara complains that one has no friends in misfortune (*ibid.* 559):—

> φίλοι γὰρ εἰσιν ἀνδρὶ δυστυχεῖ τίνες[3];

They are numerous, however, in prosperity (*Rhesus*, 319-320):—

> πολλούς, ἐπειδὴ τοὐμὸν εὐτυχεῖ δόρυ
> καὶ Ζεὺς πρὸς ἡμῶν ἐστιν, εὑρήσω φίλους.

Friends, says Isocrates, are tested in misfortune as gold is tried in the fire (*Ad Demon.* § 25):—

> δοκίμαζε τοὺς φίλους ἔκ τε τῆς περὶ τὸν βίον ἀτυχίας καὶ τῆς ἐν τοῖς κινδύνοις κοινωνίας· τὸ μὲν γὰρ χρυσίον ἐν τῷ πυρὶ βασανί-ζομεν, τοὺς δὲ φίλους ἐν ταῖς ἀτυχίαις διαγιγνώσκομεν.

Friends should remain friends in weal and in woe: they are unworthy of the name who are friends only in the hour of prosperity.

A friend who will share both prosperity and adversity is an εὕρημα (*El.* 606-607):—

> εὕρημα γὰρ τὸ χρῆμα γίγνεται τόδε,
> κοινῇ μετασχεῖν τἀγαθοῦ καὶ τοῦ κακοῦ.

---

[1] See Paley's note *ad loc.*
[2] Cf. *Andr.* 985-986; *Ion*, 935; *Tro.* 51-52.
[3] Cf. *Phoen.* 403; *El.* 605, 1131: Lysias, *Epitaph.* § 74.

Hateful is the friend whose friendship is cooled by adversity
(*Her. Fur.* 1223–1225):—

> χάριν δὲ γηράσκουσαν ἐχθαίρω φίλων,
> καὶ τῶν καλῶν μὲν ὅστις ἀπολαύειν θέλει,
> συμπλεῖν δὲ τοῖς φίλοισι δυστυχοῦσιν οὔ.

So also *Orestes* (454–455):—

> ὄνομα γάρ, ἔργον δ' οὐκ ἔχουσιν οἱ φίλοι
> οἱ μὴ 'πὶ ταῖσι συμφοραῖς ὄντες φίλοι [1].

A similar sentiment we find in Isocrates (*De Pace*, § 21):—

> τὸ δὲ μέγιστον, συμμάχους ἕξομεν ἅπαντας ἀνθρώπους, οὐ
> βεβιασμένους ἀλλὰ πεπεισμένους, οὐδ' ἐν ταῖς μὲν ἀσφαλείαις διὰ
> τὴν δύναμιν ἡμᾶς ὑποδεχομένους, ἐν δὲ τοῖς κινδύνοις ἀποστησο-
> μένους, ἀλλ' οὕτω διακειμένους ὥσπερ χρὴ τοὺς ὡς ἀληθῶς συμ-
> μάχους καὶ φίλους ὄντας.

And in Lycurgus (*Agst. Leocrates*, § 133):—

> κακοὶ γὰρ καὶ πολῖται καὶ ξένοι καὶ ἰδίᾳ φίλοι οἱ τοιοῦτοι τῶν
> ἀνθρώπων εἰσίν, οἳ τῶν μὲν ἀγαθῶν τῶν τῆς πόλεως μεθέξουσιν, ἐν
> δὲ ταῖς ἀτυχίαις οὐδὲ βοηθείας ἀξιώσουσι.

Friends possess all things in common (*Or.* 735):—

> κοινὰ γὰρ τὰ τῶν φίλων [2].

Similarly *Andr.* 376–377:—

> φίλων γὰρ οὐδὲν ἴδιον, οἵτινες φίλοι
> ὀρθῶς πεφύκασ', ἀλλὰ κοινὰ χρήματα [3].

Even sorrows are common property (*Phoen.* 243):—

> κοινὰ γὰρ φίλων ἄχη.

We find the idea in the speech *Against Neaera*, § 2:—

> ... ἡγουμένου τῇ ἀληθείᾳ οἰκείους ὄντας κοινωνεῖν πάντων τῶν
> ὄντων.

I will add only a few passages bearing on the duties of
friendship and the treatment of friends.

---

[1] Cf. *Suppl.* 867–868; *Iph. Taur.* 709–710; *Or.* 665, 727, 802, 1095; *Iph. Aul.*
345; *Cycl.* 481.
[2] The phrase passed into a proverb. Cf. Plato, *Phaedrus, ad fin.*
[3] Cf. also *Suppl.* 296; *Cycl.* 533.

A man should entertain righteous anger on a friend's behalf (*Her. Fur.* 275-276):—

> τῶν φίλων γὰρ οὕνεκα
> ὀργὰς δικαίας τοὺς φίλους ἔχειν χρεών.

When Heracles, after slaying his wife and children, urges Theseus to depart and avoid pollution, the latter refuses, because (*ibid.* 1234):—

> οὐδεὶς ἀλάστωρ τοῖς φίλοις ἐκ τῶν φίλων.

A man should not save himself by sacrificing a friend (*Iph. Taur.* 605-607):—

> τὰ τῶν φίλων
> αἴσχιστον ὅστις καταβαλὼν ἐς ξυμφορὰς
> αὐτὸς σέσωσται.

A friend, says Pylades, should die with a friend (*ibid.* 684-686):—

> κοὐκ ἔσθ' ὅπως οὐ χρὴ συνεκπνεῦσαί μέ σοι
> καὶ συσφαγῆναι καὶ πυρωθῆναι δέμας,
> φίλον γεγῶτα καὶ φοβούμενον ψόγον.

He should shrink from no friendly offices (*Or.* 794):—

> ΟΡ. οὐκ ἄρ' ὀκνήσεις ; ΠΥ. ὄκνος γὰρ τοῖς φίλοις κακὸν μέγα.

He should share a friend's grief (*Iph. Aul.* 408):—

> ἐς κοινὸν ἀλγεῖν τοῖς φίλοισι χρὴ φίλους [1].

The advice and consolation of a good friend is a remedy in grief (*Frag.* 1079):—

> οὐκ ἔστι λύπης ἄλλο φάρμακον βροτοῖς
> ὡς ἀνδρὸς ἐσθλοῦ καὶ φίλου παραίνεσις [2].

A good man, says Lysias, should benefit his friends, even if nobody is ever to know of it (xix. § 59):—

> καὶ τοῦτ' ἐποίει ἡγούμενος εἶναι ἀνδρὸς ἀγαθοῦ ὠφελεῖν τοὺς φίλους, καὶ εἰ μηδεὶς μέλλοι εἴσεσθαι.

The marks of a lasting friendship, he says in the *Phaedrus* (233 B-C), are to look not to present pleasure but to future

---

[1] Cf. *Or.* 296-300.
[2] Cf. *Frag.* 962: and for other thoughts in Euripides concerning friendship see *Hec.* 1226 ; *Her. Fur.* 1338 ; *Iph. Taur.* 497-498, 650 ; *Or.* 1015 ; *Iph. Aul.* 334 ; *Phoen.* 1659 ; *Heracl.* 895.

benefit, to practise self-restraint, not to become an enemy on slight provocation, to pardon involuntary wrongs :—

ἐὰν δ' ἐμοὶ πείθῃ, πρῶτον μὲν οὐ τὴν παροῦσαν ἡδονὴν θεραπεύων συνέσομαί σοι, ἀλλὰ καὶ τὴν μέλλουσαν ὠφέλειαν ἔσεσθαι, οὐχ ὑπ' ἔρωτος ἡττώμενος, ἀλλ' ἐμαυτοῦ κρατῶν, οὐδὲ διὰ σμικρὰ ἰσχυρὰν ἔχθραν ἀναιρούμενος, ἀλλὰ διὰ μεγάλα βραδέως ὀλίγην ὀργὴν ποιούμενος, τῶν μὲν ἀκουσίων συγγνώμην ἔχων, τὰ δὲ ἑκούσια πειρώμενος ἀποτρέπειν· ταῦτα γάρ ἐστι φιλίας πολὺν χρόνον ἐσομένης τεκμήρια.

Isocrates also inculcates the duty of benefiting friends (*Ad Nicocl.* § 19):—

τὴν μεγαλοπρέπειαν ἐπιδείκνυσο μηδ' ἐν μιᾷ τῶν πολυτελειῶν τῶν εὐθὺς ἀφανιζομένων ἀλλ' ἔν τε τοῖς προειρημένοις καὶ τῷ κάλλει τῶν κτημάτων καὶ ταῖς τῶν φίλων εὐεργεσίαις· κ.τ.λ. [1].

Friends are not to be betrayed, says Aeschines, for the friendship of the powerful or for personal advantage (*On the Embassy*, § 152):—

ἐρωτῶ γάρ, ὦ 'Αθηναῖοι, εἰ δοκῶ ἂν ὑμῖν πρὸς τῇ πατρίδι καὶ τῇ τῶν φίλων συνηθείᾳ καὶ ἱερῶν καὶ τάφων πατρῴων μετουσίᾳ τούτους τοὺς πάντων ἀνθρώπων ἐμοὶ φιλτάτους προδοῦναι Φιλίππῳ, καὶ περὶ πλείονος τὴν ἐκείνου φιλίαν τῆς τούτων σωτηρίας ποιήσασθαι. ποίᾳ κρατηθεὶς ἡδονῇ; ἢ τί πώποτε ἄσχημον ἕνεκα χρημάτων πράξας ; κ.τ.λ.

Isaeus (i. §§ 6–8) censures men who treat relatives and friends as though they were enemies.   Injury to friends, he declares (*ibid.* § 20), is madness [2].

The part of a good friend, says Demosthenes, is to act for the welfare of both, and sacrifice present pleasure for future good (*Agst. Aristocrates*, § 134):—

ἔστι γὰρ φίλων ἀγαθῶν οὐ τὰ τοιαῦτα χαρίζεσθαι τοῖς εὔνοις, ἐξ ὧν κἀκείνοις καὶ σφίσιν αὐτοῖς ἔσται τις βλάβη, ἀλλ' ὁ μὲν ἂν μέλλῃ συνοίσειν ἀμφοῖν, συμπράττειν, ὁ δ' ἂν αὐτὸς ἄμεινον ἐκείνου

---

[1] For other passages in Isocrates bearing on friendship see *Antid.* §§ 122, 134.

[2] Cf. *Frag.* 4. For the ordinary view as to the treatment of friends and foes see above, pp. 77–79.

προορᾷ, πρὸς τὸ καλῶς ἔχον τίθεσθαι καὶ μὴ τὴν ἤδη χάριν τοῦ μετὰ ταῦτα χρόνου παντὸς περὶ πλείονος ἡγεῖσθαι[1].

If a friend is thought to have committed a crime, he is sufficiently punished in forfeiting your friendship for the future: leave prosecution to aggrieved parties and to enemies (*Agst. Midias*, § 118):—

μετρία γὰρ δίκη παρὰ τῶν φίλων ἐστίν, ἄν τι δοκῶσι πεποιηκέναι δεινόν, μηκέτι τῆς λοιπῆς φιλίας κοινωνεῖν, τὸ δὲ τιμωρεῖσθαι καὶ ἐπεξιέναι τοῖς πεπονθόσι καὶ τοῖς ἐχθροῖς παραλείπεται.

But there should be no excess in either friendship or enmity. Here, too, μηδὲν ἄγαν ought to be the rule (*Agst. Aristocrates*, § 122):—

ἔστι γὰρ οὐχ ὑγιαινόντων, οἶμαι, ἀνθρώπων οὔθ' ὅταν τινὰ ὑπειλήφωσι φίλον, οὕτω πιστεύειν ὥστε, ἂν ἀδικεῖν ἐπιχειρῇ, τὸ ἀμύνασθαι σφῶν αὐτῶν ἀφελέσθαι, οὔθ' ὅταν ἐχθρόν τινα ἡγῶνται, οὕτως αὖ μισεῖν ὥστε, ἂν παυσάμενος βούληται φίλος εἶναι, τὸ ποιεῖν ἐξεῖναι ταῦτα κωλῦσαι· ἀλλ' ἄχρι τούτου καὶ φιλεῖν, οἶμαι, χρὴ καὶ μισεῖν, μηδετέρου τὸν καιρὸν ὑπερβάλλοντας[2].

These words recall forcibly the language of Ajax in Sophocles (*Ajax*, 678–682):—

> 'And I—this lesson I have learnt to-day,
>   To hate my enemies so much and no more,
>   As who shall yet be friends, and of a friend
>   I'll bound my love and service with the thought,
>   He's not my friend for ever[3].'

---

[1] Cf. Lysias in Plato's *Phaedrus*, 233 B–C (quoted above, pp. 185-186); and for another passage on friendship see *On the Crown*, § 269.

[2] Cf. Euripides, *Hipp.* 253 ff. see above, p. 73.

[3] Whitelaw's translation.

CHAPTER X

CONCLUSION

In most cases it would not be an easy task to deduce from the preceding investigation the steady development of any general principles or tendencies during the time between the age of Pericles and that of Demosthenes; but it may perhaps be well, in conclusion, to gather up the threads of that investigation in a brief summary, taking the subjects in the order in which they have been discussed.

With regard to physical theories Euripides and the Attic Orators furnish little ground for comparison; for though in the former we find a good deal bearing on the subject, in the latter there is almost nothing. Isocrates regards such studies as astronomy and geometry as a good mental training for the young, but as of little account otherwise. The passages in Euripides, however, are interesting in themselves, and show that he had devoted some study to the Ionic physicists, and above all to Anaxagoras.

In the matter of religion the field for comparison is wider, though still comparatively limited. Euripides here shows three distinct stages of development. In the first he accepts the popular religion, though now and again he gives hints of rationalistic tendencies: in the second these tendencies are fully asserted, and he is at open war with the popular religion: in the third, while he does not return to his original position, he has grown weary of the campaign and ceases from active hostility. The Orators show almost no interest in religion. If there was (as Prof. Mahaffy maintains) a reaction to orthodoxy in the fourth century B.C., the orthodoxy was not a vital one, but one rather of outward semblance. It is mere commonplace with which the Orators furnish us. Even where religious beliefs are expressed hypothetically, the hypothesis is a mere form of language, and not indicative of a questioning scepticism. But in at least one passage Isocrates is at one with Euripides, when he maintains that the poets' tales of the gods are impious and incredible, and that the gods can do no evil: and so also is Demosthenes when he declares that it is against the divine nature to lie.

What has been said of religion may also be said of their views of death and a future life. While here Euripides, with his usual indecision, wavers between the popular notions and those of the physicists and philosophers, we find in the Orators only commonplace. Of the Greek feeling as to the importance of burial, and the religious element in that feeling, both the poet and the Orators furnish us with numerous illustrations.

Reflections on life in its general aspects abound in Euripides. He is melancholy and pessimistic, strongly impressed with the sadness of life. The Orators very seldom linger to indulge in such reflections. When they do, it is to speak in a commonplace way of the uncertainty of the future, sudden reversals of fortune, and the like.

In the case of ethics also, it is in commonplace maxims that the Orators furnish a means of comparison with Euripides. They never think of inquiring, as the poet did, what the origin of evil is, or to what standard conduct is to be referred. But they agree with him in extolling virtue as the highest of all things, in inculcating temperance and moderation (σωφροσύνη), in deprecating excess (ὕβρις)—which they see to be frequently the result of wealth and prosperity—and in recommending a brave endurance of what fortune sends. And both in Euripides and in the Orators we find fully illustrated the Greek law of retaliation. Neither the one nor the other ever rose here to the height reached by Plato.

When we turn to public and private life, a comparison of Euripides with the Orators is more fruitful. In education

Euripides was among the first to try to lessen the undue prominence—as he conceived it—given to gymnastics. His ideas had gained strength in the next century, and are frequent in the Orators. That mind is superior to body, wisdom to physical strength or beauty—views like these are of frequent occurrence.

The Orators agree with Euripides in maintaining that as wealth in itself is no reason for pride, so poverty is no disgrace. Wisdom is superior to wealth: the latter is fleeting, the former abides. But Euripides with far greater emphasis and frequency than any of the Orators speaks disparagingly of riches, and he is full of pity for the poor.

While it is true that in several places Euripides attributes importance to nobility of birth, he more frequently asserts that high or low birth matters little—that true nobility consists in goodness. Isocrates and Isaeus both agree, but there is in the Orators very little bearing on the question.

In no Greek writer do we find so strong an advocate of slaves as we do in Euripides. True, he says much in disparagement of them, but he is also awake to the good that is in them. He pities the hardness of their lot, and sees that frequently the disgrace is only in the name. The ordinary Greek view, that a slave was in every way an inferior being, is what we find frequently in the Orators. Even Euripides never sees clearly that slavery is a violation of nature.

On the more general principles of political life there is a strong agreement between Euripides and nearly all the Orators. In Euripides and Isocrates there is this important point of resemblance, that both held aloof from active public life. But how alien this was to the Greek idea of a citizen is proved by the fact that both feel it necessary to excuse or defend their action. And neither of them, although they took no active part in politics, was indifferent to his country's welfare.

They agree also in the strong love of country which they exhibit. To the public welfare the dearest private interests, even parents and life, must be sacrificed. On the other side there is a peculiar horror of exile. Of all evils it is the worst.

The Greeks are regarded as a peculiar people, to whom 'barbarians' are in every way inferior. The former are free, brave, law-abiding, pious; the latter are impious, lawless, cowardly, slaves.

The general feeling of patriotism is found in its greatest intensity in the manner in which Athens is regarded. The Athenians are autochthonous, renowned for wisdom, piety, and justice, the champions of the injured and the weak. Freedom and equality find their home in Athens. She is the school of Hellas. But in the fourth century B.C. Athens had degenerated. She was no longer the Athens which had repulsed the Persian invader. Isocrates and Demosthenes continually bewail this fact, and pray for a revival of her ancient spirit.

The obverse to this love of Athens is the hatred of Sparta —a hatred which is, however, stronger in Euripides than in the Orators. The actual relations with Sparta in the time of each are sufficient to account for the greater or less intensity of the feeling. With a few exceptions, Sparta is regarded as presenting in many respects a direct contrast to Athens. Her citizens are treacherous, impious, illiterate. There is no freedom in Sparta. Secrecy and restraint characterise all her dealings.

Almost all the Orators are at one with Euripides in maintaining that democracy is the best form of government. Theseus, the ideal ruler in Euripides, is rather the President of the Democracy than an irresponsible king. But it is seen that the Demos is not free from faults—that, in fact, its character depends on its leaders. The tyrant and his life of injustice, suspicion, terror and cruelty are continually regarded with deep hatred. It is only in a democracy that one finds justice, law, freedom, clemency. Laws are the safeguard of a democracy, and a democracy is the safeguard of laws. The greatest blessings to a state are temperance, moderation, orderliness, harmony.

The worst curse in a democracy is the demagogue—the

charlatan who with specious words leads the people astray. This class is fiercely attacked by Euripides and also by the Orators—by none more fiercely than by Demosthenes. Their only motive is self-aggrandisement. They are cheats and impostors, ravens, serpents, monsters who seek to enslave the people. They pander to the popular wish: all their words have one aim only—to catch the popular ear.

What class of citizens they conceive as forming the back-bone of the state the Orators nowhere say. The state's salvation, according to Euripides, lies with the μέσοι πολῖται, the moderates in wealth, rank, politics.

Of that cosmopolitanism in the widest sense, of which Euripides has occasional glimpses, we find absolutely nothing in the Orators. It was later that the idea was fully developed.

In ideas on private life there is again considerable material for comparison. There is, naturally, much less of general sentiment in the Orators than in the poet, but what does occur is usually in the way of agreement. As to actual facts of private life as it then was we find much the same thing in both.

References to the seclusion of women are numerous. The best woman was the one who stayed most within doors. It was not a good sign in a woman that she should leave her own house, or be seen in male company. It was only the hetaerae who sat at table with men.

Of general blame or praise of women there is little in the Orators. When the latter does occur, it is usually from a utilitarian point of view. In Euripides there is a good deal of both; but, while he is full of pity for the hardness of a woman's lot, and unstinted in his praise of good women, women as they should be, the prevailing tone—due to his observation of the Athenian women of his own day—is one of disparagement.

Beauty and its power are sometimes the theme both of the poet and of the Orators, but both agree in assigning to it an inferior place to goodness.

The evils of love are described by both: it is a disease,

folly, madness. But Aeschines, like Euripides, reminds us that there is also a proper kind of love. Moderation in love—τὸ σωφρόνως ἐρᾶν—is alone the right thing.

On marriage the Orators have little in the way of general opinion. They tell us that the penalty for adultery was death, and Euripides agrees that this was the proper penalty. Isaeus—from the legal point of view as to the failure in succession—regards childlessness as a misfortune. Euripides also, from a more human point of view, does in a few cases speak of the misfortune of childlessness, but more usually he looks upon the lot of the unwedded and childless as a happy one. In his opinion marriage is a mixed blessing. Unanimity and chastity he regards as the indispensable conditions of happiness in married life. And here also moderation must be observed. A man should marry in his own rank.

The poet and the Orators are quite at one on the subject of kinship, its blessings and its claims. Family affection on all its sides should never cease to exist. There are no quarrels so disgraceful and terrible as family quarrels.

On friendship they are again thoroughly in agreement. Like to like should be the rule in friendship; and there is no choice in which a man should be more careful than that of friends. Only those are true friends who are friends in adversity as well as in prosperity. It is a duty to aid a friend when he needs aid. Injury to friends is madness: friends should bear and forbear. They should share all things—κοινὰ τὰ τῶν φίλων. But one should remember that a friend may become a foe, and a foe a friend. Here again moderation is best.—*Manum de tabula.*

THE END

O